# Ways of Virtue

# Ways *of* Virtue

*A Novel*

Liz O'Neill

SHE WRITES PRESS

Published in 2025 by
She Writes Press, an imprint of The Stable Book Group

32 Court Street, Suite 2109
Brooklyn, NY 11201
https://shewritespress.com
Library of Congress Control Number: 2025909425
ISBN: 979-8-89636-024-7
eISBN: 979-8-89636-025-4

Interior Designer: Kiran Spees

Printed in the United States

*For D. Dill and the Dupper*

So if I tell here the story of how the young planet Earth acquired an ocean,
it must be a story pieced together from many sources
and containing whole chapters
the details of which we can only imagine.

—Rachel Carson,
*The Sea Around Us*

ISLAND QUEEN
Vineyard Sound
N
W
E
S
HATCH'S FARM
WEST TI
GAY HEAD
CHILMARK
AQUINNAH

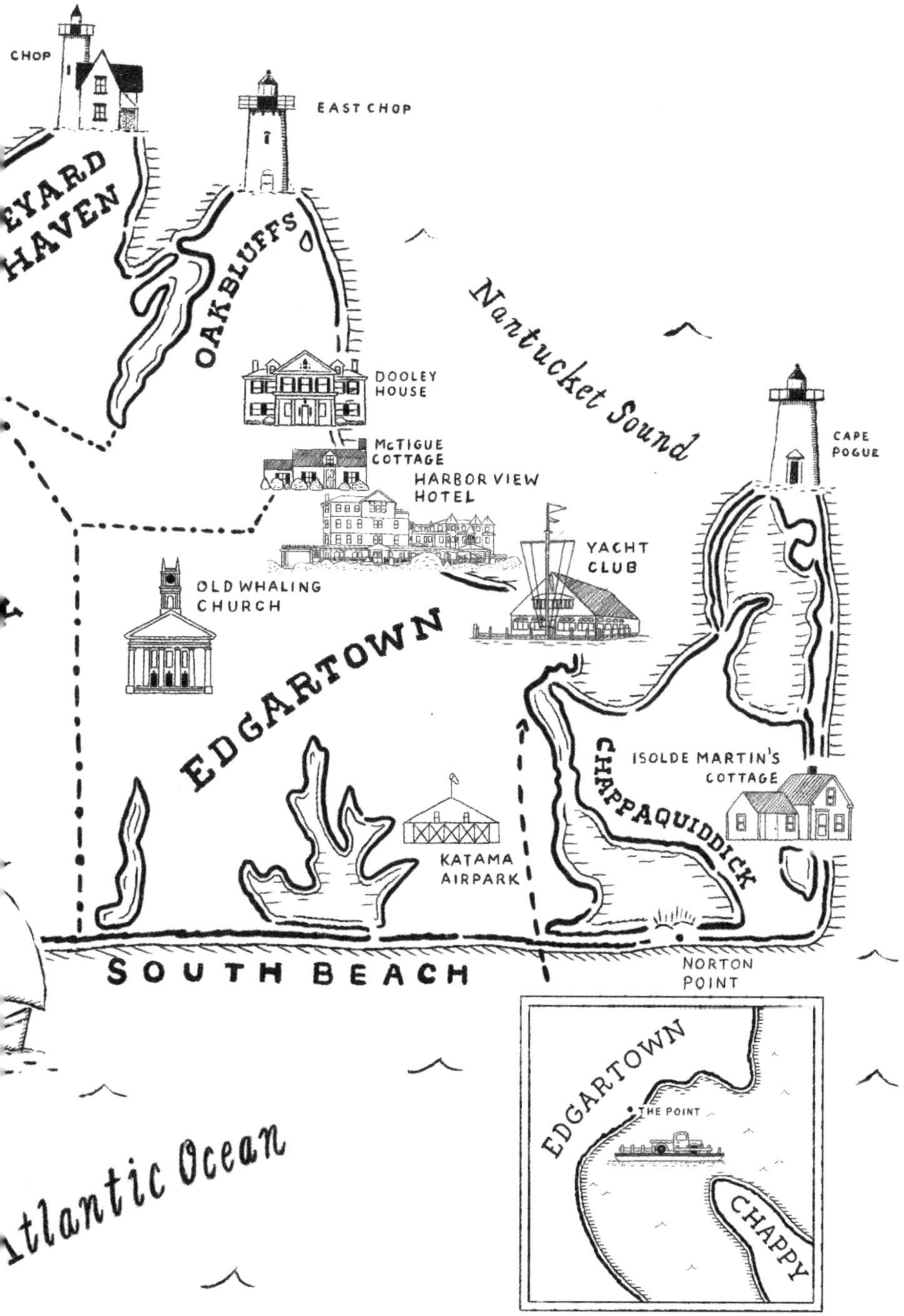

CHOP

EAST CHOP

EYARD HAVEN

OAK BLUFFS

Nantucket Sound

DOOLEY HOUSE

McTIGUE COTTAGE

HARBOR VIEW HOTEL

CAPE POGUE

YACHT CLUB

OLD WHALING CHURCH

EDGARTOWN

CHAPPAQUIDDICK

ISOLDE MARTIN'S COTTAGE

KATAMA AIRPARK

SOUTH BEACH

NORTON POINT

EDGARTOWN

THE POINT

CHAPPY

tlantic Ocean

## SATURDAY, AUGUST 28, 1954

## Damages Mount, Airplane Missing After Surprise, Season-Ending Storm

EDGARTOWN, MA (AP)—In the wake of Hurricane Carol's unforeseen ferocity, island residents today struggle to collect and reassemble the pieces of their properties, many of which remain underwater.

The first accounts of Carol's impact were recorded Friday morning, from Squibnocket Bass and Surf Club, where several skippers caught unawares sought refuge at Squibby Bight.

Witnesses report twenty-foot waves usurped the bridge to Gay Head, leaving at least fifty families stranded without milk or bread. The Menemsha Fish Market collapsed like a card house and ferry service was canceled, as Vineyard Haveners watched the ocean swallow the steamship pier. Lagoon Pond spilled into lawns and roads, while merciless gusts carried all manner of spoils—dories, chaise lounges, the Edgartown Yacht Club's grand piano—to entirely new anchorages.

A single-engine Beechcraft airplane, said to have lost its course just minutes after takeoff, is feared crashed somewhere in the Cape Cod Bay. Officials declined to release any further details. An air-sea recovery team was on the scene this morning. Ground parties will comb coastal beaches and shoal waters.

As rebuilding efforts begin, local police are also asking homeowners to be wary of insurance scams.

*STORM cont. page 5.*

# JUNE 1954

Three months before the storm

# ONE

"Sabina!" A shrill voice called from the wooden landing above the seawall. It was Aunt Poppy, of course, looking especially severe. "We've only three hours until the Dooley's bruncheon." She pantomimed a number three and a dramatic wristwatch gesture. "Exactly when do you intend to wash your hair?"

"I can't hear you," Sabina McTigue yelled up from high tide, fibbing. She unfastened her swim cap and turned her gaze toward the dawning sky. The morning was simply too pretty to quarrel, and yet—

"Drain the brine from your ears, for pity's sake!" Aunt Poppy hollered, pressing her kerchief to protect six careful rows of pin curlers. Aunt Poppy was not very much an ocean enthusiast. Instead, she was the sort of woman who believed in wearing foundation garments to the beach, along with one's best pearls and stockings.

"I'll be right up!"

"Honestly, Sabina," her aunt droned presently, hovering above the beach rose hips that threaded the stair rails and sprouted like tiny tomatoes. "Had you any sense a'tall you'd be reviewing your syllabi instead of wasting precious hours rehearsing for the Aquacade. You're like that Million Dollar Mermaid on the television. That Esther Somebody. Lolling about all day—only quite without the benefit of her curves, I should add."

"Swim club is an *athletic* team, Auntie," Sabina smiled up with effort. "It is not the *Aquacade*. And it's the only bit of college I'm actually keen on starting."

This much was true. In vain, aunt and niece had spent the early spring touring Radcliffe, Barnard, Smith, and the like. After shrugging off all Seven Sisters—seeing nothing among the students or the coursework that inspired her—Sabina had only conceded to Weston College, at the last, for the compromise of its competitive swim club, eliciting from Aunt Poppy a steady succession of cringes and shudders, tsks and frowns.

Despite these, Sabina now made a strict routine of her morning practice sessions: daily contests she waged against herself and the dark waves driving shoreward. As a matter of taste, Sabina didn't care for novels, but sometimes, reaching for ever greater lengths, she borrowed strength from accounts she'd read of different sea creatures—skates and rays, sharks and squid—how they flexed and flapped and flew and jetted across the vast stretches of open ocean. Evidence of progress showed in her well-defined shoulders, her back, her legs. She was getting stronger by the mile. And although she wasn't one for attention seeking, she couldn't help but brag a *little*—mostly in letters to her father, who was away for the summer, building large computing machines in California.

*Dear Bud,*

*Hope all is well on the West Coast. It's an unusually warm start to the season here, perfect for swimming. You'll be proud to know I made it halfway to Cape Pogue today. Well, maybe not halfway. I can't tell exactly unless Denny anchors some buoys for me. He says "not today" and that I should remind you about his graduation present (again!). He says a Beechcraft is more reliable than a Bugatti, and that, besides, commuting to the state house would be more convenient if he could fly there himself.*

*Aunt Poppy got stung in the yard last night. She's lying down right now with a cold compress. The bee got her good, square on the nose. Her face is actually quite swollen. Don't worry though, I didn't laugh. And yes, I am being cooperative!*

*I took another book out from the library on Monday. Mrs.*

*Lyons recommended it because she knows how much I like little glimpses into marine environments. Did you know that female dolphins often live their entire lives bound together with the family pod, whereas the males of the species break off on their own once they reach maturity? Lucky them, I suppose.*

*Anyway, enjoy those navel oranges! I'll just be here, swimming along with the pod.*

*As ever, Bean*

Sabina's father, Bud McTigue, was well-known in Boston circles for being equal parts rich and brilliant. Work took him across the country, sometimes overseas. And though he cared deeply about Sabina's ultimate happiness, he also borrowed much of his parenting philosophy from the old sailing precept: "A helmsman must be wary of steering too much." In this way, he trusted his daughter to choose her own academics, her friends, her hobbies; he stood clear to give her space. Aunt Poppy, meanwhile, stood by to yank it back.

When at last Sabina had reached the cottage landing, her aunt began anew. "Sabina, please don't keep me waiting this morning. I've promised James we'll be ready to leave by nine."

"*I've* not promised James anything."

"Yes, well, that's perfect ingratitude on your part. For myself, I shudder to think what might have happened if not for James putting in that kind word with Dean Budge. Why, your application was nearly two weeks late!"

"You do realize," Sabina smiled thinly, ringing out a cold drizzle from her curls, "there's a whole world of things and places to study. Dean Budge does not preside over all of them."

"She runs the only girls' college in Boston you didn't snub."

"And what does that signify? Whoever said I was bound to Boston?"

"Like flowers, my dear, we women must bloom where we are planted."

As it happened, Sabina McTigue had been planted in Boston. For most of the year, she and her family inhabited a slender brownstone in the

South Slope neighborhood of Beacon Hill. It was a snooty block without many young companions since the children of the other families had all been whisked away to boarding school, returning years later, just in time to get married off before the age of twenty-two. Were it not for the island and its promise of relative freedom—a slackening of curfews and dress codes—Sabina might have surrendered in spirit long ago.

Mercifully, every May, the McTigue family migrated to Edgartown, on the island of Martha's Vineyard, to a little street off the thoroughfare called Starbuck Bay: a lush, shady haven, lined on either side with sweet viburnum hedges and canopies of mature maples.

At the island Sabina found plenty to do, though aunt and niece often diverged on what might constitute a proper schedule. In Poppy's view, Sabina was meant to spend long hours socializing at the club—sailing, powerboating, and generally being seen with Edgartown's better set—young people whose parents did not *rent* but of course *owned*.

For Sabina, the yacht club invariably proved tiresome. She much preferred to roam the beaches—vacant but for the company of the ring-billed gulls at dawn—or wander off to Chappaquiddick, with her dip net and a tin pail, to survey the many kettle ponds and clear lagoons. Above all, she preferred the rare days when her father left his machines and found his way back to them, back to the Starbuck cottage and their badminton games on the lawn, back to fish dinners on the sleeping porch and a short row across the outer harbor each night to sing the sun down over Edgartown. While she awaited these visits, she found consolation in his letters and parcels, including the swift reply she'd received just yesterday, containing a Rosemary Clooney album and a card penned in Bud's compact, left-leaning cursive:

*Dear Bean,*
*Enclosed please find a record album that was recommended to me by a young colleague. Do you have a phonograph at the cottage? If not, send word. I can have one delivered.*

*Tell your brother I said for him to set up your buoys. Just so long as you remember progress isn't always measured along a straight line. As for his so-called graduation present, you can tell him I don't recall ever promising so much as a Buick, never mind a Bugatti. And now he's onto Beechcrafts? I'd feel a lot more comfortable buying him an airplane if I had even the slightest indication that he knew how to fly one.*

*Finally, I never have to worry about your being cooperative or not, but I feel compelled to write it just the same. Be good to your dear Auntie! These days she needs you in her "pod" more than you need her in yours.*

*As ever, Bud (Dad)*

"Ahem!" Poppy cleared her throat. She stood eyeing Sabina's pruned fingers with grave distaste. "I cannot imagine the Dooleys will be impressed to greet you in this bedraggled *state*. What do you think, Connie? Whatever can we do with her?" Poppy turned to interview their housekeeper, who'd just arrived on the landing to deliver Sabina's beach towel and robe.

"I think she's a lovely girl."

"Yes, well, we are attending a formal bruncheon today. Not the Kennel Club's sheepdog conformation show."

"Can you explain," asked Sabina, ignoring this latest critique, "why we are attending an engagement *brunch* before going to the trouble of redressing for an engagement *dinner*, all on the very same day?" She squinted at her aunt, her trademark expression. Sabina had her mother's eyes—cool green ringed with navy. Also willfulness, curiosity, and a fearlessness of the ocean—the push that sent her racing all the way out to the harbor's Middle Flats: all of these came from her mother too.

"Every woman should change her clothes for dinner, regardless of the occasion."

"Yes, yes, I know. But aren't these celebrations meant to be spaced out a bit more? Lenore and J. J. only just announced in the papers last week.

Why do you suppose such a terrible rush?" Sabina winked at Connie. Some days she couldn't help but rile ole A. P.

"Never ask questions that provoke unflattering answers," Aunt Poppy grimaced. "It is not your place to know why. Suffice it to say the Dooleys and the Shreves would like to arrange an *expeditious* trip down the aisle."

"Ah, because of Lenore's delicate condition?" Sabina pretended to catch on slowly.

"Circumstances notwithstanding," Poppy cleared her throat again, "Lenore is your best friend. And it's your duty to wish her well."

"She's not my *best* friend," Sabina corrected. "She hasn't been my best friend since we were eleven years old. What's more, I doubt she'd notice my being there or not. Her parents invited half the island."

"The rich half," whispered Connie, giving Sabina a little pinch.

"That's enough guff. *Both of you.* I am done discussing the matter," Poppy asserted. "We were invited. We are attending. We are all very excited to share in this happy event."

"Hardly that. I never have anything worthwhile to say to these people."

"Don't be ridiculous," Aunt Poppy snorted. "You are an elegant, well-educated young lady. You could certainly hold your own on the topic of *bridal fashions*. Or what about that new wicker porch furniture they've put out at the Harbor View? And Sabina, dear, if you find yourself *truly* at a loss, one can never go wrong, conversationally, by praising the success of the pastry."

Sabina saw no point in arguing. She had promised to be cooperative. And she really was something of a friend to Lenore Dooley, despite the girl's outsized ego. Lenore was the sort who liked to imagine boys waging fistfights over the lounge chair next to hers. She spent her summer afternoons poolside, maintaining a diary of all the ones who owned their own convertibles and all the ones who owned their own hotel chains. All the ones who'd begged off Patsy Walliston, and all the ones who *claimed* they had but still took an awfully keen interest whenever Patsy dropped her swim robe to reveal that holy show of a French bikini underneath. Now, with a wedding on the horizon, it would've appeared this endless zeal for masculine attention had succeeded. Then again, knowing the true push behind a rather hurry-up affair, Sabina doubted her old friend was reveling in victory at the moment.

"All right, A. P.," Sabina surrendered. "But I should confess to you now that I only packed two party dresses for the summer. And if you're expecting me to wrestle myself into a girdle tonight, well, my swimsuit will have to do."

"Please *pretend* to be a lady, Sabina. Just until I'm dead and gone," sighed Poppy. "You'll have your whole life to flit about in faded dungarees and this, this—" She closed her eyes to the offending sight. "This *thatch* of unset hair."

"What's wrong with my hair?"

"Peculiarities of style may make a man notice you, Sabina, but not favorably. We'll have to trim that length considerably before September comes."

Sabina drew in a great breath. The reality of the fall—and an extended sentence at Weston College—cast a pall across even the island's sunniest days. In her mind, Sabina could see it all unfolding: the next four years of her life, like a series of grim snapshots. Shopping for the right campus clothes. Chemical waving her naturally curly hair. Sitting through the class spirit contests, the annual pageant for the best-looking "frosh." Worst of all, the endless hours wasted inside yet another set of classrooms, learning life's supposed essentials: how to balance a household budget, how to stock a respectable linen closet.

"You might be pleased to know," Aunt Poppy broke into her niece's thoughts, "James has offered you the front seat in his Austin-Healey this morning. I'll ride over with Dennis, but you *must* be ready on time!"

Sabina was not pleased. James Whelan was an acquaintance from the yacht club, a Columbia University medical student and—in her umpteen years of summering in Edgartown—unrelenting in his quest for a date to the annual Regatta Ball. Aunt Poppy mostly liked him because he brought gifts of hats and scarves from Sybil Connolly's collection on Fifth Avenue. Also because they both followed their weekly episodes of *Dragnet* with breathless anticipation.

With aunt and housekeeper on her heels, Sabina wrapped her towel around her head before padding barefoot across the lawn, still wet with its sparkling dew. She hugged her robe around her shoulders and carried herself into the cottage, already thinking up ways she might evade James Whelan and his lousy convertible.

# TWO

Colin Hatch scanned the yacht club crowd—fancy people, decorating fancy plates with finger food they'd no intention of eating—and wondered again what the hell he was doing here. *This is supposed to be a breakfast buffet?* He didn't see anything that looked like an egg or a hotcake. On the other hand, he spied plenty of noteworthies: the lieutenant governor and Lew Hoad, that whole tired lot. They all stood gathered under the broad A-frame of the Edgartown Yacht Club, anchored at the edge of a long pier, just off Dock Street. The morning was warm but windless, so Hatch supposed none of them felt too sorry about missing early hours on the water.

"When I heard that Lenore had accepted my son J. J.'s proposal, my first thought was: *How did he manage that?*" A ripple of laughter filled the room as the yacht club commodore, John Shreve, addressed his out-of-town guests and fellow members. "My second thought," Shreve continued, "was thank God he's a *boy*, and I don't have to pay for it!" This time peals of laughter swelled up to the rafters. "Good luck, Dooley! They've both got rather expensive taste!"

The fathers nodded at each other in mirthful commiseration over the cost of a proper wedding these days. The real joke, of course, was that Bill Dooley was a prominent real estate developer; John Shreve owned half the textile mills in New England. Either one—the guests well knew—could have afforded ten weddings with just the cash in his pocket.

"But wait, wait just a second," Shreve commanded, quieting everyone down again. "Before you laugh too hard at poor Bill's expense, I feel compelled to warn you, those of you who've never been to the island before, this trip won't be cheap for you either. Your wives are already making inquiries at Seagate Realty. And your husbands—I've seen them, ladies—they're sizing up the sloops with the Burma teak planking."

The commodore rubbed his fingers together in the universal sign for money. Everyone, it seemed, was having a splendid time.

"So let's raise our glasses to Lenore and J. J.," Shreve concluded his toast. "Sorry, fellas, it's strictly tomato juice for now. We've got these damned blue laws in Massachusetts!" Here again, more laughter, a few groans of complaint. The commodore lifted his juice. "To the wind that blows, the ship that goes, and the lass who loves a sailor!"

Hatch had no glass to raise, so he fished in his pocket after his cigarette case instead. He pressed the clasp below his father's monogram and, well, there she was again. Her portrait. Adele.

"Something to drink, Mr. Hatch?" A waitress touched his elbow.

"A coffee would make my day."

"She's pretty," the waitress nodded at the old photograph pressed into his case. "Wouldn't have pegged *you* for the memento-carrying type. Long-lost love?"

Hatch snapped the lid closed. "Just the coffee, thanks."

She gave him a loaded grin. "How do you take it?"

"Black, if you don't mind."

"I should've known. I'm exactly the same."

"That so?"

"Ask anyone. I'm a cinch for keeping things *uncomplicated*." She laughed too loudly, squeezing his arm, earning them both some looks from around the room.

Swell. Just what he needed: more looks. Hatch understood by now that when the people at these sorts of parties stopped and regarded him, what they saw, mostly, was a scandal. He was twenty-nine now, after all. Cloudy service record. No wife. The question of who he took to bed and how often might as well have been a column in the *Vineyard Gazette*. It meant he didn't mix well with the club wives. And he didn't feel quite comfortable chatting up the well-heeled debs—rich girls who, anyway, he found to be more and more implausible dates as the seasons went by.

"An uncomplicated woman?" Hatch's eyebrows lifted. "I've heard tell, but I've never encountered one in real life."

The waitress smirked. "Be right over with your coffee, hon. Less than a trice."

Hatch struck a match against the bottom of his shoe and lit his cigarette. He stepped outside to pace the dock, where strands of floating oarweed skirted the piles then disappeared underneath. The sun climbed higher in the sky while the guests raked portions of poached salmon and chilled prawns onto their plates. Even under the umbrellas, the heat felt inescapable.

He stood thinking about his midday flight to Boston today—another last-minute favor to appease Bill Dooley—when he heard his name from above. He looked up to spy Denny McTigue waving him to join a circle of guests. Hatch climbed the steps to the building's upper deck.

"What's the good word, McTigue?"

"Colin Hatch! So nice of you to dress for the occasion," Denny slapped his back, referencing the pilot's crisp uniform. "Bristol fashion, ay?"

"That just shows how much you know." Hatch grinned at the group. He recognized Bill Dooley's wife and daughter, and then there was Denny's aunt standing between them. But he was unable to place the other two, neither the young man in the madras sport shirt nor the last face—a girl with light eyes and dark lashes. "As it happens, I fetch a decent number of compliments in this getup."

"I shouldn't doubt it," Denny's aunt murmured to Mrs. Dooley. Hatch watched the women exchange glances. This was not the first time they'd discussed him, apparently.

"Have you just come in from the city?" Nola Dooley, the bride's mother, interjected.

"No, I came from home. I have a place in West Tisbury."

"Colin bought the last decent lot out by Lambert's Cove," Denny added.

"Oh, that's right! It's a farm of sorts, isn't it?" Mrs. Dooley asked.

"I'd like to think so. Vegetable beds are a work in progress. But the place came with a healthy orchard, some decent rootstock. If I can find the time I might try to bottle my own wine this year."

"You don't hear that much from a bachelor, do you? It's so . . . *agrarian* of you," said the old aunt, grasping for a comfortable segue. "Mr. Hatch, forgive me. I haven't introduced our group properly. This is Mr. James Whelan. He's a medical student. From *Manhattan*."

This Mr. Whelan nodded an impassive hello, scrunching his nose to inch his eyeglasses back into position. He had a big, round face with eyes, nose, and mouth all crammed together at its center—as though, somewhere along the way, his chin, cheeks, and forehead had gone right on growing while the key pieces stood pat. Whelan sat sidesaddle, on a wrought iron café table, twirling a sailor's lanyard around his freckled knuckles.

"Lucky thing our James is a doctor in the making. Someone's liable to faint in this heat! Am I right?" Denny's aunt tittered at her own polite conversation. "Colin, you know my nephew Dennis already, don't you? This is Mrs. Nola Dooley, of course. Lenore, *the bride*—"

"Morning," Hatch doffed his twill cap in semicircular fashion. "We have met."

"You may also have heard Dennis mention his sister? Sabina?" The aunt raised her eyebrows expectantly. Following these words, Hatch saw two things happen almost simultaneously. First, the grinning Mr. Whelan sidled up to Denny's sister, clamping a hand down on her shoulder. Second, Hatch saw the girl stiffen and recoil at being claimed.

He locked eyes with her. "Oh sure, Denny *mentioned* a little sister. But clearly—well, I only wish he would have said more."

The three women gaped. Sabina squinted. She dug both fists into her dress pockets, ignoring his tanned forearm and outstretched hand. "On a day like this you must be so busy ferrying the tourists, Mr. Hatch. I hope we're not delaying you from getting back to the airfield."

"Gosh, Bean, that's a real swell how-do-you-do," Denny admonished his sister.

"I only meant to say, he might not have time for these endless introductions." The girl studied her fingernails, swallowing her first attempt at changing the subject. After a moment, addressing Hatch again, she said softer, "If you haven't already tried some, the raspberry Danish this morning is exquisite."

"You've sampled it, have you?" Hatch winked at her. "I didn't think you ladies ever ate the pastry at these sorts of affairs. Just used it as a point of conversation."

"*Clever as a crow*," the aunt murmured to Mrs. Dooley, who hid her reaction behind a slow sip from her teacup.

So he'd hit the mark. They'd discussed him all right. And wherever there were holes in the narrative, Hatch could see, these women were generous enough to supply patchwork with their own imaginations. Unfortunately, the club waitress found him at that very moment to deliver his coffee, not before giving his arm another familiar squeeze. A meaningful pause fell upon the circle.

"Hey, I heard you bought a third vee tail," Denny deflected. "Airpark must be running out of room to park your birds."

"A *third*? Oh my. How many birds—rather, airplanes—can one man fly?" the old aunt asked rhetorically, eyes trailing after the waitress' swaying hips.

"Actually," Hatch began, clearing his throat, "it was Mr. Dooley who bought that newest Beechcraft. He's expanding, always expanding. I needn't tell you, Mrs. Dooley, about Bill's appetite for business. And to your point about the tourists," he said, smiling at Sabina, "I don't expect to be at their beck and call much longer. Bill's hired us two fellas to help manage the peak season."

"But don't you *enjoy* flying?" Nola Dooley looked surprised. "I gathered from Bill you liked nothing better."

Hatch smiled in reply. He didn't *hate* his job exactly. He was too good-natured to view the horizon through such a dire lens. Besides that, being partners with Bill Dooley, it wasn't ever clear exactly what his job amounted to—piloting, gladhanding, taking orders. Some days he could admit—long term—the charter company was his smartest play. That he ought to stick it out, swallow his pride, save his money. Eventually he'd be able to buy out Dooley's share. But then again, flying—even running the business side of flying—wasn't what he wanted. Not really.

Because, sure, the club guys all laughed at his jokes, his stupid Charles Laughton impressions. And yeah, they thanked him like heck for helping dodge the fuss of a commercial flight. Their nephews and sons were even sporting enough to invite Hatch to lose his shirt at their weekly card games. But the truth of the matter came down to this: When the wind rolled in at a steady fifteen knots—kicking up gorgeous whitecaps across the sound—the bankers and the lawyers would all decide to play hooky at two thirty on a Wednesday afternoon or quarter till ten on a Thursday morning or at right-now-o'clock and *gee whiz, can't you be here any sooner?* And then it was his service that they—Dooley, Shreve, all of them—*expected*. Because ultimately, he was their chauffeur.

"Eh," Hatch made a little shrug. "Flying is one thing. Making dozens of milk runs for smart guys in suits, no offense"—he held up his free hand with respect to Denny, a regular commuter—"isn't exactly what I dreamed about as a kid."

"Yes, well. Not everyone can be Ted Williams," the smirking doctor mused. "World needs transportation workers too."

Hatch rubbed his brow with the back of his wrist. *Christ, it's humid.* He felt his starched shirt sticking to his shoulders. He thought, too, in a wordless moment, maybe he comprehended something of Sabina, seeing her frown at the remark.

"You might consider extending some gratitude to those smart guys in the suits," Whelan continued. "Lest you'd prefer towing blue plate–special ads for the Scrod Hut. 'Ahoy! Five ninety-nine lobster and spuds!'" Whelan swept his left hand like a trailing banner in the sky, looking altogether pleased with himself.

"Thanks for the advice, Jim," Hatch answered coolly.

"Hey, don't get salty, Captain. I'm sure everyone in Boston is falling over himself to book a seat on your airplane."

"I'm sure too," the aunt agreed, frowning. "Everyone except for Sabina, of course."

"Don't you fly, Sabina?" Mrs. Dooley looked quizzical.

"Poor thing. She's a reluctant flier," Whelan confirmed in a low voice.

"I'm not reluctant. I *won't* fly. Categorically." Sabina glared at him. "On the other hand I'm very comfortable answering for myself, thank you."

"Is that right?" Hatch studied the girl more intently. "You won't fly?"

"The only ones who *ought* to be flying are birds and bees. And winged insects. Some spiders. Seeds, of course."

"Spiders don't fly, dear," the old aunt clucked.

"Oh, but they *do*. On filaments."

"Filaments?" Denny mouthed the word to himself.

"That's right. Miles up in the sky. It's how arachnids came to be established in so many distant places. The remote Pacific, even."

Despite her standoffishness, there was something in her manner that captivated Hatch, or maybe it was precisely *because* of that same quality that he couldn't take his eyes off her now. At the piano inside, someone began teasing out the strands of a familiar song. Hatch wondered how he'd never crossed paths with McTigue's pretty sister before.

"I happen to think airplanes are divine," Lenore Dooley suddenly interjected, unaccustomed to being sidelined for so long in any conversation, let alone a conversation taking place at her own engagement brunch. She wedged her dramatic figure in between Sabina and Hatch, helping the spotlight to land as it normally did. "I think every man should learn how to fly one. Wouldn't you agree, Colin?"

Colin liked Lenore Dooley well enough, though she had a habit of following him around the club, hunting after an offer to buy her another scotch and soda. Sometimes she tagged along when he flew her father to Boston, arranging herself in the copilot's seat like a beauty queen on a parade float.

"Now that I know you don't fly," Hatch refocused on Sabina, "I guess I can't expect I'll see you at the airpark anytime soon. Where might I expect to see you instead?"

Whelan hopped off the table. "Look, if you're handing out social invitations you'd better take your place at the end of the line. Sabina has promised to crew for me this season."

"Uh, James." Poppy McTigue took up the young man's arm with overtaking volume, saving the group from any escalation of tensions. "How did you enjoy your drive up from the city?"

"Abysmally. Ferry was as crowded as I've ever seen it. Seems like the tourists are getting wise, bringing their station wagons in droves. Can't say I blame them. Nothing worse than pedaling around Edgartown on a *bicycle* all summer. Specially in this weather."

"Bicycling is better for the air," Sabina murmured.

"Better for the air?" Whelan shot out a laugh. "What are you, some kind of naturalist?"

"It's called human ecology. You ought to read about it."

"Too hot to read," Whelan puffed. "Damned near too hot to think."

"An inspiring sentiment from the future doctor of medicine." Hatch grinned, checking for Sabina's reaction. Barely, with something like complicity in her eyes, she smiled back.

"Look, I'm slightly asthmatic, just so you know." Whelan coughed into his fist. "Given the Weather Bureau's forecast, I am resolved to spending the next five days avoiding all unnecessary exertion."

"Gee, that's tough." Hatch made a face of grave disappointment. He squeezed the ridge of his chin. "It just occurred to me you all might like to take advantage of strawberry season at my farm. Ladies? I have more berries than I could ever use. Even the rabbits can't make a dent."

"We'd love to visit!" Lenore Dooley gushed while the older women exchanged looks. "What a charming idea."

Hatch found himself studying Sabina again. The slightest of raindrops had begun to land on the girl's arms and shoulders.

"For our part," McTigue's aunt stonewalled, "I'm afraid, my niece and I are *constantly* on the move. Hither and yon, hither and yon—we are just as two roadrunners for all the summer, aren't we?"

A distant thunder rumbled.

"Strawberry picking is my favorite thing," Sabina said quietly to her shoes. No one seemed to hear her as the other men commented on the heat flashes in the sky and the women gathered up their hats and embroidered clutch purses.

No one heard her except for Colin Hatch, who waited to catch her eye again before speaking. "Hopefully I'll be lucky enough to see you all at the party this evening?" he said.

"Oh yes," Lenore agreed, crowding in to kiss both his cheeks, Continental-style. "You can count on it."

Meanwhile, Nola Dooley sprang to the excuse of the rain. "We'd better head that way now. I've got caterers to oversee. It was a pleasure to finally meet you, Mr. Hatch. My husband says such nice things. And we're sincere about hoping to sample your strawberries," she added, less than sincerely.

"I should shove off too," Sabina mumbled, following suit. "I have some letters to write."

"Be a lamb and bring the car around, Dennis," the aunt instructed. "I'd say the sky might open up any moment."

Colin checked his watch. "S'pose I'm off to Katama. Mr. Dooley has a business meeting in town. It's been a pleasure." He tipped his cap again, allowing the ladies to go on ahead.

The group descended the balcony staircase one by one, while Hatch surveyed the fleet of boats parked at their moorings—the Chappy coastline trembling in the haze on the opposite shore. He watched them disperse across the patio, smiling his chauffeur's smile, offering cheerful waves and more promises to engage them later that same night. He wasn't exactly waiting to see if McTigue's pretty sister might look back at him. But wouldn't you know it? She did.

# THREE

"Bless me, Father, for I have sinned," Bill Dooley rasped, crossing himself mechanically. "It's been one week since my last confession. You won't believe it, but I'm afraid that, well, I may've stolen again."

"What have you stolen, William?" Father Keneavy sighed behind the clover-patterned screen. He did believe it. Through the dim light, the priest could see his parishioner sweating in his suitcoat, ashing his cigar into a hymnal. Beads of sweat flowed from Dooley's pores, along with the lingering impression of four or five Drambuies.

"More money for the Wasque development."

"The island again? I thought you'd given that up."

"I did. I mean, I *had*, earlier. But then I got to thinking . . ."

The project in question, Wasque Winds, LLC, was a ninety-acre stretch of beach and dunes, backed by grassy countryside, skirting the elbow of an island—a separate island—just barely connected to the larger isle of Martha's Vineyard. Ten years ago Dooley had bought the acreage and its rustic homestead for a song—a real ditty, it had seemed at the time—relieving some old school teacher who was tired of having his boat shed blown over every fall.

From the start, Bill's usual investors had been unimpressed. This particular parcel of land was entirely without roads, no utilities, not a single place to buy a beer after a long week of work in the city. To say nothing of its inaccessibility—there was no reasonable way to get there.

Still, Dooley had seen raw potential. He saw the natural extension of

Cape Cod's building boom, where available oceanfront lots wouldn't last forever. In Wasque he'd envisioned thousand-foot cottages, simple and compact enough to stand side by side, row by row—maybe four to an acre. He pictured, in time, a little marina and a boardwalk, just like the scene in Ocean City, with a penny arcade and a carousel and a brightly decorated bandstand under the stars. So while the War smoldered distantly, Dooley had pulled together his advertising kit—promotional letters, sales blanks—waiting for the men and the market to return.

Except now that they *had*—now that every GI and his growing brood had the means to purchase investment property—suddenly the rules on Chappaquiddick were changing. Concerns over the rapid introduction of numerous new dwellings ("Dooleyville," detractors called it) prompted the formation of the Island Commission. They'd stitched together a first attempt at zoning laws in the pathetic, rudimentary fashion of five people at a living room potluck. And if they had their way, if Edgartown officials *gave* them their way, soon enough, the chances of Dooley covering his hide—let alone turning a profit—would be nil.

It was all quite silly, really. Hysterical fuss about the traffic, the groundwater. So much hue and cry had the effect of complicating access to any more than just a handful of building permits. Only five or six opportunities to break ground in '54. That was it. Meanwhile his new investors—neighbors, friends, a few enterprising members of Nola's sewing circle—they were all getting itchy, wondering when they'd see their cut. And for a little while, even Bill Dooley couldn't imagine a way out of the jam.

"You've overextended yourself," scolded the priest mildly. "First those sky balloon rides. Then the doomsday bunkers and the fallout kits—"

"The kits are actually selling quite well," Bill put in.

"You *could* cut your losses, William."

"The losses aren't just mine to bear. Not anymore." Dooley took out his handkerchief and blew. He may have been crying a little. "Playing the ponies like I do—that hasn't helped."

"I see," nodded Father Keneavy. "Shall we pray on it then?"

Bill Dooley twisted his wedding ring. He thought of his wife, his three daughters, their perpetually outstretched hands wanting for things, always bigger and brighter. He thought of facing them back at the island, before tonight's party. They'd be knee-deep in china patterns by now. He pictured himself firing the band, firing the caterers, adios-ing that goddamned florist, and then announcing—maybe apologizing—he would have to sell the Edgartown beach house; the Sugarloaf chalet; their two saddlebreds, Smutty and Big Jim . . .

Oh sure, his wife had money. Heaps of it! Piled up high enough to cushion the chandeliers in the Barclays vault. But for access she still needed her ancient father's permission and—*No.* Bill shook his head in revulsion. That kind of surrender simply wasn't in him. He'd sooner run away to Panama.

Instead of praying, Bill Dooley pushed aside the privacy screen to face the priest directly. "Have you heard what they're doing now in Hawaii?"

"Surfboarding?"

"No, Father, I mean the *builders.* They're going vertical! Apartments to own. Twenty, maybe thirty units *on a single foundation.*" This particular pivot was not a new one, but it was the first time Bill had proposed it out loud. He liked the way it sounded, if only, at the moment, in this dark, echoic space built for the very purpose of exalting fantastical ideas.

The thing was, Bill had just taken a much-needed vacation—a Honolulu golf retreat with some friends from the club. And he'd come back with an inspired, albeit sketchy sort of a solution to the island problem. He needed more money, of course (which is why he'd accepted Jack Crowder's check at brunch today), and he'd need some creative writing skills from the lawyer he ate dinner with on Wednesdays. But the legal croquet required to get the job done was not so complex that Bill was ready to give up. His mind—despite being closed off to so many hallways of art and science—was masterfully limber with the law and the apertures of a Massachusetts building proposal. When he closed his eyes at night he dreamed in contract clauses—of winding tendrils and subtly complex anthers bursting forth from the potentiality of his empty, undeveloped land.

The more he talked, the easier it became to set aside his idea of a simple subdivision of bric-a-brac cottages. Now he could picture something really remarkable: a self-contained *vacation community.* He imagined an Olympic-sized swimming pool. Golf lessons. A fitness gymnasium staffed by bronzed young men and women. Flotillas for every holiday. Waterskiing. Stage shows. Everything you might find in Tahoe, Fort Lauderdale, or Hilton Head—only better.

"They are called *condo*-miniums," Dooley explained to the priest. His blue eyes flickered with a hectic, galloping sense of ambition. "The town has only given me five permits, sure. But I could still build dozens of houses. I'd just stack them up, up, up! And for the buyers, it'd be like living in a luxury hotel! With a view of the ocean and a balcony right off the kitchen—"

"William," sighed the priest, consulting his wristwatch. His favorite radio program was set to begin in five minutes. He couldn't have cared less if Dooley were building another Great Sphinx of Giza in the middle of Mass Ave. "I can tell you're excited. I have counseled you through similar positions before. I don't doubt your ability to fully realize these plans for your *condo*—what did you call them?"

"Mini-ums."

"Okay, fine. Yes. And so it seems to me this is more of an accounting problem than a cause for penance. Maybe you've put some money where it doesn't belong—*temporarily.* Let's say you build your *mini*—your modern houses—and in the end every cent is returned to your investors, threefold."

"But that's the problem, Father. I'm running low on funds, you see. At this point I can't actually *build* anything without securing purchase agreements, *down payments.* And I can't sell the notes without a bridge." Dooley leaned into the sill of the open window. He was waiting for something divine.

"A bridge, you say?"

"That's right. For the cars. A bridge between Edgartown and Chappaquiddick. I know this type of buyer, Father. I can picture his superior, Park Avenue mug. He'll pay for the oceanfront, all right, but not the hassle. Imagine how it'd look. Can you? Me bringing them 'round to survey their new property on a fisherman's launch, getting their good shoes all pickled with seawater?"

"Sounds like quite a bind." The priest scratched at the back of his ear.

"Two ferries, you understand? *Each way?* Even I can't honey that." Dooley shifted on the kneeler. His bad knee was stiffening.

"In that case, son, I might suggest that you've come to the wrong place."

"But there's no place else for me to go," Dooley rasped.

"That's just the gray sky talking." Father Keneavy removed his eyeglasses and squeezed the bridge of his nose. "Anyroad, go home to your family. Get back to work tomorrow. You'll find a way."

"It's like I said, Father. I haven't a shot in hell without a bridge between these two islands—"

"I'm surprised I have to remind *you* of all people, William. God doesn't build bridges. Not lately, anyway. It's politicians that do."

# FOUR

"Talk about a gift for the couple that has every material thing," Aunt Poppy marveled in a well-practiced stage whisper. "What in blue blazes will they ever do with *that*?"

Sabina and her aunt stood staring in front of a gargantuan gift table, swathed in damask cloth and tulle bunting. The table marked the entrance of a multi-peaked marquee in the Dooley's backyard. The family's Edgartown "cottage" was easily the largest on the block. Its lawn rolled downhill in broad, contrasting stripes. A cupola-topped carriage house sheltered a small fleet of sports cars whose tires never touched pavement, only the herringbone brick drive, which was itself kept clean enough for the cuffs of men in white trousers.

Tonight, a veritable fortress of boxes stood carefully arranged, all in wrappings of familiar department-store hues. To the left of the table, propped up on a silver sawhorse, was what appeared to be a massive toy airplane—with a wingspan nearly six feet wide.

"Isn't she a beauty?" Bill Dooley exclaimed, lurking behind his newest guests. "I saw one on my last trip to Chicago, and I said, *Bill, if you don't bring one of these babies home you'll be kicking yourself all summer.* The kids think she's wonderful!"

"Yes, but what *is* it?" Aunt Poppy asked. "Does it fly?"

"You bet your bonnet she flies," Dooley huffed, looking a little offended. "This here is a radio-controlled Trixter Bolt. Navy uses a similar instrument for gunnery targets."

"Oh my word."

"Look, you can steer her from the ground with this little control panel. We're gonna give old Lois a spin in just a few minutes. I named her Lois," he beamed.

"You're going to fly this? In the air?" Sabina repeated, incredulous.

"Not *me*! I can't fly a flag. I've got Mr. Hatch on the job. Have you met him yet?"

Just then Sabina spied Lenore Dooley, careening across the lawn. At events like these, Lenore normally looked like a dream. Her city hairdresser made the trip to arrange her blonde waves into smooth back rolls that exposed the elegant length of her neck, her pink Tahitian pearl chokers. Given the opportunity to greet a new male guest, she would typically glide over and strike up all sorts of dramatic faces, like the Scandinavian model in the Pond's advertisements. Tonight though, the bride looked worn. Her red lipstick was feathering. Her forehead shone. Ample curves tested the mettle of her silk taffeta seams, while dark crescents of perspiration underscored her armpits.

J. J. looked worse. Practically limping behind his fiancée, J. J. Shreve looked every bit as though he'd spent the day consuming alcohol under a direct, beating sun. He gave Sabina a perfunctory up-and-down glance before emitting a jaded yawn.

"Daddy," Lenore scowled at the radio plane, "you said you would get us a skywriter. *This* is not a skywriter. It's barely more than a child's toy."

"The skywriters were all spoken for this weekend," Dooley explained, unconvincingly, without looking up from his plane's controller.

"I wanted a plane that could *do* something. After all, it's meant to be a bit of entertainment. And why aren't there *two* of them? One for John, and one for me?" As she carped, bejeweled charms slid up and down her long doeskin gloves.

"Have another glass of champagne," Bill Dooley suggested. "Have three or four. Eventually you'll see two of them."

Not wanting any part of the Dooley family squabble, Sabina excused herself faintly, sneaking away toward the tent's massive interior. She stepped up onto the parquet dance floor, where a few older couples waltzed. Gloved waiters carried hors d'oeuvres on antique trays. The eight-piece band, elevated on a red-carpeted stage, wore immaculate tuxedos with tea rose boutonnieres. Strings of fairy lights illuminated the Dooley's massive white oaks.

As the engagement party was the first big event of the season, Sabina could see the women making careful study of their neighbors' ensembles. It was a good year, evidently, for cocktail dresses in silk brocade, hibiscus prints, halter necklines. The band drowned out the low rustle of crinoline underskirts, but nothing could detract from the effects of so much shapewear. Sabina stood up a little straighter as some extreme examples happened her way, their bullet bras as sleek and streamlined as Cadillac fins.

She was watching just such an example pass by when she heard a familiar voice at her back.

"Miss McTigue?" It was Colin Hatch, of course. His baritone voice—warm and vaguely British—met her ears as if she'd been waiting for it. She turned around to face the charter pilot from West Tisbury.

"Hello," Sabina nodded. And then, involuntarily, "You look so nice."

"Do I?" he laughed, his smile impossibly handsome. "Came straight from the airpark. I missed my evening shave." He ran the backs of his fingers against his five o'clock shadow, a little self-conscious it seemed. But it was true; clean-shaven or no, he looked rather striking in the dimming daylight.

"My aunt likes to say that appearance is all about choosing one fine accessory."

"That's an interesting theory. Is *he* your one fine accessory?" Hatch smiled conspiratorially, tilting his head in the direction of James Whelan, who was seated at a nearby table, buttering a dinner roll with a good deal of aggression.

"He's not such a bad fellow." Sabina felt herself blush. "He was my first tennis partner at the yacht club. I think maybe we were nine. Haven't quite managed to shake him since."

"Sounds serious." Hatch whistled. "How does he play?"

"Truthfully?"

"Eh," Colin Hatch sized up the medical student. "Maybe you ought to cushion it a little. For his sake. We owe him that much."

"Do we owe him something?" Sabina squinted.

"I think we must. He'll be so discouraged, after the long run he's had as your partner, to see you and I dancing together."

The Dooley's property—perched on a steep, commanding rise—backed into Edgartown Harbor, lording over the dunes below and the lights of the motorboats distantly roving the bay. Overhead, the moon was so perfectly halved, it looked like a new quarter tucked into a seam of the sky. The day's earlier storm had blown away all humidity, and now the air held perfect for an evening outdoors with bare shoulders. The band segued into something by Sinatra. Sabina accepted Hatch's hand with a volt of nervous energy. Everyone she knew, no doubt, was watching.

"So." Sabina breathed in. She attempted to hide her tentative dance steps with the very first question that materialized in her head, the one she overheard most often at events like these. "What brought you to the island? Originally, I mean."

"My first flight base was here. You won't remember. You would've been, what? Six or seven years old? But after basic, a group of us flew training missions at MVA. It's a beautiful place. Even when you're here to simulate combat missions."

"And how was it that you got into flying?" She gave in to his lead with somewhat steadier feet. He was a good dancer. She relaxed her shoulders.

"Well, my father was a pilot. That's where it started."

"He wanted you to follow in his footsteps?"

Hatch shook his head. "No, you might say Jerry forced the issue. See, I was at the Gunnery in '41, not really sure where I'd end up. And then the war broke out. Allies needed all the boots they could get. We would have boarded the boats that winter if they'd let us."

"But you were too young?"

"Only sixteen then," he nodded. "Boy, was my mother ever boiling, come spring, when they decided to graduate us juniors a year early. I remember the day they lined us up in the gymnasium, telling us to pick a side—Army over here, Army Air Corps over there. That's when it felt like we were finally getting ready to do something."

"You chose the Air Corps?"

"I already had my pilot's license. And . . ."

"And?" Sabina felt herself hanging on to his words.

"And I prefer a good vantage point, I guess."

"You must be very comfortable with heights."

"You could say that." He paused again to consider this assessment, looking off to the parterre at the side yard, then back into her eyes, maybe deciding how much he wanted to elaborate. "When I was a kid, my cousins and I used to play hide-and-seek in my grandmother's backyard. She had a big English garden, full of high yews and rhododendrons. I figured out my odds were better if I climbed a tree, so I could see everyone's position."

"Ah, you were the smart one of your group."

"I was the *competitive* one, more like."

"You like to win?" Sabina raised a fine dark eyebrow.

"Everyone *likes* to win." Hatch grinned. "Don't you? I just make it a habit, more than a preference." His blue eyes surveyed the guests around the tables. He tapped his fingers against her back in time with the drummer's closed high hat. "Anyway, Air Corps said I was too tall for combat duty. Said I'd never make weight. They assigned me to the bombers at first. Had to learn twin engines, prove myself to some of the gruffest instructors you'd ever want to meet. Not to mention cut out second helpings in the mess hall." He smiled again. "Eventually I got sent to fly fighters, Mustangs, where I really wanted to be."

"Weren't you terribly nervous?" Sabina asked.

"Oh, I don't know. Probably too cocky to be. We pulled a lot of stunts without thinking in those days. Do you know of the East River in New

York City?" he asked. Sabina nodded. "Another student pilot and I—well, he was a real wag. One day we took our birds on an unsanctioned detour *below* a few bridges down that way. I caught some heat for that little mission."

"And then what happened?"

"The war, do you mean? That's a longer story." Hatch sighed. "Too long for one dance, I'm afraid."

"Of course." Sabina swallowed. "I'm sorry."

"What for? Thorough interrogation keeps a guy like me on his toes. Are you on the school newspaper, Miss McTigue?"

"No." She blushed reflexively. "I'll be on the swim club, though. At Weston College."

"Are you going into schoolteaching then?"

"Hardly. I worry I'm too impatient with grown-ups who don't care to understand me, let alone children."

"Something tells me, whatever you take up, you'll outshine every girl on campus." Hatch squeezed her hand inside his ever so gently. She felt goosebumps radiate from her wrist to her shoulder. She ducked her head a little to regain her bearings. "Uh-oh, you've gone quiet," Colin Hatch noted. "Did I overstep?"

"No, no. Not at all. I was just thinking . . . I . . . what kind of a tree was it?"

"Pardon me?"

"The tree. The one you used to climb in your grandmother's backyard. To improve your vantage point."

"I'm not sure I remember," Hatch said, looking at her a sideways. "Why should it matter?"

She shrugged. "I'm interested in those sorts of details. Places. Natural things. Right now I'm reading Peattie's *Complete History of Trees*."

"Sounds riveting."

"Oh, I know how it sounds. A lot of the girls tell me I shouldn't be so dull. Certainly I don't *mean* to be." She gulped a little in confessing her flaws. And yet from somewhere, somehow, she'd gotten the impression she was talking to a longtime friend.

"All right then, let me see." Hatch resumed tapping his fingers on the small of her back, where his palm had been resting. His eyes twinkled in refracting the outdoor lights. "That old tree must've been a thirty-foot Cleveland pear tree. With a view that spanned all the way to Narragansett Bay. It was planted in 1926, housed one squirrel's nest, and had a slight case of the sooty blotch. How's that for detail?"

"Now you're just humoring me," Sabina swatted her dance partner. Through his sport jacket, momentarily, she felt the heat and the firmness of his chest. She inched a step closer toward him. "But I do appreciate the effort. Is that where your family is from, then? Rhode Island?"

"My mother's people, yes. My father hailed from England. Another reason for you McTigues to dislike me," Hatch joked, drawing out a long "i" sound at the Irish pronunciation of "McTigue."

"*Dislike* you? Whoever said I . . . we . . . didn't like you?"

"You were ready to hand me my hat when we met this morning."

"That's not true!" Sabina protested. "I merely suggested a Danish."

"Fair enough. In that case, let's start over. Could we?"

Sabina was about to apologize for her earlier tone. The truth was she hadn't liked being teased—least of all in the presence of Lenore Dooley, a far-superior candidate for male flattery. But the party's host cut her short. Just at that moment, a red-faced Mr. Dooley approached them with his aggressive, lock-kneed stride. His fists opened and clenched and reopened as he walked.

"Now's our moment!" Dooley announced, ignoring Sabina altogether. "The women are inspecting the gifts, and we've just enough daylight left to make a go of it."

"I don't know, Bill." Hatch shook his head. "Miss McTigue and I are having a discussion. Give us a moment, will you, please?"

"I've already gathered the people—all the *key* people, I mean—over at the seawall. The Nashes, the Crosbys—everyone is waiting!"

For the second time in one night Sabina looked to avoid a battle. She lifted her hand from her dance partner's shoulder. "Don't worry, Mr. Hatch. I think I see someone who will gladly cut in for you."

"Aw, hell, don't tell me it's your old tennis mate." Hatch furrowed his brow. His fingertips lingered on her back, even as Dooley hovered, intent on marching him off toward the impromptu air show. "The good doctor may be smarter, but remember: I'm the more *competitive* one."

It was true, in fact. Everyone *was* waiting on the grassy precipice overlooking the Dooley's end of Starbuck Beach. Mr. Ewing had his box Brownie camera at the ready. Mrs. Noble clung to her birding binoculars. Aunt Poppy and her clique of club wives sat on the stone benches nearby, exchanging looks.

"Quiet, now! Everybody, quiet!" Dooley waved his arms in a downward motion. He sold the show like a carnival barker. "What you are about to witness is a historic launch! First time ever attempted on the island!"

Hatch scratched at his ear and stuck out his lower lip. On bended knee, he studied the shape and heft of the model. Hundreds of lightning bugs blinked among the hedgerow—a first act of sorts—while the crowd waited in obedient silence.

"Guess I'll start her from the hilltop," Hatch shrugged, dusting his pant legs. He flicked a switch, and the plane exploded into life with a loud, grating, mosquito whine.

"Can't see this stunt lasting more than a minute," Walt Ewing laughed to his neighbor.

A frowning Dooley poked the man's ribs. "I've got fifty bucks says she flies for at least five."

"Five minutes? This thing? I'll take that bet for two fifty!"

As the men produced bills to clinch the bet, the guests let out a triumphant cheer in watching the radio airplane dive down over the staghorn and the bearberry shrubs, leveling her smooth red wings into a glide above the beach. Under Hatch's control, she swung left toward the boulders of the jetty, most of them now submerged beneath a high tide. She buzzed the masthead of Dooley's sailboat—a showy cruiser he liked to dock at the house whenever he knew there were guests coming 'round to absorb the full picture of his success. Farther afield, the plane performed a neat little loop around the Athertons' flag pole, prompting everyone to clap wildly. The band struck up the William Tell Overture, and then people really got excited—breaking into the sort of two-fingered whistles they usually reserved for Fenway.

Among the cluster of rapt admirers, shoulders and elbows lined up endways, all swiveling their heads in unison, Sabina felt a tug at her wrist. She turned to meet her aunt's familiar rebuking expression.

"Be wary, young lady." Aunt Poppy wagged a finger. "Bad company corrupts good character."

"What is that comment supposed to mean?"

"Ask the girls he romanced at last year's parties. There are certainly enough of them to survey."

"Oh, honestly, A. P. That's a lot of hollow gossip and nothing more."

"Ask the man himself then." Poppy pursed her lips. "Go on! Ask him about that odd little charter company he doesn't actually own. Or the way he makes his living, flying airplanes he doesn't especially care to fly."

"If you have an opinion about Colin—about Mr. Hatch, I mean to say, why not come out with it directly?"

"My point is that he's *undesirable*." Poppy exaggerated the individual syllables of the word. She dragged Sabina a few steps from the gathering, continuing with a sharper tone. "If it weren't for Mr. Dooley taking pity, *that* young man wouldn't have a pot to piddle in. Wouldn't have a *paycheck*, I'd wager. Did you know that men with, with . . ." She sputtered her distaste. "With *blue tickets* can't even get a simple bank loan? No higher education, so forget about landing a decent job elsewhere . . ."

Sabina did know, thanks to Lenore's self-important gabbing, that it was Dooley's seed money that allowed Hatch to start up the charter company. She had a cloudy notion of what an army blue ticket meant. She recognized "other than honorable" discharge as a term sometimes used in the newspapers—a formal way of degrading a soldier. But she couldn't believe it'd been rightly applied to Colin Hatch. Even if she didn't exactly know him well, she knew him *enough*. She looked away from her aunt to spy Hatch's suit-coated back and broad shoulders. *Be cooperative*, she reminded herself of the promise to her father. *Be cooperative.*

"Hear this, too," Aunt Poppy went on. "*Undesirable* stands to say he's a man incapable of providing for a wife. And here you are, cheapening yourself to *dance with him*? A fine way to waste your reputation. Very fine, indeed."

This final declaration nearly incited the desired argument. Sabina was at the point of biting back, but in the few short moments of air show they'd missed, the tone of the audience had shifted. The guests stood much quieter now, mouthing solemn observations behind Hatch's back. With each new maneuver the plane's lost altitude became more pronounced. Sabina could see Hatch concentrating to straighten Lois's course with a gradual climb. But the model was too flimsy and too small against the backdrop of the gusty Atlantic.

"You're losing her," Dooley flustered, grabbing the controller from Hatch's hands.

"It's the wind," Hatch asserted.

"It's the signal," Dooley countered, steering his prize into the southeast breeze. And yet, the addition of more tailwind did not improve the situation. Instead, the replica plane skidded and stalled, porpoised and spun. A wing snapped off, plummeting earthward.

"She's gone now." Hatch frowned.

"Christ," Dooley swore. "Some pilot you are."

The mosquito whine grew distant. A few anguished gasps filled the silence in its wake. Through the gathering dusk, Sabina saw Hatch's jaw tighten. His Adam's apple pulsed in a hard swallow. All around the guests stood judging, and not for the first time.

In that moment, she would have liked to touch his hand or at least repay him with one of his own trenchant winks. But she'd already gotten the business from her aunt. And how much did she really know about the pilot anyway? Maybe he wouldn't appreciate a petty gesture at this particular moment. Maybe, a small voice in her head conceded, Aunt Poppy *did* understand some dynamics better than she.

These were the rational sort of thoughts that should have diverted her back to the party tent and the decorum of its waiting dinner tables. These were the facts that should have drawn her into some useless discussion, no doubt happening somewhere, about the merits of a fingertip veil or a ballroom bustle—to politely admire Lenore Dooley's treasured charm bracelet collection, even. To *any* path other than the one she presently chose, which was straight down the backyard beach stairs and into the Atlantic Ocean, on a mission to retrieve a lost aircraft.

She heard Aunt Poppy call her name only once, as she stripped down to her swimsuit and dove into the black waves. She didn't dare look back to see who was watching. The ocean current, like the wind, had strong ideas about what it would carry—and where. Instead of progressing very far forward, she felt herself fighting a determined tide. This was a very different kind of swim than the ones she performed at daybreak. Decidedly, this test had no precedent. Still, she realized—muscles burning, eyes stinging, as she approached the floating wreckage with altogether new levels of daring—this time she hardly needed any borrowed narrative to will her body back to shore.

# FIVE

## WESTERN UNION

W. P. MARSHALL, PRESIDENT

The filing time shown in the dateline on telegrams and day letters is STANDARD TIME at point of origin. Time of receipt is STANDARD TIME at point of destination.

1954 JUN 12 3:36PM 1954 JUN 13 1:12PM

EDGARTOWN, MA=P.O. BOX 2200

BILL: HEARD YOU NEEDED SOME HELP WINNING AN APPEASEMENT FROM THOSE DAMNED LITTLE ISLANDERS. BLAME IT ON FISHERMEN'S EYE; THEY LACK VISION. DON'T FRET, THOUGH. I'M SENDING ALONG SOMETHING SO BIG AND SO BLONDE EVEN A HALF-BLIND SCALLOPER CAN'T MISS HER. SHE'S GAME TO BUY THAT OLD CHAPPY HOUSE ON YOUR LOT. SHE'LL BE IN TOWN NEXT WEEK. BOOKED A ROOM AT THE HARBOR VIEW. I IMAGINE YOU AND YOUR BRIDGE WILL BE BACK IN BUSINESS SHORTLY THEREAFTER.

HARRIS

# SIX

Isolde Martin made it very well-known, at least once each day, in case it might be her last, that when she died she wanted to be buried in a size 2 Balenciaga silk suit. Byzantine blue, to match her eyes.

Except she wasn't dying. Not according to the doctors, anyway. And so what she wanted, *more immediately*, was to play the part of the teenage milkmaid in Frank Capra's next picture, scheduled to begin filming in September. To do so realistically would mean losing ten pounds along with the tired half-moons shadowing her eye sockets. It made sense, therefore, that she'd defected from Manhattan and come to this little resort town, on the recommendation of her boyfriend Harris—a rising Massachusetts politician with a thick accent and, somewhat inconveniently, a pencil-thin wife.

At first the move had sounded like an inspired plan. Harris knew of a man who was selling an old beach house—a tidy saltbox with a wood-burning stove and the dinner plates of someone's forgotten grandmother already inside. "Turnkey" was the expression, she believed. And all of that suited her fine.

She would spend the summer on the more-remote peninsula of an already remote island—Chappa-something, the guidebooks said. She would enjoy ten weeks removed from her prying fans. (Well, not *all* of her fans—mainly the sloppy, unattractive ones.) She would cut out the pills. Cut out the lunches. Maybe breakfasts too. On an island, anything could be possible! And golly, just think: all this majesty just under an hour from New York!

Except that so far, her island adventure, starting with the flight from LaGuardia, had proved nothing short of harrowing. Turbulence cracked her Swiss sunglasses against the ashtray. Her Perrier was stored in an eighty-degree footlocker. Before takeoff, the boorish charter pilot refused to fly her two prized cockatiels on his plane, which meant sending them with her driver, who'd subsequently gotten pulled over (*twice!*) in Connecticut—on account of all the squawking and swerving—only to be denied transport at the Cape Cod ferry. After six phone calls to the statehouse and a favor from the coast guard, finally, Isolde and company were at last assembled to enjoy their getaway destination. And then this latest crisis: no ripe cantaloupe. No cantaloupe at all, in fact.

"What's that, you say? No one can *find* a cantaloupe?" she'd demanded of the front desk. "Send me someone who could outwit a cantaloupe, then. Shall we just start there?" She slammed down the hotel room receiver. Her head hurt. Her heart ached. She'd hoped Harris would have been on scene to offer a surprise reunion. Flowers and a string quartet, at least, waiting for her in the suite. The absence of both drove her straight to her pep pills.

Isolde Martin was not an unreasonable woman. But she had learned how readily people respond to drama, and unless she was dead tired or truly aggrieved she found it best to ratchet everything to its most extreme degree. On the day she signed her three-picture contract with MGM, for example, she'd held a $5,000 funeral for Myrna Martin, the landlocked former version of herself, who had escaped greater Cleveland only by dint of a sudden snow squall that forced the emergency landing of a big-screen executive en route to LA. He had found her selling tuna fish sandwiches in Terminal A. *Could she act?* With her wide eyes and wondrous, high-shelved breasts, that detail was almost beside the point. And besides, if "acting" meant looking wholesome and serene in church every Sunday alongside her debauched parents, then, yes, absolutely, she could act.

A loud knocking roused her from her gloom. Koji, Isolde's bodyguard, intercepted the visitor.

"Isolde!" boomed the red-faced Bill Dooley, who barreled in past Koji with forced familiarity. His busy eyes bounced between the actress and the appointments of the room. Dooley drank in the fabrics, the fixtures, the jewels about her neck. Gilt salon chairs in emerald green velvet stood at opposite sides of the armoire. A large cane headboard, painted with gold flourishes and rose garlands, faced a wall of windows looking out at the ocean's rolling waves, with the Edgartown lighthouse in the center of the frame.

"Hello, Bill. I wasn't counting on you so soon." She adjusted the belt of her robe. "Harris said you would call to arrange *dinner* plans."

"No point in putting off the island's most important business," Dooley beamed. "Anyhow, I've got Baker downstairs. And Doc Kemp has a launch—a private motorboat, is what I mean to say. He can take us all to the lot *right now.*"

"*Who* is downstairs?" Isolde dropped her jaw with disdain.

"The builder."

"*Baker,* you said?"

"Yes, Baker."

"The builder?"

"Yes! That's right. Leave it to me, and we'll have you luxuriating on your widow's walk by August."

Isolde scowled at the little man standing in her space. He was shorter than her, which somehow made everything worse. "Harris told me the house was already built."

"Yes, my dear, of course the *house* is already *built*!" Dooley turned to Koji, seeking some form of alliance—man-to-man. He got nothing. "But you'll need a proper road. A *paved* road, I'm saying. Electrical lines, a telephone cable—and the water well that's in place now won't accommodate more than just a handful of guests. I know you're more popular than that." Dooley winked.

Isolde held her hand defensively to her forehead, as if his words were driving nails into her skull. "I couldn't handle another trip at this moment, be it by plane, train, or rickshaw. Just getting here was an odyssey."

"Bad flight?"

"*Bad?*" Isolde laughed lightly, twirling her finger at Koji for a cigarette. From their twin mahogany cages, built to resemble gothic cathedrals, the cockatiels echoed Isolde's reply. "With no exaggeration, Bill, I can tell you it was monstrous."

"Bit of weather is all," Dooley grinned, rocking on his heels, jangling the loose change in his pocket. "Low-level, uh, wind shear."

But Isolde shook her head. "I am beginning to think that an *island* retreat is perhaps inconvenient beyond the boundaries of reasonable comfort. Anyway, Harris told me we'd be able to *drive* to the property."

"Well. Yes. He *is* right. At a certain time of day, when the tide is out . . ." The wily developer spoke haltingly. "It is possible to take a beach buggy along the sand spit at Norton Point, but—"

"In your letter you mentioned a bridge."

"And certainly we are still working on *that*. The selectman and I have a proposal for the next Town Meeting and—"

The actress stood and exhaled at the ceiling. "I don't know about you"—she crossed the room to glare out the window—"but I've heard many good things about Vermont. The Berkshires, even."

From the corner of her eye she could see Bill Dooley getting ruffled at this threat. His face screwed itself into a pink, disconsolate knot. No doubt he had already made deals and promises that hinged on her presence. All the more reason, she thought, to renege and go home. Sell the house back to him. Rent it. Raze it. Tear it apart by the board. Who cared what she did? Certainly not Harris.

"I doubt I should need an airplane and a limousine *and* a rowboat to get myself to East Hampton."

"What if I told you I could lend you a better pilot?" Dooley blurted. "I'm talking about someone *dedicated* to your needs. I happen to know an impeccable flier—Army Air Corps veteran. He's easy on the eyes, as well. Or so my wife tells me. *Ha!* Come to think of it, Harris wouldn't like me recommending this particular fellow. Bit of a playboy, he is. I know you and Harris are only friends, of course."

"I'm not a schoolgirl, Bill." Isolde snapped her head around, exhaling smoke. "Are you really trying to sway me with the town flirt as my escort?"

"Hardly that, no! You misunderstand me. It's just that I wouldn't want to feel responsible if you missed out on the island's full, uh, scope of hospitality. Or if I let you defect to Vermont with all the damned cluster flies. *I* think"—he grasped at his shirt's breast pocket—"given the chance, you will find the atmosphere and the company here to be infinitely more suitable to your tastes."

Isolde lifted a bird from the cage. She smoothed its chartreuse crest feathers, which were raised in alert over the presence of an unfamiliar guest. She'd grown up in a blue-collar Ohio town where her father sold upright vacuum cleaners to seniors who could themselves barely stand upright. She knew the cadence and tenor of an opportunistic speech when she heard one. And yet, she also knew how Harris would feel about a young, able-bodied male joining up with her entourage. She recalled a recent outing in Boston: screaming through the streets of Chinatown in his Maserati A6, past the groceries, the restaurants and brothels; hitting a pothole and blowing a tire. He was useless, this supposed man of the working people. She could have replaced the thing herself, but of course he wouldn't allow it. Instead they sat in the car, while a light rain evolved into a downpour, both silently lamenting his mechanical ineptitude until a Good Samaritan stopped to help. Without question, Harris would be threatened by an army pilot assuming a regular presence in her life.

"All right," she relented, making sure to look no less put upon. "I will meet your pilot next week. I have a voice lesson in New York on Wednesday. If he gets me there in one piece I'll be ever so grateful. As for your Baker, he can start tomorrow."

"Brilliant!" Dooley exclaimed. "You'll be very happy, my dear. I can promise you—"

"Yes, yes, yes, that's fine. But, Bill? Do me one favor."

"Name it."

"Find me a bottle of 1938 California chardonnay and some *ripe* cantaloupe, diced small and thin. I don't want to see a single seed on the plate."

"I'll have it for you within the hour."

"That's all I ask."

"Lunch of white wine and cantaloupe, eh? Not much to subsist on," Dooley chuckled his way toward the hotel hallway, manically opening and clenching his fists.

"The cantaloupe is for the birds," Isolde replied, closing the door.

# SEVEN

As they jounced along the road to West Tisbury—young ladies in the back, Auntie and Nola Dooley in the front—Sabina prayed that Colin Hatch did not subscribe to the island newspaper. "Rescue at Sea" had been the cover story on Monday. And her photograph, thoughtfully supplied by Mr. Ewing, told the tale of a skinny girl on a ridiculous quest to save her host's ill-fated hobby plane. The only thing that made it halfway bearable was the author's last line: "With such enviable vigor and tenacity, Miss McTigue is certain to find success in her college career and beyond."

"I think it was a nice story," Nola Dooley attempted from the front seat. "My Bill always says there's no such thing as bad press."

"Your Bill sells real estate," Aunt Poppy countered. "The Boston marriage market is a trickier business, I can assure you. Bad enough she's as bony as a scad. To go off imitating one besides—"

"Don't worry too much, Bean," Lenore offered. "I'll bet everyone will forget how awfully goofy you looked by the time the wedding rolls around."

Sabina held her tongue, concentrating on the trees rushing past her window. On a better day, she might have questioned out loud her aunt's motives—how the very same woman could be scandalized by a passing association with Colin Hatch and nevertheless, now, be on her way up-island to sample strawberries at his farm. But she already knew they were going because Lenore wanted to go and because uncannily, in the Dooley household, and quite often beyond it, Lenore got exactly what she wanted. Aunt Poppy, for her part, trailed after Nola Dooley like the tang on a tailor's tape.

The Dooleys were the right kind of Irish, according to Poppy McTigue, who had long ago dropped her brogue but not her provincial prejudices. The island neighbors with roots in Cavan or Longford were as unappealing as sand fleas. Nola Dooley, meanwhile, had grown up on Ailesbury Road, earning her a place on Aunt Poppy's social calendar. Brunches, teas, impromptu deliveries of floating island meringue—these house calls patterned her days whether Nola liked it or not. So it was no surprise to Sabina that her aunt would seize on an opportunity to further ingratiate herself, even if it did mean deigning to visit Colin Hatch's farm.

Now Sabina's stomach dipped and fluttered inside her aunt's yellow Studebaker. She couldn't tell if it was Poppy's skittish braking or legitimate nerves. Normally an afternoon of strawberry picking would've sounded sublime. But right now she hardly knew what to feel. This morning, all throughout her swim, she had replayed her most recent exchange with her father, looking to extract something useful.

*Dear Bud,*

*I might as well address the Dooley's party. I think you've already heard a version from Auntie. But I would like to emphasize that I was trying to do something nice by saving Mr. Dooley's radio plane, and also by helping Mr. Hatch, who looked terribly discouraged in front of all the guests. I think it was unfair of Mr. Dooley to ask him to fly such a clumsy plane. But Auntie says my display is the offense people will remember, and that it was very "gauche" of me to steal the spotlight at Lenore's event.*

*I also want you to know that I apologized to everyone (the Shreves and Dooleys both) as soon as I was dry and redressed. Luckily, they'd had enough cocktails to laugh at almost anything. Except for Mr. Dooley. He says the plane is rubbish now.*

*Have you ever wondered how you come across to other people? I know it's maybe an odd question I'm getting at. It's just that yesterday I happened on an old postcard. Addressed from you to Mother.*

*I found it tucked inside a magazine. (Do you remember the boxes in the basement? Mother's issues of Popular Mechanics? Auntie wants to pitch them, but I'm stalling her for now.) Anyhow, you were in college still, and she must've been working. You'd written all about fixing up your trusty Pierce-Arrow. Dual-valve engines and vacuum brakes, et cetera, et cetera. How did you know she wouldn't cry from boredom?*

*If I had to write a postcard, to an older man no less, I can't even think of how I'd begin. I doubt he'd be very interested in my swim chart. I certainly wouldn't start in about dual-valve engines. No offense, Bud.*

*Hope your computing machines are cooperating better than your "gauche" daughter!*

*As ever, Bean*

Since the party, Sabina had endured her aunt's retelling of the airplane story ten different times, mostly to the Saint Andrew's ladies—women who Poppy called on to report controversial items in the church bulletin, as well as to detail plans for retrimming her summer hats. Sabina's practiced patience waned. As often as the weather allowed, she'd escape to a swim, far out along the buoys Denny had anchored for her. Other days, if her timing was right, she could walk the spit to Chappaquiddick, a narrow sandbar—just a skeletal stretch of land—reaching eastward to Norton Point.

On cloudy days she'd drag Connie into a few hands of rummy on the porch, watching cold raindrops clog the cottage's wire screens. Most nights, before dinner, she'd grab her old Shelby from the boathouse and spend an hour pedaling around the wharf, up toward Cannonball Park, where she gathered fruit in her bike basket for Connie's beach plum jam. She liked to sit at the marina and survey the disembarking ferryboat tourists: newlyweds who held hands, seniors who held tight to their purses and luggage, big families with parades of children and crying babies, short men with their shorter sons, dainty women chasing toddlers in sunsuits that matched their traveling scarves. This patchwork of people made her own family seem less peculiar, and after an hour or so she'd ride home with a temporary sense of relief.

But the calendar was always encroaching. And she felt, acutely, the perpetual stress of the coming fall. As the smells of sea air and cut grass wafted through her window, she was sometimes overcome by the sense that she should be doing something more important with her time—something bigger than swimming the harbor, bigger certainly than flipping through bride magazines with Lenore. Falling asleep to the boom and hush of the waves, the cantos of pastel color across the poem of the sky, she struggled to rest easy. The world was moving. Somehow she was missing all its important clues.

Finally, her father's reply had arrived in their post office box at the market. Since it absolved Sabina entirely, she left it lying open on the coffee table, just before *Dragnet* began, so her aunt could see the verdict.

*Dear Bean,*

*I did hear about your display, as you put it, and I have spent some time contemplating a suitable "punishment." Your sentence is as follows: The Shreves are hosting their Fourth of July clambake soon, where many of the same guests will be gathered. Go! Dress elegantly. Try to enjoy yourself. You are old enough now that I can be honest about the facts of life, and they are these: You will never again be as vibrant or as energetic as you are today. Don't waste this time hanging your head in self-doubt (or locked in the basement studying mildewed magazines).*

*As to postcards and the question of corresponding with (older?) men, I think you already have all the material you need. Keep in mind that men are people. Even the tamest, most brooding among us need the whimsy of a girl like you for balance.*

*Yours, Bud (Dad)*

*P.S. Your mother was the one who started that conversation on dual-valve engines. The only thing she loved better than cars (before you kids were born, of course) was talk of breaking them apart and rebuilding them all over again. I learned pretty quickly my letters got answered fastest when I asked for her mechanical advice. It's called leveraging common ground. Good luck!*

Generations of sun-bleached oyster shells paved the drive to Colin's farm. His house wore neat rows of shingles, weathered to a silvery patina, beneath its hipped roof and old stone chimney. Along one side of the house, eyebrow dormers interrupted the steep roofline. Sabina could see lace curtains billowing on either side of the upstairs windows. She wondered who'd chosen them, and the thought suddenly spawned a million other questions about how Hatch lived, kept house, ate his meals, and with what sort of napkin.

"Good *mawhnin*! So nice to see you all!" A heavyset woman of middle age ushered the party along a pea-stone path, bordered by wide-brim hosta and lavender. "I'm Florence. Mr. Hatch's secretary. He's just down at the barn for a moment. May I take your *otters* for refreshment? Lemonade? Iced tea?"

Were it not for her laughing eyes and obvious warmth, Florence's voice—loud beyond any conceivable necessity—might have rang offensive. Her New England accent gave an unduly long stretch to the word "garden." She pronounced "order," Sabina perceived, like the name of one particular aquatic mammal. She wore a Boston Red Sox baseball cap—something Sabina had never seen on a woman—and a polyester blouse in a bold floral print. Sabina heard Aunt Poppy emit a faint, dismayed tsk at the offending lid.

*Otters* thus taken, the visitors walked through a gate, past an old garage with a flagstone terrace. The land dipped down a grassy hill, and where it flattened again Sabina spied an enormous barn painted in cardinal red. Outside the barn, a little clearing of hardpan looked like welcome ground for goats or chickens, though there were none to be found. The afternoon ballgame droned from a nearby radio.

"Hello there! Welcome," Colin Hatch shouted up the hill, emerging from the barn with a handkerchief at his brow. He stopped to lean against his tractor mower, lighting a cigarette behind the shield of his palm. Sabina held a hand across her lids to take in the view of the farm—the grass mowed in neat coils, the aster and ryegrass beyond, bowing at the suggestion of a breeze. Fifty yards downhill, grape vines huddled together in even lines, their frog-footed leaves entwined with rows of chicken wire, pulled taut between weathered fence posts. Opposite the grapes, on the other side of the slope, young apple trees crouched low to the ground. Mussed, frazzled branches grew at odd angles, already weighted down by a promising crop.

Aunt Poppy took one look at the uneven terrain and opted to enjoy the view from underneath the arbor, where a pitcher of iced tea was now waiting. Here, too, grape vines grew from gnarled arms and legs that embraced the frame of the arbor. Leaves cascaded down from the lattice roof, dripping delicate, cat's-eye-colored clusters of grapes all around the shaded seating. Poppy had battled polio as a child. Its effects still showed in her slightly labored, off-balance gait. She owned a cane—three of them actually—designed to scale with the formality of her attire. But she refused to use one whenever Nola was present.

"Help *yehselves* to tea, ladies," Florence gestured. "I also brought out some nice *crackahs* with English Stilton in port."

"Yes, thank you," Poppy frowned, lowering herself into a wicker chair.

"Don't worry, Miss McTigue. We'll bring you plenty of strawberries for your jam," Lenore promised.

"Bring some for the both of us, will you?" Nola said to her daughter. "I'll keep Poppy company up here in the shade. You young people have things well enough in hand."

Thus dismissed, the trio set off over the little footbridge that separated the lawn from the orchards. Hatch led the way, and the girls trailed after, their steps exciting little white moths that fluttered about the purple clover. Overhead, warblers whistled in trills, as if vying for someone's attention. Here and there, maple leaves on low-hanging branches twisted like hands waving hello.

"However did you afford all this *land*?" Lenore demanded of their host. She swiveled her head back and forth between the acreage and the structures on the hill, apparently making a real estate assessment in her head. Sabina rolled her eyes at the ground, amazed and also not amazed by her friend's degree of gall.

"When my mother died, my sister and I sold the house back home. We each inherited a little something—"

"There were only two of you?"

"By blood there was only one of us. I was a state boy. My folks adopted me when I was four."

Lenore nodded as if piecing together a puzzle. "Must have been a pretty big 'little something' she left for you."

"Yes, well," Hatch swiped his brow. "Your father's loan helped bridge the gap."

"Is that a fact?" Lenore smiled knowingly at Sabina. "And have you lived here long?"

"A few years now."

"Always all by yourself?" She looked dubious. "What a shame."

"Luckily Florence lives next door, down that way." Hatch pointed. "She answers the phone for the charters, books the flight plans, usually brings by a plate of whatever she cooked the night before."

"And your *laundry*?" Lenore persisted, as if she'd read Sabina's earlier thoughts. Evidently, the life of a bachelor intrigued them both.

"My laundry?" Hatch laughed. "I send it out. Why?"

Lenore stopped short, fists on hips. "Well, now don't go taking this the wrong way, Colin. But if I were you, I would think about hiring dedicated help. Someone younger than old Florence, *obviously*. You need a full-time girl for the everyday chores and things."

"Lenore, I will take that advice into serious consideration."

"Good. And in the meanwhile," Lenore shot him a flirting grin, "you're looking terrifically browned these days." She swung her empty trug around her wrist. "Getting to the beach much?"

"Nah. Farm keeps me pretty busy."

"Sometimes having a bit of fun is the best way to keep busy."

"*Lenore* is very busy with her *wedding* plans," Sabina blurted out. "Laboring over the cake selection, isn't that right, Lenore?"

"Yes, the cake business is still quite unsettled. John Joseph favors a black fruitcake for the groom's option, which to me seems awfully drab . . ."

Sabina felt relief to hear her friend running with this bait. She checked Hatch's face and caught sight of his amusement as Lenore prattled on.

". . . On the other hand, little *boxed fruitcakes* for the departing guests, well, those can be charming. But to serve at the reception I'm leaning toward something a bit classier—Bavarian cream in between layers of *silver* cake. I found a confectioner in Baltimore who can sculpt our likeness exactly into miniature marzipan figurines—"

"Lots to think about." Hatch gave Sabina a wink. "Will you get it all done before summer's end? What's the wedding date again?"

"The twenty-ninth. August twenty-ninth at the Harbor View Hotel. I would've preferred September, mind you—the Kennedys were married in September. I happen to know because my parents attended the reception at Hammersmith. If you ask me, I'd say Jacqueline is much too beautiful for the senator, even if she is a brunette. What do you think, Colin? Are you partial to blondes or brunettes?"

"And for the honeymoon," Sabina cut in. "Tell him about your grand tour."

Lenore blew upward at her bangs. "Mother and Daddy are sending us to Europe for an extended holiday."

"Where will you visit?" Colin turned his back to the orchards, walking in reverse and holding out his two hands to steady the girls as they maneuvered the high grasses of the hill. Sabina tried not to grip too tightly or too long. And she told herself, when he released Lenore's hand first, at a more level spot, it was only by meaningless chance.

Now Lenore looked flummoxed. "Darn if I can remember where. Geography is such dull business. Nice little countries by the sea, anyway. I can say for certain one spot has a heated swimming pool with its very own artificial waves! Say, I've already shown Sabina, but would you like to see the terrific tan line my engagement ring is making?"

Hatch laughed to himself. He shook his head at the ground, stopping to squat by the trough that divided his raised beds of strawberry plants. "What I'd really like is a cigarette. I forgot my case back in the truck."

"Someone ought to go fetch them for you," Sabina suggested, perhaps a little too quickly. Hatch caught her eye.

"Are you volunteering?"

"It'd *have* to be me, I'm sure. We couldn't expect Lenny to find her way without help."

Hatch looked from one girl to the next. "Let's not bother with them."

"You think I can't manage on my own?" Lenore challenged.

"Look, it needn't be any kind of contest. I'll go myself." Hatch stood.

"Meanwhile, Sabina thinks I'm too fussy to climb up that hill. Isn't that right, Sabina? You think I can't manage?"

"Not without an escalator."

Hatch laughed. Lenore curled her lip. She dropped her trug at Sabina's feet, charging off to attempt the high grasses without the aid of Macy's rising staircase at Herald Square. Neither of them watched her efforts for very long. She was forgotten before she was even out of earshot. And Sabina soon felt her stomach loop the loop like a traveling carnival ride.

"Well," she said, trying to remember whatever it was her father had advised about common ground.

"How's the swimming going?" Colin asked. He picked berries. She followed his lead.

"I'm so embarrassed about the party," she confessed.

"*Embarrassed?* What for? The way you cut through those waves—heck,

I thought maybe you were part seal or something. How d'you swim like that?"

She shrugged. "Practice."

"I'll say." He whistled. "I know *I* couldn't hold my breath that long."

"You certainly could. It's just about getting at it every day. Going a little bit farther every day."

"How long can you stay under?"

"Oh, I don't know." She blushed. "Close to two minutes, I guess."

"That's quite a talent."

"I'm not so sure I agree." Sabina shook her head. "Maybe if I had some useful way of employing it. In this case—at the Dooley's, I mean. Trying to solve a thing that didn't really involve me—well. That's the sort of talent that echoes of my aunt. Although she certainly wouldn't have jumped into the ocean in the middle of a cocktail party."

"Sabina, if anything about you resembled your aunt," Hatch said as he let his shoulder collide with hers, reaching for a cluster of berries, "I wouldn't have been so glad to steal you away from your tennis partner."

"Who's that? James, you mean?" She laughed to cover the tiny screams of joy going off in her head. He liked her. He was telling her that *he liked her.* She had no earthly idea how to respond. After a moment she said, "You shouldn't talk so conclusively, you know. James is not an easy man to put off."

"Well, you *do* owe him a sail." Hatch crossed his arms and scrunched his nose, doing a bit of a James Whelan impression. "I'd say he's pretty brassed off about it by now."

"Yes, I did promise to crew for him," she nodded. "He makes the invitation sound pleasant, but it's actually a risky proposition. Last time he wound up racing the Shreve boys home from Squash Meadow. Complained the whole way my weight was slowing him down. He made me jump ship at the harbor."

For a long time they worked together—shoulder to shoulder—without saying much. It had rained the night before, so now the air, the plants, everything around them smelled washed and new. They settled into a kind of rhythm. His right arm and her left reaching out for berries, bending back—wrists grazing—dropping fruit into the trug.

"Denny says you're a whiz at sailing," Sabina offered, noting an unusual shakiness in her voice. She'd already started and stopped so many conversations in her head she had to remind herself to actually say the words out loud.

"I've been called many things, but never a whiz at anything." Hatch shook his head. "Anyway, I always find my way home. I guess that's what counts."

"Does your boat have a name?"

"She's called *Riprova*."

"That's lovely. What does it mean?"

Hatch shrugged off the compliment. "It means 'try again.'"

"Any special significance?"

"It's silly. I shouldn't bore you with it."

"Oh," Sabina nodded, remembering how meddlesome Lenore had sounded, deciding to let the point drop.

"What about you, then? What are your plans for this summer?" he asked. "I haven't known you long, but I doubt you're spending too much time working on your, uh, your tan lines."

"Are you saying I'm not like the other girls around Edgartown?"

"I don't think anyone has to *say* it. It's pretty well apparent to me. You are much more attuned than other girls your age." The compliment delighted her, and yet Sabina bristled at those last three words: "girls your age."

"Well, I've been swimming quite a bit. I usually read an hour or two every day—"

"Oh? What are you reading now? My sister—she lives out in Sheboygan with her family—she's keen on those Perry Mason novels. Do you like mysteries?"

"Sometimes, I do. But mostly I read about the natural world. Case studies or scientific reports. Real things that matter to real people. That's my preference."

"I remember now," he snapped his fingers. "You like details. Peattie's *Complete History of Trees*, was it?"

"I finished Peattie. Right now I'm reading the Nagelmackers report on the Roman ship discovered at Bruges."

"At where now?"

"Bruges. *Belgium.* Roughly five hundred meters from the sluice gates of the Ostend Canal." Sabina tilted her hat up to look at him. Besides her father and Mrs. Lyons, no one ever asked her what she was reading or why it piqued her interest particularly. "You see, right around the turn of the century, canal excavators stumbled upon an ancient ship—oh, maybe as ancient as Caesar, they think. But they hadn't really the right tools to assess the materials in those days."

"Go on." Hatch looked at her with a curious expression.

"Well, Nagelmackers and his crew, they've since been able to study the original shipwrights' work quite closely. The characteristics they've seen are more akin to the Celtic tradition as opposed to the Scandinavian clinker method or a carvel construction—"

"Clinker method, huh?"

"Yes, but that's not what interests me."

"Clearly not."

"What interests me actually," Sabina set aside her trug, "is the fact that Nagelmackers had to halt his excavation, on account of the Black Stench."

"You'll have to explain that one."

"Dirty, foul-smelling water in the Ghent. You can't even imagine how bad. And all the fishing boats flaking apart with rust. Thousands of bream and barbel gone belly-up. Happens every summer, they say. It's bad out-water from the French flax mills."

"Damned French." Hatch shook his head. "And yet some people still claim they don't stink."

"You shouldn't joke about pollution," Sabina chided him. "It's really a very serious matter. Even here in Massachusetts. Before they modernized the plant at Moon Island, the fumes from the Charles were so bad they could peel your wallpaper. And just last month—I don't suppose you've read it, but just last month the papers printed a new report from Dr. Gerald Wendt who says all man's burning of coal and oil is actually heating the planet by measurable degrees. Not so much that you and I would ever notice, but—"

"If you want my opinion," Colin Hatch lit a cigarette, for it seemed he had one on hand after all, "I'd say you're too pretty to worry over bream and barbel and factory fumes. Why do you go on reading about such things?"

Sabina stared at him, somewhat disbelieving. "*Why read about such things?* How else to know what's important in the world? How else to fix it?"

"Very true," Hatch nodded. "And damned enlightened for a girl who's never left—have you ever left Boston?"

"Not really," Sabina confessed. "I've been to New York City once. Aunt Poppy and I. But still, it's a funny thing about the studies I read," she continued, softer. "After I learn a bit about here or there, I feel just as if I'd actually traveled to that place. And that's why I . . ." She stopped to check his face, to be sure he was still listening. "Well, that's why I'd like to keep a map on my wall one day. The kind with those little red pushpins? I've been to all seven continents by now, in a manner of speaking. And I think it would be nice to keep track of my travels."

Hatch studied her face, his eyes twinkling as they did whenever he was about to say something droll. "I'm a little worried about you, Sabina McTigue. But mostly I'm worried for the professors at that college of yours. Which is it?"

"Weston," Sabina swallowed.

"Weston, right. Once those Weston professors meet you, I think they might be done for. Kaput, you know?"

"Like the bream?"

"Yes, exactly like the bream."

"I'm not *always* reading," she hastened to add. "Just yesterday I packed some sandwiches and rode my bike to Felix Neck. You wouldn't believe all the different birds you can find up there. Heron, plover, kinglets, and orioles—say, this would be a nice place for a picnic," Sabina noted, getting to her feet as if to examine the full scope of the land better. "The view is wonderful."

"You should see it in the winter." He stood to join her. "Last year all of this ground got a good, clean blanket of snow. When the trees are bare, you can see James Pond over there, and a piece of the Sound through that clearing. Maybe it's the Englishman in me, but I do so love being out here in the cold."

"I've never been to the island in winter."

"You're welcome anytime. Any *season*, I guess I should say. In fact"—he looked at her with a question in his eyes, pausing an unbearably long time—"would it be too forward of me to ask you back for lunch? Without your aunt or Lenore and the gang?"

"I think poor Lenny might feel left out." This was all Sabina could say to conceal her glee. *A date with Colin Hatch—just him and her alone?* She had no idea how she'd ever square it with A. P. She had to put aside the invitation he was making, just a bit longer, until her brain could find means to piece together some restrained counteroffer. "Lenore is awfully interested in you—in your circumstances, I should say."

"My 'circumstances,' eh? Makes me sound like a Dickens character."

"I didn't mean—"

"Now, look, McTigue. I have a job that needs doing over in Menemsha. And I know you're keen on details—clinkers and bream, fellows like me and the types of trees we're apt to climb." He winked at her. This time her heart jumped straight into her throat. "Maybe we could collect some new details along the way?"

"We'd better get back," Sabina deflected, brushing the dirt marks from her toreadors. "Aunt Poppy will be fretting about the bees by now. She hates bees something fierce."

"You're going to make me wait for your answer, is that it?"

"I'll bet Lenore is riffling through your medicine cabinet as we speak."

"You should know"—he lowered his voice—"I haven't much practice in holding my breath."

"Well. Everyone has to start somewhere."

"All right. I catch your drift." Hatch relented, taking the full trug from her hands. "But, Sabina?"

"Yes?"

"Will you tell me more about the flax mills?"

# EIGHT

Sabina was awake. Sunlit patches climbed the pattern of her lords-and-ladies wallpaper. Outside branches, come to life in shadow, dappled and danced across the pinewood floor. Instead of bounding out of bed, as per usual, today she lay contemplating, watching the day emerge. From their nests among the heather, the plovers called her down to swim. Off in the distance a tugboat sounded faintly.

After a time, she heard the sounds of Connie rising—starting the coffee in the percolator and scalding the ceramic teapot with a rinse of boiling water. Still, Sabina felt like lingering in bed. She felt a pleasant warmth expand the space inside her chest. It was the same sensation she'd discovered in the strawberry patch and carried all throughout yesterday's car ride home, while the ladies had offered varying assessments of their host.

"Overall, I do think he's a nice boy," Nola Dooley had concluded.

"And I think he's slippery," Poppy tacked on. "Nice *boy*, my foot."

The conversation had ambled on like that without holding any real importance for Sabina, who knew something that none of the other passengers did. She had a date. She'd been invited—*without* Lenore in tow—on an actual date with Colin Hatch.

"My! This is a nice change," Aunt Poppy looked up from her *Ladies' Home Journal*, remarking on her niece's spruce appearance. Sabina wore a sleeveless blouse in lavender check, kidskin sandals, and a pleated linen skirt.

Her hair had allowed itself to be tamed into a thick fishtail braid, with fine, curling wisps playing at her cheekbones. She wore her mother's gold earrings—a sure sign this was no ordinary outfit. "By the looks of you, I take it you are going somewhere, miss?"

"I am," Sabina nodded with quiet resolve. "I have plans to go to Dawson's Market."

"In Menemsha? Whatever for? You'll never make it on your bicycle."

"I'm not taking my bicycle." Sabina swallowed. "I'm going with Colin. To deliver fruit."

"Oh?" Poppy closed her magazine and took a slow sip of steaming breakfast tea. She grasped at the buttons of her house dress in a far-off, musing way. She hadn't yet pinned her hair or done her face. In the mornings, without any powder applied, Poppy's freckled complexion made her look a bit softer than usual. It lent Sabina some mettle.

"It's all right, Auntie, really. Bud knows Colin from the club. And you heard Mrs. Dooley say yesterday what a nice person he is."

"I'll thank you not to refer to your father as *Bud*." Poppy reopened the magazine. A young model on the page sat smiling from a cream-colored davenport. Sabina could see her aunt lamenting the choice of fabric—even for a made-up household in an advertisement. "And you needn't persuade me on Mr. Hatch. I've come to terms with the fact that you'll do as you like. Be it rational or otherwise." She flipped the page like a punctuation mark.

"Truly?" Sabina wasn't sure what to say next. Her aunt never surrendered so fast. More likely she was feigning armistice, saving strength and strategy for some future battle.

"I cannot tell you what to do anymore, Sabina. My nerves are frayed with trying. Swim the ocean! Become a fruit peddler! Go ahead and elope with Luis Romeau and the entire Copacabana Chorus—"

"Oh honestly, A. P.," Sabina attempted.

"No, no. This is where we've arrived. You have outgrown my authority, and I've small heart to fight it. You'll be pensioning me off to the old folks' home soon enough. I might as well learn to accept a new role—perhaps a bit like the Queen of England," Aunt Poppy reflected into her teacup. "Strictly ornamental. No power."

"Yes, but think of the exotic goodwill tours Her Majesty enjoys," offered a low voice from behind them. Colin Hatch stood smiling outside the screen door, carrying a woven basket full of fresh greens. Morning glories in deep purple climbed the porch trellis as high as Hatch's strong shoulders. Behind him, Sabina could see yesterday's bed sheets arching and snapping on the backyard line. Behind those she saw the blue of the harbor and the distant sails of the boats she'd grown up counting on her fingers. Altogether the picture was a perfect collage of happy, lovely things.

"Good morning, Colin." Poppy rose from her chair to get the door.

"Good morning, ladies. Pardon me for interrupting."

"Not at all," Poppy smiled wanly. "A touch of British sarcasm to start the day. It's absolutely topping, as they—*the Brits*—might say. Do come inside, please."

"Thanks. I brought you these." He held out his offering.

"Goodness. Been a long time since a man brought me flowers." Aunt Poppy twisted her earring, deciding on a tone. "Much longer I should think since one of them brought me rhubarb."

"I'm glad I didn't bring you flowers. I doubt any florist could compete with the blooms you've got outside," Hatch replied in his charming way. Aunt Poppy seemed mollified almost to the point of a sincere smile. "And for you," he grinned, turning to Sabina, "a book of details." A small hardcover wrapped in butcher paper appeared from behind his back. Sabina opened it to find *The Guinness Book of Superlatives.*

"Thank you." Sabina blushed, turning the book over in her hands. "This is for me?"

"It's a reference guide," Hatch explained, "full of worldly facts. It was thought up by the same fellas who make that terrible Dublin stout. Leave it to the Irish to write a book on one-upmanship."

"Leave it to an Englishman to poke his nose into Irish doings," Poppy rejoined.

"This is so thoughtful of you," Sabina mumbled, her head suddenly crowded with excess words and emotions—unsure how to convey her appreciation fully and at the same time aware of Aunt Poppy grading her reaction like an oration instructor.

"*Competitive*, more like," Hatch winked at her.

"Will you stay for some coffee, Colin?" Poppy asked.

"No, we'd better head out." Sabina spoke for the pair of them, self-conscious about everything in the small, bright kitchen. "I'd hate for the fruit to get warm in the sun."

"But you haven't had any breakfast," her aunt objected.

"We'll stop for something on the way. I won't let her go hungry," Hatch promised, demonstrating the perfect balance of deference and decisiveness. Sabina felt herself melt a little. Up until now the only man she knew who could subdue Aunt Poppy's raised eyebrows was her father.

After that there were words of goodbye and logistical details; Sabina couldn't help but hurry things toward the door. In the drive she saw Hatch's stake-bed Ford overflowing with wooden baskets and mismatched bureau drawers. The harvest represented a full rainbow of colors: strawberries, carrots, spinach, garlic, kale, radish, and Swiss chard. When Hatch opened the door to the pickup and helped her onto the running board, she felt like she might be climbing into some kind of dream state, certainly into a new chapter of her life.

"All right, McTigue," Hatch instructed as he turned the key in the ignition. "Two rules of the cockpit. One: the captain sets the itinerary. Two: the copilot never gives him any lip."

"Agreed. But meanwhile I'll be testing you." Sabina waved her new superlatives book in front of him.

"I'd expect nothing less."

This was not her first date with a boy, and Sabina was prepared to tell Hatch as much, in case he started up, dropping hints about her age again. She'd gone to the Saint Andrew's Spring Fling with Carl Wheeler, a bookish

Republican who'd nearly tripped her down the doorsteps and then spent twenty minutes talking politics with her father. The two kids stayed out until midnight. Carl insisted she wear his tennis sweater home, though it was eighty degrees. After that he tried telephoning her two or three times. Sabina sent back a brief note that said she had enjoyed his company very much, which wasn't true, and that her father wanted to see an increased focus on her studies—an even bigger lie. Eventually Carl conceded the race.

Before Carl there was Eddie Danton. She'd met Eddie a few summers prior, when a group of island kids formed a kind of beach club down at the Dooley's end of Starbuck. They all paired off into couples: Sabina and Eddie, Betty and Chipper, Trip and Midge; Lenore and Denny were actually an item back in those days. But soon enough, Aunt Poppy moved to squash the attachments for all involved—far too much "unaccountable gadding about town," were her exact words. By the fall, Eddie's family had sold their cottage anyway.

Sabina was not sorry. For all his good looks, Eddie Danton had suffered from an unfortunate misapprehension: the idea that *force* is a fine proxy for sentiment—any sentiment—including fondness. And so Eddie Danton kissed as though kissing were a contest of strength. He kissed as if confronting a football sled. He kissed, more or less, in the style of a Saint Bernard. He hooked his thick, athletic arms around her neck and pressed with all his weight, so the seal of his lips on hers never broke or varied or allowed any room for the intake of breath. What he imagined to be moments of intense devotion, Sabina braced for with eyes squeezed shut. She sometimes thought to tell him where he was going wrong but decided that was a task better left to the next girl. Maybe some sort of female lumberjack.

"What is the world's most expensive perfume?" Sabina began her quiz for Colin.

"Unless they sell it at the A&P, you'll have to give me a hint."

"It's called Joy, by Jean Patou. It's made with over one hundred flower essences. Do you want to guess how much it costs?"

"More than I would ever pay," he nodded, turning onto Dock Street.

"Not even for the right woman?"

"Not even for two of them."

"Forty-five dollars an ounce!" Sabina marveled, ignoring his sarcasm. "Seems like a crime. All the money some people will pay for glamour."

"The real crime is the lack of imagination. Most of them can't think of any other way to spend it."

"How about this? What's the world's fastest snake?"

"James Whelan in his ridiculous Austin-Healey convertible."

"Very funny. It's actually the black mamba. On a favorable surface, the mamba can reach speeds of seven miles per hour."

"That *is* fast. But I still think Whelan might move faster if there were a sale on Bermuda shorts happening somewhere."

"Okay, you sore loser. Here's one that's up your alley. What's the longest homing flight ever completed by a pigeon?"

"*This* is the question that's meant to be *up my alley*?" Hatch looked incredulous.

"Why not? It's flight related."

"You overestimate me, McTigue. But it's okay. I like that. I'll say three thousand miles."

"The correct answer is fifty-four hundred miles—from Ichaboe Island in Africa all the way to London. Although it says here the authors suspect the actual distance might have been more like *seven thousand* miles, since the pigeon would have wanted to avoid the Sahara."

"Indeed he would. I hope the poor bastard packed a brown-bag lunch."

"He died." Sabina frowned. "Just one mile from his doorstep at Nine Elms."

"That's a very sad story." Hatch snatched the book from her hands. "I won't allow it on a beautiful day like this. You'll wilt the lettuce."

They drove the beach road in pleasant silence. The truck rolled past the matchstick fences and the tidal estuaries, where the island boys toted fishing rods and invaded the marshland in knee-high waders. Shirtless teenagers manned tilting catboats. In between glimpses of water, vines climbed the arthritic pines.

Hatch pulled into the lot for the airpark diner—a small, noisy place already bustling with tourists and small-plane pilots. Hatch ordered a grilled English muffin, bacon, and two fried eggs. Sabina relayed her order by way of Hatch, as good etiquette commanded, opting for oatmeal and a fruit cup. The waitress gave Colin an extra-long smile every time she visited the table. Sabina pretended not to notice.

"You know something?" she offered, as they chewed across the table from each other, "I've been thinking about your farm."

"Have you?"

His eyes square on hers gave her a quick shiver. She sipped her coffee, which was too strong and tasted vaguely of cigarette smoke. "I think you ought to get some chickens."

"Hmm. *Chickens.*" Colin Hatch stuck out his jaw, repeating her word with sarcasm.

"Don't you think markets and hotels would be glad to have you deliver them fresh eggs?"

"How do you suppose Bill Dooley would react to that demotion? Coming in second place to my gaggle of hens?" Hatch laughed.

"All right, never mind then." She shook her head. "But for hens you would say 'brood,' not 'gaggle.'"

"Noted, thank you, Miss McTigue, Edgartown's resident zoologist. Could I count on you to help feed these chickens each morning?"

"I'd like to, but my mornings are spoken for. Swim practice, you know?"

"Every morning?"

"That's right."

"How am I to spend more time with you then?"

She shrugged at him, trying hard to look indifferent.

"I'll have to come over to your camp, it seems." Hatch made a sandwich of his breakfast, the lacy skirt of his egg dangling free. "Maybe you could teach me how to swim."

"You don't know how to swim?" she practically shouted at him. Luckily the diner was loud with kitchen sounds and doo-wop music.

"I *do* know how. But judging off your recent maneuver, I'd say you're much faster than me. Pass the salt, please."

"You want to swim as fast as me?"

"And I'll need you to teach me how you hold your breath that long."

"You're serious?" She wiped her mouth with the corner of her napkin. "You want swim lessons?"

"I could pay you in wax beans."

"I've never much cared for wax beans."

"Broccoli?"

"Eck. Worse."

"All right, summer squash. Final offer. And I will meet you down at your beach tomorrow morning."

"I'm out there very early," Sabina warned. "Six o'clock most days."

"That's good. Then we'll have time to manage my deliveries afterward."

"Oh? Are we making a regular appointment of today? I'm not sure you've thought this all the way through, Colin." Sabina forgot to be nervous around him. She chewed without the shield of her palm in front of her face. She allowed herself to hold his gaze. "Aunt Poppy will think there's something cozy going on between us."

"Well," nodded Hatch, inhaling deeply, landing his two fists lightly on the tabletop. "It's an old-fashioned instinct that woman's got." He took a long draught from his coffee and placed a crisp bill underneath the mug. "But it's fearsomely accurate."

After dropping most of the produce at Menemsha, they visited two seaside inns in Aquinnah, where the owners were indeed delighted to receive fresh items for their guests' breakfasts. The proprietors spoke so gratefully of being spared a trip to First National or the IGA market in Tisbury. It was happy work, and everywhere they went, Sabina found something lovely to take in and enjoy. She smiled at the gray and cream blotches climbing the trunks of the sycamore maples, the dusty pebbles in the road—the way they crunched beneath her steps—the piles of fading catkins, fallen from the oaks, now gathered up and down the quiet lanes like feathery snakes.

The midday sun relenting, they set off for the boathouse on the west side of Katama Bay. Hatch said Florence had a second cousin living on Chappaquiddick. She was an older woman with a day nurse to care for her. He looked in on her occasionally, bringing her fruits and vegetables for canning. Sabina was glad for the opportunity to extend their day a little longer. Every time Colin began to speak, she expected him to say he ought to be getting her home by now, and every time he said something else—something not at all focused on resuming their lives apart—she exhaled with happiness.

They arrived at the Point just in time to catch the departing ferry. Hatch drove his truck over the metal grates of the ramp, straight aboard an unassuming little motor scow. Sabina waved to George Mattos, the skipper, who she'd known since forever.

Since there was no bridge to Chappaquiddick—apart from the tenuous sand spit, passable only on big balloon tires at a certain stage of tide—getting to the minor island required a boat. And that was George's job. George served as the lone gatekeeper for all cars, trucks, and bicycles en route to Chappy. Before him, his father had done so, only with a rowboat preceding the motor-powered one. Now George, his wife, and his black Polish hens lived on the North Neck promontory. If George woke late or lunched longer than usual, the back-and-forth traffic—scant though it was—waited. At any given time, he knew exactly who was visiting the smaller island and who among its few residents was due back home from their parent town. On weekends, for example, when the Timmons' kids ventured west to the Edgartown Playhouse, he took it upon himself to round them up and see them safely home across the channel before logging his last trip of the evening. Sabina made a mental note that she needed to ask George a private favor. She'd have to catch up with him tomorrow.

"Afternoon there, Miss M.," George called out from the pilothouse.

"Hello, George. How've you been?"

"Can't complain. Not in this weather, for certain. Is that Mr. Hatch there with you?"

"Hello, George," Hatch waved. He dug into his pocket to produce the twenty-cent round-trip fare. "How are the quahogs this year?"

"Come by some night, I'll show you. This morning I filled a basket with top necks big as my boot. Can you use any?"

"No, thanks." Hatch smiled. "I had to hang up my chowder pot this summer. Too much growing in the yard." He pointed to his truck bed.

George nodded as he bent to place two wooden wheel chocks against the Ford's front tires. "You hear much about that build Dooley's cooking?"

"I haven't, no. What do you hear?"

"Don't need details to know it'll be mayhem."

"That bad?" Hatch frowned.

"Worse. Up to him, this place is as good as Coney Island. *Damned bridge*. Eelgrass is barely back to what it was before the slime mold wiped us out."

"I can't imagine folks here would let it happen," Hatch said.

"Ain't nothing or no one can't be bought," George leveled with a winking eye. "You think Dooley don't have the right backing? Already I see him carting that fancy actress to and fro. They come in on Doc Kemp's launch."

"Which actress?"

"Oh, you'd know the one I mean. She's got the real big . . ." George paused to consider Sabina's presence. "Well, she won't sink anytime soon, that's certain."

"I'll run it by the boys at the club," Hatch offered. "Take the temperature in Edgartown."

George wagged a finger. Years of island winters, shucking oysters by the gallon, had eroded the flesh on one side. Pink scars scissored across his hands. "Got a mind to go see that old crook myself."

"I have to admit I'm curious now." Hatch raised an eyebrow at Sabina. "You?"

"I wouldn't be too concerned. We've got smart people in this town. One of them is bound to make his case heard at Town Meeting."

George poked his head into the truck window. "From your lips to God's ears, Miss M."

Sabina knew the Chappy crossing as if by heart. Katama Channel stretched only five hundred feet from point to point. Wouldn't take her more than ten minutes by trudgen crawl. And yet today it felt like a sprawling adventure set to unfold in an unfamiliar land. The silvery bonito hurdling the waves were nothing short of magical. The cowbird's song seemed to guide them into the narrow ferry slip. When they reached the Chappy banks, lush with sea rocket sprouting from the sand, her face hurt from smiling out the truck's open window.

It turned out Florence's cousin was napping when they arrived. The nurse said best not to wake her. And Sabina realized, with a faint prick of shame, she was glad for it. She sat building up the courage to suggest an improvised picnic on East Beach. They still had some berries and a paper bag of hot cross buns from Mrs. Dawson in Menemsha. So while Hatch unloaded the last crate of produce in the old woman's kitchen, she borrowed the truck's rearview mirror to check her flyaway hair and choose the right-sounding words.

"This is a good place to swim," Hatch pointed out. Gentle waves climbed the incline of the beach, forming smooth, curved licks across the sand. Behind them swayed the vast acres of beach grass and willowy blue toadflax cropping up throughout the dunes. Hatch lay supine, propped on his elbows, looking out toward Nantucket. Sabina sat beside him, cross-legged, on the car robe he'd carried out for her. She took off her sandals to mash her feet against the sand: tiny pebbles of tan and white and rust.

"I didn't bring my suit," Sabina shrugged.

"Do you mind just sitting and talking?"

"Not too much, I guess."

"Your enthusiasm is flattering."

"Oh, I didn't mean to sound indifferent," she blushed. "It's just that I—"

As if he hadn't heard her, he reached out to take hold of her earlobe. "These are lovely," he remarked.

It took her a moment to remember she was wearing earrings. "There's a bracelet to match. Belonged to my mother. But the clasp is broken."

"You ought to bring it by the farm one day. I could fix it for you."

"You're quite busy enough, I'm sure."

"It's no trouble," he said, smiling. His fingers—rough, but warm—still held a little piece of her ear. "Your mother is passed, I take it?"

Sabina nodded.

"Sorry to hear. You were close?"

"I was five when she went away. I don't remember her all that well." Sabina shrugged.

"What happened to her?"

"Did you know, way back when, the Coast Guard used to patrol this beach, on the lookout for U-boats?" Sabina spoke as if she hadn't heard his question. "Fifteen or twenty men actually lived up in the Pogue lighthouse for a time. I used to ride over on George's ferry. Then bike out here to watch the soldiers practicing their drills."

"Is that a fact?" Colin Hatch smiled.

"Anyhow, since the war," Sabina watched a cloud overtake the sun, "more tourists are finding Chappy every year."

"You say so like it's a bad thing."

She shrugged. "Can't stop the world from changing, I suppose. But I do miss how the island used to be."

"Oh? For instance?"

"For instance there used to be sheep out in the pasture. Ducks on Poucha Pond. Before they breached the dike. Some 'big-idea man'—another Bill

Dooley, I suppose—said a breach would be good for the fishermen—drawing in more scallops by letting in the salt water, you know? But I think they mostly just wanted to bring in the bigger boats."

"So what happened?"

"The pondweed died. All the freshwater fish disappeared. And soon enough no more ducks or geese either."

"Did the big-idea man get his scallops?"

"Not a single one. Plenty of new boats parked out there, though."

"You think the same thing might happen with Dooley's bridge?"

"I don't know." She hugged her knees, waiting for the sun's warming light to return. "But I do intend to ask a few questions."

"When you've got a handle, will you explain it to me? Over dinner?"

"We'll see." She couldn't help but grin at him.

"I suppose I'm back to holding my breath again?"

The wind blew at their faces. Sabina brushed a hair behind her ear. "Why is it you'd rather be a farmer than a pilot?"

"It's complicated. I don't know if you'll understand."

"Why shouldn't I?"

"Because your life has always been your own. You haven't got any anchors on you, so to speak."

"Ha!" Sabina pushed his chest. Unbraced, his elbows caved beneath him, and he toppled flat onto the beach. He sat up smiling. She reached to brush the sand from the back of his hair—a velvet-soft, even crewcut. Impassioned as she was, she barely paused at her own forward gesture. "I'm sorry, it's just—do you know how many years of piano lessons I've been badgered into? Then ten seasons of tennis at the club. And now that I'm graduated, it's this endless push for me to find some meaningful *direction*, as Aunt Poppy expresses it."

"Be careful which one you choose. You might find yourself stuck."

"That's what worries me. I've no idea where I'll be or what I'll happen to enjoy in five years' time."

"I've been flying for Bill Dooley nearly twice that long," he sniffed.

"And I know for certain I don't happen to enjoy it. Not even for Lauren Bacall when she's in town."

"Does Lauren Bacall telephone for you?" Sabina marveled at the idea.

"No, she whistles." Colin dropped his head flat on the car robe to look up at the clouds.

"Well," Sabina said, laughing, "believe it or not, I *can* sympathize with what you're saying."

"Can you?" He looked relieved to hear her say it.

"I think so. Except . . ." She caught herself staring down at him. His blue-green eyes were sporting, as always, but vivid with something else now too. She felt his eyes drawing her in—if that was possible—to succeed at a plan she hadn't quite consciously made. It occurred to her that she wanted to kiss him. Instead, she heard herself asking, "Why don't you just give it up?"

"Piloting?"

"Yes, why not give it up? What's to stop you?"

"Well. It's like this." He sat up straight again. "Farming's not exactly a foolproof venture, financially speaking. I'm not sure how well I'd manage off the land alone. Crops need to be fed and pruned and mulched. You have to watch for disease, blotch, black rot. Spray for codling moth, dust for weevils, mites, crown borers. And all that's before the weather throws you a curveball."

"You've got to believe in yourself is all."

"Says you and Earl Nightingale." Hatch patted his pocket for a cigarette. "I spoke to a man from Concord Land Bank last year. Do you know what he told me?"

Sabina shook her head.

"He told me just about every orchard loan in New England has been foreclosed on since the war years. Said he wouldn't lend me a nickel even if I wasn't—even under the best of circumstances."

"Colin." Sabina stretched her legs against the sand, bearing down so that her heels carved out two ruts that were instantly erased by the rising water crop. "There are a hundred reasons you might fail, but none of them matters if you're certain about what you want."

"Bill Dooley and his bank note matters. If I walk away now, he can take back all the equity in my farm." Hatch picked a flat stone from the beach and skipped it on a wave.

Sabina felt sorry. She didn't know what to make of his new expression. She wanted to take her opinions back, to be a less-chatty type of talker, but it was too late now. Heaven only knew what he'd be thinking after he dropped her at home.

"Sabina, there's something I ought to tell you."

"It's none of my business," she replied, burrowing deeper with her heels.

"Maybe one day you'd like it to be."

Sabina bit her lip. In truth she would have liked to know just about everything a person could know about Colin Hatch. "It's about your blue ticket?"

He laughed without smiling. "So you've already heard?"

She nodded. "What does it mean?"

"Having that kind of a record." He balanced his cigarette between two offset lips. Sailed another rock into the crest of a wave. "Makes things very difficult for a man. Financially speaking. If I quit flying for Dooley now, I lose the farm. No bank will ever help me repay him. So I'm on his hook until we're square and then some. That's what the blue ticket means."

Sabina stood to rinse her toes in the encroaching water. She felt an anger firing her blood. "But you didn't *deserve* the blue ticket, did you? What could you have done to warrant it? I'll bet you just need to find the right person, the right sort of authority to clear it up. Bud, my father, knows plenty of lawyers, I'm sure—"

Colin shook his head. He looked so grim, she didn't dare ask which of her ideas he was dismissing.

Just then, thankfully, a man's voice cut into the quiet constant of the ocean wind. "Hey there! You kids!" Hatch turned on his bent elbow to see a gentleman in seersucker swimming trunks now trotting toward them.

The man carried a tin gas can in his hand, a towel draped over his shoulders. "The missus and I, we ran out of fuel about a half mile back. Mind if I siphon a bit to get us on over to Edgartown?"

"Not at all." Hatch stood. "We'd be happy to drive you back."

All together in the cab of Hatch's Ford, Sabina tried to sit as unobtrusively as possible. Mr. Lawrence—that was the tourist's name—was built like a professional weightlifter. He joked about his struggle to walk as far as he had while his wife waited with their empty Oldsmobile. Now, wedged between him and Hatch, Sabina narrowed her shoulders and nearly held her breath until the strain of it felt painful. Gradually, she let her left side retreat into the edge of the space where Hatch sat driving. She turned her body the slightest fraction of a degree away from sweating, wheezing Mr. Lawrence, who kept swearing he was the last person on earth you'd guess would run out of gasoline. Eventually, her bare arm relaxed against the cotton of Hatch's shirtsleeve. In response to the occasional bump in the road, her left knee collided with his right thigh. At a hard left turn she had to grab hold of his arm.

Hatch made no reaction. He gabbed with Mr. Lawrence throughout the short drive, asking where he was from, how long he was staying on the island, and all the usual things. If he was aware of Sabina's internal struggle not to press herself in any way against him, he didn't let on. But when the Lawrences' black car came into view with a relieved Mrs. Lawrence waving happily from the roadside, Hatch didn't jump out to oversee the refueling operation as Sabina had expected he would. Instead, he offered a friendly goodbye while executing a quick three-point turn, tires scratching over the loose sand. As he put the truck in gear, without Sabina noticing, his free hand found its way beneath her braid and settled around the nape of her neck, as smoothly and sweetly as if he'd held her that way a thousand times before. Neither one took their eyes off the road ahead.

"This was a fun day," he said. "I had fun with you."

"Me too," she said, mostly because it was all she could muster. And also because, for that moment, and for the days to follow, it was all that mattered.

# NINE

"*Hatch!* Hold up a minute!" Bill Dooley wrestled his body out from the back seat of his town car. Rain fell in sheets. Katama Airfield was a bog of pudding-brown puddles. The little businessman teetered to avoid them.

Hatch lifted his cap. "Let's go, Dooley!" He clapped his hands from the open door of the Beechcraft. "Jig time!" They both knew Hatch couldn't leave without him. Still, wouldn't hurt for Dooley to show a little hustle.

"Sox won an awful dogfight last night. Did you hear it?"

"No," Hatch answered, adjusting his headset. "I've been getting to bed early."

"That so? Who with?" Dooley snickered, ducking his head into the plane, dragging his briefcase behind him.

"A farmer leads a solitary life, my friend."

"I'm not buying it." Dooley shook his round face. "Give me the straight stuff."

"Nothing to hear, Bill." Hatch scowled at his engine ops checklist: oil pressure, fuel pressure, instrument air, ammeter plus, fuel boost off.

"Listen, before you get going there," Dooley said, gesturing to the cockpit controls, "do you mind if I ask you—see, it's really more of an *opportunity* than a favor. Happy news for both of us."

"Let me guess. You've been nominated *Time*'s Man of the Year."

"Isolde Martin." Dooley spoke the name like a quiz-show clue.

"The actress?"

"The very one. She's your newest client."

All at once Hatch remembered George Mattos's report from last week. Dooley's trips on Doc Kemp's launch. The actress. The little island. "What's the angle you're playing now?"

"My God, she's *beautiful*, Hatch. And she's here!"

"This is to do with your bridge business, is that right?"

"The girl bought a house from me. Now *I'm* helping *her* get set up with some other, uh . . . amenities. That's neither here nor there. The thing is, she needs a pilot. She'll pay triple."

"For when?"

"*When?* 'For when' you're asking me?" Dooley balked. "How about 'wow' or 'gee whiz, thanks'?"

"You know me, Bill. I don't get hysterical about fancy people. And of course I'm grateful, but the truth is I'd prefer to come out here less. I've got beds of spinach that are already bolting—"

"Beds of spinach!" Dooley doubled over and slapped his knee, though he wasn't actually laughing.

"Look, Bushmick can help her. Got another kid on the way. He's been asking for extra runs."

"No, that's the point. It has to be *you*, Hatch." Dooley leaned closer. His breath, even at 9:00 a.m., smelled of pearl onions and cigars. His exhalations fogged the plane's small windows. "She's already had a very bad experience with some amateur from Mayflower. Treated her worse than fourth-class mail. And now she's talking about leaving the island for good if she can't secure decent transportation."

"So what if she does?"

"I'm not sure if you're *hearing* what I'm *saying*." Dooley's pale eyes narrowed into darts. He pulled the *Globe* from his briefcase—the massive wingspan of the paper nearly reaching either side of the Beech's fuselage.

Hatch considered the consequences of saying no to his longtime benefactor. True enough, he owed the guy money. But didn't he already do him enough favors? Besides, it'd been months since the last time Bill really went bugshit over something silly. More than once this summer the club had let him out golfing again—in the presence of ladies, no less. On the other hand, Bill Dooley had a way of queering things whenever he was disappointed. He'd given up screaming at people maybe, but he certainly wasn't through cooking up his quiet punishments on the side.

"I'll have to think about it," Hatch exhaled.

"Good. While you do, think about this: What if I could find your girl for you? The Italian. The photograph you've got glued to your heart. I'm friendly with the ambassador, you know."

"I took that out," Hatch lied. He turned in his seat, giving his back to Dooley and the whole conversation.

For the record, Hatch was not *saving* Adele's photograph. Not per se. Nearly ten years removed, saving her photo would be about as foolish as plucking petals from a daisy. He knew this. But getting *rid* of it had proved a complicated chore. Somehow (with what tools, he couldn't remember), she'd fitted the edges so damned perfectly against the corners of his cigarette case that prying it free required, well, more effort than he was willing to give.

Hatch replayed their last day as he always did when Adele's name came to mind. He still remembered watching her do up the buttons of her new blouse, the sounds of the courtyard outside the hotel: young boys peddling their trinkets, the *arrontino* clanging his bell, the growling of distant engines as soldiers passed through the mountains beyond the town. The plan was in place, but he hadn't fully trusted it. They were late and he was hanging on to her fingertips, worried. She stood facing the door. "*Dai*," she'd complained, tugging her wrist away, meaning, "Come on," or "Give," really. And so he'd let her go.

Dooley persisted. "You've had a lot to say about her in the past. I know how men exaggerate when they get tight, but be honest, son. She's important to you. And I know people who can find her."

"We should get moving." Hatch looked at his watch, did a panel scan.

Altitude gyro. Altimeter set. Com frequencies, all good. Hatch radioed into ground control.

"Of course, if they found her—I mean, if *my guy* found her, it could go a long way toward reversing that blue ticket you've got."

"Katama ground," Hatch repeated. "This is Beech 2-2-0-2-2 at the east gate. Requesting taxi eleven for departure to Logan."

"Maybe, in fact," Dooley pressed, "you'd have a good case for the Military Discharge Review Board. Might change some people's minds about you."

"I'm not interested in changing anyone's mind," Hatch replied.

"Aren't you, though? Wouldn't you like to win back your veteran's benefits? Own that scrappy little farm of yours outright?"

Hatch cleared his throat. "You don't know what you're talking about."

"My wife says the same thing." Dooley smiled into his paper. "She's never managed anything on her own either."

"I said I'd think about it."

"That's good. Because it's all been decided anyhow. They're combing the Italian countryside as we speak. And you're on the flight log with Isolde Martin for July fifth. So be here, waiting."

The percussive rain continued beating against the plane's metal roof. At times it assumed an almost dizzying tempo, like a protracted crescendo, like a boxer's last series before surrendering the prize fight. Hatch said nothing. Instead he released his toe brakes and centered the clipper with the rudder pedals. He set the flaps to takeoff position. He watched the rotation speed, pulled back on the yoke. Without another word to Dooley, he prepared for ascent.

# TEN

"Lenore, darling, why don't you walk yourself down to the market to fetch this morning's mail?" Nola Dooley sang out in the sunny, decorative voice she saved for company. "It's the perfect day for a stroll—don't you think so, Ethel?" The two island neighbors nodded. Lenore glared into the Frigidaire, hunting for a plate of last night's fried chicken.

This, Lenore decided, was her mother's great talent: a contrived way of speaking that allowed her to manage two discrete conversations at the same time. Something she'd learned from her husband, probably. The innocent meaning and then the subtext, layered together and baked smooth. So while Mrs. Crowder was visiting the cottage for tea, and while Lenore was routing 'round the kitchen, looking (apparently, in her mother's eyes) a bit snug in her sundress, Nola could satisfy two agendas at once.

"Pick up a newspaper for Mrs. Crowder while you're there, won't you? I'm sure she'd appreciate the favor." More nodding. More smiling. More tea.

Outside the presence of company, earlier that month, Nola Dooley had been more direct with her concerns.

"A little plumpness is still a nice look for a bride, but honestly, we do need to start restricting," she'd warned. "No more bread and butter with dinner. You will have grapefruit for breakfast. And you will—don't scowl at me like that—you *will* start walking into town every day."

"Shall I carry a shoulder yoke as well?" Lenore had replied. "Perhaps I could haul the groceries home on a drag stone."

"Lenny, please. It's a mother's duty to improve on her daughter's appearance. It's not as if I'm trying to punish you." She'd made a quick sign of the cross. "But in the long run, I do think you'd be angrier with me if I *didn't* impose some kind of program for you. Really, a little dieting is not so difficult."

Now, nine weeks before the wedding, nine weeks before Europe and a long list of impossible goodbyes, Lenore Dooley found herself grasping. Her hands had reached out, scrabbling for bearings, and had somehow come back to her clenching secrets. Exquisite pearls of information that did not belong to her, but which she nonetheless carried—clung to, even.

By late June and a half dozen of her mother's imposed mail runs, this is what she knew:

Her father was planning the construction of a bridge between Edgartown and Chappaquiddick. The engineering sketches, drawn up by R. S. Baker & Sons, revealed a riveted steel truss design, like a lank cat arching its back over the channel. Hardly one tenth of a mile, from point to point, plotted down harbor from the club, where Katama Bay was at its narrowest. The Chappaquiddick Island Association intended to fight him on it. And yet, if Lenore was reading well enough between the lines, the bridge was happening anyhow, already preceded by a $30,000 paving contract, invoiced care of Miss Isolde Martin, for two miles of "mechanically stabilized gravel base/dense-graded asphalt surface." Already coming into being as disparate piles of brackets, pins, beams, and plates on the ground of an Alleghany steelyard.

From the same daily errand of the mail, Lenore also knew that her father was broke. His accountant diagramed the matter, in increasingly simpler terms, finally resorting to red-ink imperatives and handwriting the size of her old primary school readers. So much money going out. So much less coming in. A series of question marks surrounding several LLCs on the ledger. It appeared the accountant was losing patience with William Dooley's inattention. Or, more accurately, with the inattention of a certain Mr. Noel Wunholm, a perfectly make-believe administrator her father had invented and employed in order to buffer himself from any unpleasant correspondences.

At any other point in her life, these overlapping controversies might have alarmed Lenore. But she'd discovered—somewhere in the aftermath of her first missed period—one's threshold for panic rises only so high before descending, mercifully, into a realm of detached bemusement. And so now the grim facts of Dooley business took turns on a stage that came to life, each day, with the ritual of collecting the family letters.

Lenore's walk into town carried her along the water, past the scalloped fences and the rose-bushed verandas of the Harbor View Hotel. Most days the sidewalks were crowded with tabloid photographers and low-grade vacationists haunting the hotel steps, waiting for a glimpse of the island's newest celebrity in residence: Isolde Martin. On the opposite side of the road, a gathering movement convened with placard signs and megaphones to protest her father's bridge. In between, throngs of families toted their shade umbrellas and nylon dip nets, en route to Lighthouse Beach. And all along the main drag, teenagers in convertibles—carefree kids in a carefree season—honked their way through the foot traffic.

Lenore felt dizzy. She eyed the balcony seating at Alouette's, where she'd often—in a past life, it seemed—sat lunching and pointing out the ladies with the rather obvious home-done permanents. She elbowed past soliciting street artists—city men all selling alike canvases of quaint ocean scenes. Lenore sometimes wished she could step into one of those scenes. Step in and keep right on walking.

"Yes, fine, hello," she mumbled preemptively to the man who held the door for her at Mayhew's Market. Inside, she could see, the aisles hummed with more vacationists, stockpiling the usual household staples: milk, bread, soap flakes, bug spray. While the women shopped, their children crowded round the penny gum machines. The babies waited parked outside in a row of identical buggies.

"*Lenore Dooley!* Why, hello yourself! How did you like my gift?" the man at the door replied.

“Beg your pardon?”

“My engagement gift. For you and John. The antique tapestry?”

Lenore Dooley shook free from her private thoughts long enough to regard this man on the doorstep. She came to recognize James Whelan for his large glasses and fatuous grin. Lenore forced a smile back at him. “Yes, a very unique piece, to be sure.” She imagined the pile of gifts stockpiled in the cottage’s spare room, most of them still unopened. “I hope you can excuse me just now, James. I’m afraid I’ve—”

“The marriage of Cupid and Psyche,” the student doctor continued.

“Cupid and what?” Lenore rubbed her forehead.

“That’s the scene the artwork depicts. Woven into the tapestry, I mean. The story of the marriage of Cupid and Psyche. You remember! He was a god with a history of sordid liaisons, and she a mere mortal. Beautiful, yes, but unequal nonetheless. Why, Lenore, you look perplexed. Don’t they teach Greek mythology at Vassar?”

“I must have been sick that day.”

“I got it at auction. From the atelier of Pieter van den Kecke,” he clucked, embellishing the accent. “You really ought to have it appraised. For insurance purposes.”

“We will treasure it, truly.”

Whelan beamed at this assurance. “My mother had suggested a silver soup tureen, but she grew up very bourgeois. You can’t go by her standards.”

“Mothers can be difficult,” Lenore swallowed.

“Are you picking up your mail? I’ll wait for you.”

“That’s kind of you, but I need to shop a few items, and I’d really hate to keep you.”

“It’s no trouble,” the young man replied, pushing his glasses to the bridge of his nose. “I’d been meaning to track you down at the club, actually. To ask for your opinion.”

“*Mine?* What about?” Lenore eyed him suspiciously.

“Well, it’s about Sabina, you see.”

“Oh.”

"And Colin Hatch," Whelan added bitterly.

"Oh!" Lenore perked at the pilot's name. "Wait here a moment, then."

Inside, Lenore absently managed some pleasantries with the market cashier. She tossed the change for the newspaper in a way that sent her nickel spiraling. It landed against a jar of wax-wrapped Necco wafers. "I'll take two of those," she commanded. "And a Charleston Chew."

"Certainly, Miss Dooley," the cashier smiled.

"And a quarter pound of peanut butter fudge."

Lately, Lenore's queasy stomach could tolerate only two food groups: white and brown, which loosely translated into starch or chocolate. Or root beer. Sometimes a root beer was the only possible antidote to the hot, disorienting waves that washed over her body not just in the mornings, but *all day*, at hourly intervals, with a wicked punctuality and an uncompromising demand for simple sugars.

Toward the back of the market, Lenore found her family's post box among the grid of silver squares. She unlocked the little door with a key around her neck and tugged out a stack of bills and letters, most of them curled inside the U of an oversized buff envelope marked, CONFIDENTIALE. For a moment she stood and puzzled over the Roman return address. Something to do with her honeymoon perhaps? A secret admirer of her father's? Forgetting Whelan for the moment, she rushed to tear it open.

**Cliente:** *Sig. Noel Wunholm*

**Indirizzo di fatturazione:** *PO Box 897, Edgartown, MA - Stati Uniti*

**Numero del caso:** *6547*

**Investigatore:** *Pacifico Vento*

**Servizi di traduzione:** *Speak Easy Inc., Via dei Serpenti, 247 – 00184 Roma, Italia*

*Roma, 7 giugno, 1954*

*Dear Mr. Wunholm,*

*Your request, it seems, will be somewhat more difficult to fulfill than I had originally anticipated. The girl in question must not have been truthful about her surname, or else she was traveling under her married name, which seems unlikely, given that she was said to be fleeing a violent marriage. In any case, there is no record of an Adele Buontempo born in the city of Naples, nor any of the surrounding villages.*

*Enclosed you will find a copy of the photograph you sent me along with several false identity cards that were confiscated from Neapolitan gappiste and returned to the local commune. Some similar faces in the bunch, no? Perhaps your soldier can examine them with more familiar eyes. The bad news, I must tell you, is that all of these women are dead. The good news, of course, is that if your target is not in fact among them, she may not be so very badly off.*

*In the second case, please do not despair. As you know from our mutual friend, I am connected with many of the prominent people across my country. Their access and influence will be a great aid to us, as we unravel this case on behalf of your colleague, the airman.*

*Regrettably, my fee must again be addressed. I will require the £300,000 we discussed in order to broaden my investigation outside the province. Please confirm you have received this report, and please remit payment promptly (invoice enclosed) within thirty business days. Failure to reply will result in a closure of your case number.*

*Cordially,*

*Pacifico Vento*

Lenore considered this information between long, grinding bites of candy bar: Colin Hatch was looking for a woman. A married woman, gone missing. And Lenore's own father was meant to be financing the investigation.

She stood in the back corner of Mayhew Market and pondered this latest stolen secret while giving herself a little absolution: It was never her intention to spy on anyone. She was not a nosey girl. No one could accuse her of being that, not even her worst enemies (although several of them had, at one time or another, accused her of it). Instead, this news had quite literally fallen into her lap, and only after her mother insisted she be the one assigned to fetch it.

She folded the letter back into its first-class envelope and stepped outside to reconvene with the insufferable James Whelan.

"Anything good in the mail?" He eyed her shoulder bag.

"Could be." She flashed him a smile. "What was it you wanted my opinion of?"

"It's this situation between Colin and Sabina. They are *seeing* each other, you must know? *Carrying on*, some might even say."

"And you disapprove?"

"Oh, I don't know. It's more that I *worry.*" James Whelan smoothed his hair. He gestured to help Lenore with her shoulder bag, but she clutched the strap tighter, shrugging him off. "Heck, Lenore, I worry about her future."

"You don't like the pilot," Lenore corrected him. "Tell me truly. You think our girl can't handle him."

James Whelan needed no further coaxing to confess. "Not without a hunting license, she can't. Look, you must agree. Colin Hatch is a square in our social circle. He's so much worse than just *wrong* for Sabina romantically. His influence, his stupid grinning—why, if I had her father's ear I'd argue the man is an actual *detriment* to a young woman's personal growth. Putting her behind the curve, when it comes to life's quote-unquote 'dating game' and to understanding the specific kinds of exposure she needs to gain—Lenore? *Lenore?* Why are you laughing?"

Lenore couldn't help herself. The day's dismal start had given way to an amusing afternoon. And yes, the chocolate had helped considerably too. "I'm sorry to laugh," she admitted. "It's just that your timing is so funny." She threw her head back and laughed at the sky. "It's so funny, I'm practically weak from laughing."

"Funny? How so?"

"I happen to know something about Colin Hatch that might make you worry a whole lot less, at least insofar as his prospects with Sabina are concerned."

"*What* do you know? Something about his history?"

"Why should I tell you?"

Whelan shrugged. "Go ahead and keep it to yourself, then. See how this budding summer romance shakes out naturally. See how well you like the scene, come August, at *your* wedding, when the two of them can't be kept apart, and all the guests are watching the prettiest couple they've ever chanced to admire gliding across your parquet."

And there it was. At Whelan's deft instigation, Lenore felt it again. Felt it all over. Not just the nausea, but that woozy sensation, the tilting—like a slow-motion fall. A feeling like the sidewalk beneath her feet, or her very life itself, were edging away in small, certain breaths. Another ounce of the inevitable. A thing coming: the way new seasons swell and erode, one leaf at a time—that was now the terrifying fate of her good skin, her perfect figure. And John too. Lately she felt him slipping away along with this same grim undertow. Extracting himself every day with quieter complaints, simpler apologies, long stares out the car window and carefully removed from her gaze. Did he still love her? She couldn't bear to ask herself, let alone ask John directly. So what else could she do? What else but to go ahead as she'd always been: smiling, sarcastic, indelicately attuned to everyone else's tough luck.

Lenore produced the Italian letter from her shoulder bag and tapped its sharp corner to her chin. Later today she would place it, along with the others, in the tray atop the credenza where her father retrieved all his business papers. He would not wonder about why the mail was now suddenly, neatly opened for him. Letters from his office often appeared at the island, along with urgent telegrams for the illusory, made-up assistant, Mr. Wunholm. And her father regarded them in much the same way he frowned at the Boston ivy burrowing its vines into the cottage's untended chimney cracks. When, if ever, her father's partners were answered was rather a mystery, like so many other mysteries jockeyed around his desk blotter all the live-long day—mysteries to abscond with via taxi cab, streetcar, or chauffeured Lincoln; to burn in the fireplace of his den, watching the words waft away as minute curling particles, soon to settle, imperceptibly, into a hanging cloud of dust.

But first, she handed the Italian letter over to James.

# ELEVEN

Ani's Tiptop Tailoring was perhaps the last place on earth Sabina wanted to spend a precious summer afternoon, and yet she couldn't help herself from smiling. Only five more minutes to endure—Sabina willed the clock's slow hands to march forward that much faster—and then it would be time to meet up with Colin. Meantime, Lenore Dooley stood in her Spanish heels and alençon lace atop the seamstress' overturned whiskey crate. Ani knelt at the bride's feet, an army of straight pins clasped between her lips as she deftly navigated the hems of nine different petticoats.

"Are you almost through?" Lenny groaned down at her feet. "Honestly, it's hot enough to scald a loon in here."

Ani gave no reply, only a murderous glare and a firm tug at the dress' silk lining.

"Can I bring you a sorbet?" Sabina offered, eager to escape outside. The shop window looked out onto North Water Street, across from the granite steps of the bank and the striped awnings of the ever-crowded drug store, where vacationing families milled around for zinc oxide and chocolate frappés. Ani looked up again to glare at Sabina. "Perhaps an ice water?"

"Don't bother," Lenore sighed. "If I put another thing into my mouth I'll end up right back here next week, so she can turn the screws that much tighter. This gown might as well be a duck press."

"Well, you *look* lovely," Sabina affirmed. "You'll be the prettiest bride since Kay Banks married Buckley Dunstan."

"I'd better be. Seems some of my guests are already more interested in *your* appearance at the wedding. Yours and Colin's, I should say."

Sabina frowned, spinning around from her watch post at the shop window. In doing so, she caught sight of Lenore staring. The bride's expression revealed a grim combination of criticism and envy, that particular look women save only for one another, for the unavoidable comparisons they make—appraising advantages both physical and otherwise—dozens of times each day.

"That can't be true."

Lenore sighed, smiling down at the enormous diamond on her finger. "You must know how people are *talking*. The girls at the club have crowned you this summer's biggest flirt."

"I beg your pardon," Sabina said, blanching. This was her aunt's pet phrase, the begging of pardons. She only wished she'd thought up something smarter to say.

"He's not hard to look at, I'll give you that much. But it's gotten awfully exclusive, awfully fast, wouldn't you agree?"

"I do see Colin often, yes. In the mornings we're out at Starbuck. I'm teaching him to swim and to hold his breath underwater . . ." She trailed off.

"*Hold his breath?* That's rich. I didn't know you had it in you, Sabina."

"Lenore, I don't like your tone."

"Like it or not, what kind of friend would I be if I didn't even *try* to dissuade you?"

"Dissuade me from what?"

"Heartache. Embarrassment. Complete social disaster." Lenore fanned her glistening forehead. "You're no end of a brick, dear. Why do you suppose Colin Hatch suddenly dotes on you?"

"I suppose it's because, well, because he's fond of me."

"*Fond* of you?" Lenore covered her mouth to stifle a laugh. "That's darling. And nothing at all to do with your father's big-time money?"

"I think I'd better go." Sabina gathered her sunglasses and straw bag.

"Wait, Bean! Please!" Lenore attempted a contrite expression. "I think I've gotten us started off on the wrong foot."

Sabina straightened her mother's bracelet—the one Colin had gone and fixed for her after all. "Where is it we're meant to be going?"

"Look, I know the idea of going off to college weighs heavy on you. You've never lived away at school before."

"And?"

"And you've no older sister to prepare you for—well, to be quite direct, there are certain campus rules a girl's got to follow. *Parietals.*"

"I'm familiar with parietals. What are you getting at, Lenore?"

"I have to get down for a moment," the bride informed her seamstress. "*Now*, if you don't mind."

"You can hold it," Ani murmured, her lips clenching pins.

"No, this can't wait." Lenore tugged her skirts up, hopping off the crate.

"To go outside in your gown is very bad luck for your wedding."

"Bad luck," Lenore jeered. "Don't be thick."

"If you dirty this dress . . ." the seamstress threatened as she stood, pushing her sleeves up over her elbows and plucking the remaining pins from her mouth.

Lenore paid no mind, kicking off her heels and grabbing her bridal robe from the changing room hook. She tiptoed out the front door in a half-hearted attempt to keep the dress from dragging, followed by Sabina and the jingle of the shop's silver bell.

The girls walked to where the Dooley's driver waited with his long, polished Lincoln, parked beneath the frothy blooms of the Japanese lilacs. Bits of white petals scattered over their hair and shoulders as a warm wind blew. Lenore's head disappeared into the back seat while Sabina stood fuming, hands on hips, wondering whatever absurdity Lenore was about to reveal.

"Your aunt asked me to give you this."

Sabina accepted the small package still bearing its stamped postage and brown paper wrapping. "But it's addressed to *me*. A. P. has already opened it? *You've* opened it?"

Lenore shrugged in her maddeningly casual way. The breeze kicked up again, setting her blonde curls aloft while the passing bank patrons wondered at her odd attire—the silk robe doing little to conceal the enormous train of her wedding gown, which she'd gathered messily into her fist. "Lately it's been so difficult to get hold of you. I'm sure Poppy worried this needed your immediate attention."

Sabina unfolded a sheet of stationary bearing Weston College's distinctive gold-and-navy crest.

*Dear Miss McTigue,*

*As we look toward the happy beginnings of the Class of '58, we must also remember the traditions that define our rich legacy. Weston girls pride themselves on their individual goodness and collective esprit de corps. But it is hardly by accident that we see these attributes thrive, year after year. Enclosed herein, please find the Weston College Freshmen Ladies Guide. I trust you'll find time to put these parietal rules to memory before the fall semester.*

*More importantly, as I know you are capable, I trust you will read between the lines to arrive at a clearer feeling of what Weston scholarship truly means. For while it is all well and good to remember our hats and gloves when heading out of doors and to confine our smoking habits (if we must have them at all) to our private living quarters, rules are quite useless without a deep, personal commitment to reinforcing them.*

*Weston girls, I am proud to say, do not sprawl themselves across the lawn on sunny days, nor do we entertain members of the opposite sex past ten o'clock. And yet again, it seems to me, the most powerful tool for cultivating honest, upright citizenship is not any code that mandates outward conformity but an ongoing survey of one's own attitudes toward manners and refinement.*

*It has come to my attention you may have already formed some, shall we say, unsavory "attachments" in your hometown. I do not relish the idea of policing my students or their campus guests, so I'm requesting you find means to sever said ties inside the boundaries of the summer break—to make the right choice inwardly, as well as publicly. Take it from a fellow Weston gal, to do so will serve us both for the better.*

*Yours,*

*Gertrude Budge*

*Dean of Students, Weston College*

"Well?" Lenore demanded.

"Well, what?"

"What do you think?"

"I think," Sabina said, swallowing and folding the dean's letter in half, "I think that you're jealous."

"Jealous!" Lenore threw back her shoulders. "Jealous of what? *You?*"

"Of all the, the . . . the low-down stunts!" Sabina stuttered over her words. "You reported me to the dean, didn't you? Because Colin hardly notices you, and because you're jealous."

A family of tourists gave wide berth to the girls squabbling on the sidewalk.

"I did nothing of the sort. James Whelan's cousin's second wife is a Weston alumnus. It was she who placed the telephone call, I'd wager. And besides, who on earth would be jealous of a bland little nit like you?"

"A nit like me!"

"Yes, *you!* That's what I said. You, who for nineteen years has had nothing better to do than hide her dental bands inside some old nature journal! A girl who—who spends her Saturday nights going birding on Felix Neck, for heaven's sake!"

"You sound awfully defensive."

"Do I?" Lenore had this particular way of standing—very tall and haughty—with her nose tilted up like a coneflower tracking the sunlight. "Then perhaps I am jealous. Jealous you're getting chucked from college over some war criminal who you haven't even kissed yet!"

"That's not true." Sabina's voice came out choked. She suddenly felt the hot sun burning on her cheeks. Tears of anger stung her eyes. "He's not a criminal."

"You don't know the half of it," Lenore smiled meanly.

"And *you* do?"

Just then a dump truck advertising "R. S. Baker & Sons Hot-Mix Asphalt"—well-caked in its own grime—chugged and hissed down North Water Street, replacing the usual smells of Edgartown in the summer with a momentary whiff of sulfur and coal-tar pitch. The two girls watched it jitter and jounce in the direction of the ferry point. Just behind came Colin Hatch, quietly pulling his Ford against the curbstone's smooth lip.

"*Colin!* Such a pleasure to cross your path again." All too quickly Lenore became her composed, flirtatious self, making it her business to lift the green tarpaulin from the truck bed, inspecting his crops with a studious eye. "Are you here to retrieve Sabina, then?"

"That's right. I took your advice and hired myself some help. She's a good scout, but you have to feed her constantly."

"Oh, Colin, you slay me! Just so long as you remember, she's only a *temporary* worker. Come September, it's off to college with her."

"Never mind us," Sabina cut in sharply. "Shouldn't you be back inside by now, Lenore? You're not dressed for public."

"A *bride* should get used to attracting public attention. What's your excuse, Sabina?"

"I don't need any excuse."

"I think Dean Budge might beg to differ."

"Who's Dean Budge?" Colin asked.

"Nobody." Sabina glared. She strode off to escape into Hatch's truck, hoisting herself in the cab with a well-practiced skip. Colin stood by whistling as he pressed the door closed behind her.

Later that night, she tried to remember just how it'd happened next. Later that night, she lay in bed—contorting her face, this way and that—trying to recreate whatever expression had decided the moment.

Wondering how she must have come off looking—*too clumsy, too silly, too bold; and which one of those would have been the worst?*—from Colin's side of the exchange. His face had been so close, so handsome, and her temper was so fired. In a way, it felt obvious—the only thing *to* do. She had reached through the open window with one un-gloved hand, taking hold of his scratchy cheek. Then he'd leaned in and pressed his lips to hers. Lightly, for a start.

In that moment, with Lenore looking on—not to mention the whole of North Water Street—Sabina finally kissed Colin Hatch. She kissed him solidly, with purpose, with notes of passion and defiance and maybe something like revenge playing out in her head. She kissed him in the unforgiving light of a Tuesday. Before lunchtime, even! She kissed Colin Hatch as though paying homage to Hedy Lamarr in *Algiers*: with a brave, desperate expression and a fully tilted head. It went on rather a bit longer than was proper. (Later that night, before falling to sleep, this recollection also burned up her cheeks.) Her fingers climbed his face and took hold of his earlobe—surprisingly soft beneath the stubble of his sideburns. From his neck she found traces of mint and sweet basil and citronella soap. From his lips she found encouragement to stay just as she was—just as *they* were—maybe for all the summer. Naturally, though, Lenore demanded the attention right back. Sabina was just pulling away from Colin's surprised smirk when she heard the girl calling again at the sidewalk.

"Oh, Colin! Excuse me, Colin? Don't keep this date going too long, will you? My father has something more important waiting for you."

# TWELVE

"You don't like me very much, do you?" Isolde Martin smiled. "Well, that's all right. Not everyone has to be friends." She wasn't sure whom she was addressing, but the observation landed soundly, given the context, in either direction. To her left stood the acclaimed builder Baker; to her right, the taciturn ferry tender, manning the wheel of his tattered old boat with a sunbaked scowl. Among the company of normal strangers, Isolde wasn't used to anything short of complete adoration. And yet for their own private reasons, *these two men*, much like the Academy members back in Hollywood, were not Isolde Martin fans.

*But still it is a lovely day!* The Katama Channel glistened, topped with an expanse of fresh blue sky. On shore, pairs of dragonflies hovered about the daylilies. Sea oats danced around the footing of the dock. Hardly the moment, Isolde sighed, to dwell on whatever silly prizes she hadn't won. Because today she wondered if perhaps she wasn't getting something much, much better. Something stronger than a bronze statuette, more permanent than cinematic praise or critical approval. More practical and altogether *real*: Today she was getting a road.

A road.

"My own road! What more flattering tribute could there possibly be?" she turned to ask Baker, the builder, a city contractor connected to both Harris and Dooley by way of some nondescript government projects. The fact that he couldn't be tied to any reliable schedule didn't seem to trouble anyone except Isolde. He was cutting them a terrific deal, Harris had told her. And if he sometimes showed up to work at ten, or twelve, or one fifteen, *well*, that was just the price you paid for getting a job done right. This Baker stood slumped against the scow's rail, reaming the cake from his Kaywoodie pipe.

"Beats me," he grunted without looking up.

"A brand-new roadway, built entirely in *my* honor." She swiveled to address the ferry man, who went by the name of George. "There's a good chance they'll even name it after me, Bill Dooley says."

"Swell." George coughed.

"Can Greer Garson make such a claim? I'd very much doubt it. Why, she's got nothing to stand on but fan mail."

Baker spat into the wind. George scratched beneath his cap.

"Now consider *asphalt*, by comparison," Isolde rhapsodized, abandoning Baker for the starboard rail of the vessel, performing the dip-toed walk of a tightrope artist as she skirted the stern. "It's a verified statement piece." In proclaiming this, she almost believed it well enough to forget the other woes that presently plagued her: the elusive Capra role, the Harris situation, the remaining pinch of fat that refused to dissolve above her kneecaps.

On her road, though, the immediate future sparkled. She loved each new day's length of progress better than the last. And so what if her collaborators—she regarded Baker and George again—insisted on stewing along the way? So what if she hadn't a friend? An ally? The thing of it was, she now had *inspiration*.

On the first day of the build, the crawler tractor had arrived promptly at nine. For all the fanfare it attracted, it might well have been the first Atlas elephant chained and dragged into a waiting Colosseum. The incongruence was striking: a bright yellow machine encroaching on the plains of a chaste, wind-swept prairie. The tourists watched from the benches of Harbor Light Pier. Across the bay, at the beach club, sunbathers left their sand chairs, wading out ankle-deep, where they stood to marvel at the crossing.

For the first week of paving—despite the swirling grit and the clouds of acrid smoke—she'd attached herself to the proceedings, every morning, dressed in a Western-style blouse and high-waisted dungarees. Every morning she walked the three blocks along North Water Street, inhaling the heavy white air rolling in off the water. At the ferry berth she'd exchange six cents with George, the skipper, who asked her nothing—except for a ten-cent fare that first day she boarded with the moped.

Once arrived at the little island, Isolde now rode her awaiting Lambretta—no need to chain it; no *place* to chain it!—about two miles to the grassy bluff where the defunct cottage stood. Her new homestead amounted to a plain rectangular box, built from old shipwreck timbers and weather-rusted boards. Dooley had arranged for a whole battery of subcontractors to meet them on-site: men to shine up the floors, men to apply fresh coats on the walls, men to gussy up the bathroom, more men to stand ponderously beside their varying trucks—men who looked virtually identical to any witness save their own mothers and who were, Isolde observed, brutally intent on leaving ten thousand half-finished cans of Moxie behind at day's end. Bill Dooley dropped by occasionally to engage these men, the bosses among them at least—to rap his red knuckles on whatever task they'd recently completed and thereby declare it a fantastic success.

Her plot was a flat parcel in between a small lagoon and a stunning vista of marsh grass, nodding off toward the sea. When she sat on her porch step she could see everlasting hummocks of cool sand cresting at irregular intervals. In the mornings, the gray knolls woke up pocked with small craters formed by last night's rain. In the light of day, the mounds revealed their spots: flecks of blue and white and purple-black shells. Here she'd sit and rehearse her milkmaid lines, patiently listening for the gravelly breath of Baker's engine, the chorusing grunts of the workmen loading hot mix into the front hopper, the smell of the bituminous dust, which—depending on the direction of the wind—usually arrived first of all.

Contrary to what any of her city associates might have guessed, Isolde was actually soothed by these rote stages of her day. In New York or LA, hopping from cab to limousine to airport terminal would have exhausted her nerves faster than Fred MacMurray at a wrap party. But here, the promise of her quiet island life was already taking effect. Looking past the mechanical din and the omnipresent cans of Moxie, she could see that Chappaquiddick was as charming as it was spare. As busy as it was sedate—active with surly marsh hawks evacuating families of smaller birds from the cedars; with blue crabs slinking across frothy tidal pools; with shy voles peering through the fragrant, creeping mat of Plymouth mayflowers.

Here, her chronic neck pain was gone. Her dieting was effortless. In fact, her midsection was narrowing below her ribcage to such an extent that she'd sent her driver into Boston just the other day to buy a belt from the Young Miss department. Her skin felt warm and taut from all her time outdoors.

She liked the white-uniformed ice man who made his rounds in a truck with a painted cartoon igloo. She like the boys who hunted periwinkle by the wharf, begging after tourists to toss them loose change. She liked the little sign by the boatyard that advertised mumpers for a nickel. No question, she found everything about this life easy. Beyond easy; she found it obvious. Here, she nearly fell down in her swooning love for this place of basic words and tones and scenes. She was even feeling sympathetic toward her Harris lately.

Yes, Isolde had to hand it to herself, buying the Chappy house—sight unseen—was not the disaster her various advisors had predicted. It was not just another impulsive, defiant purchase. Admittedly, she made plenty of those. To Isolde's mind, there weren't enough diamond brooches or alligator bags on all of Via Condotti to shed the legacy of frugality she'd endured as a child. She could still, quite uncomfortably, picture her mother's tentative hands—the way they trembled before a cashier to pluck the required coins from her change purse. She could picture the sad scraps of curtain swatches—the birdsong, the toile, the unattainable Essex check!—tacked against the kitchen wall for at least two years, while her mother lost sleep over the eight-dollar decision at hand. Little wonder Isolde used her money at will, without pause or guilt. And if the island house had turned out to be another giant flop of a buy, she wouldn't have let her mind dwell on those dollars lost for any longer than it had taken to whisk her signature across the purchase papers.

*But look!* It was not a flop. This house, in this place, was so explicitly *right*, it bordered on fated. She could tell by the way her fingers fit around the cottage railing. The cheery pink of the Carolina roses—*her* roses—growing wild along the old stone wall. The way the cowbird sat on the edge of her water well, winking its tender affirmation. And she could tell by the very *feel* of the beach at dusk—its low-tide invitation drawing her out to revel in the corrugated bedform of the sand. Those smooth, elongated ripples proved the earth itself was rising up to meet her every footfall, to cushion her every step.

Now today, as she basked in the trade wind that traversed her front porch, watching butterflies graze in the milkweed, watching Baker's men dump and smooth another thousand pounds of hot crushed stone, she congratulated herself once again. She was humming Donizetti, in fact, when the clomping of heavy hooves broke her from the trance. A long-legged shadow darkened her yard's sandplain grass. A man atop a gray horse (*Good God*, she thought, *what century is this?*) appeared in silhouette before the sunshine.

"Happy to help you clear the yard if you'd like, Miss Martin," the man ventured. He wore a Scottish-style cap and an abashed hint of smile. From his perch on horseback, he was trying valiantly not to look down Isolde's blouse.

"Do you live here?" Isolde inquired.

"Oh sure. Forty years now. Name's Roon. Hayden Roon. Guess I forgot to introduce myself, since I feel I already know you so well. From your pictures, I mean."

"Yes, well." Isolde nodded. "That happens. This is your pony?" She gestured to the animal, which stood harnessed to an ancient-looking plow.

"Pony? Ha! She's all grown now. Not too old for mowing dry marsh, though."

It occurred to Isolde then that her island neighbors lived a very different kind of life here. On the dusty road behind Roon, now floating into view, appeared another four men carrying hand tools and hay rakes. Two lawless dogs ran their mottled muzzles along the dirt, sniffing after the horse tracks. Mr. Roon followed her eyes to where his countrymen made their slow approach. "We figured you could use a hand. Lord knows that old woodstove of yours isn't what it used to be."

"Yes, but how do *you* know that it isn't?" Isolde eyed him.

"Small neighborhood." He shrugged. "Comes with the turf. Still waiting on electricity?"

"Yes." Isolde nodded. "After the road is complete they will bring in my power lines."

"*Your* power lines?" Roon laughed at something amusing in his head.

"Listen, Mr. Roon, it's awfully nice of you folks to volunteer your help, but I don't think I ought to accept. I'm just not sure—"

"Having second thoughts about staying?"

"Well, no. None at all, actually."

"Can't say I blame you. This island used to be a quiet, private place. Simple living. Now with Dooleyville moving in—"

"What *Dooleyville*? What do you mean?"

"The apartment houses. Sky towers, more like. Right over there, Doc Kemp says they're going in. Don't tell me you didn't know." Hayden smacked his forehead with a stultifying smack. The horse shifted its muscular form beneath him. Isolde reached for the porch rail to steady herself as she stood but quickly pulled her hand away, realizing she'd landed it in a wet splatter of bird shit. She cursed loudly, frightening her new neighbor and his horse.

"Gee-whiz, I hope I didn't—we'll come back another time," Roon promised, tipping his cap to the actress, who now stood flailing the sullied extremity like an object on fire. "We were all just as buffaloed as you," he offered contritely. "It's like I said to my wife when we first saw the steamrollers. I said, 'Helen, why do you s'pose anybody'd fork over all that cash just to live in some pell-mell tenement on the beach?' And she said, very wisely to her credit, she said, 'Well there, Hayden, I expect they'd just as soon live in a garvie tin if it meant they could be neighbors with that pretty Isolde Martin.'"

# THIRTEEN

The day of the fourth dawned so lovely Sabina almost couldn't bear to stay inside, watching her beach sit empty, the low-tide stretches of sand freshly delivered, smooth and clean. But the Shreves' party was tonight. And she would be there, on Colin Hatch's arm. Together she and Connie spent ages setting her long hair, polishing her nails, practicing her walk up and down the cottage hall in a pair of precarious bare-back heels. Connie took in Sabina's new black peplum—a proper cocktail dress from Bonwit Teller, no less. Denny's girl at the office picked it up and brought it all the way from the city to the ferry at Woods Hole.

A month ago Sabina would have laughed to think of herself standing before a mirror, makeupping her lips and eyelashes, spritzing perfume along the hem of her skirt—and all just to impress a boy! But things were different now, of course. Something inside her kept fizzing up all day, like a tonic bottle shook and opened too soon, making it nearly impossible to sit still or wash the lunch dishes or even read a book without rereading the same line over and over again.

"He ought to pick you up at the door," Aunt Poppy lectured from her rocker, her main contribution to the evening's preparations. Aunt and niece were more or less on non-speaking terms since the revelation of the Weston College letter from Dean Budge, which Sabina accused Poppy and James Whelan of instigating—a charge her aunt did not deny.

"Thank you for your opinion."

"It's hardly an *opinion*. I'm referencing the simplest rules of civility. If he were any kind of gentleman, he'd insist on escorting you himself."

"He's flying some tourists in from Boston," Sabina explained for the tenth time. "He won't be home until nine."

"Then why not take you at nine?"

"Because I'm happy to take myself on time."

"I'd say it's boorish behavior. To the extreme."

"And *I* would say I don't mind meeting him at the party. It is my decision, you know."

"Women who make excuses for men are the saddest of the sad." Aunt Poppy stood with the help of her cane and shuffled off to find her knitting. It occurred to Sabina, not for the first time, that her aunt knew rather a lot about sadness and disappointment.

The Shreves owned an old whaler's mansion on a stately street downtown. As the tourists passed with their sightseeing maps, they paused to admire its quintessential Federal style: white clapboard siding, bright emerald shutters, neat dentil ornaments all around the length of the cornices. On one side, an elegant porte cochere shaded any guests who arrived via the semicircular drive. On the other side, a curved portico looked out over the soft carpet of lawn. Massive stone planters extended the garden to the second-story porch, where trailing ivy and sweet potato vine poked through the sculpted balustrades.

Sabina waved goodbye to Connie, who dropped her alone at the gate. She straightened her dress and inhaled deeply under the brace of a new girdle. Long lavender clouds stretched low in the sky. The air smelled deliciously of bonfire and the woodsy vanilla of the men's pipe smoke.

"Sabina McTigue!" Mr. Dooley barked, fists opening and closing as he moved in to kiss her cheek. "Where the hell's your father? That old goat ever getting out of the hoosegow?"

"For the wedding, I'm sure," Sabina smiled. Mr. Dooley had a black peppercorn lodged between two incisors. She willed herself not to stare at it.

"Listen, now. If you hear from him"—Dooley's body listed like a coble boat—"tell him I was asking."

"If you like, I could try telephoning him. It's only four o'clock in San Jose."

"*Now?* Don't be silly!" Mr. Dooley slapped her wrist and then kept his hand there, gripping. "It's no emergency. Time sensitive, you might say, the way these rare opportunities can be, but not *urgent*."

"All right," Sabina said calmly, noting the contrast between their voices.

"Hey!" Dooley barked again. His skin looked especially porous, damp. His breath smelled of Smirnoff. "One more thing there, love. Tell your old man I said his front grass looks like dead kelp."

Sabina smiled. "I will relay that message."

"I say again, it is *the* outstanding tension of our society: not enough women in the sciences." Mr. Ewing was preaching to an audience by the outdoor bar. "The Russians graduated *fifty thousand* engineers this spring. And here? We're lucky to prepare half as many."

"But why is it that *women* should pick up the slack?" Mrs. Crowder puzzled. "Hasn't our sex got quite enough to manage already? What with the home, the children, the endless needs of our husbands, we have to learn atomic science now too?"

"No one's proposing atomic science. I'm merely suggesting—"

"What do you think, Sabina?" Mrs. Crowder called her over. "You're a bright young lady. What's your view on women's involvement in the sciences?"

"Well," Sabina waded in slowly. It wasn't too long ago, at these sorts of parties, the hostess would rely on her to go check the children. Or even refill a water glass, in the absence of a maid. "For myself, personally, I would say that scientific study is a top priority. Science gives us new ways of *doing* things, whereas other areas of study—literature, history, philosophy—mainly sharpen our skill for discussing things. And so, I suppose, I would rather be a doer than a talker, in the long run."

"But darling, you're too pretty to be a scientist."

Sabina bit her lip in consternation. "I'm very keen on nature conservation," she continued all the same. "I've been following the career of a local woman—her name is Hughes—she's just earned some prestigious honors in the field of human ecology. And—"

"And I'll bet her husband's pleased as punch," James Whelan broke in on the group, giving Mr. Ewing a convivial elbow to the arm. Whelan wore his usual plaid sport coat and his Edgartown reds. He held a champagne glass in either hand, offering one stem to Sabina, who shook her head to decline.

"No, really, James. Ecology is a fascinating bit of science. Dr. Hughes works at Woods Hole. The Oceanographic Institution, just over in Falmouth. I've read her papers on how it is that our most valuable local resources are too rapidly getting sold off into private ownership. On behalf of the wildlife, she argues the state ought to be acquiring more beach frontage—in Duxbury, Marshfield, Sandwich—by way of eminent domain."

"Eminent domain, huh?" Mr. Ewing swigged his gimlet. "If the state's intending to seize my property, they'd better plan on taking my mother-in-law too. Talk about wildlife."

"Sabina, I'm eager to hear your aunt's opinion of this *human ecology.*" Mrs. Crowder lifted her chin. "Last I heard she expected you'd study classroom instruction."

"Yes, I don't doubt that's what she expects," Sabina smiled.

"Where is Poppy, by the way?" James asked. "I haven't seen her tonight."

"Oh, she's got a headache. Or *will* have, I should say. She's putting herself to bed before the firecrackers get going. Could you excuse me for a moment?"

"I know the way to the WC. Allow me." The young doctor volunteered his bent arm with too much enthusiasm. Together they passed through the Shreves' screened porch. Whelan closed a pair of pocket doors behind them. She sensed something crooked coming.

"Sabina," he leveled. "I think it's time you and I had a serious chat."

"I already know about your Weston College handiwork, thank you very much. And I don't appreciate the intrusion."

"I suppose you'd prefer social ruin?"

"It's a party, James." Sabina sighed. "Let's steer clear of personal politics. Especially if you're in league with Auntie and Lenore—and now your *cousin's wife*, apparently—about this Colin Hatch argument. I've already read the letter from Dean Budge. And I don't care what she says about *severing my ties*."

"Your aunt certainly does." James dealt her a concentrated stare. "If you can't make a go of it at Weston, I don't doubt she'll send you packing. Tuck you right into the next overhead sleeping berth to Switzerland."

"What are you driving at? Finishing school?" Sabina grit her teeth. "I'd rather eat paste."

"There, there. Don't go histrionic," James tutted. "You have alternatives. After all, *Lenore*'s not going back to college this fall."

"And the Braves aren't coming back to Boston. What's your point?"

"I'm saying, there *are* other options for a young lady. Other avenues besides college. You ought to let me help you find a different path. Things with Colin are over, after all—"

"Who says things with Colin are over?"

"Oh, haven't you heard? Colin has agreed to be Isolde Martin's private pilot for the summer, while she's vacationing on Chappaquiddick. Can't leave much time for swimming lessons."

Whelan's delivery caught her in the gut. Sabina flinched. *Colin Hatch and Isolde Martin?* Sabina remembered the first time she'd seen Isolde Martin on-screen. She and the girls from Latin Day had all gone to the Cambridge Zoetrope for a Saturday matinee. Afterward they'd sipped frappés and obsessed over the actress' impeccable style. *How did her hair hold its shape all throughout the motorcycle chase? And that wild finale on the rooftop!* Sabina could see Isolde Martin was lovely, of course. But she wasn't the least impressed by her cloying dialogue or exaggerated pout. The next time the girls picked a show, Sabina had opted to see Audrey Hepburn play Princess Ann again.

"That's—why, that's wonderful news. I mean, for the charter company. Such a noteworthy feather in his cap."

"Another notch in his bedpost, more like."

"I'll ask you to take that comment back." Sabina frowned. "It's insulting to both of us. And it's categorically unfounded."

"It's a pattern," Whelan said flatly. "Bird-dogging left and right, that's his MO, all right. I won't just stand by while you insist on wearing blinders."

"No one's asking you to stand by," Sabina replied. "He didn't *bird-dog* me from anyone, anyhow."

"And what about his sweetheart overseas? From the war? Bill Dooley is pulling strings to help him find the girl. Hardly a 'girl' by now, I should think."

"I don't know anything about a girl from the war."

"Don't you, though? Imagine my surprise."

"You're inventing stories." Sabina swallowed.

"I wish I were. But this Italian bride is very real. I saw her wedding portrait, in fact. Apparently your valiant pilot snared the girl in Tuscany. They say he's *desperate* to find her."

"Colin was married?" Sabina asked quietly, mostly to herself. "And she went missing?"

"Romantic, isn't it?" Whelan grinned. "Bill's now working to locate her on account of his connections with the Italian ambassador."

All at once, the house shook as if with cannon fire. Lamp cords rattled against their ceramic bases. The twelve-light panes shuddered inside centuries-old window frames. The Shreves' Welsh corgi zipped across the wide-plank floors and disappeared up the stairs. Outside, the fireworks had just begun.

# FOURTEEN

On the cool, clear evening of the Fourth of July most everyone in Edgartown was celebrating the holiday outside. Boaters took to their watercraft. Families gathered on beaches, watching the town's display smoke up the sky over the lighthouse. Inside the restaurant of the Harbor View Hotel, only a few odd couples remained dining by candlelight.

"How's Baker treating you?" Harris asked, distracted more than usual.

"Inattentively," Isolde replied. She wore a bandeau swim top beneath a satin-trimmed swing cape. Her dinner consisted of chardonnay and romaine leaves topped with herbed crostini, which she raked about the plate. "Given the choice, I think I'd have much preferred the butcher or the candlestick maker."

"Give him a chance. He'll get it done."

"I imagine he'd better. Sounds like your apartment houses depend on it."

Harris set down his highball glass. "Who mentioned apartment houses?"

Isolde smiled like a sphinx. "Does it matter? I know all about them now, which means I also have a good idea why I was invited to this lousy island in the first place."

"It's so we can spend more time together," Harris petitioned.

"It's so you and Bill Dooley can hook, line, and sinker a wealthier set of fools, I'd say," Isolde muttered.

"You've got to keep an open mind, darling." Harris shot her his varsity grin. "Why can't it be both?"

"That's just you all over." Isolde nodded in accusation. "*Both*."

"Don't let's get started."

"Started on what? You were the one who brought up Baker."

"Yes, and now *you're* bringing up unpleasantness we've already put to bed." Harris surveyed the dining room. A woman of about eighty sat hunched over her bowl, fighting to balance her soup spoon while her husband wheezed into his handkerchief. Two priests looked on as the waiter opened their second bottle of red.

"You promised, Harry. Ten times over. You promised you'd have done it by now."

"I'm not dawdling for the sport of it. In my line of work, divorce is bad for business."

"It's been two years." Isolde stabbed at her lettuce.

"Even still. You don't understand the perception about it."

"That's why I'm so grateful you're here to explain things to me." She sipped her wine.

He took her remark, incorrectly, at face value. It subdued him for the moment. He reached his hand across the table, as a gesture of compromise. Isolde stretched her forearm toward him in reply. The crook of her elbow still bore a tiny bandage from her last intravenous catheter. The hospital nurse had struck a nerve again. So lately, when she unfolded her arm this way, like a drawbridge, she felt the tug of an invisible thread—a tight, stretching sinew that threatened to snap or recoil at any moment.

"Look," Harris was saying. "I'd like for us to proceed as friends, just for the time being. Give me time to tend to my career. Another year or two—"

"Another year or *two*?" Her arm catapulted back.

"Please, Isolde," Harris whispered through clenched teeth, hoping to moderate her volume with his own. "Reelection is four months away. I'm desperate for your discretion." He pressed the lines around his eyes and stared at her beseechingly. He might actually have believed he was desperate. But Isolde was used to his iterant begging and the pathetic swoon of his male dramatics. She touched her throat and pressed her décolleté against the pristine linen table cloth. From the neighboring table, their waiter stood transfixed, spilling ice water onto one of the priests.

She said, "If you're so hell-bent on discretion, why did you just follow me into the powder room?"

It was a reasonable question. As usual, Harris seemed to be having trouble distinguishing between what he wanted and what he could logistically contain. There were days he acted as if these elements might somehow overlap. Then there were other days, when he'd come to her defeated, his wife having hurled some piece of heirloom crystal across their dining room in the sort of display that suggested he was wrong.

He said finally, "The governor keeps a surplus jeep at the airpark. Until the Chappy bridge is built, I can drive it over Norton Point. To see you occasionally."

Isolde raised her eyebrows. "Oh?"

"*Occasionally*, I'm saying. Until the election."

"Mr. Roon says that little sand spit washes out whenever a storm comes in." Isolde tapped her choker with the smooth tips of her manicure. Harris gestured for the check. "I was saying," she continued louder, "*occasionally* sounds very much like a temporary solution."

"Ah, but life's temporary, Isolde. So I'm afraid *temporary* is all that's on offer."

"In that case, you needn't bother with your crummy offers. Maybe I'll sell the damned place after all. I'm not especially keen on helping you and Bill Dooley scam the wealthy duffers. Playing the part of the tourist bait." She sniffed.

"You've certainly played lesser parts. Why get discerning now?"

Isolde didn't blink. She held her glass, wet with condensation, close against her rouged cheek. She recrossed her legs beneath the tablecloth. The clips of her stockings dug into her thighs. "I'm all through with you, Harris. Do you hear me? *Through*."

"You're only saying that to be cruel."

"Ah, but life's cruel, Harry."

Harris stretched his fingers against the table, hiding his wedding ring under the big, furry paw of his right hand. After his long pause, he whispered hoarsely, "Just stick around until September, Isi. Can we agree to that? I'd like to see you again this summer. Truly, I would."

And so she replied, at a volume often urged by her voice instructor (*"Make sure they can hear you in the back row!"*), "Gosh, Harry, *seeing* me is probably the least scandalous thing you've done tonight." She watched his shoulders cave in defeat. She was gorgeously inappropriate. It drove Harris wild. Her dialogue was always all about sex—except on Sundays, her sad days, when she was about repeated hang-up phone calls or maudlin poems of suicide or threats that involved tell-all letters to the press.

Harris let his eyes wander over the tableware. He closed them for a moment before saying, "If you stay on until September, *I'll* buy the damned place from you. Pay you double what you bought it for. How's that for a duffer?" He pushed his chair away from the dinner table and stood slowly, pinching at his shirtfront to invite a bit of cooler air inside. His buttons were done up wrong. Isolde watched as he nodded at the dismayed waiter with a luminous smile, for this was how he told his most impressive lies: lavishly, *wordlessly*, connoting a mountain of good intentions.

Next to the bread basket, Harris had forgotten his wallet. Isolde slid the wallet into the pocket of her cape and finished her glass of wine, a distant smile on her face. It satisfied her to think of her new pilot, the handsome young veteran she'd been promised, waiting to help her in and out of his airplane. Surely he'd also be willing to help her in and out of other things. She laughed aloud in anticipating how Harris would think of him too. Harris would come to know what it felt like, after all, to sit opposite a person who wanted *both*.

# FIFTEEN

Sabina craned her neck as if to admire the golden bursts dripping from the sky. In reality, nothing of the display registered. Lenore Dooley offered her a sparkler and she refused. James Whelan offered her a whiskey sour, which she drained in two quick swallows. Instantly, he brought her another. She considered Aunt Poppy only briefly before consuming this second drink. Inside, something heavy and fierce had burst open. She found she couldn't lock it back up.

His name materialized before she actually saw him. It was Mr. Shreve's loud gabbing about their best clambake yet. The tenderness of Hatch's new potatoes. Then it was Colin shrugging off the praise, explaining his early crop—how he'd planted earlier than usual because of the mild April. She heard the club men toasting his arrival, offering cold drinks to their favorite pilot. She didn't realize how close she stood listening until Hatch was directly behind her, resting his hand on her back in his easy way.

"It's not fair for you to look so lovely," he whispered in her ear. "Once they see how high you've set the bar, these other woman will stop trying altogether. Tell me, what did I miss?"

"What did *you* miss?" She spun around. "I hate to quarrel, but it seems I'm the one who needs some catching up."

Hatch was about to object, an injured look contorting his handsome face, when James Whelan magically emerged, out of nowhere, flicking a spent cigarette behind him.

"Colin Hatch. You make such wonderful entrances. Everyone's always guessing when you'll finally arrive."

"I promise you, Jim, I couldn't give a fig what people are guessing."

"Right," nodded Whelan. "Well, that's part of it, isn't it? Your intrepid loner routine."

"Do me a favor and give us five minutes alone," Hatch replied with a withering look.

"Tell me. Who's listed on your flight log this week?" Whelan grinned. "Anybody special?"

"That's not the kind of information I publicize," Hatch replied, his gaze fixed on Sabina. She could see him asking for latitude with his eyes.

"Come on, Captain America. You don't have to mention *names*." Whelan adjusted his tortoiseshell glasses. "How about just confirming the rumor is true? Hell, everyone knows already."

"I told you, Jim. I don't disclose passenger information."

"What else don't you disclose?" Sabina shot back.

"'*Les jeux sont fait*,'" Whelan triumphed. "*Casablanca*. Do you know what it means?"

"Sure," Colin smiled. "It means your legs better move as fast as your mouth, as you're no longer needed in this conversation."

Sabina felt herself tilting off-balance. Her high-heeled stance wobbled. Whelan took the opportunity to wrap an arm around her waist. She wrestled herself free and abandoned them both, striding off with great effort to keep her ankles from folding. When she reached the bench at the garden, it was Hatch who sat down beside her.

"What did you hear?" he asked, taking her hand in between both of his.

It was hard to avoid looking at him, though she tried. "Did you ask Bill Dooley to help you find a . . . a woman from your past?"

"I didn't ask. He offered."

"Were you married to her?"

"No! Of course not."

"Do you love her?"

"That was ten years ago."

"But you loved her then?"

"I don't know. I was very young."

"Nineteen? Like me?"

"Right now it's probably better if we didn't talk about Italy."

"Better for whom?" Sabina carried on, unconvinced. "It's obviously very important to you that you find the woman." This was not a question. She refused to allow any objection on his part. It was true or else he wouldn't have made any new bargains with Bill Dooley.

"*You're* important to me."

"I had hoped so. But what do I know? After all, I'm so very *young*."

Together with the whiskey, emotion blurred and divided her thinking. Like accounts she'd read of people floating outside their bodies during near-death experiences, it almost seemed some part of her was merely a spectator at the scene, while another part, simultaneously, was the young girl speaking too quickly, too hotly, complaining of injuries she hadn't quite earned.

Why should she be surprised? Other women were everywhere. Tall ones, gorgeous ones, exotic Pacific beauties of the sort her uncle, the navy veteran, had tattooed on his arm. *Of course Colin Hatch has loved before*, counseled this spectral Sabina, whose sympathy floated in and out of focus, while far off and away the boys with small crackers launched tin cans off the Shreves' fence posts.

"Look," Colin said weakly. "I can tell you this much. She was a girl I carried on with during the war. Only for a very brief time. In the end, I had to shove off and, well . . ."

"You got her in trouble?" Sabina felt a chill snake down her spine.

"No! Nothing like that. Please don't imagine it's at all like that."

"But what *can* I imagine, Colin, when you're talking so cryptically?"

"I'm not trying to be. Don't you see? It was a complicated time. In some ways, it still is." He ran a hand over his hair. "Can you trust me when I say I made a well-meaning mistake? And now my only goal is to learn that she's all right."

"And this girl, this woman—she's the cause of your blue ticket?"

Hatch paused. He sat very still and uncertain, in the manner of the gray squirrels Sabina sometimes interrupted, walking the pokeweed path around the pond. "Yes," he admitted. "I caused her harm. The extent of which I still don't know."

"I see." A part of her wanted only to embrace him. Another part—this part she didn't understand—could not abide the specter of a secret now looming between them. She blinked through the mounting silence. She counted: *Two, four, six*. How high would he let her go? Her blood rushed. Her throat felt so full and so tight she thought she'd gasp before she spoke.

"Sabina?"

"When were you going to tell me about your new assignment?"

"What do you mean? Isolde Martin?"

"There seem to be a lot of girls in your orbit these days. Maybe one too many. Even for you."

"That's low." He shook his head. "And you know better. You think if I was that sort I'd have wasted three weeks on cold swims?"

"*Wasted three weeks?*"

"That came out wrong. It's not what I meant."

"I certainly hope the second half of the season"—Sabina wiped her eyes—"heats up for you."

Colin set his jaw. "You don't want to see me again, do you?"

"Maybe not for a while, anyhow."

"You think he's right?" He hurled his arm in James Whelan's general direction. "That I'm some no-good cad on the make? Is that what you think?"

She couldn't meet his gaze. She couldn't speak. She knew Colin Hatch was not the person James made him out to be. That wasn't what stung her. Still, the right words would not come. Instead of answering, she looked off to where the children played, the littlest ones now whirling sparklers on strings. A thousand tiny embers jumping and falling to the grass.

"At least let me take you home."

She shook her head. “It’s not necessary. I’ve a late date planned elsewhere.”

“Since when?”

“Since things between us got too complicated for me to understand.”

“Sabina.” He braced his forehead. “If you’ve made up your mind about me, I can take it. But I can’t let someone else make it up for you. I won’t.”

“I brought you a gift,” she cut him off. “It’s waiting inside, in J. J.’s cellar. A velvet hatbox by the boys’ old trophy case. Take care not to leave it behind tonight.”

He took hold of her hand and pressed it again. “You ought to know me by now.”

Her throat kept throbbing with that awful fullness. Her eyes again swept over the yard—the black mass of treetops swaying against a charcoal sky; orange flames from the climbing, spitting torches; a smattering of faint stars, where clouds of smoke had parted overhead. She hadn’t made up her mind, not hardly. What she ought to say, what she ought to *do* next—these were ideas as undecided as the tiny midges flying zigzag all around. Still she answered him only, “It’s *you* who’s undecided. Otherwise you could tell me everything.”

After that the evening had devolved into a jumble of isolated, inchoate moments. When Sabina tried to reconcile them the next morning, she could only retrieve a few shameful fragments. There’d been more whiskey at the Seaside Saloon. Singing. Dancing. James Whelan had driven her home. She’d gotten sick somewhere. *In the pot of geraniums, was it?* He and Connie coaxed her from the comfort of the drive, where the cool brick pressed against her cheek as she felt the earth’s rotation beneath. At some point she’d unfastened her girdle. At another she sat crying at the foot of her bed. She’d definitely flung her Guinness superlatives book out the bedroom window.

The next morning she tried to imagine, as she gathered her pillows behind her head—an attempt to sit upright and sip a bit of coffee—that there was humor to be mined from the evening, if not today then certainly once she'd settled into her life's next chapter—whatever that might be. But the earlier confidence extracted from her heels, her stockings, her damned Dior was vanquished now—reduced to a sad heap on the latch-hook kitten rug on the floor beside her bed. From the hallway, someone knocked at her door.

"May I come in?"

"Yes," Sabina croaked. "Only please don't tell me how you could have predicted this."

"Not *could have*." Aunt Poppy folded her arms inside the doorframe. She cast her eyes from one side to the next—her affected way of trying to recall a fact she knew outright. "I believe I *did* predict it."

"I don't quite remember what happened."

"I do," Poppy frowned. "You emptied all but your regrets, my dear."

Sabina melted beneath her coverlet. "I'd like to go back to sleep for a while if you don't mind, Auntie."

"Does this mean you've already replied to Dean Budge's letter?"

"No."

"You *owe* her an answer, Sabina."

"That *is* my answer. *No.* I'm not going to conduct my life according to some old dean's bidding."

In short order, Aunt Poppy's neck erupted in hives of frustration. Her pink oval nails twisted a pearl stud. "Do I need to remind you what a small world we live in?"

"I'll work it out, A. P. Believe me, I will."

"See that you do. And quickly. Because I'm telling you now, come the fall it's either Weston College or the Institut Montreux. I have a letter to the headmistress already waiting in my study, so do not test me. I won't have you loafing about the house once September rolls round."

"Finishing school? Oh honestly, A. P. It's a wonder they'll propose to *finish* me when I haven't even started anything yet."

"Your father agrees with me on this point. And if you're not satisfied with my word, you can ask him yourself. *Connie!*" Aunt Poppy yelled for the housekeeper. "Do run and get Mr. McTigue on the wire."

Sabina issued small utterances in reply.

"Go ahead and groan, but any young lady of *your* age, in proper society, ought to have some sort of academic occupation—unless she's already got an engagement ring on her finger. And let me point up, taking residence at the public library does not qualify as *occupation*."

Sabina lifted her head long enough to meet Poppy's hard stare. "I just want for you to know, despite everything, Colin Hatch is a good person. He never had any of those ulterior motives you and James imagined."

"Sabina, don't befool yourself. Sometimes I'm sorry for your being as smart as you are in the classroom. I think it makes us all forget—myself especially—how naive you are in the world."

Sabina burrowed beneath her pillow.

"*Everyone*, my dear, has ulterior motives. That goes for you, and me, and the birds in the trees. Even the wind." Poppy pointed a slender finger toward the bedroom's ocean view. "This very wind has its designs on something crafty."

## SUNDAY, AUGUST 29, 1954

## Widespread Devastation Across Cape and Islands, Plane Remains Missing

EDGARTOWN, MA (AP)—A state of emergency was declared today by Lieutenant Governor Harris Shields, who began his briefing with a prayer for those lost, injured, or missing since Carol swept in Friday morning.

Asked to describe the scene, one observer reported Oak Bluffs' streets have cracked and separated "like a cake baked too hotly." Cars left parked along the curbs now sit tire-deep in floodwater. Mr. Lawrence Farraday, vacationing with his family from Milton, recalled watching his prize ketch ride the breakers ashore until a wharf spile punctured its hull.

When the storm's eye passed over Chappaquiddick, a Mr. and Mrs. George Mattos, two residents brave enough to venture outside, say they discovered dozens of massive yawls—"just like beached blue whales"—strewn across the wasteland of an extreme low tide.

The savage storm blew itself out somewhere over Canada late last night, but not before destroying tens of thousands of homes and upward of five thousand watercraft. National guardsmen will begin patrolling Commonwealth streets, inclusive of downtown Edgartown, while Red Cross volunteers arrive on the island in waves, manning a few scarce boats donated by private citizens, until ferry service resumes.

Back on Massachusetts's mainland, under the cover of widespread blackouts, ten prisoners at MCI-Norfolk escaped from their dormitories on Saturday.

At the state capital, the steeple of Boston's Old North Church canted for hours before toppling neatly onto Hull Street. "For the first time since the Revolutionary War, Sunday services will be canceled," said Rev. Peck.

Fog-penetrating searchlights were pressed into service yesterday, as local authorities worked to locate a small airplane and its pilot feared to have crashed in the Boston Harbor.

*STORM cont. page 7.*

# JULY

Seven weeks before the storm

# SIXTEEN

Colin Hatch arrived at the hangar early, taxied the Beech, and set down a welcome mat for his newest client's first boarding. He pretended to be busy removing his cowl plugs and wiping down his windshield so as not to appear too interested in her limousine's arrival. He was aware of his pilot friends, across the parking lot, glad-eyeing the actress from inside the greasy windows of the diner.

It was her perfume that greeted him first. From a full five yards away.

"Well. Hello then," Isolde Martin began, sizing him up with either mild approval or disdain; Hatch couldn't tell. "You're unexpected." She wore a knit dress of pale blue, a patent leather belt strapped around her impossibly narrow waist. Her red lips cushioned the end of a long cigarette, while her hair—an otherworldly shade of blonde—held firm against the ocean wind. "I was imagining you'd be another reprobate like the fellow who first brought me here. His costume . . ." She invited herself to pick up Hatch's tie and run it through her fingers. "Well, his was more like a cowboy's. Yours is rather like a bellhop's."

"Not a costume," Hatch frowned, rubbing his temple. He felt like he'd spent the previous night eating plates of sawdust. The waitress at Mel's twice asked if he was all right, the way he'd sat guzzling waters before heading outside to untie the plane. "This Beech is my office, Miss Martin. I'm here to do a job."

"Don't most men bother to shave before going into the, uh . . . *office*?" Isolde asked.

He could tell she was used to allowances of all kinds. But he didn't have the strength. His head hurt something awful. Suddenly, desperately, he had to piss. "I shave in the evening."

"Ah. For your nightlife," Isolde smiled.

"I'm not big on nightlife."

"Bill Dooley told me there was quite a party last night. Weren't you there?"

"No. *Yes*. I mean, I dropped by."

Isolde Martin scrutinized his face. "I heard the whole thing from my room at the hotel. The firecrackers and the music. Bill asked me to go, but I'm taking a break from parties at the moment. I'm meant to catch up on my sleep. Lately, I've just a flirting relationship with the sandman."

"You ever try sleeping pills?"

"*Try* them? I own stock. Anyway," she sighed, leaning back against the edge of the plane's low wing. "What about you, Bellhop? Did you catch any nice girls with your smooth complexion?"

Hatch considered the fallout from the party. From the moment Sabina left him sitting alone, in the shadows of Shreve's darkened yard, he could see what he'd done. He'd played his hand all wrong. Ought to have given it to her straight: Adele, their bad bargain, the truth behind his blue ticket. A better man would have fessed up to everything, come what may. A better man might have trusted Sabina's constancy, believing she wouldn't run away in disgust from the story on record. All he could do now was hope he hadn't blown it for good.

When it came to women, Hatch knew most men had their types. Even subconsciously, they veered this way or that, if not outright pronouncing a preference for blondes. For dimples. Slender ankles. Curves enough to fill a catcher's mitt. Hatch was not categorically biased in this way but for the fact, he now realized, he'd been waiting around for someone constant. Someone *accepting*. And yet, how could you blame a girl for not accepting a history like the one he was dragging?

He'd tried once, hadn't he? And once was enough. Two or three springs ago, by now. He'd been courting this very nice girl, easy to smile, easy to laugh. (If he *did* have a type—come to think of it—he supposed that sort was it. Easy to laugh.) And so they'd gone out a few times, and they'd talked by and by. The kind of talking where a man can sense the girl's feet coming off the ground—it's just that easy and light and pleasant to go on talking. And she'd asked him what had happened. In the war. It was Fourth of July weekend. And she asked him, in fact, why he didn't don his dress blues like the other young men for the town parade. She was always smiling, he remembered. Her face was pretty and soft, with little lines at her eyes when she smiled. He took it for granted, he supposed, her easy smile would return no matter how hard the truth. But as soon as the words were out—the grim fact of his situation—he could see, those eyes fell. Her mouth went straight as a seam. Her feet touched down. Their words—anything either one of them attempted after that—plodded along, flat and heavy. She *did* smile again, but the way she had about her was different—cautious. Charitable, maybe.

He knew he couldn't make any dates with her after that. Even if she'd wanted to keep his company, to keep lending her sympathetic ear, how could she ever feel romantically toward him? How could she give up on a perfectly spotless future, all full of goodness and light, only to become a party in his sad story?

Although Hatch didn't like to dwell, God help him, he sometimes thought he'd have been better off to have come home missing an arm or a leg, like some of his buddies had done. It would have been easier to lose a piece of himself, he thought, than to gain this extra weight—this heavy, invisible weight—impossible to explain, impossible to sever.

But finding Adele—that *could* bring a conclusive ending to the Italy affair. Or at least a small part of him dared to hope as much. Not through an upgraded discharge, nor the reinstatement of his pension as Dooley had sold the deal, but just through knowing—if it were a thing that *could* be known—the girl had made it out alive. A bad idea, after all, is one thing.

A fatal idea is quite another. And a man who once—long ago—orchestrated merely a bad idea isn't one who deserves to go on punishing himself forever. A man with a bad idea can persist, in due time, to outshine the past with better, smarter acts. He can build his way back up to shape, like any other kind of fighter. Trusting in himself and his work—a comeback that Hatch, so far, was never quite able to muster.

"Look after her, will you?" he'd asked Alex Shreve, pressing two dollars into the kid's hand to make sure Sabina landed safely home, wherever her supposed "late plans" might take her.

Mr. Shreve had already given Hatch a bottle of Lagavulin from the bar, having witnessed the row. "This is for the potatoes, my friend. Escape while you can."

Next he'd gone down to the Shreves' basement to retrieve the hatbox Sabina mentioned. Inside were three baby chicks scampering over scissored strips of magazine: chickens for his farm. He'd gone home and started building a proper brooder house, digging out the heat lamp they would need from the musty corners of the old barn loft. By midnight he was sculpting like Bernini, humming a tune he came back to whenever drinking scotch—a song he learned from two of the Haitian Red Tails he'd met in Ramitelli. The chicks settled in, and his lathe work wasn't half bad. By two in the morning he was passed out. He woke to Florence's voice, reminding him he had a flight with Miss Martin in one hour's time.

Returning to his celebrity charge, Hatch lifted his cap, wiped his forehead. "Look, Miss Martin, I think we're getting off track."

"You're the pilot," she shrugged, shifting her gaze to the clouds. "Feel free to lead the way."

"Naturally, I will. I was only saying—"

"You were saying you normally shave in the evening."

"That's right."

"Because a lion always hunts at night."

His mouth was too dry to form words comfortably. He reached into his pocket and pulled out a pack of Life Savers. "Just a habit of the old-time pilots. You know the ones with the white scarves and the flying togs? Biplane is awfully unkind to a freshly-shaved face. It's what my father taught me, anyhow."

"Then you're a second-generation professional? That's encouraging. Hopefully a marked improvement over the cowboy."

"What's under the cape?" Hatch gestured to the cargo her driver had deposited between them.

"My birds."

He lifted a scarf to reveal two cockatiels sitting primly on their swings.

"I hope you'll find a comfortable spot for them on board."

"Couldn't they just tail us?"

"Ha," Isolde said dully. "I don't expect people to understand—people without birds—but mine are like family. Laurel and Hardy, I call them. I won them in a game of White Elephant."

"I have chickens," Hatch volunteered, and the recent fact of it made him smile for the first time that day.

"Chickens aren't birds, Mr. Hatch. They can't fly."

"Well, that's just the point. They're meant to help me stay grounded."

"I've heard that flyboys are an arrogant lot. Is it true? What did the girls at the party make of you, by the way? You never got round to saying how well they liked your smooth face last night."

"Lot of good it did me." Hatch reached for the birdcage. He hadn't intended on revealing personal troubles, but his comment opened a door nonetheless.

"Were you rejected, then?" Isolde's face brightened. "Do start with her name and her complete physical description. I'm a sucker for a real-life love story."

"I'm sure you've got plenty of love stories of your own," Hatch called over his shoulder. He stowed the baggage behind the passenger seats, climbing back out of the plane to catch sight of the actress frowning.

"Everybody assumes that about me. But it's not true. Not really. All the best love stories are reserved for poor people. I'm afraid I've missed my window."

"Never too late to be poor." Hatch looked at his watch.

"Yes, but while I waited for the love story to arrive I suspect I'd get awfully uncomfortable."

"Well," segued Hatch, who was tired of talking, tired of standing for that matter. "I think you'll be very comfortable with me—with the flight," he clarified, a little too impatiently. He extended his arm toward the mat on the ground and the Beech's lowered staircase. "Shall we?" He was suddenly aware that he wanted to be looking at the clouds and not at her face, which—more than his hangover—was the cause of his floundering.

"That's such a relief." She flashed him the broadest of smiles. Instead of constricting her features, Isolde Martin's smile seemed to magnify her beauty: her turquoise eyes widened and glimmered; the apples of her cheeks rose into soft pink mounds. "I was beginning to think I might not like this island."

# SEVENTEEN

Sabina waited to board the ferry under a stirring, sunless sky. A damp heat found its way beneath the cloud cover. Passengers in line shifted their weight and adjusted their baggage, sweating and restless. The steel gangway groaned as it wandered and recoiled against its tether on the wharf.

"You've got your blouses wrapped in tissue paper, haven't you?" Aunt Poppy began fretting all over again.

"Yes, A. P. And my good shoes in the velvet pouch, and my weekend slacks folded along the crease. I've even packed clothes hangers in case the barracks haven't got any." Sabina felt warm and unsettled. Her aunt wasn't helping things any.

"*Barracks.*" Poppy shuddered and sighed. "What kind of young woman lands herself in a *barrack*?"

"My mother, for one," Sabina replied. "How was it she volunteered to help with the war?"

"Sabina, please don't provoke me right now. The constant *questions*. And so early in the morning. It's unsettling for the stomach." Her aunt pulled a painted hand fan from her bag, batting it wildly against her nerves as much as the July heat. She turned hopefully to her niece. "I don't suppose you've changed your mind about Dean Budge? Confirming your place at Weston College?"

"I don't suppose it either."

"Just as well." Poppy fanned harder. "They'll know better what to do with you in Switzerland. I'll finalize everything just as soon as I'm back at the cottage."

"It's a wonder you'll have me shipped halfway around the world, all as so I can learn, what? Where to set my oyster fork?"

"Sabina, what is so awfully unpalatable about studying to improve your poise and self-expression abilities?"

"Oh, A. P., if you don't already know why I'd hate it"—Sabina wilted against a rail—"I can't even begin to explain."

"Well, there you have it. You've proved my point exactly. Anyhow, Switzerland will only be temporary for you."

"Only temporary until what?"

"Eventually we'll get you married, with children," Poppy whispered, looking her niece's thin frame up and down. "God willing."

"Oh, I see, and *that's* meant to stimulate me in the long run? Marriage? Children?"

"Don't be foolish." Aunt Poppy pushed her along the plank just as the hulking ferry *Islander* hove into view. "Being a wife and mother is meant to make you worry over someone else's stimulation for a rare change. Safe travels, dear!"

At the sound of the horn, the ferry sighed into the dock, unloading a crush of inbound passengers. Babies in bonnets, tired of being held for an hour, wriggled down the fronts of their parents. Men walked ahead of their wives, maps in hands, white socks pulled high. A few family dogs strained on their leashes, panting and curious. On the whole, they all looked bright and expectant. And when they strode past Sabina, pursuing the sacred places she was about to leave, it almost felt like inviting them to a time that had already happened. She wished she could go back herself.

Hardly a week removed, the night of the Fourth still felt like a bad dream. She didn't know who she blamed more: Colin or her own stubborn self. Most mornings she had to remind herself she wasn't going to meet him at the beach, wasn't going to picnic on the lawn, where that soft skirt of moss wrapped the cottage's tallest oak. She wasn't going to ride alongside him in the truck, wasn't going to rest against his arm, watching well-dressed city anglers fish from the bass stands, their shrimp chummers in heavy black aprons, tossing chop into the bight. The days that followed the Shreves' party felt empty and drab, though her aunt kept pushing her out into the sunshine, delivering her to the yacht club each morning with ready-made plans she'd arranged on her niece's behalf. Fortunately, Sabina had thought to wire her father in the midst of her gloom.

*Dear Bud,*
*How's the Wild West treating you? I'm sure you spend most of your time inside a dreary office, but I'll bet the change of scenery is still quite nice. Everything here is exactly the same, except Denny is growing his hair long and drowning it in Brylcreem. Aunt Poppy is convinced there's a bees' nest lurking in the porch roof. She went outside to investigate with a broom and a lobster pot on her head. Would you believe she didn't find anything?*

*Speaking of the Wild West, I read that Ike and Mrs. Eisenhower are vacationing in Denver this summer. The papers say he brought his trout fishing rods. Did you know they use airplanes to stock the lakes out there? I can't imagine how one would contain a freight load of live fish on an airplane. Sounds like slippery business. I find it very alarming for the trout.*

*Today I went sailing with James Whelan. Do you remember him from the club? He's a nice person. The wind was fine and we had a nice time. I'm getting better at heeling, James says. No dog jokes please.*

*As ever, Bean*

Boarding the ferry, Sabina spied a farm truck from Bolton in the line of disembarking cargo vehicles. She wondered if this delivery man would be turned away anywhere along his route because of Hatch's expanding service. She wondered about all the things that might have been different if she'd stayed around to witness the pilot's next move. As it was though, for good or ill, her latest exchange with Bud was sending her on an unexpected course.

*Dear Bean,*

*It's funny you should mention the merits of fresh scenery. I was just talking to an old college friend last night. He's helping to launch a very sensitive project on the Cape. He needs a research assistant. It would be tedious work—lots of details. Naturally I thought of you.*

*I know you're having a "nice" time with your friends at the island, but maybe there's room for improvement on that score. If you're willing, he'll need you in North Truro by week's end. Denny can help you with transportation. I can start working on the necessary security clearance. (Are you intrigued yet?) There are comfortable barracks for civilian volunteers I am told. Even clubrooms and television dens! Sounds a bit like camp, eh?*

*I know you are fond of your daily swims and are a creature of habit in so many other ways. Yet I'd be very distressed to think of you wasting your energy on sailing dates that don't interest you. Reach out to Dr. Marshall Bassett directly (MIT's Lincoln Laboratory) if you're up for the change. I'll square it with Aunt Poppy.*

*Yours, Dad*

Sabina had no trouble finding Denny at the port in Falmouth. He stood out from the crowd, dapper with his dark waves slicked back and a white sailing sweater knotted at his neck. Denny had boyish cheeks; they flushed pink whenever he was hot or embarrassed. At the dock that morning he may have been a bit of both. He hadn't been at the Shreves' party, but that was no reason why he wouldn't know of her trouble with Colin Hatch.

"Happy Fourth of July." He took Sabina's suitcase from her hand before drawing her into a firm hug.

"Little late for that," she smiled over his shoulder.

Sabina wondered if this was how all families talked—or, rather, *didn't* talk. This funny kind of shyness mixed with pride, where she couldn't possibly come out and just *say* the thing that was bothering her. Not really.

They drove along Route 6, following the state's bent arm, through a string of hamlets each staking claim to the world's best ice cream or hot dog stand. They passed three dozen motor inns and as many signs for rental camping cabins with water views. Up ahead, the traffic slowed. Smoke rose from the engine of a long blue coupe, blocking the way north. Sabina saw the driver popping his hood. A blurred, wavy heat stirred up from the pavement. The cars behind idled and stacked. Impatient horns honked. A few drivers exited their cars, rolling up shirtsleeves to preside over the trouble. Denny lit a cigarette.

"I'm not too sure about this place we're going," she murmured, eyeing the line of stalled traffic.

"That makes two of us," Denny smiled at her. "You couldn't get much farther away without joining the navy. Say, you're not joining the navy, are you?"

"Dad arranged it."

"It'll be all right then." He squeezed her shoulder. "At least, you do know how to march, don't you?"

She smiled back at him. Sometimes she recognized her brother, with a mighty relief, as the only person on earth who shared her unique makeup. They were very different still, but having him around—a perfect ally—it helped.

"Too bad Mother wasn't here," Denny remarked. "She could get that old clunker running again." He nodded ahead at the overheated coupe.

"She was good with engines, wasn't she?" Sabina brightened.

"Yeah, I guess some folks thought she was an awfully strange bird that way."

"Did *you*?"

"Did I what?"

"I mean . . . you were older than me. You knew her better. Did you think—?"

"Hey, Bean, look where we are!" Denny craned forward in his seat. "Isn't that the Orleans VFW up ahead? That old haunt! Remember it? Remember the time Eddie and I took you girls to try out the Orleans Jubilee?"

"I remember." Sabina looked down at her hands folded in her lap.

"The Orleans barn dance. That was a hoot. Only it turned out we had our weekends mixed up? When we got there, the dance floor was covered with banquet tables on account of it was bingo night instead?" Denny slapped his knee. "You and Lenny spent the whole day getting primped to reel with the hayshakers. Ended up helping two dozen old folks read the call numbers on their bingo cards. Boy, can you beat that?"

"I didn't mind too much." Sabina shrugged. "And *I* was the one who helped with the cards."

"Come to think of it, that's true. Lenny hitched a ride back to Falmouth." Denny's face got lost in the memory. "We never did make it back for the actual barn dance, did we?"

"I think they called your number not long after." Sabina checked her brother's face, regretting her words.

"I'll bet Lenore got up to bigger stunts that summer." Denny exhaled smoke.

Sabina looked out her own window. She wished the old coupe would get out of the road so they could pass.

"Hey, and how about that time you and Lenny planned to camp out, all night, on the beach?"

"*That* was ages ago. We still had Jib then."

"Sure was. We had Jibby and Lincoln the rabbit. Remember his hutch out back, where you and Lenore kept your seashells?"

"I do! Oh, how A. P. stewed about the flies."

"Us guys watched you pitch your tent and hang your silly curtains that Connie made up—all that homey nonsense you dragged inside."

"The curtains were Lenny's idea."

"Then you went to bed and we dug that moat all around you. Filled it with buckets of blue claws, bushels and bushels of them. Boy, she screamed so loud. Lenore did. I had to carry her out. Remember that?"

Sabina nodded. "She wouldn't come back to the beach for weeks."

"I guess it was a stupid prank after all," Denny said, mostly to himself.

"You seem to have quite a few rosy remembrances featuring Lenore Dooley. Maybe you ought to give a toast at the wedding."

"Nah." Denny's cheeks turned to cherries. "Not really much of a story. Anyhow, I doubt she remembers those old days as well as I do."

"Too busy adding charms to her charm bracelet."

The squad of helpful passersby had pushed the coupe up onto the shoulder by now. The traffic began its slow crawl forward. Denny flicked his cigarette out the window. He threw Sabina a look. "It's not all her fault you know, Bean."

"That's right. Nothing ever is." Sabina hated to sound so spiteful, especially having glimpsed her brother's mind, once again, on his fondness for an old flame. But she couldn't help being cross with Lenore. Not after that Weston College, Dean Budge business.

"She puts on an act, I'll give you that. But it's not her fault. I mean, consider the father. If he's talking, he's lying. The mother's out to lunch. And the only thing they—any of them—care about is looks. You and I, we're lucky. We've got A. P. to mind us—well, you mostly. And Dad to set us straight, and . . . Sabina, I've been wanting to ask you something." Denny blushed again.

"Oh?"

"Yeah. Well, I mean . . . do you suppose she really loves him?"

"Who?"

"Lenore and John, I'm saying. I know Lenore can be trying and all, but when you think of *John*, as a person . . . do you suppose . . ." Denny turned to look at Sabina. By her face he must have judged himself wrong. "Aw, hell, Bean. I guess it's pretty crummy of me to ask a thing like that, huh? Forget I said anything, how about?"

"I don't think it's crummy." Sabina patted her brother's arm. The gesture seemed to remind him of something he wanted to hear on the radio, for he made a very fast grab for the dial, tinkering with different stations until he found an upbeat number he liked. Sabina thought she ought to say something more—about Lenore, about the past, about *something*—but the right words escaped her. They drove the rest of the way without talking at all.

"Welcome to the 762nd Aircraft Control and Warning Squadron," an officer greeted them at the gate. Two massive spheres emerged from the trees behind him, like perfectly shaped great horned owl eggs. A plane roared overhead. "You a new filter station volunteer?"

"My sister is," Denny explained. "We were told to ask for the GCI director during his duty hours."

"Sign in at the personnel office. Building 8. You can wait there for in-processing."

The McTigue siblings stood for some time in the bleak lobby of Building 8. Sabina studied the base map she found tacked to the bulletin board and made at least one happy discovery. The base had its own library, open each morning until noon. Another notice outlined the theater's schedule, which offered movies three times a week. There were barracks for single men and women on separate floors of different buildings, depending on their military or civilian status, plus apartment houses for married airmen and families.

"Oh good, you're here," remarked the young woman who finally approached them. "At last." She wore wing-tipped eyeglasses and an ill-fitting dress, which she tugged downward when she walked. She had a thin, wiry frame; Aunt Poppy would have begged this girl to imbibe some Poundex caloric malt.

"Am I late?" Sabina turned to Denny, confused.

"You're not early," said the young woman, apparently somewhat vexed by the question. "Controller told me you'd be starting *today*. So I prepared these notes for you." She thrust her hand forward, dangling a sheet of paper with five or six line items typed in all caps. "I took the liberty of ordering you a coffee. Three hours ago." She rolled her eyes. "My name is Bev, by the way."

“Thank you, Bev,” said Sabina, accepting the typed agenda. “This is my brother Denny.”

“You can skedaddle, Dennis. I’ll take her along from here.”

Denny accepted his marching orders after depositing a quick kiss on Sabina’s cheek. As he rounded the corner of the hall, he shouted back a final thought: “You won’t try to swim this beach, will you? The riptides here are treacherous.”

“I swim the ocean in preparation for my school team,” Sabina explained to Bev, waving in agreement to her brother. “Well, I’m not sure if it’ll be my school team after all. There was an issue with the dean, you see. But I do swim quite often.”

“Congratulations. I do crossword puzzles in my bed jacket. Let’s not burn daylight, dear.”

Bev towed Sabina around the places she “needed to put to memory,” walking two steps in front and barking backward when wanting to emphasize a point. *Absolutely no running in the corridors, even if you’re late for your shift. Cigarettes should be smoked outside, during designated break times, unless you are offered one by a supervisor. No walking on the lawn in front of company HQ!* “The first sergeant combs it with his toothbrush practically,” Bev explained, narrowing her eyes. “He can be a real SOB if you fuss up the grass.”

They toured the motor pool, the day room, the chapel, and the chow hall. Back outside Sabina glimpsed a green band of ocean. She stepped away from her guide, wandering closer to the Clay Pounds—steep cliffs worn jagged by weather and time. A group of men in glossy sealskin sat anchored in a skiff, helping one another shrug into their heavy packs.

“Who are they?” she wondered aloud.

“Who, the frogmen?” Bev followed her gaze. “They’re divers, what else?”

“Divers?” Sabina looked on with interest. “What are they diving for?”

“Got me.” Bev scratched her head with the pencil she kept behind her ear. “Shipwrecks maybe. There are lots out this way.”

“Shipwrecks?”

"You sure came armed with plenty of questions."

"Say, do you know exactly what I'll be doing here?" Sabina responded with another one, as they headed back toward the offices.

"Well"—Bev blinked back the wind, unable to shake her stricken expression—"you *do* whatever you're told. We're not meant to know more than that."

"Maybe I should ask to see a supervisor, then? Dr. Bassett, maybe?"

"Wedging yourself in with the boss on your first day, huh? Let me give you some free advice, Miss Swim Team. We are dealing with national security at this base. No one's impressed by your pretty face."

"But I'm not trying . . ." Sabina shook her head. "I only asked about Dr. Bassett because my father—"

"Oh I see," said Bev, nodding fiercely. "*Your father.* Well I guess I'd better shoot you on over to see Dr. Bassett. I don't have time to stand here arguing your nobility all day long."

Sabina tried to apologize—for what, she wasn't sure—but she was facing Bev's back now, following her guide's plaid dress through the double doors of a building titled Operations. Inside, they threaded through aisles of work tables. Sabina tried to catch the eye of someone sympathetic. It was no use. All the men wore preoccupied expressions, like students on test day. Walls of instrument panels slanted from ceiling to floor, at obtuse angles, dotted with knobs and blinking circuitry. Sabina caught herself falling behind as she absorbed the energy of the room. At last Bev stopped at a door with a figured glass window. Soft classical music played behind it.

"Here's your man, cupcake. You understand, I'm not trying to be unwelcoming, don't you? I'm actually very well-known for orienting our new girls as quickly and efficiently as possible. But when you come in asking *so* many questions . . ." Bev rolled her eyes. "Well, there's only so much I can do for you."

"I understand." Sabina nodded. "Thank you for your help. I'm sure I'll fall into the swing of things soon enough—and without getting in your hair," she added.

"Let's hope," grumbled Bev, who executed a rigid about-face and walked briskly—elbows pumping—almost without her heels meeting the floor.

Dr. Bassett called for Sabina to come inside after her third feeble knock. She straightened her seams and smoothed the back of her hair before entering. The room was startlingly cold, thanks to a whirring air conditioner machine positioned in the window. Right away she noticed the walls of his office were decorated with framed photographs of various seabirds. She recognized the sooty tern. A flying gannet. A frigate bird with a crab claw in its beak.

The doctor followed her gaze. "I took those after the storm of '44." He had a placid voice and a very slow, thoughtful way of speaking. "It's amazing what you can find—petrels and xemes, all kinds of lost souls—after a wind like that disrupts their flyways."

Sabina nodded. "I enjoy the birds at the beach very much."

"Do you? You must get that from your mother. You look just like her." He smiled. "How are you doing?"

"I'm well. Very glad to be here."

"Good. Your father said you had an interest in science. I must say, I was envious. My own daughter is interested only in film stars. You've met Beverly I gather?"

"She was very helpful," Sabina affirmed.

"Don't let her frustrate you. Terrible pill, but she's a demon typist."

"That's wonderful," murmured Sabina, perceiving a delayed onset of seasickness from the ferry.

"So, tell me. What do you know about Truro?"

"It's the easternmost point in the United States, apart from rural Maine?"

"Yes." The doctor smiled, removing his glasses. "It's also home to an outfit known as the Lincoln Laboratory. We're from the Massachusetts Institute of Technology, here to help the air force engineer a defense system capable of identifying and intercepting hostile aircraft."

"Airplanes carrying atomic bombs?" Sabina's skin rose with chill bumps.

"Precisely. You've heard of the Ground Observer Corps? Operation Skywatch?"

"I read something in the newspaper. One of my cousins mans a volunteer post in Hull. The *Globe* says Massachusetts is still twenty thousand people short of its goal."

"That's true. The military is working on recruiting more airplane spotters. We rely on their efforts in watching the skies. Our filter operators field the calls from the GOC posts and track any unidentified aircraft on a map—a plotting board, we call it."

"All right," Sabina nodded. The early pricks of low-grade panic emerged. She felt her pulse quickening as her eyes misted over. Was she excited? Afraid? Even viscerally she was confused, caught between the meaningful aims she imagined for herself and the nagging self-awareness that she was, after all, a girl who still sometimes chewed on the end of her braid.

"Our base is unique, and very important, because we're also a GCI station." Dr. Bassett spoke evenly, seeming to sense her thoughts were wandering. "No doubt you've seen the domes outside?"

Sabina nodded yes. The more he explained, the more she wanted to run from his office and phone her father. What on earth had he gotten her into? What was she doing here?

"Those ray-domes house powerful antennae," Dr. Basset continued. "So in addition to relying on civilian eyeballs, we're using electrical means to monitor the skies. The men outside this door are watching radarscopes. You understand?"

Sabina willed her head to nod again, but it mustn't have obeyed because Dr. Basset sat back down behind his desk and started on a different tack.

"Let's put it this way. We do two things here. One is that we test the radar's capacity by tracking our own birds—some flying high, some low, some awfully fast. We're trying to judge how well the machines work in these different scenarios. And how quickly we can pass the information along to other bases in the area."

"I see."

"The other thing we do is field telephone calls from the GOC. Civilian observers with posts all up and down the seaboard. An observer calls us to say they see an airplane in the sky. They've been trained to recognize a few key details about different models, and they use an instrument"—he held up a small ring—"like this one, to gauge altitude. In the Operations Room, *you* are the operator who will take that call. You plot the sighting on a board and check it against all regional flight plans, confirming it's a friendly."

"A *friendly*?"

"That's right. A flight we're expecting."

"And if it's not?"

"That's what the men outside are here for. They're in constant communication with interceptor aircraft, who are at the ready to, well, intercept, if necessary."

"To attack any enemy planes?"

"To ensure that there's never another Pearl Harbor," he edified. "Now then, are you ready to get started? I know the men can use another smart young lady such as yourself."

"Okay." Sabina forced her face into a smile.

"That's fine. I'll make sure you get your badge, which you will need for gaining access to the bunker. Are you bothered by confined spaces?"

"Not especially." She shifted her weight. "At least I don't think so."

"And everything makes sense to you now?"

"More or less." She gulped. She knew she lived a privileged life, a *protected* life, in so many ways. But she also understood—and understood it acutely, in this moment—she was not immune to failure. Things could go badly for her here. Probably *would* go badly, given how lost and uncertain she felt. And what then, if all the notions she held about thinking and doing "big things" were merely that: just a young girl's notions? What if Lenore Dooley really did have the jump on her, after all? Getting married. Starting a family. Sabina felt her heart sinking with embarrassment, to think of the accusations she'd hurled at Lenny. Calling her jealous.

Claiming somehow, indirectly, to be better, smarter. Soon enough, Lenore would have a husband who loved her. A good, respectable husband. A well-defined place in the world. And what exactly would Sabina have?

"Wonderful." Dr. Bassett rapped on his desk. "Let's go get that bunker badge."

# EIGHTEEN

Denny McTigue circled the block four times before a space materialized. It was a fashionable hour for late lunch in downtown Edgartown—the weather perfectly composed for taking up a sidewalk table, a glass of beer, a plate of steamers served with butter bowls for two. Well-known and well-liked as he was, Denny would have no trouble claiming and keeping a table like that, defending his turf against all comers—the beach crowds, the souvenir shoppers, the parched and the weary—even at prime hours. He could nurse his beer, savor his clams, stay on all evening if he liked, without any waiter or busboy hanging over like a meter maid, trying to turn the table in time for another tip. On the other hand, finding the right girl to go and camp there with—well, that was always the difficult bit.

"Where've you been all week, McTigue?" J. J. Shreve shouted across the yacht club dock. He sat with his long legs straddling the bow of his dinghy, bent practically in half to swipe at the scum below the waterline. For the purpose of scrubbing his keel, he'd rigged himself a broom-length cleaning paddle, buoyant with cork backing so it'd float snug against the bottom of the boat. "Hell, I know you're some kind of government big wheel these days, but even Dick Nixon skips work occasionally in the summer."

"You'll have to pardon me," Denny called back. "Statehouse is a Monday through Friday gig, so you know. We don't all work for our fathers."

"Lucky for you." J. J. spit at the thought.

"Truth is, I had to drive my sister out to Truro this morning." Denny took a seat on the opposite end of the cat-rigged Finn. He pulled a peach from his pocket, watching his friend scrub.

"Truro, huh? What's she doing way the Christ out there?"

"Volunteering. At the air base."

"Boy, you McTigues. You're the limit, you know that? Whoever heard of such daffy business?"

"My father thinks it'll do her good. Give her a dose of perspective or something like that."

"Must be nice," J. J. sniffed. "Being a woman." He lifted his paddle onto the deck and swung his legs into the green water around the mooring. Hopped overboard with a bit of sandpaper and toweling under his arm. "Trying on *perspectives* while we men do all the sweating. Would you look at this lousy scab?"

Denny didn't answer. He ate his peach, staring out at the waves. J. J. was always griping about his boat, its upkeep, this never-ending battle.

"You know it only takes a heartbeat—half a second, maybe—for a barnacle like this to spoil a boat like mine?"

"You've told me before." Denny kept chewing.

"One lousy, *tiny* barnacle—just like this menace, right here. Can ya see that?"

Denny nodded.

"You're not careful, this one tiny son of a gun turns into an entire fouling colony. Digs its hooks in, eating last week's paint off, adding drag time in the bargain. You want to know what kind of sailor shows up with a hampered keel?"

"Not you, pal. That's for sure." Denny heard the mounting aggravation in his voice, even if J. J. didn't.

"Damn right, not me."

"How much longer you plan to be?" Denny leaned over the grab rail.

"Long as it takes."

Denny watched and waited for the end of the extraction routine. J. J. scrubbed for slime twice a week, sluicing his lines, warding off the larvae of the acorn barnacles, the yellow sponges, the spidery limpets and sea squirts, and the shining chartreuse mane of algae that claimed every inch of roping just below surface level. On clear afternoons at the harbor, with the sun beating hot on his neck, the business of tending to his boat was always J. J.'s foremost complaint. But also, from where Denny sat, his favorite distraction.

"I saw your old man playing mixed doubles with the Beaumonts on my way over."

"That's not playing," J. J. snorted. "That's politicking. I'm supposed to take the daughter on the boat afterward. Say, you wouldn't want to take her, would you? She's a real scarecrow."

"Nah, I've got a flight lesson this afternoon. At Katama."

"Still on your airplane kick?" Shreve laughed. "There are easier ways to catch a decent girl, you know. Come to my bachelor dinner tomorrow night, I'll show you. In fact, I'll bring you a butterfly net. We'll catch plenty."

"How are things going?" Denny ventured. "By the way. With the wedding, I mean."

"Dandy." J. J. spit again. His sunburned shoulders were peeling. The backs of his ears—typically specked with freckles from fall through spring—had arrived at the point of summer where nothing of his natural coloring shone through. Today they looked to be on fire.

"Did you speak with Lenore yet? You know, that new direction you were considering?"

"Pipe down, will you?" J. J. scrubbed.

"Can't imagine it's an easy decision." Denny lowered his voice. "For either of you."

"It's not difficult." J. J. reached his arm up to trade his toweling for a beer. Denny handed one down. "But she'd sure find a way to make it so."

"So you *haven't* asked her?"

"Not exactly."

"Well look, what did you call me out here to talk about then?"

Of course, Denny already knew what J. J. wanted to talk about. When you boiled it down, J. J. Shreve was always talking about the same thing, more or less. Himself. His ideas. His priorities. His great big plans. For instance: Marigot.

Denny supposed it was just his luck he'd been at the club the day that J. J. got the phone call—an old crew mate from Exeter, Randall Simms. Randy had phoned to say he was cutting a deal with Hotel Marigot down in French Saint Martin. Tourists newly discovering the archipelago of the Leeward Islands: Saint Barts, the Virgins, and thereabouts. First-class types were asking after more intimate excursions. They wanted midnight sails, deep-sea fishing, hidden swimming beaches accessible only by catamaran. Randy proposed that J. J. come down to partner with him, to help skipper the boats and give their private touring company a handsome face, to share in the windfall while pursuing the very same pastimes they already loved.

Only one small wrinkle: none of this aligned with the postmarital plans J. J. had been prescribed. Not by a long shot. His father and his father-in-law had mapped the next nine to twelve months of his life as clearly as any nautical course chart, including an extended sojourn in England and France where, ostensibly, he would be mastering the "French fold" technique for manufacturing greeting cards and bringing this rare science back to his own family's printing factories. In a year's time, he and his bride—plus one—would return to America, take over the company in Needham, raise their children as Irish Catholics, buy one house in the city and another at the island, ever ready to smile for group photographs printed in the EYC yearbook. A pretty picture, indeed. But J. J.—Denny knew by now—had already decided on something else.

"Heck, I thought maybe *you* could tell her."

"Me?" Denny leaned backward.

"Sure. Give her a good sit-down. Like an older brother would."

Denny heard himself make a sound like a muted laugh, though this idea was not especially funny. In the first place, whenever he thought of Lenore Dooley—whenever he *had* thought of her, in the past of course—it wasn't anything in the way of how he saw his sister. And in the second place—

"She could see reason, coming from you. And you could make the case real clearly. How much she'd hate Marigot. The tropics. How she really ought to stay here with her people."

"Do you mean to say that you intend to go *without* her? What about—Jesus, what does Randy say?" Even as he was asking, Denny didn't want to know any more. He suddenly had an uncomfortable feeling—the feeling that consumed him whenever folks on the beach took to speaking on serious matters, not realizing how keenly others could hear them. He'd clear his throat to demonstrate the nearness of every carried sound. Still, sometimes you just had to get up and walk away.

"Nothing. Randy doesn't know anything."

"He doesn't know you're engaged to be married?"

"Oh *that* part he knows. It's the other thing. Well, my folks don't want me discussing it really. I shouldn't even bring it up now. Except, it makes a difference of course. Calling off the wedding—in this situation, Lenore's situation—would mean injuring a lot of other things too."

"So, I have to ask you again. What are we talking about, John?"

For a long, chill moment the sun shrank behind a cloud. Denny closed his eyes as the ocean wind mounted. With the Finn's sheets lowered and bound, just the edges of the sails lifted and flapped.

"I wouldn't be the first guy to back out on a girl." J. J. kept on scrubbing. "Papers are full of stories. Husbands going AWOL. Husbands marrying their stenogs. Anyhow I'd rather be the sort that backs out early than the sap who sticks it out and surrenders himself to . . . to . . ."

"To what?"

"That awful . . . I don't know. The *drudgery* of it all. Nine-to-five workday. Weekends mowing the lawn. Bridge night on Saturday. Church on Sunday morning. Weekly dinners with the in-laws. Choked into some corny necktie. Saddled with a set of his-and-hers drooping midsections. Wailing kids. Regular table at Durgin-Park. Condemned to talking up my friends' orthopedists instead of even noticing their pretty wives. That's how it happens—believe me, I've seen this story before."

"Your family's name would be mud," Denny leveled, giving in to brutal honesty. "Your father would lose clients. You couldn't show your face again *here*."

"I know all that," J. J. fumed, spitting seawater from his mouth. "Why don't you tell me something I haven't considered?"

"I don't think you've considered Lenore at all."

"Bullshit, I haven't. I've considered how this is maybe the best thing that could happen for me, and she'll only foul it up on account of there's no Bergdorf's in the Caribbean."

"You asked her to marry you, John. And she said yes. And now you owe it to her."

"Listen, I'm not worried about Lenore. If there's one thing that girl can figure out on her own, it's how to replace a man. If not, her father can buy her one."

"I don't think she's as frivolous as all that."

"You'd be surprised." J. J. pulled a pair of goggles over his eyes, ducking his head underwater to feel for rough patches. When he resurfaced, he hadn't forgotten his point. "Your buddy Colin Hatch has her checking her powder compact every six seconds these days."

"I think you're wrong there." Denny shook his head. "Colin's got eyes for Sabina."

"Oh, wake up, McTigue. That wolf? He's got eyes for every kind of skirt that saunters by. Not that I begrudge him the right of way. I'm only saying, tell your sister not to get too attached."

"She called it quits."

"Good for her." J. J. drank from his beer can. "She's got the right idea, I'd say. Get out of Dodge while the skies are still clear. That's my plan—if you don't mind helping me out a little."

Denny threw his peach pit against the smooth plane of the water. He threw it so hard his arm stung. "You want *me* to break off *your* engagement, while you hightail it to Marigot?"

"Don't say 'Marigot' out loud." J. J. scanned the harbor for anyone in earshot. "But yeah, I mean, you're the best man for it. She had a major case on you once—don't think I didn't know. Puppy love, sure. But that nonsense carries over with girls."

Denny stood up to stretch his legs. "Sometimes, John, the way you talk—it's like you're frozen inside."

"Well all right, McTigue. Forget it then. *Jesus.*" J. J. slapped the water. "What's the good of having a buddy if you can't even ask a favor now and then?"

"She's got a good heart—that kid. And I won't help you break it."

"Look, if you love her so much, why don't *you* marry her?"

"Yeah? Maybe I ought to."

"Yeah?" John shot him a look of pure amusement. "Except maybe you're right. Maybe she *isn't* as frivolous as all that."

The boys let the wind intervene as it gathered big and loud in their ears. J. J. inspected his brushwork while he frowned and treaded. Denny watched the charter boats chugging off, decks awash with fresh crews of summer anglers and their rented tackle. He'd never been in a fistfight his whole life—excepting Korea, but that was a different kind of scrap. Sometimes he liked to think his zero-for-zero record was among the few facts that truly defined him, set him apart from other men. And then other times—other times he so much hated that it did.

When J. J. finally spoke again he was calmer. "Next full moon. I'll take the yawl to Miami."

"Be serious."

"I *am*. If I hug the coast, I could sail her there myself. She can hold her course for hours without any hands on the wheel. Some nights I wouldn't even have to pull into port. Randy and I will meet up stateside, do the last leg together. I have some cash set aside—enough to fix me for a year." The constant flutter kicking made his sentences breathy. He sounded to Denny like a child who'd run all the way home from school.

"And your parents? *Her* parents? You're just going to *announce* this gladsome plan after church one Sunday? Because I'm sure as hell not delivering the message."

"Maybe I won't do it in person then. Maybe I'll leave a note."

Denny sat down quiet again. "That's just about the worst thing I've ever heard."

"What's so awful about it?"

"You can't just sail away, John."

J. J. brushed his wet hair back, scowling at the houses along the shore. "This island is a stinking lath pot, you know that?"

"You can't just leave them behind."

"What's to hold me?"

Denny rubbed his eyes with his palms. He tried digging around his brain for some measured response. Some sage bit of advice. But J. J. was already back at the cork paddle: pushing, pulling, emitting small grunts of exertion, determined to beat back the encroaching ocean, denying the smallest trace of any creature intent on slowing him down.

# NINETEEN

"Mr. Dooley?" Wanda buzzed. "There's a man here to see you."

Bill Dooley rocketed upright in his chair. He set down his cigar and scowled. Behind him stretched the misty view of Boston's Back Bay—a grid of neatly plotted avenues alternating in their tri- and disyllabic appellations: Arlington, Berkeley, Clarendon, Dartmouth, Exeter, Fairfield, Gloucester, and Hereford. From Berkeley Street rose the cloud-ringed weather beacon of the John Hancock building, flashing blue to signal a coming rain.

Any number of men Bill didn't wish to see presently were looking for him—most, foolishly, would be surveilling Suffolk Downs; another few might be kicking at cans in the alley that flanked Flynn's. But none he could think of would be quite so crafty or else quite so misguided as to seek him out here, in his office, on a weekday afternoon in July. It was precisely the reason he'd chosen to hide here.

"Who is it?" Bill coughed into the intercom machine.

"Says his name's George. George Mattos. From the island, I believe."

Bill shuffled a pile of financial papers into a thin, drop-front drawer, slamming it twice to contain them with finality. "All right, show him in."

Too quickly for his comfort, there was Wanda and there was George looming beneath the transom. The presence of George Mattos in Bill's city workplace proved deeply unsettling. As the ferryboat skipper marched into the room, hat in hands, smelling faintly of diesel and fresh bait, Bill suffered a momentary wave of disorientation. He felt for his cufflinks and found them smartly protruding at each wrist, heavy and solid with their sharp little corners. Relief prevailed. He was who he was supposed to be.

"George!" Bill stood to receive the surprise visitor with his typical garrulousness. "I didn't think they gave you leave but once a year for Christmas. Who've they got minding the Point? How's that delinquent brother of yours, anyhow?"

"I didn't come for small talk, Bill." By his expression—an inward searchingness—it was clear George Mattos was afraid of getting derailed. "I'll be direct, if you don't mind. I think you know too well how the Chappy crowd feels about your bridge business. And I think it's only right we discuss it like men."

"Say, does your wife ever stir up a batch of old-fashioned noodle salad?" Bill replied, chin in hand.

"Come again?"

"George, if I may tempt you, there is a *cafeteria* downstairs." Bill circled his desk. Pulled his pant legs before sitting, inertly smiling toward the window. "Wonderful *hidden gem* sort of place. And let me tell you, the noodle salad they compose is—well, I'm nothing if not honest, George." Bill shook his head at this elliptical detour. "The noodle salad downstairs, with bits of olive and paprika, I guess it is—it's better than my own mother's, truly. You eat lunch yet today?"

"I know how the Chappy scam works." George leaned into Bill's desk. "How you intend to keep squeezing your profits out of these good-hearted people."

"Two minutes," Bill mouthed to the skipper, his desk phone now cradled against his pink cheek, spidery with its red and blue vessels. "Wanda? Wanda, are you there? George and I have a hankering for that terrific noodle salad from downstairs. Could you—? Right. Yes, please. Just bring them in."

"I've seen the Wasque contract papers, Bill. For your gimcrack houses, or however they're meant to be called."

"Say, George, I could go for a quick snort. You?" Bill reached for his carafe of Glenfiddich, but George was brooking no such pleasantries or stalls.

"You make bogusness into a real art form, you know that?"

"What you're saying sounds awfully unkind, George. Let's have lunch before we ruin our appetites with insult."

"You've ruined more than my appetite, Dooley. If your bridge gets built, I'm out of a job."

Dooley laughed. "Did you really want to go on skippering that tired barge forever?"

"And *now*," George raised his voice, "Doc Kemp tells me he's actually considering *buying* one of these atrocities from you. I've got the contract you gave him right here. On top of his loan, says he's got to pay for something called a 'rec lease,' is that right? Attached to the property deed for *ninety-nine years*?"

"Ninety-nine . . ." Bill whistled. "That *is* a long time."

George pulled a creased page from his ticket pocket. "There's also something called a 'management contract' and a 'funding fee.'" He pointed, a mystified expression crossing his face. "I'm no lawyer, but this says—well, if this is correct, you can raise these provisions, just by fancy, for the term of the lease. And your buyers have to keep on paying. Every year?"

"I'm not prone to fancy, George." Bill relit his cigar.

"Maybe 'larceny' is a better word for it then."

"Look," Bill sighed, emptying his midday drink down his throat and, with it, the remaining ounces of his indulgent mood. "Mattos, I want you to consider your own home for a moment. That old shack of yours couldn't fetch a plug nickel right now, on account of no one and his grandfather can *get to it*. But in ten years' time, *your* property is going to be worth double what it's worth today, all thanks to Wasque Winds, my bridge, and the traffic it brings. You'll be *thanking* me then. *Doc Kemp* will be thanking me then."

"What about our bay scallops?"

Bill studied George with a serious, constricted look. His eyes lingered on the man's frayed, umbering pant legs, on the length of his silver-sprouting ear hair. He so much hated this absurd and jangling problem of the bay scallops.

"Honestly, George. To hear it from your side, these poor sons of guns have been dying since Christ left Chicago. First it was the sea star attack, when all your moaning inspired a state bounty on starfish. You remember that? Then the eider ducks, then the scoters—you brought in sharpshooters that year, if I recall. Now you expect me to believe my digging up one little seed bed in the bay—"

"That one little seed bed feeds four hundred families, Bill. Mine included."

Bill leaned on his buzzer. "Wanda? How are we coming with that noodle salad?"

"Your bridge means raking up Outer Harbor. We've all seen that before: '43, '44. Navy comes out, digging up the flats for the crash boats. Do you remember how it went?"

"Vaguely," Bill conceded, a tired expression overtaking his face.

"Kicked up enough silt to swamp Lake Superior. The eelgrass never recovered. Scallops were gone from that bed for two, three—for how many winters the catch was thin? Things are *just now* getting back to normal."

"You natives," Bill chuckled, though he could feel his hackles rising. "You'd sooner part with your wives than your sweet-eyed scallops."

"Scallops are worth more than a million dollars a year to the town. That's a fact, whether you want to recognize it or not. Your bridge, your big, fancy build—they'll end us, Bill."

"This is a mesmerizing story, truly."

"I say it's a *fact*."

"All right. So, where's your *proof*?"

"I don't need proof. I know what I know."

"I'm sure that'll make a convincing case for the voters at Town Meeting."

"We want you to sell the land back to us."

"How's that now?"

"The land at Wasque. Sell it back to us."

Bill pushed a great breath of air through his lips like a trumpeting elephant. His face was by now an azalea shade of purple. "Jesus, George. You must keep the gals in stitches, sense of humor like that."

"We know what you paid for it," George leveled. "The Island Association has that much raised. Plus five percent. It's a damned decent profit, if you ask me. Not that a man like you needs any more profit. Sell it to us and forget about Chappy. Forget the bridge. Forget the apartment houses. You can stay right here in the city where you belong, swilling your . . ." He gestured to the Waterford carafe. "Having yourself another *snort*."

Bill Dooley sucked his teeth as if to extract a lethal venom. From deep within he felt his stomach acid roil, devoid of any lunch, now climbing the steppes and rills of his gut in search of so many aforementioned noodles. He exercised a bit of quick math. Selling out would certainly offer immediate financial relief. With some gold-medalist public relations, a pivot now could almost be sold as philanthropic. *But then what?* Bill's instinct for profit demanded. He owed on more than just the cost of land. A lot more. And he wasn't feeling especially charitable.

"No," he said at last.

"No?" George bridled.

"That's right, *no*. I'm willing to gamble this bridge business will work out in my favor. I'm sure of it, in fact." His right knee bounced like an electric sewing needle. "Would you like to make a wager?"

"If that's all you've got to say, s'pose I'll see you at Town Meeting then."

"And I'll wear my best suit. Just for you, George."

"I think you'd better. We've got the full Chappy vote behind us."

"Congratulations. Two more and you could field a ball team."

George Mattos smiled. "I'll see you back at the island."

"Wanda!" Bill shouted through the open door, over the fumes of George's exit.

"Yes, Mr. Dooley," the young woman chirped through the insufferable desk machine. "How can I help you?"

Bill bit his inner cheek. *Wanda.* Thin. Pretty. Wholesome, but in a pliable way. She wasn't much older than his youngest daughter. And yet here, the girl had herself a full-time *job.* A legitimate marriage. No rich heirs to buffer any unfortunate mistakes she might choose to make in life. Probably no hideous bruncheons and luncheons involving an absurdist set of in-laws, whom her own father was meant to befriend. And so Bill, God help him, often extracted some twisted pleasure in trying to make this delicate creature cry.

"Where is my mail?" he bellowed. "I'm looking for a contract proposal—"

Presently the girl appeared again in his doorway, twisting the skin at her wrists. "I had it forwarded to your post box at the island."

"At the *island*? Why?"

"Well, because you're not here in the summers."

"Aren't I?"

"Well, no, Mr. Dooley."

Bill felt with two hands down the front of his person. "Am I an apparition then? A holographic illusion?"

"I'm so sorry, Mr. Dooley." Wanda shrank. "I'll have it fixed right away."

"Never mind," the developer grunted as he stood, snatching up his hat and his doweled *Boston Globe.*

"Mr. Dooley?" Wanda bleated.

"Yes?"

"My last week's paycheck wasn't cleared by the bank. Shall I ask Mr. Wunholm to look into it, sir?"

"*Who*?"

"Mr. Wunholm, sir. Noel Wunholm. Your accounts payable assistant?"

Dooley chuckled past her. "Knock yourself out, Wanda. Go ahead and ask him. See if that doesn't do the trick."

# TWENTY

Sabina woke to a blue and mellow morning light rising outside her dormitory window. Rain clouds gathered full and low, but little swallows still twittered in the trees. An oriole flew past to claim the bit of orange peel she'd left on the sill—a small scrap of a habit they both now shared. Another new habit: She kept her slippers camped close beside her bed, for the tile floor proved awfully cold in the mornings. But she rather liked the other kinds of newness about the place—the sounds of the volunteer girls making small movements up and down the hall, the tinny pops of rain jumping off the gutters when it stormed. She felt warmed somehow by this little nest she'd built for herself, with her Truro postcards—still blank, still unaddressed—taped to the cinder block wall. The cozy closeness of her space made it all that much harder to report for bunker duty in the morning, where things were also close but never cozy. She reread her most recent letter to her father before gathering her basket of bathroom things and heading down the hall to her shower.

*Dear Bud,*

*Things are just fine here in Truro. I spent my first week learning the ropes on the gap-filler radar and a little light gun the boys use to select tracks for identification and display. The work is fine and the time passes very quickly during the day.*

*After work, some of the fellows organize softball games. I've been made an honorary manager of sorts. I learned to keep scorebook from the dugout. Then on Sunday morning a group of us drove to Corn Hill Beach, where the water is perfectly flat and warm on account of being bayside. I tagged along for swimming and sun. The boys here call me "Sally."*

*Back at the island, I'm told, Denny is unbearable these days talking up his pilot's license. He's coming and going two or three times in a week now for lessons. Connie thinks he's trying to impress a girl.*

*Speaking of girls, Bud, do you ever think you'll try again at marriage? Are you meeting any blonde, arty women in California? Or maybe cowgirls who wear those tall rancher boots? It's okay if you want to tell me "none of your beeswax." I just get to wondering sometimes. About second chances.*

*It's easy to forget how many people there are in the world . . . until you come to a place like this, that is, and you see all the different kinds of men. I don't just mean tall or short either. I mean quiet and serious or else loud and jokey . . . oh, never mind what I'm trying to say! Rain makes me sentimental, I guess.*

*As ever,*

*Bean*

*P.S. I'm not sure why you recommended the AFB exactly. Aside from the lending library, there's not much here that interests me.*

"Good morning." Sabina stepped into the bunker. She'd taken careful pains, as usual, to look neat and tidy, for she often heard the senior men bawling out the volunteer girls who let appearances slip on account of the beachy weather. Eleven faces looked up without answering. Elbow to elbow, the team milled around a pair of observation screens.

"Who are you? Where's your access badge?" A twelfth man—brand-new to Sabina—barked from his seat in the corner. He was tall and lean when he stood, with a long, sharp nose and accusing eyes. If he meant to be terrifying—Sabina swallowed—he was remarkably successful.

Sabina held up her ID card for him to see. “Volunteering?”

“Volunteering, sir,” he corrected her. “Volunteering to do what?”

“Help with the radar project, sir.”

“Are you a student at the college?”

“No, sir. Which college? Well, no sir, in any case. I only just finished high school.”

“Then what are your qualifications?”

“I have none, sir.”

He checked his watch. “I thought as much. You know teletype?”

“Not really, no.”

“How about shorthand?”

“But shorthand is for secretaries, sir.”

“Of which you are *not*?”

“That’s right.”

“Do you understand azimuth synchronization?”

“Excuse me, sir?”

“Digital radar relay. Have you studied it?”

“No, sir. So far I’ve just been observing—”

“So.” He crossed his arms. “Let me ask again. What are *you* doing here?”

“I’m here because . . . well,” she attempted, being careful not to mention anything about her father. That explanatory detail seemed to upset the airbase people most.

“Don’t stammer. Don’t tell me any tales. And for God’s sake don’t waste my time, would you, please?”

Sabina straightened up tall and spoke as quickly as possible. “I’m here because I’m meant to find some sense of direction before my aunt ships me off to Swiss finishing school on account of I’ve burned a bridge with every women’s college from here to Poughkeepsie.” Remembering, she added, “Sir.”

This new man in charge, whoever he was, snatched off his glasses. His accusing eyes shrunk to a less formidable size. “That sounds about right,” he sighed. “Read this.” He tossed her a sheaf of handwritten pages.

"Translate it into proper English. Come back tomorrow with a typed transcript."

"But I haven't any typewriter."

"That's all for now. Dismissed."

Sabina walked back to the dormitory without having eaten any breakfast or mailing her father's letter, without stopping to ask wherever it was she was supposed to acquire a typewriter. She avoided the first sergeant's lawn and took the long route along the Clay Pounds cliffs, where down below, the frogmen were again out maneuvering in their skiff, looking darkly busy with their flippered feet and faceless masks. Sabina hardly wondered about their dive this morning, running up the stairs of her dorm. She missed her island. She missed her cottage. She missed the fine crape myrtle in the side yard that'd be blooming like a summer bride just now. She missed the old craggy juniper that always looked so parched, even after it poured. She missed the bittersweet that struggled and clung and reached and wrapped around the splintering fence rails as if it feared where the wind might take it otherwise. She missed Connie and ole A. P., even. She crashed back into her bed—a cot, really—opening the envelope so as not to tear it, and carefully scratching out last night's postscript. She took up her fountain pen and revised:

*P.S. I'm not sure how much there is for me to learn here. I don't care anything at all for radars or air defense systems either. I worry all I'm getting good at is defending myself against gruff people.*

She sealed the envelope and decided to mail the letter after lunch, perhaps when the sun came out. Maybe then she'd feel ready enough to ask around after typewriters. For the time being she found her way beneath her blankets, listened to the birds, and cried.

# TWENTY-ONE

Isolde had it in her head she would work with Hitchcock one day. Eventually. They both shared a certain taste for the absurd, or so she'd been told, indirectly, by multiple film executives who had, in various ways, accused her of being insane. For this reason she had a man she hired to hide small, dead animals around her New York City apartment. Just two or three, whenever she traveled. It stunk up the place something awful, which tended to dilute the surprise. Still, at the moment when she actually stumbled upon a stiff carcass—starkly naked in a wash basin or bathed in the shadows of the bread box—she would practice clawing at her cheeks and screaming out open windows until authorities of some kind were dispatched to help her.

Oh, there wasn't too much harm in it—her own curated brand of the Method—especially considering the kinds of career paths that awaited girls with strictly nonsense résumés. She was tired of the comparisons drawn between her and Marilyn. Tired of being asked to burst into song and shuffle-hop-step, while women of lesser talent snatched up all the serious parts opposite serious men. The very mention of Grace Kelly made her livid.

And still, for all her concentrated screaming, the world had yet to take her seriously. To force its hand, she sometimes took to dressing all in black: black cigarette pants, a London smog-style turtleneck underneath a funereal trench, a black headscarf tied tight enough to cramp her jaw (only a serious person would endure so much self-inflicted agony), black leather gloves in the swampy heat of a midtown afternoon.

This was how Isolde Martin arrived at LaGuardia, twenty minutes before departure back to the island. Her appointments in the city had not gone well. Her agent scolded her for spending so much time in the sun. Scandinavian milkmaids, apparently, were ever so much more convincing *without* bronzed cheeks and deeply-tanned cleavage. Her weight was at last under control and her complexion looked fresh, but her voice rang as pitchy as ever. The instructor dismissed her with a pile of exercises to complete before their next session. Harris hadn't returned a single one of her phone calls.

"Where's your luggage?" her private pilot inquired, strolling out from the terminal, dusting sandwich crumbs from the pockets of his neatly pressed shirt. He began unknotting the plane from its tie-down points at the wings and tail.

"I don't know," Isolde answered honestly. She was tired. She was restless. In moments such as these she often relied on a bargaining sort of conscience. Most of her decisions—especially borderline immoral decisions—hinged on the outcome of silent, "if then" scenarios she concocted in her head. *If he lets me sit next to him, then I shall make him fall in love with me.* "Do you always remember everything you've left behind? Every *one* you've left behind?"

"Sorry I asked." Hatch shook his head.

"I thought, in fact, maybe I could share the cockpit with you this afternoon," said Isolde, ignoring his reply.

"Suit yourself." Hatch gestured to the aircraft door.

"May I borrow some headgear?" she asked, while her pilot took his seat beside her.

Hatch helped her place the band over her head, guiding the audio wire to its port. Suddenly her ears filled with the crowded party of Northeast air traffic control. *Three two Charlie Victor. Requesting runway two four. Go ahead clear. Runway two four cleared for takeoff.* When Hatch spoke, above the chorus, she could hear his voice inside her head—low and sure, hinging on that occasional Southmead lilt of his. As they taxied and took off, she focused her eyes on the movement of the propeller, drawing its hazy gray arc out in front of the windshield. But her head was connected only to his voice.

The trepidation she'd felt during earlier small-plane flights fell away. In its place, tucked snugly into the cockpit next to Colin, she felt something much more akin to thrill. She hardly noticed when they left the ground, and yet the mounting sensation of buoyancy gripped her like magic. Her vital organs seemed to take their cue from the plane, defying gravity, floating as if unmoored from the necessary bits of connective tissue. Hatch turned his head and winked at her.

"Can they hear us when we're talking?" She pointed to her ears. "The men in the tower?"

"Not unless I press this button."

"Good."

"Why's that?"

"I've been meaning to ask you something." She settled her shoulders against her seat. "Well, I'm told Bill Dooley is planning to build something monstrous in my backyard."

"Yep," Hatch nodded. "Half of Edgartown is invested in it too. What did you think he'd do with all that empty land? Raise mink?"

"What's he building anyhow?" Isolde drew her string of pearls between her teeth. *If he winks at me again, then I'll ask him to dinner.*

"Some kind of complex for the deep-pocket crowd, I guess." Hatch squinted, adjusting buttons on the dash. Terse non sequiturs from the control tower crackled in their ears. *One eight two Hartford approach. Maintain two thousand, expect six thousand.*

"How *many* apartment houses?" Isolde pressed, laboring to envision something like her New York building in the middle of Wasque.

"Who knows? Fifty? Sixty? Whatever he can get away with. I'm surprised you're not sore at him."

She sank her forehead against the passenger-side window, only halfway aware she was quoting a scene from her last film. "When big things are underway, certain lapses should be expected. History always forgives its great men."

"Jesus, I hope you don't mean Dooley. A great man?"

"No, not him. Maybe some of his friends though. Haven't you ever put yourself out for a friend?"

"I find that good deeds are overrated. And underpaid."

"Well, it's a damned shame, anyhow." Isolde stretched her arms above her head. "I had a spot for my private sunbathing all picked out. Someplace I could be comfortable without any prying eyes in the vicinity. And now . . . do you know what I mean by *comfortable*?"

Hatch shifted in his seat. "Naked?"

"You needn't be crass, Captain."

"Look, I'm not the one getting undressed on the beach."

Isolde licked her glossy lips. "What about up here then?"

"Up where?"

"Here." Isolde twirled her finger in the air. "In your little flying machine."

"What? Do you mean have I ever—? *Never*," he shook his head.

"Are you telling me *nothing* untoward has ever gone on in this space? Not much room to maneuver, I suppose, but—"

"Oh, there's room enough," Hatch confirmed without thinking.

"You see?" Isolde clapped her hands together in triumph. "I knew you had a playboy streak in you! And all this time you've been misleading me with your straight-laced, good-soldier routine."

Colin Hatch laughed at himself then, and Isolde saw he had a sheepish side, very unlike his usual air of quiet strength. "As long as we're speaking of misleading . . . how's that new Chappaquiddick road?"

"Still unfinished."

"I see the trucks go by some days. That Baker crew."

"They're criminally inefficient."

"You do realize"—the pilot paused to check her face—"I mean, you know that you're financing a key piece of Dooley's neighborhood, don't you? You're paying for the road and the power lines he needs to build up his skyscrapers."

"What are you saying?"

"I'm saying that you're getting rooked, kid."

Isolde shrugged. The sunlight on the open water trembled like a follow spot, like a beam of light cutting through a hazy theater. "You've a right to your opinion," she said haughtily. "I don't expect you to understand what's actually happening."

"Try me."

"The truth is that I'm cultivating an experience from which I can subsequently draw an emotional *sense memory.* It's called research, Mr. Hatch. And it's all soon to enrich my characterization of Inga, a poor and exploited milkmaid."

Hatch shook his head. "Back up. I am confused. Is it that you're doing a favor for a friend? Or is it that you're *letting* Dooley bamboozle you, just to improve your acting chops?"

"Don't go and ruin it!" Isolde ripped off her headgear, replacing the earpieces with the defiant cups of her hands. "If I'm altogether *conscious* of the situation it diminishes the effect."

In truth, she supposed her tolerance for Bill Dooley was owed to a bit of both motives. Her hopes for a life with Harris Shields lit up and went dim directly alternate to her rising and falling confidence in her career. So when the one pursuit seemed fruitless, the other burned brightest in her imagination.

"Of course, I don't know you too well," Hatch ventured, "but it sounds like you might be deluding yourself."

"Inga's character is also quite delusional, in her way." Isolde spoke at her window, watching the plane ascend through shearling clouds. "It's a very complex role. Very difficult to play her brand of 'good,' if you know what I mean."

"No, I think you lost me again."

"It's very difficult to portray the quality of *goodness*. There's very little substance to demonstrate. Morally flawed characters have certain ticks. Wicked laughs, maybe. A depraved sort of sneer. But good? Blameless? A good character is without any definition at all."

"Oh, I don't think that's true. I think there's substance to good."

Isolde crossed her arms and shook her head free of the pilot's dissenting opinion. "Haven't you ever noticed how all the best scenes are set aside for villains? No? I'll tell you what for. It's because you can't ever count on a good character to do very much that's interesting. Why, she might as well just sit here in this airplane with you, looking terribly dull, keeping her hands folded in her own lap." Isolde unclipped her seatbelt. Slid her shoes off beneath the dash, maneuvering to her knees. "Whereas a more villainous sort of minx would creep in closer. Breathe her dastardly lines into your ear. Maybe brush her lips against your cheek, where I do believe there's color rising just now—"

"You ought to stay buckled."

"I'm showing you how easy it is to play bad."

"So what happens to her exactly?" Hatch interrupted the demonstration. She couldn't help but notice a subtle distancing from her touch. "What happens to this Inga character you're studying? Are you sworn to withhold the film's ending?"

Isolde swallowed an ounce of disappointment. She didn't answer. She sat back down on her heels, shrinking her chin and nose into the jersey of her turtleneck. It was a sweater built specifically for evading bad air. Ever since the Great Smog of London, she owned five. After twenty minutes of punitive silence she put her headgear back on. "What are those dark hills there?" she asked.

"Those are the blue hills of Boston."

"They look like the end of the earth."

"Over there, that's Newport."

"What's down that way?"

"Nomans Island. It's closed to the public. Still littered with live munitions from navy training."

"Wait now. You're going too quickly," she complained. "Can you circle back? I'd like to explore a bit more."

"You wanna drive us for a while?"

"No, I couldn't! *Could* I?" She looked to see if he was teasing her. But his expression was neutral. "I'd probably land us in Alaska."

"No chance of that," Hatch's assurance came through her earpiece. "There's nothing you can do wrong that I can't fix."

It was just a quick, offhand remark. Probably something all trained pilots say to their passengers up in front. But Isolde thought she heard a promise inside. It warmed her face. Her mouth curled up on one side. She ventured to touch him again—this time petting his arm above his wristwatch, where a current of blondish hairs converged into a neat, masculine stripe. *If he takes my hand in his, then I won't think of Harris again. Not for the rest of tonight.*

And he did. For a moment, at least. He took her hand to place it on the copilot's yoke. She added her right hand for balance. The control was not unlike a steering wheel, and yet, when she gripped the thing, immediately, she felt her seat shudder.

"That's just a little oscillation," Hatch assured. "Loosen your grip. Let the plane fly first."

She followed his instruction, and the plane's steady glide returned. Through the windshield, all around them, she saw the cornflower blue of a midsummer sky. Here and there, sprigs of clouds bowed like ribs. As they made their approach, the tops of individual trees sharpened into focus. Hatch radioed the tower. Four little lights planted in the grass switched from white to green, the island's promise it was safe to land.

"The truth is," Isolde suddenly resumed speaking in her autocratic way, "I don't actually *know* what happens to Inga in the end. They haven't given me the full script to review. I suppose I'm not the director's first choice."

The airpark tower interjected. *Beech 22022 turn right heading one eighty. Wind two-four-zero at niner. Runway fife, right. Cleared to land.*

"Cleared to land and going down now, sir. Beech 22022," Hatch replied to the towers. Turning to Isolde, he offered, "Hard to imagine a world where you come in second place to anyone."

"Yes, well, you know what they say . . ." Isolde slipped her hands back inside her calfskin gloves. The airplane was nearly on the ground now. She could see the sprawling airfield with its high grasses brushing against miles of split-rail fencing. Wheat-colored lanes bore the faintest tracks of nose wheels, up and down for acres. The Atlantic waters shimmered like cobalt sequins, and as suddenly as summer rain, she started to cry.

Her hired car would be waiting at the gate to take her home. Back at the Harbor View, her hotel room would greet her with darkness. Minus the birds or Koji, there'd be nothing to do but practice her voice instructor's breathing exercises, hands and knees down on the floor, filling her lungs completely with great swallows of air.

"No, tell me." Hatch's voice softened as he extended his handkerchief. "What *do* they say?"

"It doesn't matter anyhow."

"Sure it does. I'd like to know. What do they say?"

It was another line from her old film. Now that he seemed to care so much, she felt silly borrowing it. "The world is a rotating frame of reference."

"I've never heard that. *Who* says that?" He smiled. He winked. The pilot seemed, in that moment, to understand all her silent bargains.

"People who know that nothing lasts. But everything comes back around again."

# TWENTY-TWO

*Dear Bean,*

*Maybe I never told you . . . My father sent me away for the summer once. To learn chemistry, I was told. In truer terms, he sent me off to scale herring at the Bodman fish factory, where they were cooking up fake pearls from some kind of fish-skin emulsion. I smelled of low tide until October that year, but believe it or not, I learned quite a lot. Don't count out radar science or air defense or scaling herring, for that matter. All of life becomes relevant eventually. Meanwhile, take a little taste of everything.*

*It's Friday here and, as I write, some of my associates are mixing Tom Collinses out by the reflecting pool. (Did I tell you we have a pool at the office? Not for swimming, mind you. For reflecting.) I'll confess to having had a few, lest you think I'm always open to entertaining questions about my love life. For tonight only I'll say this:*

*Here at the company, there was a project once that had us scratching our heads for years. We worked on it in New York. You were still in braces then. For a full year we hated this project. We moved on to other things. We went back. We attempted calculations that hurt our heads harder than what to say to a girl who's just suffered her first heartache. Eventually, we got it done. And now there is a formula, inside a computer, that can tell you where the moon is cruising right exactly now—in relation to just about everything.*

*What I'm saying (I think) is that there's more than one way to try again. Sometimes it looks like starting over on a blank page. And sometimes it means taking the old, impossible problem and turning it upside down to find another way through. This will sound silly to you, but I haven't given up on finding your mother. I don't mean heaven, somewhere over the rainbow, or any of that . . .*

*She and I, you understand, traded plenty of letters. Our courtship was a long one. She lived so far away. Her family was in automotives, in Detroit. I was in Boston, of course. Well, I saved them all—all of her words. I've kept them, and I revisit them still sometimes. (Rain makes me sentimental too.) Anyhow, computers can learn languages. I don't see why, one day, they couldn't learn the one your mother and I shared between us. I don't see why I couldn't one day write to her again, and she write back. A different kind of togetherness, maybe, and 100 percent pure science fiction, but it's the only kind of "try again" that would ever appeal to me in this lifetime.*

*Hopefully I haven't dampened your evening. By the sound of things, there are many (different!) shoulders available for you to cry on. Keep them all at arm's length, please—and not just metaphorically.*

*Still in California,*
*Bud (Dad)*

*P.S. Gruff people are everywhere. Don't learn to defend yourself. That's the coward's way out. Learn how to convert them.*

"McTigue!" Captain Ford boomed across the bunker. He was forever twisting his face into his eyeglasses—hooking the temple tips around his ears—and then snatching them back off again, so that sometimes—such as now—they sat crooked across the bridge of nose, giving his head an amusing off-kilter effect. "My six-year-old daughter could compute these sums with better accuracy." He was waving a copy of his latest report on the gap fillers' detection ranges.

Sabina hardly glanced up from her notepad. "You have a daughter, sir? How old?"

"Don't you think you'd better stick to correcting these numbers?"

"I'm only surprised a girl hasn't softened some of your bite. She'll be venturing out in the world one day too. I imagine you'd hope for *her* a kinder reception than the one you've given me."

"Imagine less." Captain Ford handed Sabina the red-lined report. "Refigure these sums."

"But those aren't my sums, sir. Those are Kaplan's. He left them on your desk this morning."

"Oh?"

"That's right." Sabina grit her teeth into a smile. *Learn how to convert them.* "But I'd be happy to correct his work."

These were her typical afternoons in Truro.

And still, each morning, it was impossible to sleep very much past dawn. One curious phoebe called to another, like a record skipping on the hi-fi, belaboring the same idle question, again and again—never finding an answer. Sunlight dazzled the narrow peel of water visible from her window. And one day she woke up to realize it'd been weeks since her last decent swim.

So what if Denny had cautioned against the rip current here? The tides, she reasoned, couldn't possibly be more gruesome than the officers. So she packed her beach bag and padded barefoot out the dorm. It was a fine, warm day, capped in exhilarating blue, and her walk along the hilly road, fringed with windswept sand, proved long enough to reset her outlook on the place. The dunes here loomed much higher than back home at the island. Turning off the main road and through a break in the cliffs meant navigating a steep descent. It was as if she'd wandered over the edge of a massive, spouted sugar bowl. She had to run for fear her knees would come down ahead of her feet otherwise.

By the base of the path, the beach spread out before her in long, stunning licks. She dropped her bag and tugged off her dress, right there, bookmarking that steep, exposed crease in the earth. She made out for the waves, spilling forth in their vast, ruffled tiers, each tinged a bit bluer or greener, more peacock or steel, than the one riding its collar. The tide fanned out, low and far, and so took its time climbing higher up her legs as she ran. It seemed she'd been running for a very long time before the crystal-clear layers darkened and deepened enough to allow for a dive.

Going under gave her a chill shiver of satisfaction. It seemed her skin could *feel* the salt almost as surely as her tongue could taste it. All the familiar chemical reactions—ocean minerals rushing through her pores—tingled along her arms and legs, reviving her no less powerfully than a fresh canteen might restore a shipwrecked man. She was home again, even here, so far removed from Edgartown.

When she resurfaced, she turned to survey the shore. Brilliant sunlight drew out the full color of every natural thing. The dunes looked back at her, tall and ancient, cat-scratched and ragged. She spied her red dress, like a tiny, far-off map tack. There was no one on the beach. She decided then she ought to come back to this place every morning. More than that, she knew that she would.

A powerboat motored into view. Sabina made herself tall in the water, treading hard with her legs. The skipper saw Sabina then, for he waved and arced his course, steering his outboard wide around her position. She waved back, too late to realize it was them.

It was the frogmen.

"Ahoy!" The little white skiff idled windward carrying four black-suited men aboard. Three wore their rubber hoods drawn tight around their faces. The skipper's suit stopped about his neck, where a coil of tubing, like an Electrolux hose, draped a flat glass oval edged in black rubber. He cut the engine. "You come here often?" he shouted. The other men laughed and set about dropping anchor, gathering lines, clamping their noses with odd metal grips.

"No, actually. I'm new in town," Sabina shouted back. She pushed the hair from her face. "I volunteer at the AFB."

"AFB know you're out swimming alone? We've got sharks in these waters."

"I'm not afraid of sharks." Sabina swam in nearer, to save her voice, but mostly for a closer look. The skipper lifted a black box, a little larger than a transistor radio, onto the gunwale. His face was warm with sun and good humor. She could tell he was a "smart aleck," as A. P. would say, from his faintly sarcastic smile, upturned on one side. "Nor the jellyfish or the rip currents."

"Oh, you're one of *those* girls."

"One of which?"

"The kind who calls her own shots."

Sabina didn't object. She swam in closer still. "Are you hunting for treasure?"

"Something like that."

"Do you mind if I watch?"

"Free country," the frogman shrugged. He placed a heavy headset over his ears. A thin black wire connected the hearing aid to his black box.

"What are you listening to?" Sabina pointed to her own ears.

He pulled off the headset. "Beg your pardon?"

"I said, what are you listening to?"

"Oh," he smiled. "Fish."

# TWENTY-THREE

"They're coming around again! Keep it slick there, pal," Bill Dooley called to his hired chummer. The developer stood watching shoveled fish carcasses land and descend—in a blurred, bloody staircase—below the water's surface.

"How's it going at Wasque?" Harris practiced his subtle, disaffected brand of information gathering. The heat of the afternoon lingered. The sky beyond the bight and above the trees of Money Hill flickered with silent lightning, like muzzle flashes buried in the clouds. "You making any progress with buyers?"

"Eh." Dooley spat splintered cigar bits into the slick. "You know this business. Always a fight to the finish. It's either we could bring home the crown, or we could be next week's dog meat. Never can tell. Guess that's why I like it so much. For the suspense."

"Huh. I thought it was for the complete absence of effort."

"That's very funny, Harry. I'll remember that remark next time half of Brighton dies in a gas blast and you can't be rousted from Monte Carlo."

"I was in *Cannes*," Harris frowned, winking at his scope. "You've got *some* people on the line, though. Right? There is *some* money coming in, isn't there?"

"*Some? Loads!* Outside Boston, the buyers just about climb into my lap. You should have seen me working the course at Dorset last week. At least another twenty on my prospect list." Bill turned to survey the sporting column of the *Globe*. "Although . . ."

"Although what?"

"Did you know they had *six* daily doubles at Flemington? A quinella on seven races? You could lose all of Belmont in just a corner of that place. Over 250 bookmakers too. You ever been to Australia? I wouldn't mind a trip out that way . . ."

"Although *what*, Bill?"

"I won't lie." Bill folded his paper. "I'm in a ticklish position with the close. Chappy's lack of infrastructure right now, people can't see Wasque for what it will be, no matter how many artist renderings. It's too new even for the new money."

"I keep telling you, Bill. State needs another lunatic hospital. Couple more corrections facilities. If we move in before the zoning laws come to pass—"

"Harry, we can't get this town on board with a bridge and a square-dancing pavilion. You think a sanitarium's going to win hearts and minds?"

"What about Isolde? Is she helping you any?"

"Oh, hell. She's an incentive, that's sure. For the women, mostly. They want to buy their beef from the same butcher."

"Isolde doesn't eat beef."

"There's no butcher either. Who's checking? Thanks for getting her here, by the way. Have I thanked you yet?"

"You can thank me when that bridge contract gets signed. The *real* one, from Falmouth, I mean. Not this Tinkertoy version across Katama. You can thank me at the Paradise Club."

"Jersey?" Dooley snorted. "Jesus, I hate Jersey."

"That's just because you don't know how to dress for it."

"Look, Harry. To be honest. I'm gonna need another few weeks on the first installment. And I know that's not the timeline we discussed. But my builder's loan is on hold at the moment."

"So you need more time?"

"A few weeks."

"On top of my getting Isolde here."

"Twenty days. *Max*. You can raise the interest."

"Sometimes I wonder, Bill. Do you even know where the line is?"

"What line?"

"Between your friends and your mugs. Do you even know where it is?"

"Oh, that line," Bill laughed uneasily. He cast his gaze out to sea. The wind and sun, bearing down on the waves, painted the water with contrasting stripes, like the coat of a jungle animal.

Harris sniffed. "You're lucky the syndicate's not after you."

Bill grunted. "I pay my debts. Always have."

"Your investors pay for them, more like. Don't forget how long I've known you, Bill. I know how you think. That is, you *don't*."

Bill whistled at the wind, changing the subject. "I'll tell ya, Harry. When you're bankrolling a wedding like I am, well, you'll see how these women bleed you, mark my words. Your girls will grow up, get themselves engaged. Next thing—"

"I think you have me mistaken for your friend, the priest." Harris squinted, aiming at a dark mass gliding beneath the bass stand. He squeezed the trigger. Blood and surf exploded skyward. "I'm not interested in Bill Dooley's confessional hour."

"Tell you the truth, priest's not all that interested either," Bill exhaled.

"I'll give you a month. Consider it an early wedding present. But after August . . ."

"Would you do that? That's swell of you, Har, I mean it. You're a charitable guy. In fact, I'll tell ya, you *should* have been a priest. Honest to God. You have a soul for salvation."

"Don't bullshit me, Bill. I'm not your priest and I'm not your bookmaker either. But I can keep score just as well as they can."

# TWENTY-FOUR

"You're out of your depth again," the skipper called over from his skiff. Sabina swam toward him, hauling out with the tide. She'd become a familiar sight to him, and likewise the other way around. She timed her daily trips about the backside beaches in hopes of catching him along a course that shifted from Longnook to Newcomb Hollow, and everywhere in between.

This particular morning was cool and, Sabina judged, deceptively sunless—the winning sort of July beach day that starts out a foggy gray only to dazzle all the more when its clouds burn off, giving way to electric-blue skies. Along her walk, she'd breathed in the day's potential. Spied the wild raspberries in full bloom. The brown rabbits munching. The Queen Anne's lace erupting from the roadside bramble—just the buds yet—tightly puckered like little lion faces fringed in fresh green manes. Next week their white frothy flowers would spread open for the sun, offering a delicate dust at every kiss of the wind.

"Says who?" Sabina bantered back. "Anyhow, I don't answer to frogmen."

"Who are you calling *frogman*?" the skipper yelled. The shadowed crease of a smile broke out across his unshaven face.

Overhead, a small plane puttered and purred westward. The early gulls let out plaintive cries, combing the shallow rock pools, hunting after blennies and smelt. Sabina shivered. The ocean still held a few final stores of its winter chill.

"I didn't mean any disrespect." She wiped the water from her eyes. "It's just a silly name from a comic strip."

"If you think we're such a silly bunch, don't cry for our help when some rogue, ten-foot man-eater gets you in his jaws."

"I told you before, I haven't any worry over sharks." She dove and kicked down deep enough to press the ocean floor with her hands, resurfacing on his starboard side. "But I could use your help, as it happens." She was grateful to find the skipper out alone today—no fellow frogmen to embarrass her into fumbling her words.

"Oh?"

"Did you mean what you said before? That you're out here listening to the fish?"

"I always mean what I say."

"I didn't know fish were much for conversation."

"Fish, *as it happens*, cook up all kinds of chatter. Whales sing, shrimp snap, and even clams—oh, you can't discern much of their poetry. But sure enough you can intercept the size of the stock, where it's headed."

"Could I listen with you?"

"What, right now?"

The circumstances were not ideal, true. And yet, Sabina reasoned, right there in the water, she was as comfortable and confident as she'd ever be. So she launched into the plea she'd been forming in her head ever since their first encounter. "I probably sound terribly eager and impetuous," she began, hearing in her voice those very qualities on display. "I'm quite interested in the sea—how it moves and what it carries. And to think of all the different types of fish—*talking!*—some we don't even know about. Why, if I had just an ounce of your instruction—how to dive with one of your Aqua-Lung packs—I could be very helpful to you. I'm a quick study and a strong swimmer—"

"Is that a fact?"

"You'll only ever need to show me something once."

"What'll I get in return?"

"How about the satisfaction of enriching a young woman's life?"

"*Satisfaction.* Listen, miss. This isn't a hobby boat. I sank two years of graduate study into this project, not to mention two months of scuba training. And even as pretty as you are, you can't expect I'll drop everything and bring you up to speed all because you happen to be a curious girl who showed up in the water one day and now persists in tagging after me. I don't even know your name."

Sabina swam 'round the boat to better organize her thoughts. "From that perspective, the idea *does* sound awfully presumptuous. But how about looking at it from my side?"

"*Your* side?" The skipper scratched at the beginnings of his blue-black beard. "Say, what's your story anyhow? You running away from home?"

"Not exactly."

"You *are* quite the swimmer."

"I agree. Not to sound immodest, of course. But wouldn't it be an awful shame if I got shipped away to some la-di-da boarding school? Every day in full skirts and petticoats, in a landlocked country, no less?"

"I guess that would be a shame."

"So you'll help me?"

He frowned. "You have to understand. This sort of work, it's not recreation. It's—dangerous."

Without reply she slipped under the waves, her even strokes aiming shoreward.

"Miss? Where are you going now?" he called, just as she emerged.

"Back to safer depths!" She executed a quick flip turn, where her feet touched down to meet the bottom, so she was facing him again when she yelled, "My name is Sabina, by the way. Sabina McTigue."

"All right, Sabina," he shouted back. "Tell you what. If you're so keen on fish, there's a class you ought to take. Meets weekday mornings at the Y. In Boston. Early train into the city should deliver you there in time. Ask for the Sea Rovers. They'll get you started."

"Get me started on what?"

"Becoming a frogman."

# TWENTY-FIVE

Lenore stood leaning into the icebox for relief. She wiped a mass of hot, frizzed curls away from her face, while her mother unpacked the latest round of wedding gifts.

"You and John are certainly well-equipped for a dinner party," Nola Dooley enthused. "So far your guests have gifted no fewer than one dozen sherry glasses, one dozen cordial glasses, one dozen champagne flutes with the solid stems. Two dozen *punch* glasses. One dozen highball glasses and—oh, look, only half a dozen for sherbet. Unless . . . let's see . . ." Nola reached down to her elbows in denatured packing popcorn. Wooden crates from Marshall Field's, Arnold Constable, and Best & Co. still waited at her ankles.

Lenore could not imagine dusting seventy-something pieces of glassware every week for the rest of her life. Couldn't even imagine paying someone to do it.

Outside, the sky rained without sound, without defined drops, but in a clinging mist that suffused the cottage air, breathing through the open windows, crimping the magazine pages, dampening the upholstered chairs and the white chenille bedspreads. The rain was so slight and the ground so hot, little puffs of steam rolled across the front walk.

"Well, I suppose the flowers can use a drink anyway." Mrs. Dooley frowned at the weather from the sidelight window. "You'll have Burns drive you to the mail?"

"I'm actually rather fond of the walk." Lenore flexed her face into a smile. "I'll be fine to go down with my umbrella."

"You're sure? Let me go with you then," Mrs. Dooley offered. "It'll be like the days when I walked you to your kindergarten school. And we sang that old song about the peat bog."

"I'd rather go alone, Mother, if you don't mind. Gives me time to think about things, how it'll be after the wedding."

Lenore's mother smiled weakly and resumed unwrapping a set of milk-glass egg cups.

Outside the house, the battle at hand was much clearer. More vocally fought. Rather than sort the piles of wedding-guest replies—*Yes, yes, Mr. and Mrs. Hartley Sneed will gaily attend. Seafood medley, beef tenderloin*—Lenore liked to evaluate the points and counterpoints of a more comfortable divide: Katama Bay and its unbuilt bridge.

The little islanders—the Chappy crowd—had issued a series of broadsides in the *Gazette*. The big islanders launched counterattacks with handbills tucked into screen doors. The boating clubs knew no shortage of opinions. Passionate dialogue spilled over from one beach blanket to the next. Some days there were fistfights. At Reynolds' Coffee Shop the two impassioned camps—for and against—occupied opposite wings of the counter.

Hundreds of silk-screened signs garnished the fence posts and utility poles all about Edgartown. Half of these, sponsored by the Automobile Owner's Association, urged town voters to clear the way for a thriving, modern seaport. "Did you know there are only ten automobiles on all of Chappaquiddick?" Lenore overheard two neighbors speculating. "Frightening how intolerant they're being, barring bridges and paved roads. In point of fact, it's a form of bigotry."

The other half, sponsored by the Chappy Island Association and the shellfish constable, pled the fishermen's case, by way of cartoon-drawn bay scallops linked to quotation bubbles that read, "Save the Shellfish, Not the Selfish!" and "I Pay for Your Schools!" Activists turned vandals took to the streets—to the Edgartown Golf Club, in one embarrassing case. High schoolers ventured to spell out their view, VOTE NO ON BRIDGE, funneling fifty pounds of rock salt onto the green. Eventually their opinion burned bright orange across the bent grass of the club's third hole.

And both campaigns, the yeas and the nays, reminded property owners of their duty to attend August's special session of Town Meeting.

Down at the market, Lenore was routinely summoned to see the store clerk, where she retrieved an entire laundry bin full of envelopes addressed to her father's company. Most of these she threw away in the trash pail outside Mayhew's. The protest letters proved boring, unvaried. But today, finally, after an eternity without word, correspondence from the Italian PI topped the pile of mail. Lenore stuffed it in her shoulder bag before hazarding outside into the fine warm spray.

"Splendid weather we're having, wouldn't you say?" James Whelan shouted his opportune hello from the corner of Cottage Street. Lenore paused to regard him. The young man wore a fisherman's slicker and a bright white rain hat—humid air beneath its brim fogging up his lenses.

"Hello, James," Lenore exhaled. As she embarked for home, she walked carefully, sidestepping the divots in the road where shallow puddles now swam with washed-out earthworms. Careful, too, to keep her hands shielding her middle, conscious of the very small bulge lately formed beneath her sash.

"May I escort you to your door?"

"That's not necessary," she declined, forgetting her manners. Or ignoring them, more like. Since Sabina had gone to Truro and Colin Hatch had all but vanished from the club, she and James's mutual interests seemed lacking. And she didn't much care for his timing at the corner, either, which could only have been intentional.

"Wait up! Just a second there, hot rod," Whelan huffed, traversing the road with an effortful jog. "I need to ask you something."

"I don't think you need to worry about Colin Hatch anymore," Lenore replied. "Last I heard he's instant-glued to Isolde Martin."

Whelan huffed onto his eyeglasses, rubbing circles with his shirt cuff. "That's a good sign, I suppose. But still. I don't trust him. Isolde Martin won't be touring New England forever. Fall's coming. And I guess I'm curious—well, I guess I'm hoping you'll help me stay abreast of whatever that search in Italy uncovers."

Lenore smiled. "I'd like to, James. But as it happens I am very busy, in case you hadn't heard, getting ready for my wedding."

"Of course you are," Whelan agreed, too gamely, replacing his glasses. "I won't keep you. I certainly wouldn't expect to encroach on your time without giving back something of equal value."

"What sort of *something*?"

"Oh, I don't know," Whelan mused, falling into step with Lenore. "What is it that you're interested in these days?"

"Calisthenics," Lenore replied, accelerating her pace.

"I see," nodded Whelan, looking her up and down. "Working on that honeymoon figure?" he winked. "Or *maybe* . . . heck, I'm a friend, Lenore. I wouldn't hazard such a bold guess otherwise. But maybe it's a *post*-honeymoon figure that's got you running away?"

Lenore stopped short on the sidewalk. "I don't know what you're talking about. I'm not running away from anything or anyone. I am very eager to marry."

"In some ways that's apparent." Whelan studied her again, his eyes lingering at her midsection. "Some might even say your eagerness is showing."

Lenore moved in closer. Her eyes narrowed. She glared at the soon-to-be doctor of medicine. She wished she'd never shown him the Italian PI's letter for Colin or gotten involved in that Weston College business.

"I'm not like my father, do you understand? Whatever it is you *think* you've heard, or presume to know about me, I don't make deals with shady men."

"All right then." Whelan backed away, hands pantomiming surrender. "I'm sorry to have misjudged you. And I'm sorry your opinion of me is so low, especially after all the years we've known one another. You are right about one thing, though." James Whelan spun the cane of his belted umbrella. A cold spray leapt from its cotton fringe. Cars passed, stirring up the brume at their feet. Tiny droplets from the leaves overhead fell onto Lenore's lashes, stinging her eyes, trailing her cheeks like tears. "You *are* nothing like your father. He's a man, after all. And that means he'll always have escape routes you haven't got."

"What do you want?" Lenore leveled.

"I just wanted for you to know . . ." He shook his head dolefully, as if his better judgment precluded him.

"Know *what*?" she demanded.

"Just that I'm here for you. As a friend."

"Golly. I'm touched."

"I mean it, Lenore. I am here for you, if all of *this*"—he waved his freckled hand before her, like a papal blessing, across her wet face, her very slightly pregnant middle—"ever gets too much to carry. I'm here to help."

"I don't need your help."

"No? And what if he left you?"

"Left me? Who? *John?*"

"Forget I said anything." The doctor subsumed his lower lip. "It was wrong of me to mention."

"What an absurd thing to say." Lenore brushed at her cheeks. For a moment she was glad for the dampness in the air, the ambient wet on her face, in her eyes, for it could have come from anywhere.

"Is it? Is it really so absurd?"

Lenore stuck out her chin. It wasn't absurd at all. It was, in fact, the very change she felt, in little inches each morning—almost as imperceptibly as the movement of the earth toward a coming colder season.

"Just so *you* know, I'd be fine if anyone left me anyhow. Last summer I had eighteen invitations to the Regatta Ball. *Eighteen!* There wasn't another girl on this island with so many."

"Last summer you had a different, er . . . way about you. A certain lightness. I daresay things are different now."

"You're an odd boy," Lenore sneered. "Everyone thinks so."

"Would you like to know what *I* find odd? Getting a telephone call from a young man—a young man who *you* happen to know—bound for a European holiday. I find it odd to the extreme such a man would tell me, in addition to the usual traveler's inoculations, he's interested in yellow fever serum. *Yellow fever serum.* Of course, you can guess what I told him. I told him no one's dying of yellow jack in Paris these days. On the other hand, if he expected to find himself in South America or, say, the tropics, gladly I would help him prepare. Six weeks ahead of his departure. And wouldn't you know . . . this young man took out his calendar and counted down with me still hanging on the line. What do you know of South America and the tropics, Lenore? Perhaps a little port of call called *Marigot*, Saint Martin?"

"Nothing I care to know."

"Well, maybe you'll feel differently in six weeks. I don't suppose John's ever mentioned the two of you jetting off to the Caribbean, has he?"

Lenore didn't answer.

"Is it possible he'd skip town—*alone?*" James pulled a handkerchief from his pocket. She didn't take it. "Some women, in your situation, would find a way to start over."

"Start over how?"

"Oh, have I gotten your attention?"

"No. No, you haven't. I find this whole conversation revolting, frankly. All your plotting and conspiring—" She scowled at him through pleats of rain.

"I could help you."

"In exchange for *what*?"

"For Sabina, of course. You must know that I intend to make a go of things with her. And since she's not likely to see my way of thinking all on her own, I'd like her brought home from that ridiculous girl scouting camp in Wellfleet."

"She's in Truro," Lenore corrected. "It's an air force base."

"Whichever backwoods drill hall she's out junketing." He fussed up his face. "It's my intention to have her home in time for the Regatta Ball. She owes me a dance."

"How do you propose I manage that? With a vaudeville hook?"

Whelan chuckled, as if imagining Sabina juggling rings, Lenore guessed. "Why not write and tell her you've got a crisis at hand? Too much time in the pool, and now your hair's gone green."

"You're proving how little you know the girl, James. She wouldn't even understand the emergency in that, let alone rush home to revive me. It's all right though; I know well enough what would compel her."

"So you'll write to her?"

Lenore lifted her chin. She didn't fully understand this bargain. "And then you're going to do *what* exactly? Once she's here, I mean. You're going to mousetrap her? Tie her up and drag her off to the Upper West Side?"

"I won't need to try half that hard," Whelan countered. "Sabina's a sensible girl."

A true rain began in earnest. Farther down Water Street, women scattered inside the souvenir shops. Café waiters hurried to disassemble the sidewalk tables, stacking patio chairs beneath the awnings, while the gulls set off for dry eaves, retired from scavenging for the day.

"She doesn't love you, James."

"You see now, *this* is the very problem." Whelan pushed the silver runner up the shaft of his umbrella. Its little ball spring popped for emphasis. "*This* is what happens when you girls go off to college without a ring already waiting on your finger. All these notions of life's potential for you *emancipated* women. Romantic foreign affairs! As though some cad in Chicago or Philadelphia or . . . or Abyssinia, for that matter, is going to treat you better than your own hometown beau. It's ludicrous."

"Colin Hatch is her hometown beau," Lenore baited. "Not you."

"Colin Hatch," Whelan reddened, "is a transient wolf with a goddamned pilot's cap decorating its head. And I'll have you know, Lenore, that every last club girl he has duped—*every* gal, from Bunty Fay to Midge Cheney last summer—has subsequently taken up with and gotten herself engaged to the *very next man* who crossed her path. When it comes to Sabina McTigue, 'that man' is going to be *me*."

"That's an interesting theory. I didn't take you for a superstitious fellow."

"When a girl gets jilted hard enough, her taste in men changes pretty fast. I've got facts in my favor too."

"Like what?"

"Poppy McTigue will insist she be in school or else engaged by this fall. I think Sabina'd sooner accept a baguette-cut Cartier than an open-ended sentence at that Swiss finishing school."

"I wouldn't count on it."

"Look, maybe I haven't got the pilot's height or his *laborer's physique*, but I can give Sabina something even better: three hundred miles between her and a lifetime lived in captivity. I can give her new museums, new libraries—independence, in a word. I think Sabina could find consolation in a free and busy place like New York. Besides, I'm an enlightened man. It wouldn't have to be marriage right from the start. I wouldn't press her to love me, only to give the city a chance. As a place for her to land."

Lenore stared at him, wide-eyed. She'd spent so much of her life laughing behind James's back, it'd been difficult to ever take the young doctor seriously. But he was, she could see, dead serious about this.

"Regarding my situation. Can you really arrange to . . . help me?"

"I have a friend in Washington Square. He's a women's doctor. Does procedures all the time. It's not complicated."

"I haven't got any money. That sounds pitiful, I know. But I can't ask my father for more allowance."

"I'll cover everything."

"Why should you?"

"Because we're friends."

"All right," she said, huddled under the bowed ribs of her own black umbrella. The rain clicked and pecked at its dark canopy. "Let me think about it."

# TWENTY-SIX

Lenore didn't want to think about it. She didn't want to think about John, nor James's accusations. She didn't want to be at the club, didn't want to see anyone at home, either. So she ducked into the cottage conservatory, a quiet room affording a door that locked and the ruse of an incomplete floral bouquet she had begun shaping that morning.

At least, she breathed, there was new mail from Italy. She sliced through the letter's seal and dumped its pages across the marble pedestal. She listened for footsteps. Hearing none, she breathed deeper, letting her hands arrange loose stems in one of the umpteen Tiffany vases her wedding had inspired.

**Cliente:** *Sig. Noel Wunholm*
**Indirizzo di fatturazione:** *PO Box 897, Edgartown, MA - Stati Uniti*
**Numero del caso:** *6547*
**Investigatore:** *Pacifico Vento*
**Servizi di traduzione:** *Speak Easy Inc., Via dei Serpenti, 247 - 00184 Roma, Italia*

*Firenze, 15 luglio, 1954*
*Dear Mr. Wunholm,*
*I am delighted to inform you I have located the records of an Adele Buontempo born in the city of Salerno, on 11 May 1926, along with her two twin brothers, who did not survive the birth.*

*She was married in Naples, on 2 June 1943. Police records show she was reported missing that same year, in September, during il Quattro Giornate di Napoli, a very brave moment for our southern city.*

*Enclosed you will find a photograph of our young lady, taken by an Austrian journalist just outside Abruzzo. He remembers her with certainty for the mountain route she was attempting on bicycle. She was a courier, he believes (staffetta partigiana, we say here), among the women of the Resistance who delivered reports between our hidden fighters. Such bravery, he remembers. Determinazione, yes?*

*There is no charge for this small offering, as I think you can see now what a swift and reliable service I provide.*

*Alas, good help does not come cheaply in this economy. I still require the £300,000 I first quoted in order to staff your case with intelligence men of the quality you should expect. Please confirm you have received this report, and please remit this payment promptly (invoice enclosed) within ten business days. As a man of business, you must understand I cannot continue working for free.*

*Cordially,*

*Pacifico Vento*

Lenore studied the airmailed photograph with a critical eye. *This* was Hatch's Italian sweetheart? This frowning, sack-clad frump in desperate need of a brow pencil? Lenore had expected curvaceous, sultry—some raven beauty built like Rita Hayworth in a shantung two-piece. The reality was much less dramatic. The girl was pretty, no question. And, to be sure, a day dress paired with matching espadrilles would not have been appropriate for the precipitous dirt road hugging its ragged mountain village. But those plain, unadorned features sent Lenore's head spinning, wondering what passed for beautiful—*desirable*—outside of Boston.

Without warning, the French door of the conservatory swung open, revealing across its eighteen glass panes, just for a moment, a mirrored view of Lenore at the pedestal. She caught sight of herself standing alone, trapped behind the invented project of her flowers, contemplating the yellowed photograph of a young Italian woman, alone in the world, unencumbered, aiming to tackle a horizon of snowcapped peaks. Though Lenore's eyes moved to intercept the visitor at the door, her expression hadn't changed—the mood in her gaze, the set of her mouth. And despite whatever conscious impressions she may have formed for Hatch's distant flame, her reflection told a different story. Its hard truth was unmistakable. Her expression was admiring.

"Oh, pardon me, Lenny," Shannon mumbled. "Mother said you'd gone into town."

"It's all right. I'm nearly through in here."

"I saw Denny McTigue at the club just now. He was asking after you."

"Was he?" Lenore replied absently.

"He's a nice fellow, don't you think?"

"He's dull," Lenore frowned. "That's all there is to him."

She felt a pang of guilt as soon as she'd said it. Denny *was* something of a hall monitor type. But it wasn't fair to call him dull. Patient, maybe. Collected. A little too obliging. He was always nodding and listening, Denny McTigue. Never any back burners at the risk of boiling over. Never charging off to go do what the other boys wouldn't dare.

"What are you working on?" Shannon gestured to the table. She was the middle Dooley sister. She tried, more than the others, to be universally pleasant.

Lenore slid the pirated Italian photograph underneath the tissue paper from her long stems. "Nothing important."

"Look." Shannon took one step tentatively into the room, as if sensing something secret inside. "I think you must have dropped this reply card when you carried in today's mail." She extended an embossed ivory envelope to her sister.

"Thanks," Lenore replied without moving to accept the card.

"No, *look*, Lenore. It's postmarked from Marigot. Saint Martin! Isn't that the most? A Mr. Randall P. Simms, it says, is the sender. I didn't know you'd invited international guests."

"Randall is a friend of John's. *Marigot* did you say?" She snatched the card from Shannon, slicing its top crease with her letter opener. Reading aloud she began, "'Mr. Randall Simms will gladly attend . . . Seafood medley . . . P.S. Old pal, looking forward to ironing out our details . . . Simms & Shreve Adventure Company! How about that? You'd best get used to rum cocktails . . .'" Lenore swallowed. "'Once you've had a taste of the good stuff, you'll never go back.'"

"'Adventure company'?" Lenore's sister puzzled. "Whatever does that mean? Never go back to where?"

The bride's hands went cold. Her grip failed her. She dropped the letter opener. "Shannon, do you suppose you could help me find James Whelan's telephone number?" He's offered to help me take care of something before the wedding."

"Of course, Lenore. It's up in my bedroom."

"Would you mind bringing it down? And fetch my good stationery too. I've some correspondence I must get into the mail right away."

# TWENTY-SEVEN

Sabina snuggled deeper into her cot, watching the rain decorate the window with its long, yawning drops. Outside the sky stormed. Wind off the ocean swept the tree limbs backward and sideways, revealing the silver undersides of the leaves.

Since learning about the Sea Rovers dive class in Boston, she'd asked for and received permission to cover the night shift: fielding calls from the Ground Observers; plotting airplanes on the Plexiglas. She'd expected Captain Ford to make a fuss about the change, but when she told him what she'd be doing every morning, he actually didn't holler. Instead he'd given her a hard chuck on the arm and a nodding "atta girl," which she took to be approving.

"Knock, knock! Sugar report!" This was Bev's standard greeting with the daily mail run. The girl had mellowed toward Sabina—not unlike a chary housecat coming 'round to new guests; not unlike Captain Ford, for that matter—since their first meeting in Building Eight. Bev poked her head out from behind a wooden carton marked PERISHABLE.

"It's another carton of beans from your boyfriend." Bev deposited the package on her colleague's desk.

"He's not my boyfriend."

"No wonder. Maybe he ought to try sending chocolates."

"He ought to try explaining himself."

"Oh, honey." Bev rolled her eyes, helping herself to chew a slender bean. "They never can. You going to write him back? Thank him for the beans?"

"I don't miss him *that* much," Sabina frowned.

"But you do miss him some, don't you?"

"It's a long story. What else did I get?"

"Just this." Bev tossed her an envelope of fine ivory linen. Sabina noticed the Edgartown post office box. She recognized Lenore's monogrammed wax seal and impatient cursive scrawl. She tore it open, reading aloud:

*Dear Sabina,*

*I'm sorry we quarreled, and over something so silly! I hope you're still planning to attend the wedding. To prove no hard feelings, I've saved you a seat next to my best cousin, Phillip. Remember his dimples?*

*More to the point, I walked into quite a tempest at the club last week. Everyone arguing the Katama Bridge, and now the paper asking for expert opinions besides. They haven't got a single soul to champion the nay vote. I suppose most people are afraid to say "boo" to Daddy. Gosh, I hope you won't mind . . . I went and mentioned your name to the shellfish constable yesterday, given all that ecology business you're always spouting. I'll bet you're the only "expert" pretty enough to keep folks from falling asleep at Town Meeting. And the constable says he'd be awfully glad to get a woman's perspective. Think it over, anyway?*

*Yours in friendship,*

*Lenore*

Along with this note, Lenore had enclosed a clipping from the newspaper.

**DEBATE RAGES OVER PROPOSED CHAPPY BRIDGE. STRESS-STRAIN ANALYSIS TURNS UP PLENTY OF BOTH AMONG ISLAND FISHERMEN**

> EDGARTOWN, July 17—Twenty-five members of the Chappaquiddick Island Association took part in a demonstration last night, promoting an unfavorable stance toward Article One on the Town Warrant, which comes before voters next month. The article proposes $300,000 for the construction of a two-lane bridge, roughly five hundred feet in length, twenty-four feet wide between curbings, designed to permanently conjoin Edgartown and Chappy. The Finance Committee has gone on record as wanting the bridge plans postponed. The shellfish constable and scores of island scallopers are likewise demanding a feasibility commission to research scalloping impacts. Voters from the town of Edgartown, inclusive of Chappaquiddick, are reminded to meet at the Old Whaling Church, on the twenty-second day of August, at eleven o'clock in the forenoon. Speakers with knowledge of any potential impact are asked to share their views . . .
>
> *BRIDGE cont. page 3.*

Sabina crumpled Lenore's supposed peace offering and threw the resulting ball into her wastepaper basket.

"Bev?" she asked. "Do you ever wonder what you ought to be doing next?"

"No." Bev cocked her head, puzzled. "I keep a calendar in my diary. That way I don't have to wonder. They sell them in town, at the drugstore, if you need a bit of help staying organized."

"That's not what I mean," Sabina sighed. "I'm talking about life. Where you belong. Where *I* belong."

"You know, Sal," Beverly volunteered, a tangle of beans now puffing out her cheek. "When I first met you, I had the awfulest feeling you'd be another barmy birdbrain—the type of slouch they usually send to us from Miss Arthur's Business School for Girls. But you're all right, you know? You're an okay girl. The boys at college are going to see that about you."

"There won't be any boys," Sabina mused. "Not where I'm going."

Bev moved to sit on the edge on Sabina's cot. Her teeth crunched green beans in between sentences. "Oh. Headed off to join the Seven Sisters, are you? Smith? Holyoke?"

"Finishing school. Switzerland."

"Real blue bloods, huh?"

"That's the thing. I'd be miserable," Sabina confessed. "Learning how to reprimand the maid. How to address foreign dignitaries. Which school did you go to?"

"Miss Arthur's Business School for Girls."

Sabina smiled. "Did you like it there?"

"Better than the room at home I shared with two toddlers and an infant." Bev shrugged. "I think it was an all right choice."

"I haven't got any toddlers at home. Or any choices, for that matter. Apart from Weston College or the Institut Alpin Montreux." Sabina spoke the name of Poppy's prescribed Swiss finishing school in her snobbiest French.

"Where would you rather be going?"

"Honestly, I don't know. I always supposed college would open new doors for me all by itself. But I'm starting to wonder if I oughtn't stop to decide which doors I want to have opened in the first place."

"Well, look, what are you interested in?"

"Oh, I don't know. Birds and fish. The trees. The different blues that make up the ocean."

Bev sniffed. "Are you joking?"

"No."

"Oh. Well, say, you could teach biology."

"Not teaching." Sabina shook her head, imagining how her aunt would make merry of such a perfectly traditional choice. "I haven't the right disposition for it."

"You could be a painter!" Bev snapped. "Specialize in ocean landscapes and natural scenes."

Sabina made a doubtful face. "I'm no more artistic than Miss Arthur."

"A laboratory scientist, then? With a microscope and a little white coat?"

"Maybe. I *do* like the idea of digging into a problem. Trying to unpuzzle a thing—a *real* thing people need to know about. But then I get so tired of classrooms. The constant indoors."

"So . . . ?"

Sabina broke out in a wide grin. "Can I tell you something, Bev? What I'd really like to do?"

"Sure. What's stopping you?" Bev reached for more beans.

"Well, it's . . . it's a new idea. I don't know an awful lot about this course of study—"

"Just come out with it, already! I won't laugh. Honest. What's the big dream? You want to be an astronaut or something?"

"Just the opposite." Sabina's eyes lit up.

Bev tried to do the calculation in her head. "A coal miner?"

"I want to be a research diver."

"Come again?"

"*You know* the sort of men I mean. You've seen them. The divers! They wear those dark slick suits and the tanks on their backs. Why, you told me they were hunting for shipwrecks. But it turns out they're listening for clams—finding newer, bigger beds so the same old stocks don't get overfished."

"Oh!" Bev jumped to her feet. "The frogmen!"

"I'm already an excellent skin diver. All I need now is a little practice on the equipment. It's called an Aqua-Lung. A new friend of mine, a Mr. Malcolm Lambert—he happens to know the sport quite well. How to breathe correctly through the mouthpiece without exploding your lungs—"

"*This* is what you want to do instead of college?"

"You promised you wouldn't laugh."

"I'm not laughing," Bev contested, hiding her smirk behind her hand. "It's just, how on earth would you ever square the idea with your folks? Nothing too manicured about a girl in a rubber suit."

"I'd have to show them why that sort of work interested me, I suppose. Why it *mattered*."

"Maybe you could invite the head frogman over for dinner. You know, to explain it?"

"Or maybe . . ." Sabina stood to retrieve the crumpled newspaper clipping from her wastepaper basket. She smoothed it out against the room's cinderblock wall. She reread the update on Dooley's bridge proposal in Chappaquiddick, tracing the call for expert guest speakers. "Or maybe," Sabina waved the scrap of paper, "maybe I could explain it all on my own."

# TWENTY-EIGHT

"Stay the night," Isolde entreated. The bedsheet decorated her neck like an enormous scarf.

"I can't." Harris dressed in the dark. "I've got to get the jeep back across the spit before the tide comes in."

"Must you really?"

"Isolde, I can't control the heavens. You live on an island. As of yet without a bridge."

And it was true. She did live on an island without a bridge. Baker had finished her paved road, from point to parcel, so that each end blunted, acontextually, against the buff periphery of continental sand—and then water, on either end. A road to nowhere.

"You know," she said to Harris, sitting up on her elbow, "I'm beginning to think you turn into a pumpkin at midnight."

"That's a woman's trick if ever there was one. Looking the part just long enough to get her own way. Promptly turning into something else when it suits her. *Me?*" he crowed. "I am always myself."

"Yes," she reached for his wrist, kissing up and down his woolly arm, "except for when you're my surgeon." They had this little farce between them. A way for her to summon Harris from his public affairs, when he dined in the city or went away on long trips. She'd dial up his restaurant or resort, demanding the esteemed surgeon be delivered to the telephone at once. "Tell me, doctor. What shall I wear to the gala?"

"Which gala?"

"Your wife's event for Homestead. I've been asked to say a few words."

Predictably, Harris stirred himself up to a fighting pitch. "God Almighty. You can't possibly be going."

"I was invited."

"Sometimes I think you'll do anything for a line of print."

"I was *invited*," Isolde insisted.

"*I'm* invited to a great many places, my dear. But you'll notice I don't go about accepting every silly request. Particularly not when the organizers are intent on jeering me."

"I've crossed paths with your wife before. She never jeers."

"She plays a smooth game, but believe me, she's jeering."

"Then why did she invite me to speak at her benefit?"

"To watch you turn into a pumpkin, I suspect."

"I am a socially prominent person, Harry, uniquely poised to help the less fortunate."

"Forgive me for saying so, but I don't think your philanthropy is anything close to what's most *prominent* about you."

Isolde gathered the sheets about her shoulders. "You're a bully."

"And you, my dear," he softened his tone, "are a brilliant performer. In all productions and venues." He collapsed backward into bed, pressing his mouth to her ear. "Speaking to lines of print, I wonder if you were you able to secure that interview with *Look* magazine? Talking up your home on the island? The bridge and so forth?"

Isolde gaped. "*No!* No, I wasn't, as a matter of fact. And honestly, all this campaigning over one lousy bridge. Why doesn't Bill Dooley just sell the damned place?"

"I expect he's into it for more than it's worth at this point."

Her pencil-drawn eyebrow went up. "I know the feeling exactly."

"There's that trademark charm. From princess to pumpkin in sixty seconds flat. Must be midnight."

She threw herself across the mattress, landing her face into a pillow. She choked out a few tortured sobs before lifting her head to gauge the effect. He couldn't be talked into staying, or else he'd have lit another cigarette. "You know," she sighed, "some people *have* to reinvent themselves in order to survive in this terrible world."

"That's true." Harris stood at her bedside, looking down at her. "And some people . . ." He twirled the keys to his borrowed jeep, assessing the dark interior of her reclaimed cottage. She followed his attenuating gaze, his tacit judgment of her house, her clothes, her life. "And *some* people, I suspect, would sooner die than occupy the same reality two days straight."

# TWENTY-NINE

"Air Defense, go ahead." Sabina jolted awake at the sound of the telephone. Her wristwatch showed ten thirty. She must have nodded off.

"This is postcode RJ 485, Haverhill, Massachusetts, calling to report an aircraft flash."

"All right," she acknowledged calmly, just as the afternoon girls had demonstrated. "Proceed."

Initially, the airbase night shift had appeared nothing more than standard reception work. She sat beside a telephone and waited for it to ring. Now that it finally had, her interest was piqued.

"One aircraft observed. Bi-motor. Unknown altitude. Flying southwest," a serious young voice reported. Sabina could hear clattering sounds and muffled cursing in the background.

"Check, thank you," she replied.

"It's one of ours. Not theirs," the young observer ventured. "I know my models, ma'am."

She'd already referenced the Department of Transport's local flight plan log and confirmed this Piper Apache was right on course to Philadelphia. "Yes, I can see him on the DOT AMIS. He's expected."

"Delay two minutes. Apologies there, ma'am. We're on a party line up here. Mrs. Higginbotham is sometimes real slow about getting off with her sister." The young man cleared his throat. "Post again is Romeo Juliet four eight five."

"Check, thank you, RJ four eight five," Sabina assured him. "I got that. Everything all right up there? Sounds like a bit of a ruckus."

"Don't mind my co-observer, well, my kid brother, actually. He knocked over the cribbage table, is all. Don't let us keep you, ma'am."

"RJ 485, exactly how old *are* you?" Sabina tried to hide the smile from her voice.

"Ma'am?"

"I'm sorry, it's just you sound awfully young to be manning a Skywatch post at this hour."

"I'm twelve years old, ma'am. But please don't doubt my ability. I can tell aircraft by sound, better than anyone in town. It's why I work nights."

"And your brother?

"Oh, he's new to spotting. Still studying our recognition models at home. But he's improving, I'd say."

"And you don't mind being alone in that tower after dark?"

"No, ma'am," the boy answered emphatically. "Ma says we can volunteer until school starts back up again. We intend to be ready if any Reds fly over. No Russkies bombing Boston on our watch. Well, not unless they make a go of it after August, that is."

"Yes, well, don't go nodding off up there, will you?"

"Fall asleep? No, ma'am. Finn and I, we skipped dinner tonight. Hard to get drowsy on an empty stomach."

"I see. And when will you be off duty?"

"Twenty-three hundred, ma'am."

Sabina disconnected the line, plotted the flight's approximate coordinates on the Plexiglas. She looked around the room to see who else might notice. Lucille sat filing her nails. Rhoda was nose-deep in a copy of McCall's. Without overthinking, she picked up the receiver and telephoned the operator for the sheriff's office in Haverhill, Massachusetts.

"Haverhill police station," answered the dispatcher.

"Good evening, sir. I just wanted to let you know there are two young boys in your GOC tower tonight. Doing a fine job, I might add."

“Oh, sure, don’t I know it. The Trombley kids.”

“Would it be too much trouble to send someone over with some hamburgers? Before twenty-three hundred? They’ll be finishing their shift just about then, and they haven’t had any supper.”

“Hamburgers, did you say?”

“Yes. That’s right. It’s a request from the North Truro GCI.” Sabina held her breath for a moment. She had no authority to command police officers. No authority to do anything, really. And yet, her brief time at the base had taught her one thing very clearly: The Truro installation was an important place. Just by dint of being there, she was pocketing a little portion of consequence every day.

“Roger that, GCI. Wilco. Hamburgers are on the way. Over and out.”

# THIRTY

Isolde shook, praying for sleep. On her separate island, nighttime lasted an eternity. The electrical connections proved spotty. The cottage often blinked and went dark with just the scantest shiver of wind. More than once she awoke to an unknown hour, heart racing, disoriented, trapped inside a spiraling panic. The sugar of her white wine diet hummed through her veins, which rose and stretched along the backs of her hands like plump blue night crawlers.

She so wished Harris would have stayed, and she resolved to eat healthful things starting at daybreak. Meanwhile, she tore through her pill bag in search of something quieting. After a few minutes of waiting with no obvious effect, she felt justified in dialing his number. *If he answers the phone, then I'll convince him to rescue me.*

"Yes?"

"Can you come over?"

"Isolde?" Colin Hatch sounded confused. She tried to read into his tone beyond those passive syllables. Was there a trace of happiness? A flickering note of attraction trailing the hard consonant of her name?

"I need help, Colin. I think I'm ill."

"What's the matter with you?"

"I can't sleep."

"That's not an illness."

"My body is weak."

"At this time of night, so's mine."

The truth was, she sometimes heard her heart leaving out beats. Other times, on the verge of sleep, that same fickle organ would drill her chest wall with a seismic burst, accompanied by the blinding white light of a morgue. She often suspected she was dying.

"You ought to come check on me."

"Isolde," Hatch leveled, his voice dipped in and out of a yawn. "You live on an island."

"And why must everyone keep *harping* on it, too?"

Hatch said nothing, though she could hear his calm breathing.

"You own a boat, don't you?"

"It's a sailboat, not a magic carpet."

The glow of her kerosene lamp cast odd shadows across the floor. A rove beetle scrambled through the slanted light and Isolde screamed in honest fear, jolting Hatch completely awake on the other end of the phone.

"What happened?"

"I can't stay here alone. I'll simply die!"

Outside, Isolde's small kettle pond lay bathed in moonlight. From her crumpled pose beneath the sheets she could see its silver water—underfed by the summer's sporadic rains—where prehistoric boulders halfway revealed themselves like the backs of giant beasts, long ago plucked up and carried by a vast glacial moraine. Now they rested uneasily here, waiting for the heavens to blanket them properly. To make some suitable recompense.

"All right, let me see what I can do."

Hours later, with the dawning light, she awoke and she found him there. Asleep in the rocker on the front porch. He hadn't bothered to wake her, apparently. His head rested on his broad shoulder. His lips blew out small, invisible candles. His chest rose and sank, like a skiff on a slow-rolling tide. She pressed her palm flush against it. Her pilot.

Through his shirt, she felt a folded mass of paper nestled inside his breast pocket. Carefully, she extracted the ruled pages—ink-smeared and scratched over. At her elbow, Colin stirred, and she lurched to hide her trespass beneath a loose bit of cottage shingle.

"Good morning, Captain." Isolde spoke quietly, touching his shoulder to wake him.

"What's that?" Colin Hatch came to consciousness with an instant readiness. He stretched his eyes open wide and shook his head. "You all right?"

"Naturally, by *now* I am."

"Wonderful." He stood from the chair. "Glad I could help."

"Oh, don't go yet," Isolde petitioned. "Please?" She had realized, with the dawning light, that riding beside him in the small airplane every few days was not just a pleasant thing; it offered a dose of his calm and his strength that she very much needed. In his airplane her eyes would pore over the skin of his neck, the neat angles of his regulation burr cut, the width of his shoulders, the way his hands played across the instrument panel no less remarkably than the pianists she'd known at Ciro's. She would lean sideways, asking to know what each knob did, why he was adjusting it in just such a way. She would touch his arm and feel anchored by extension—even thousands of feet in the air.

"I can't stay." He checked his watch. "I borrowed Doc Kemp's launch to get here. And he wasn't awake for me to ask him, so ought to be getting it back by now."

"Let me make you some coffee."

"How fast can you be?"

She flashed a cover girl smile. All at once they both took notice of her mint peignoir—its thin, filmy cover accomplishing no cover at all.

"As fast as you like."

"All right then." He relented, patting his pocket for a cigarette.

"Why do you suppose people these days are so mad to live near the ocean?" she called to Colin from the kitchen. She pressed two cold spoons from the icebox just below the hollows of her eyes—a Hollywood trick to wake up the face.

"My guess? It's the bikinis."

"Do you want to know what I think?" She poured his coffee into one of her inherited mugs. "I think it's greed. A kind of sensory greed. Men are like children who've never been disciplined into choice. So they can't ever decide. Do they want land or sea? The chicken or the fish? The filet or the caviar? And the answer is: They want it all. To see it all. To *taste* it all. They want to do everything except declare themselves. That's why restaurants invented surf and turf, actually."

"Is that why you came to Chappy?" Hatch sipped at the steaming coffee she'd delivered. "Couldn't decide between a chicken and a fish?"

Isolde touched her hair. This morning it sat nested atop her head, between the X of two gold kanzashi sticks. A curtain of baby-blonde ringlets evaded the pile; these trembled about her suntanned neck. She found herself twisting and tugging the errant locks just to keep from outright falling into Colin Hatch's warm arms.

It was true, though; she couldn't decide what she wanted. Lately, at night, she'd taken to posing under the covers with both hands jammed beneath the weight of her head on the pillow. The desired effect was to achieve, in them, a certain deadness. With enough time, the pins and needles gave way to deeper sleep. Her hands numbed into heavy, foreign palms and fingers while her head dreamed solidly of nothing she remembered. And when she woke—stingingly without feeling—she would put the cold, alien plants to her face, down her neck, across her chest. When she woke, the hands belonged to someone else. To Harris. To Hatch. To Hitchcock, even. And for those fleeting moments of senselessness, she had no real control of them. No possible idea what they wanted to do.

"Yes, I suppose so," she admitted. "Maybe I'm rather like a man in that way. Maybe I've studied all their vile characters too well."

"Not all men are villains. You ought to rethink the company you keep."

"I have." She touched his chin. "That's why I telephoned you."

Hatch raised his palms in firm absolution. "Oh, no, 'fraid not. I fly airplanes. That's about the scope of my professional service. I'm no good solving matters of the heart."

"Aren't you though?" The actress leaned toward him, aware of how her nightgown clung sheerly to her body. She took up the pilot's hand and pressed it to her chest, to the true ribs mounding the skin beneath her clavicle. He didn't pull away. "Just feel what wonders you've done for mine."

"You're welcome."

"I think you've brought it back to working order, in fact."

Colin extracted himself. He studied his watch again. "I really should be going. Do you mind if I take your bike back to the boat?"

"Go ahead. But come back and save me again tonight." Isolde sat down on his lap. "I'll make you dinner."

"Can't. Card game in town."

"Then I'll go with you!"

"It's not that sort of card game, I'm afraid."

"Not what sort?"

"Civilized." He grinned and helped them both up to their feet. They stood watching the sun spread fresh light across the grass, the beach roses, the end of the pitch-dark road. Dooley's orange-topped marking stakes formed a connect-the-dots border along the better half of Isolde's ocean view. "Besides"—he nudged her arm lightly—"you've got work to do."

"Oh, what now? Rehearsing my tired old milkmaid lines?"

"Nope," he said, commandeering her Lambretta, kicking up the pin of its side stand. "*Deciding.*"

Isolde watched the moped and its rider grow small against the horizon. She stood watching until their melded form had disappeared, and eventually the sound of the buzzing engine faded to silence as well. She pulled the stolen pages from beneath her cottage shingle, turning them over in her hands. *Deciding.*

*Dear Sabina,*

*~~I borrowed a book~~ I happened to be reading a book about the natural world tonight, and I came across a detail that reminded me of*

*you. Did you know, by chance, that the largest meteorite crater in the world is about 1,350 feet deep, with a rim that runs seven and a half miles around? It's in Canada. Someplace called Ungava. And do you know how they discovered it? It was from an airplane.*

*I'll admit I don't know much about meteorites. And I'm not an ace at letter writing either. I bet you could guess that much. But I know something about ~~suffering a hole in your heart~~ all the things a person can see from the sky. I was wondering if you'd reconsider your embargo on flying. Your embargo on me, actually. I'm ready to explain my trouble from the war. I'm definitely ready to see your face. What do you say?*

*Yours in every little detail,*

*Colin*

Isolde took the letter and two blue pills back to her bed. She lay folding it, unfolding it, dangling it from the sill of her open window, where an easterly wind blew bound for Muskeget. At once she loved and hated the affection it contained. She stared dumbly at his name—at the girl's name—until all the words blurred before her drowsing eyes. This newest sedative delivered the pleasant effect of tucking her in, arms and legs overcome by a kind of quiet immobility, while her head drifted lightly along a gentle train of thoughts.

In time she fell back to sleep, her face warmed by a streak of morning light, clutching a stolen piece of the pilot, his signature pressed to her heart. His postscript—barely legible—mapped out a tactical pilotage chart she'd been too woozy to decode. But the story was there—the very story of his blue ticket—penned in military shorthand and an invented symbology, across a sloppy sketch of the Italian Alps. With a sober read, she might have understood something of the significance, but just now, from her limp and tingling hands, she let the words swim away: Colin Hatch's signed confession.

# THIRTY-ONE

"Okay, the game is four flusher. Crisscross. Spades two and three," Denny announced.

"This is six low, right?"

"No, this is Sunday-night rules. If you tie the high, you're out."

"Are we playing wheel on this?"

"Shut up, Roger. King bets."

"Raise a buck."

"Here's your buck, plus another half a buck."

"Very nice." Windsor whistled. "Very nice."

"You give everybody low cards but me. Why is that, Dennis?"

"Are you in or are you out?" Roger barked, cigar dangling.

"I'm *thinking*," whined Ellie, short for Walter Ellington. Ellie squeezed his eyes shut as though the effort pained him.

"If he's thinking, he's as good as out."

"All right, I'm out." Ellie folded.

"What'd I tell ya?"

The back room of the yacht club was a small, pine-paneled den with the card table at its center and a miniature refrigerator parked in the corner of the checkered floor. The boys chopped the pot to maintain funds for their beer supply, parceling a bit of their winnings each hand into wooden peanut bowls on the bar. This ensured they had enough Blue Ribbon and sunflower seeds to last a four- or five-hour game, which was not unusual on a Sunday night, even as the chore of the coming workday loomed closer and closer on the horizon.

As it functioned something like a part-time fraternity house, the boys referred to this space as the "goat room" and had even hung a makeshift Greek banner outside its wide picture window, through which a breeze helped to temper the summer heat. Nighttime winds carried the sounds of late-night cruisers on the water: laughter, song, awestruck whistles aimed at the glorious falling stars.

"Raise."

"Of course he's gotta raise."

"Babe's out."

"What's a matter, Babe? You don't want that ugly reject nine?"

"Oh my God, look at all the *sevens*."

"I'm gone."

"I'm with him."

"Flush."

"Of course he's got a flush!"

"You racing at the regatta?" Windsor Crawford turned to address Denny as he dealt the next hand. Windsor was born the great-grandson of someone important—important by Edgartown standards—which conferred, on the island at least, tacit permission to nudge all boundaries of common decency. He was friendly with the club boys from their shared years at prep school and also from many, many summers together spent harassing city girls on the beach—usually by depositing a dead goosefish on one's towel.

"Pot's right."

"Nice pot. Let's see if I get sandbagged again."

"Diamonds now . . . No help . . ."

"Not this year," Denny answered Windsor, straightening the five towers of chips at his wrists. "I'm bringing Gretchen out to the island. She's never been."

"This is the tall skirt from your office?"

Denny nodded. "She works in the building."

"Crew for me, will ya, Dennis? Your girl won't mind."

"Nah, I want to show her the race."

"That's not all he wants to show her," Shreve added, looking Denny straight in the eye. "Anyhow, don't bother asking McTigue for any favors. He'll give you a homily before he lends you any hand."

"Ouch."

"Raise."

"Ace."

"Buck."

"Who's turn?"

"Someone wake me up when he's ready to play cards, please."

"You know, I've half a mind to slug you, John." Denny threw a chip.

"That's just what it'd take too." Shreve winked, cracking a new beer. "Half a mind. To start a scrap with me, choirboy."

"Is Sabina coming home for the regatta?" Colin Hatch broke into their standoff, trying to sound blasé about his interests, Denny judged. Not very well succeeding. "Coming back to the island, I mean?"

"I'm not sure."

"Anyhow, this Gretchen must really be something," Windsor ventured from behind his curled hand. "Sure got you pressed to earn that pilot's license."

"We've got clubs now!"

"No raise?"

"Next victim, please."

"Hey, I've met her. And that ain't all she's got pressed." Shreve whistled. "Talk about two herring barrels."

"Is she marriage material?"

"She's *material* anyway."

Denny stood up from the table. He was about to end this bull session with finality when a low, rhythmic chanting drew all the boys' attention outside. The game scudded to a halt. Through the window, above the water, the sky glowed eggshell pink. Sailboats bobbed in black silhouette. A shadowy gang of passengers could be seen disembarking from the planks of George Mattos's inbound scow.

"Now here's a motley crew for you," Shreve said sneering, craning his neck for a better view.

"It's the Island Association. The Chappy crowd." Windsor spoke the name of the little island derisively.

Even in the pinkish-purple light of the evening, as they trooped up Mayhew Hill, it was plain to see they came from a separate place. Their clothes were all wrong for Edgartown. The women's hair too fussily arranged, the curls done up too tight. The men, looking pinned inside their suits, carried the requisite homburgs on their heads but too high, gutter crowns tilted at wrong angles.

"They're all in a lather about that dammed bridge. Going picketing at the movie theater tonight."

"What bridge?" Ellie looked up from his cards. "Who's picketing?"

"Dooley's bridge. Don't you ever read the papers?"

"The funny papers, he reads."

"That bridge better get passed." Windsor spit a seed out the window. "I've got ten acres at Toms Neck doing nothing but depreciating. Dooley's right to put a proper road in. Can't build much more than a sandcastle on Chappy without one."

"My father's got shares in Wasque. That means guaranteed interest *and* a piece of the pie when those apartment houses sell."

"Long as the bridge vote passes."

"Hey, you know what, Professor? *We* all took a vote just now, and we think you should make a bet sometime this evening."

"And here I thought this was a friendly game." Roger shook his head.

"No friends among enemies."

"It's two dollars to raise. You buying Ellie Mae?"

"Say, Denny, they teach you how to bail from that airplane? You know, with a parachute and all?"

"I'm not joining the paratroopers, Ellie."

"Still, you never know when you might need to bail. Isn't that right, Hatch? Smart guy always has an escape route. Emergency window, trap door—"

"Would that we had a trap door under your chair right now. Are you *buying in* or what?"

Outside, the crowd of picketers gained ground. They passed the clubhouse in a mob of two dozen, toting wooden signs and American flags, marching the inclined route to Main Street, toward the Old Whaling Church, where all town warrants were debated and decided.

"An early wedding present for you, Shreve." Roger followed Ellie's bet, dealing a queen on the turn.

"Thanks, but no thanks. Another lady can't help me."

"Funny thing. I hear some ladies are keeping their own names these days. After they get married. You fellas hear that?"

"Why should they bother taking a guy's name once they've taken everything else he's got? His checkbook, his opinions—"

"His will to live." Shreve spat a seed.

"A real fine way to talk before your wedding," Denny leveled across the table.

"Sorry, McTigue. I forgot you were acting defense counsel for the bride."

"I think our friend Mr. Shreve would also like some of that bail-out training." Windsor cracked a new beer. "Can you help him, Hatch? Sounds like we have a jumper."

"I've got my outs," Shreve muttered. "Don't you worry. No thanks to anyone at this table."

"All right, all right. Your attention please, gentlemen," Roger shouted over the din, tossing fresh cards. "The game is now seven-card stud. *With a pin*. And this time you have to throw something away."

# THIRTY-TWO

"Some good news and some bad news, my boy." Bill Dooley picked his teeth with a putty knife, pacing the floor in an unnerving way.

"Better than no news, I suppose." Colin sawed without looking up. He hadn't intended on starting another project. Last thing he needed, really. But the floor of his seed shed was crumbling with rot from where the rainwater kept pooling behind the door. The last time he ran the wheelbarrow over, his brogan crashed clean through, sinking into the earth between the joists. So it needed doing. Just like everywhere else his eyes landed, the shed now needed his attention.

"You're angry I haven't called." Bill made a make-pretend sorry face. "Look, if that's what's eating you, you'll have to get in line behind my wife. Ha!"

"I'm angry that I trusted you. Here I am, flying the actress around, on top of your board meeting trips, on top of your Saratoga trips. I can't catch up on the harvest, and there's still no information from Italy." Hatch flexed his shoulder into the motion of the saw. Today was the first day in a week that'd actually belonged to him. Until Bill dropped by, he'd been working to make it count, starting first with cleaning the chicks' litter, spreading their green feed. Next he'd sown the seeds for the fall crop: Big Boston, kale, radish. He'd already cut five bushels of sweet corn. Treated the springers on the shed ramp with a coat of hot creosote. And now, tending to the floorboard, while Bill insisted on pacing.

"All right, all right. Keep your culottes on, Mabel. I did say *some* good news." Bill opened his briefcase to produce a large envelope. "Take a look at this."

Hatch set down his saw. He dried his palms on a rag. He read the investigator's report—twice.

"And?" he said finally.

"*And* what?"

"Where's the photo?"

"What photo?"

"This letter says he's enclosed a photo."

Dooley shook the envelope upside down. Poked one eye into its opening. "Must have slipped out."

"Jesus, Bill. You *lost* it? How do we know it's even her, then? This 'courier' from Abruzzo could be anyone."

"No worry. I can send for another copy."

"He's not going to send you *another copy* until you pay him. Did you pay him?" Hatch took in a deep breath.

"Pay who?"

"The investigator! He's asking for his money. Did you pay him?"

"I wired something over, yes. Of course I did. Naturally, I *paid* him. But don't worry about what *I'm* doing. Your job is to keep Isolde happy."

Hatch fumed. Another bad bargain. Why hadn't he told Bill there was nothing to find in Italy? Why hadn't he told himself? Adele was gone. For all he knew, for all *anyone* knew, the poor thing really was lost to the world. It was silly to think otherwise, and now he'd wasted half the summer chasing a ghost.

If he'd been true to himself—truly holding a hope—he ought to have gone back to Italy on his own. Never mind sending some *investigatore* twice removed. He ought to have tried again, like he promised he would. If all else fell apart, a reunion in Pisa had been their plan. Before she'd gone off, before his blue ticket, if it all went south they'd agreed to reunite on the feast of Saint Anthony. At the baptistery—a place where a person's sung notes echoed and carried on for so long it was said that one man could harmonize with himself, all alone, inside the dome.

But after his discharge back home, it would have been impossible. Would she have understood that? He didn't know.

And so coming home disgraced had felt like a compound loss. For a long time Hatch just watched the world go by. Didn't feel qualified to say or do very much of anything. Someone told him they needed farm labor in Maine. Orchard owners up that way took in ex-GIs of all stripes and never asked why they'd been kicked out of camp or couldn't reenlist. So that was where he landed.

When his mother passed, he took the inheritance and escaped to the Vineyard, reasoning that an island—a life lived in the suspense—could ensure maximum distance between the separate chapters of his past. To keep the facts from eating at his pride, he pushed them off into the periphery. Left physical placeholders where the answers to important, self-examining questions should have gone. He bought two beds for the bedroom. Two dressers. A standup Sunbeam Mixmaster, even—for cakes or pies—hell, he didn't know what for. He left half his closet empty. None of it was for Adele. But the *idea* of her—he had to make space for that.

Meanwhile, his trees and vines didn't bear fruit right away. He needed tools, equipment, and constant repairs for the pretty house that met the sunrise on the hill. That drove him to Katama, looking for pilot work, where he'd run into Dooley chewing out some clod with a charter plane. Three beers later they were planning their own company—Dooley's company, by rights, but craftily established under Hatch's name. They'd sat at the club bar sorting through his farm papers and personal finances like fine old chums. They signed a contract loan for no small amount. They made a deal. At the time, it didn't seem half bad.

That day, he remembered, his chest had swelled with the air of something different. Not altogether rosy and gay, but different. Raised eyebrows at the bank and later, at the yacht club, still complicated his path. But it got easier. He understood most people looked at his life and saw the obvious absence of a wife. He didn't disagree, and yet he didn't dwell. Why should he dwell? He'd made it home alive. All he could do was wonder if Adele had been so lucky.

"I can see you're busy," Dooley elbowed into Hatch's thoughts, swinging his stingy brim fedora in a way that suggested departure. "And if you don't mind, I've just got one more favor to ask."

"No." Hatch frowned. "How's that for a firm hand?"

"That's good! That's very good. Passed the test. No, but do be serious, now. If I'm going to wire these Italians more money—"

"I thought you said you already *had* sent the money."

"I *did*." Bill Dooley crashed his hat against his thigh, exasperated. "Naturally, I have. But if I'm going to be at peace with *having done* so, I mean to say, I do need just a bit more buy-in from you."

"I'm not in the market for oceanfront property, Bill."

"It's not that." Dooley shook his head. "It's our old clients, the Norwegians. They're coming here for the regatta, you see. And I was hoping you could bring them out to the Point, maybe with Isolde along for the ride. Show them all a nice time?"

"Why can't you bring them out?"

"I'm away that weekend. Prospecting."

"Prospecting ponies, more like."

"It's all green money. Don't act like you care where it comes from."

"So now I'm also meant to be your harbor cruise guide? Is that it?"

"You're meant to find that old sweetheart from the war," Dooley smiled. "This is just a small part of the process."

"Colin!" Florence called down from the garage, interrupting the men's exchange. "Long-distance telephone call for you in here. It's New *Yawk*. That woman."

"What woman?"

"The one with the jumbo front porch," Dooley suggested with a smirk. Colin had forgotten the developer was still standing there. "Say, Hatch, I'll bet whatever's in my pocket against whatever's in yours that our friend Isolde could hold up a nine iron without using any hands."

Hatch threw his associate a disapproving look. "Take a message," he yelled up to Florence, kicking at the dirt.

"Got a prow like the *Queen Mary*, boy oh boy, that one does." Bill relished the thought.

Hatch cut him off. "Are you all finished here?"

"I'll show myself out. But look, let me put the Norwegians in touch with Florence. Just so I guess that's all taken care of. And listen, Hatch, don't be a stranger at the club. If I get any more news, I mean, when I hear more news about your girl, you can buy me that beer you owe me."

Hatch wiped the sting of sweat from his eyes. Allowed himself a momentary break on his tailgate while Dooley hobbled up the drive. Florence passed him on her way down the gravel footpath, collapsing as she reached the old wood slat bench. She moaned at the strain of bending, reaching to loosen her shoelaces.

"I'll be mighty glad when this season's through."

"Why's that?" Hatch smiled at her. "Don't tell me *you're* tired of talking on the telephone."

"It's not the job that goads me." Florence threw him a long, knowing stare. "We both know how it's been since *she* landed."

"She's all alone. You have to have some sympathy. Don't give me that face. I know. It's true, some people make their own beds. But I suppose I feel like she needs looking after."

"Hmm." Florence sniffed. She straightened the collar of her blouse. "And who's looking after *you* I wonder?"

Hatch winked. "I thought that was your job, Flo."

"I'm too old."

Hatch could see she was fighting herself not to say more. They both held their fire for a moment, taking in a merciful gust of cooler wind.

"All right then, out with it. What would you have me do?"

"None of my business, of *coss*," Florence preempted. "But I think it's a mistake the way you put off Miss McTigue."

"I write to her."

"You mail crates of cucumber. That's not the same thing."

"I tried writing a proper letter, and I left the damn thing in my shirt pocket. It went out with last week's laundry."

Florence stared at him.

"Would've been foolish to send that letter anyhow. Sabina and I have a plan to reconnect. In person. Or at least I have. Come September."

"*September?*" the old woman burst out.

"By September I'll have firm answers."

"Colin." Florence laced her fingers together in supplication. "What is it that you need an investigation to tell you? That you're a good man? That you're decent and hardworking? That the Air Corps still owes you three hundred dollars in mustering pay?"

He shook his head as if to say it wasn't as simple as all that. "All right. What about Sabina's father, then? How could I ever talk to him about a future from where I stand now?"

Florence smiled. "I wouldn't expect to find yourself in any better position. Not if you're taking Dooley at his word."

"I know how to handle Bill Dooley."

"I think he's trained you to handle him exactly as he likes. And I think—I'm sad to say it—but I think you're convinced you don't deserve anything better."

Hatch wasn't ready to own the claim. He held up his hand for an opening. "Dooley's contact over in Italy is the only way. The only way to find out if what I did—"

"Meanwhile, you leave a nice girl waiting in the dark."

"Would you feel better if I took a ride to Truro? Had a talk with Sabina in person?"

Florence rose to her feet, prompting a succession of arthritic clicks in her knees. "I'd feel better if I were twenty-five years old again. But okay, you're the boss. Go see the girl this weekend, please."

# THIRTY-THREE

Lenore Dooley checked her compact, powdered her nose, re-pinned her hat, and said a quick "Glory Be" that she would not vomit on the express train to New York City, scheduled for departure in just under one hour. She looked to her fiancé in an effort to impress upon him the time—*Is he aware of the time?*—but kept quiet for fear of betraying anything outside the manners of a casual shopping day. If she *were* going to tell J. J. the truth about where she was going, a finer time for it would have been last week, last night even. *But not now. Not*— She foraged in her bag for a bit of ginger candy and pressed her handkerchief to her lips. They were already so late.

They rode to Boston's South Station more or less in silence, past the air-cooled donut shops, through the gravelly-beach towns that linked Cape Cod to the city, now stretching into view above the morning haze. John Joseph turned his head to check her looks occasionally—as much out of concern for his Mercedes upholstery as for her comfort, she supposed. She dusted an invisible nothing from the lap of her Fred Leighton suit with the broomstick pleating. Tugged her silk-cord Movado. Gazed out the window and back to her bridegroom, wondering if she ought to tell him what this trip was all about tomorrow. Or never.

"It's going to be awfully hot in Manhattan," he volunteered, as if sensing the approach of something heavier. "I've a friend who works on Wall Street. He says sometimes the streets actually go soft in a heat like this. Pavement turns to pie dough."

"Is that right?" Lenore sat perfectly erect, modeling the picture of ladyhood, despite the bitter taste collecting at the back of her throat.

"He says the crosswalks are all polka-dotted with rubber divots pulled clean off the women's high heels. And you can't get running water inside the buildings, besides. Imagine that?"

"No water?"

"Not to the upper floors. It's neighborhood kids prying open the hydrants. Pressure's gone. All along Wall Street."

"How high up does it go?"

"What's that?" J. J. tugged at the notch of his collar. His throat looked raw from shaving in the heat.

"The wa—" She swallowed an ounce of encroaching bile.

"The wall?" J. J. stole another quick glance at her. "Honestly, Lenore," he chuckled, "it's lucky you're so pretty. There's isn't any actual *wall* on Wall Street."

"You didn't let me finish."

"I wouldn't have to let you finish if you didn't start up with silly comments in the first place."

"I was asking about the water."

"I already told you about the water. Try listening for a change. It's not difficult."

Lenore folded her hands in her lap. "It's not difficult" meant J. J. was done talking.

"It's not difficult"—a long-sung refrain, favored by the various men in her life—meant the topic at hand could be managed by any child, any fool, any old dumb Dora—herself even included.

The road test for her driver's license—no matter how many mailboxes she swiped, her father sniggered, his police sergeant friend sniggering alongside—would not be that difficult. The affair in Palm Beach, in the Shreves' poolside cabana, Easter weekend: the very event that had landed her here in the first place. She remembered J. J. kissing her neck with heightened urgency, battling her bikini's clasp, whispering above the relentless hiss of breaking waves, "Lenore, relax. It's not so difficult."

And so on and on it went. This car ride. This direction. This unstoppable current. With him two lengths ahead, while she fought to keep up.

The split-flap board switched and shuffled. "Delayed," read the status of the 9:15 to Penn Station. Lenore fanned her face and sighed. A lovely child with round eyes and strawberry hair wandered into her gaze. The girl tap-danced across the echoic floor—venturing farther and farther from the post her family occupied at the water fountain. The girl wore a brand of tatty plastic sandals also worn by her two brothers—recent acquisitions, perhaps, from a midsummer clearance sale. To Lenore she announced herself as Nell from Albany, on her way to Cape Cod, and ventured to inquire if Chatham, in fact, had any nice public beaches. Lenore was explaining all about the bay side versus the ocean side when Nell's mother swooped in to extract the girl, scolding as she went. "You mustn't pester ritzy people. In the first place, ladies like that don't care to have little children about."

Eventually the train's platform was announced. Lenore gathered her things, sweating and parched, and headed for the first open door. After passing through several cars along the corridor, she took a seat in the train's crowded dining car. She read the breakfast card and filled her order blank so robustly the waiter plainly paused to look about for some phantom companion. To evade his puzzled gaze and otherwise occupy her mind, she pulled out her favorite bit of pleasure reading. Another new letter from the investigator in Italy.

**Cliente:** *Sig. Noel Wunholm*
**Indirizzo di fatturazione:** *PO Box 897, Edgartown, MA – Stati Uniti*
**Numero del caso:** *6547*
**Investigatore:** *Pacifico Vento*

**Servizi di traduzione:** *Speak Easy Inc., Via dei Serpenti, 247 – 00184 Roma, Italia*

*Firenze, 21 luglio, 1954*

*Dear Mr. Wunholm,*

*I write to you today with great happiness to say that our team has succeeded on this most impossible quest through time. We have found her, the very girl! Adele Buontempo is alive and quite well. Enclosed you will find several recent photographs to confirm her happy fate. She has climbed a good many mountains, I can tell you. Today she is settled in a little northern town where the lakes are as blue as the sky, in a small appartamento with but one table and two chairs. She has even—in her precarious journeys—managed to save a young boy, adopted. You can see the pair together here.*

*Our guess, it seems, was correct. Your Miss Buontempo joined the Garibaldi Brigade to escape the trap of her husband's home. A mere messenger to start, she discovered some talents for concealing herself, for stamina, for courage. The notes she supplied helped the guerriglia succeed in strategic attacks against the Tedeschi. As you know, a good many key cities began to fall to us—I speak of Genoa, Turin; Alba was, for a time, its own republic. For this we must acknowledge the staffette. Italian women, you see, can clean up more than just the kitchen floor!*

*Miss Buontempo was eager to hear of your soldier and rejoiced at news of his well-being. She wished, if it might still be possible, to explain some of her doings before and since they have parted. She has drafted a letter with some details he will no doubt be seeking. And some private words, necessarily, she wished to add. Yet she remains unwilling that we should share her whereabouts, as she still lives clandestinità. I have the letter here, on my desk.*

*I daresay you could not have scripted a better ending to this nagging puzzle had you one hundred carabinieri searching the countryside with mustache combs. Imagine the skill and the service required, to have achieved it with just one man and his nephew, who is a doltish boy, besides.*

*Much as I would delight in sending you Miss Buontempo's reply today, I must regretfully redress the subject of remuneration. You have not yet paid what you promised, sir. Please remit payment in full within ten business days. I will, in turn, share the final chapter of this remarkable story.*

*Cordially,*

*Pacifico Vento*

Lenore sat stunned. She pored over these latest photographs of Colin Hatch's Adele and the child posed beside her, maybe three or four years of age. First, it was the pair of them standing on a concrete stoop. A second shot captured them setting out a meal at what must have been their one modest table and chairs. And a summertime photo. A hot day. Woman and boy splashing in a lake with a pebbly beach and a backdrop of house-dotted hills camped between thick cascades of wisteria.

This older version of Adele was still unquestionably lovely. And yet her prettiness was not where Lenore's attention came to land. *She has climbed a good many mountains . . . A town where the lakes are as blue as the sky . . . A small* appartamento . . . *Saved a young boy . . . Escaped the trap of her husband's home . . .*

Lenore reread the letter five times. She examined the photos, back and front, looking for some dashed line of print: perhaps the name of the town, the name of the boy, a blueprint for *how. How? How?* She looked around at the other passengers on the train. Like waking up from a dream, she needed a moment to establish which set of scenes was most real. She reminded herself where she'd just come from. *It's not that difficult . . .* Where she was going. *Ladies like that don't care to have little children about . . .*

Suddenly Lenore Dooley felt the scant bites of breakfast she'd managed rising to her throat. A cold sweat broke on her brow. She struggled to her feet as the train began its slow, southbound chug. The car screeched and clacked to escape the terminal. Making for the aisle, she wobbled against the escalating speed. Her seatmate offered his hand; still, she tripped over his cordovan shoes. At the aisle she grabbed the seatbacks, regained her footing, one hip pressed against a pole. Nearly heaving, she lurched toward a little depression in the wall, toward the rear of the carriage, where a taut black chain underscored the moment's blazing homophone: ALARM. Lenore's hands reached out, scrabbling for a halt. Her fingers found the communication chord. The car went black just before she pulled.

When she came to she was lying on a couch in the Amtrak administrator's office. A young woman held a compress to her forehead. A man in suspenders and a denim flat cap hovered behind.

"Look, she's awake."

"Thank heaven, she's awake. Listen, honey. You're sick. Can you hear me, honey? You fainted on the train."

Lenore lifted her head an inch off the pillow, which happened to be her own Fred Leighton jacket, rolled up like a bolster.

"Say, who can we call to come get you?

"Call over to the statehouse, please. Ask for Dennis McTigue. He'll come quickest."

# THIRTY-FOUR

*Dear Emma,*

*Can you offer any advice to a young woman who has fallen for a man with a past? I must start by explaining I am nineteen years old, intelligent, and levelheaded. Earlier this summer I found myself quite spellbound. I can't explain how or why. If I tried, I fear you wouldn't believe my claims of levelheadedness. My friends and family disapprove of the relationship. (The man is older and presents a somewhat spotty résumé.) I broke off the attachment when I learned he was asking after an old flame of his. He says the reasons for his search are rather complicated and he isn't prepared to share them with me now—maybe not ever. I've read your column, so I know you will counsel that a man never truly forgets his first love. I suppose I can't argue with that. And yet I find myself terribly lonesome and unhappy since we parted. Supposing he's sincere about finding this girl merely for answers—and not for any rekindling of their romance. Do you imagine he and I could still have a decent shot together? And if so, should I accept all the things I can't know about him?*

Sincerely,

*Pining in the Dark*
*(Sabina McTigue)*

At the sound of the train's whistle, Sabina up and ran so fast she nearly bumped the conductor off his post on the scaffold. Her class started at nine thirty and already it was—*What time is it?* A quarter past nine, and still a decent jog to the downtown YMCA. Her duffel pounded against her back as she ran. Her letter to the *Globe*'s advice columnist, Emma Dix, waved from her fist.

In the blur of the South Station crowd she flew past a pretty blonde—Lenore Dooley's twin, practically. If the young woman hadn't been so patiently engaged in conversation with a child, Sabina might have paused to take a second glance. But as it was she didn't look twice, only kept running up to street level and flying down Atlantic Avenue like the Cape's last rubythroat beating town for the winter.

"This class is closed to the public." A man with a clipboard addressed her from the white-tiled pool deck.

"But I'm not the public. I'm, well . . ." Sabina coughed at the smell of so much chlorine. "I work at Truro AFB."

"You're in the corps?" He looked doubtful.

"No. Uh, not per se. I'm a secretary. A volunteer secretary," she explained, undressing down to her swimsuit as she spoke, right there on the deck, before the instructor could say no.

"What's the trouble? Military sank all its steno pads into the ocean? They sending you down to retrieve them?"

"No." Sabina laughed to be polite. A dozen divers, already in the pool, looked on expectantly. "No, I . . . I want to be a frogman. Frog*woman*, pardon me. I'd like to train for it. With you."

"That's nice, sweetheart, but like I say. This class is closed."

"Aw, let her in, Milt," one of the divers called up from the pool. "She's got nice legs anyhow."

"Malcolm sent me!" Sabina suddenly remembered to add. "He said to tell you that Malcolm Lambert sends me, along with his most enthusiastic recommendations."

"That so? Remind me to thank him. You've got equipment?" The instructor gestured to the sack on her shoulder.

"Borrowed, sir. Yes."

"Oh, hell. Jump in."

They paired off in twos. Dive partners for the class. Not surprisingly, Sabina found herself treading next to the only other woman in the water.

"Guess we're partners," the woman smiled. She was older. Maybe in her late thirties, Sabina judged. "My name is Robin. Robin Hughes."

"From Woods Hole? The institution? Dr. Robin Hughes?"

"Have we met?"

"Oh, no, but I've read your work. I mean, I follow your work."

"You must be getting off to sleep awfully well then."

"Just the opposite. Your research is fascinating! I think I've put some to memory, actually."

"Sabina, is it?" Dr. Hughes pulled the strap of her swim cap under her chin. "If you don't mind my asking, what brings you here?"

"Two busses and a train. Which is why I'm so glad he let me in the pool after all."

"No, I'm asking, *why* are you interested in scuba diving?"

"I'm a very capable swimmer." Sabina looked about the other pairs, a little self-conscious suddenly. She lowered her voice. "And I've often thought I might like to do what you do. To report on marine life. All the ways we humans tend to muck it up. But it's been a tricky summer for me. I mean, they don't teach that sort of thing at college."

"Oh, but Sabina," Robin Hughes tilted her head, "they most certainly do. Maybe not every college. But I can tell you, at Harvard, at MIT, they most certainly do."

"I could never go to Harvard or MIT." Sabina shook a bit of water from her ears. "I just wouldn't fit there."

"And why not?"

"I'm not much for classrooms."

"And I'm not very much of a swimmer. Maybe we could help each other."

# THIRTY-FIVE

"I'm awfully glad you telephoned." Denny smiled across the table. He could feel his damned cheeks going hot and pink. Of all the dopey things to say.

"I guessed you'd be at work." Lenore checked her face in her compact mirror. "And of course the statehouse isn't too far from South Station, whereas John is—"

"Yes, I know where John is." Denny lit a cigarette, picturing the guy out sandpapering barnacles off his lousy Finn. Their waitress appeared.

"Just tea and toast, please," Lenore ordered, tugging her fingers free of her gloves.

"I'll have a malt and a hamburger. Rare."

"Oh, must you?" Lenore's pretty face went white. "My stomach—"

"Tea and toast for me also," Denny nodded, as though toast was what he'd wanted all along. "Lenore, listen. Do you suppose—I mean, once we're through eating—do you suppose I ought to take you to see a doctor?"

"I'm fine now, Denny."

"You fainted on the train, after all. You might need . . ." He reached for her hand, thought better of it, began stacking and unstacking the salt and pepper shakers instead.

"I don't need a doctor. That's the absolute last thing I need, in fact."

"Well all right." Denny looked doubtful. "We could go see a movie if you like. There's a decent matinee—a travel documentary, I guess it is—playing over at the Flick." He looked up for her reaction. "Unless that sounds too intellectual? Would you rather just go back to the island?"

"How about 1951? Back to my junior prom. Could you take me there? That was a good night, as I recall."

Denny smiled to hear her true speaking voice. Sometimes—usually at the club or one of its mixers—when Lenore Dooley spoke, she made her words go singsong and cute, like she'd drawn the Betty Hutton card in a game of Guess Who? All shoulders and eyebrows. He liked her best when she wasn't trying to act splashy for anyone.

"You wouldn't go with me then," he said quietly. "Why should anything be different now?"

"I *would* have gone with you." Lenore looked through the café's painted glass window, across the Atlantic Avenue traffic, out toward the harbor. The whir of the ceiling fan ruffled the ostrich feathers on her hat. She answered as if from someplace far away. "If only . . . if only maybe you'd been a bit more complicated or something."

"Complicated." Denny sniffed. "Is that all? And here I always thought girls went in for taller."

"Honestly, I can't go home just yet." Lenore sipped at her tea. "I'm supposed to be in Manhattan. Shopping. Say," she said, brightening. "Why not take me for a ride in your airplane? My stomach will be all right after some lunch. It always is. Aren't you parked at Logan?"

"I'm not allowed to fly solo yet." Denny added a third and a fourth heaping teaspoon of sugar to his own cup.

"You wouldn't be *solo*," Lenore took the sugar spoon from his hand. "You'd be with me, silly."

"That's not the question. I need another *pilot* to ride along still. Rules are pretty strict on that. Besides, you've gotta put in a flight plan and all. Can't just go joyriding over Boston, you know."

"Oh, Denny, is it really so impossible to break the rules now and again? Haven't you ever?"

Without thinking, Denny answered too quickly, "And that's what you like about him, isn't it? That he doesn't give a damn?"

"Him, who? *John?*"

"No, Santa Claus."

"What's got *you* so riled? I'm the one who ought to be riled. I've just made myself the spectacle of the morning commute."

These were her words, and yet she didn't look riled. She looked altogether calm, self-collected. Maybe it was seeing her outside their usual context—no familiar faces for her to follow around the room, no pertinent bits of conversation to distract her ear. But her features, too, appeared changed, now that he let himself really look at her. She wore less lipstick, maybe none at all, and still her smile seemed fuller. Her shifting blue eyes—so often difficult to take in or describe, like splices of ocean spied between houses from a fast-moving car—today they pulsed a steady, saturated hue. For once she seemed to be comfortable sitting perfectly still.

"I'm sorry. Forget I said anything."

Lenore wandered her gaze out the window again. "You know Daddy had an idea for that building over there? He says they ought to tear it down and replace it with a sky tower. All glass paneling. Windows from sidewalk to clouds, with a ballroom and an exposition center and a penthouse restaurant inside. Can you image? Fifty-something stories high—sitting and eating and looking down at the world? I think it'd be divine."

"Which part?" Denny asked. He was still studying her changed looks.

"All of it—the view, the height, that feeling of . . ."

"Danger?"

"Triumph, I guess I was thinking. I imagine it'd be something like climbing a mountain."

"I didn't know you had an interest in mountain climbing."

"I don't really. Just something I've been reading about."

"Is that right?"

"I do *read*, you know. You needn't sound so surprised."

"I wasn't surprised."

"You were too. You assume I haven't got much capacity for books—or travel documentaries either. Isn't that what changed your mind just now?"

"*No.* No, it wasn't, in fact. And even if it were, it'd be no worse than your assuming I'm too gutless to break the rules."

"I didn't assume. You said so yourself that you wouldn't."

"Well, maybe in this particular case, maybe I did. But that doesn't mean—"

"Listen, Denny, let's not quarrel. You were kind to come and claim me. And I . . . goodness knows I don't deserve it. Still, I hope I haven't used up my last favor with you."

"There's no such thing," he said. "You can have all the favors I've got to give."

Talk about dopey. There went another soppy line. He gulped at his tea, burning his tongue.

"Oh, Dennis. Would you *please* quit trying so hard?"

"Trying so hard at what?"

"Trying to hold up this rosy image of me, despite all evidence to the contrary. It's a miracle I haven't yet been struck down by lightning for all my misdoings. Already, just this summer, I've schemed and I've lied—tricked your sister—aren't you even going to ask me where I was going today?"

"New York, I thought it was," Denny puzzled. "For shopping."

"Well, it wasn't for shopping. It was . . ." Lenore shook her head. "I've learned quite a lot this summer. How much easier it is to hurt someone, rather than to help them. Suffice it to say, I'm in a position to help someone now."

"Oh?" Denny set down his cup.

"Only catch is I don't quite have all the information. There's a little project that goes into collecting it, and I'm afraid I'm going to need some money."

"I can lend you the money, Lenore. How much do you need?"

"Lots. Too much. I couldn't ask you for it, thanks all the same. I intend to get the money myself, if you can point me toward a good swap shop."

"A *swap shop*?"

"That's right. Someplace where they'll pay out cash for odd valuables. And a truck—a delivery truck that can carry a decent amount of cargo. Boxes. Do you know of anyone who might lend me a truck like that? Tomorrow night?"

"Lenore, are you intending an armed robbery?"

"Not at all. More like an exchange."

Denny crushed out his cigarette. "Whatever this scheme, I have to say, doesn't sound like anything a girl ought to be getting up to."

"Oh no? Here then, look at this." She ventured into her purse and produced a little cardstock rectangle. She tossed it across the table. "John has this old friend, Randall Simms. Randall lives in the Caribbean. His reply to the wedding invitation contained *that*. It's a business card."

"'Simms & Shreve Adventure Company,'" Denny read aloud, fingering the embossed script, the little golden sailboat. "I'll be damned. He's really going to do it."

The waitress set down two plates of white toast and assorted crocks of jelly. As soon as she was out of earshot, Lenore grabbed Denny's wrist. "Dennis McTigue! You *knew* what John was scheming at? For how long didn't you tell me?"

"It wasn't my place to tell you."

"That's a fine excuse."

"It was John's place. He ought to have done so himself, and I told him that."

"John's place." Lenore stewed. "John's place indeed."

"Lenore, I'm going to say something now." Denny set down his butter knife. "Something I should've said a month ago. Maybe sooner. Maybe, to be quite frank, the first time I ever saw you showing off his damned fraternity pin."

"Please don't. I mean, I wish you wouldn't."

"Why not?"

"Because . . ." She hesitated. Denny watched her mouth, her unpainted lips. Her eyes were soft on his but settled just the same. She wasn't acting gloomy or somber, and still she wasn't flirting with him either. "Because I've already decided what I'm going to do."

# THIRTY-SIX

"I'll need you to bring me back to Manhattan this weekend," Isolde announced in a high, clipped tone. They were embarking on their usual city trip. He'd been to her house twice in as many days—once to lower a tricky window in the rain and again on Sunday to investigate a rattling sound in the attic that proved to be the dangling roots of a long-defunct anemometer, now measuring island winds in an obvious though less precise way. "And I'll need you to bring yourself—in white-tie attire."

Hatch cocked his head and exhaled in frustration. She could see him trying to decide how best to let her down.

"I've got plans this weekend," he replied.

"*Plans?* What sort? Not your card game again?"

Her pilot parried. "No, just personal plans."

"Whoever she is I'm sure she's reasonable enough to step aside in the name of goodwill. It so happens the Homestead Benefit is a very worthwhile cause."

"She *is* reasonable, yes. But these aren't your usual circumstances, you see. I've already asked her to step aside once and now—"

"Not to mention I'd be scared speechless having to fly again with that lunatic from the Mayflower airline."

Colin Hatch stood outside the Beechcraft looking up at her. His hands rested in his pockets. With the sun at his back it was difficult to discern any clear expression underneath his pilot's cap. But she knew exactly how he felt when he said, "I hope you'll understand."

"Colin." Isolde sighed such a gust it could have come from a bellows. "The money raised at this event goes to orphans. Haven't you any heart at all for children in need of adoption?"

"I was adopted."

"*Were* you?" Her face lifted. "Why, then you'll *have* to be there. Consider the exposure for your company."

"The exposure is another thing that worries me."

"What? Getting yourself too tight to fly home? I've already thought of that. I keep a suite at the Warwick Hotel. It's no trouble."

"Trouble for me, I'd say. Last thing I need in my life is more talk."

"Don't flatter yourself," Isolde clipped her seat buckle across her narrow lap. "If I imagined us on some kind of romantic path, you'd be the one asking me to fancy evenings out and not the other way around." She lit a cigarette with her rose gold Zippo. Hatch climbed into the seat beside her. "I've so many dear, dear, wonderful friends to see, I'll very likely lose track of you once you've escorted me inside."

"Isolde, I'm afraid I really can't help. Not this time."

All at once she summoned her most troubled expression. She averted her eyes and lifted a tentative, gloved finger to the fogged square of glass at her temple. There it lingered, tracing a succession of delicate questions marks. The pilot spoke her name. She could tell he was watching her closely, waiting for a reaction, which meant at least she had regained some advantage.

"I'm terribly glad for you," she said finally. "To be so keen on a girl, so resolute. So *devoted*. When I look at your refusal from that slant, of course I can see why *my* little terrors shouldn't matter an ounce."

"Isolde," Colin brokered.

"And if I'm *really* honest with myself, I'd have to admit that I'd feel this way—sad, lonely. Despairing, even. I'd feel this way anyhow, eventually. I'm practically always afraid, living on the brink of the tomb. So why should one particular trip to New York matter?"

"Isolde."

"Maybe, in fact, the whole awful episode will be good for me. An opportunity to adjust my behavior patterns or something like that." She executed a frail laugh while climbing over her seat and creeping on hand and knee, like a wounded animal, into the back seat compartment.

"Where are you going?"

"Don't mind me. I'll just ride along with the duffel."

"Don't think I don't know what you're doing. This is—this routine is purely performative."

"Honestly, I'm very glad for you, Colin. You *should* go see that girl. Probably she's the type who takes a perfectly rosy view of everything. A lovely, confident girl who can sleep at night and wake up smiling. I'd say she's the one who deserves your attention. I've survived nervous breakdowns before. Someone always talks me off the ledge eventually. And if not this time, well, you'll remember me to my friends in California once I'm dead and gone, won't you?"

## MONDAY, AUGUST 30, 1954

# Faint Signal Buoys Hope for Recovery of Missing Aircraft

BOSTON, MA (AP)—A faint distress call, pulsing SOS, set rescue crews again into motion this morning, rallying hope for the private plane pilot presumed lost in Hurricane Carol's violent spree. The fate of the missing aircraft remains unknown, though authorities say it is believed the pilot, whose name is being withheld until next of kin have been notified, kept a seaworthy raft and synthetic green-dye marker on board.

Shrouded in static, today's signal was traced four miles southeast of Castle Island and intercepted by a Pan American transport en route to Labrador.

No fluorescent sea dye was detected in the area. Rescue conditions are expected to shift from "fair" to "poor" with showers returning this evening as well as significant cloud cover.

*MISSING PLANE cont. page 5.*

# AUGUST

Twenty-one days before the storm

# THIRTY-SEVEN

"Knock, knock!" Bev appeared in Sabina's room without actually knocking. "I've got a major newsflash for you."

"What's that?" Sabina looked up from her papers.

"It's Friday night. And we're the only two gals still sitting at home."

Sabina sighed into her tea. She set down her pencil. When she'd mentioned eelgrass research to Dr. Hughes, the researcher had encouraged Sabina to try her luck at the Woods Hole library. Dr. Hughes expected they wouldn't have every answer she needed, but then, certain permissions could be granted. And so Sabina had started by requesting the files of a group of governmental aquaculturists—she had read about them once, fellows earlier sent to investigate the burning rivers in Cleveland. Without any fuss at all, the WHOI librarian had generously duplicated this request to specified laboratories, fish farms, and university archives. In response, not five days later, and steadily rolling in still, cartons of scientific paperwork arrived at the base.

Sabina tore through the reports like a child on Christmas morning. Volumes of findings soon littered her desk and floor. Each afternoon—delivering her stacks—Bev grumbled anew. Nautical charts. Herbarium records. Fishery logs from Connecticut, Virginia, Maine.

She learned about essential scallop landings: the eelgrass. She read how eelgrass bloomed with tiny, striving flowers, reaching for the sunlight through clean, clear shallows, sheltering spat and other young mollusks. She studied the wasting disease, a virulent slime mold, a plague that came about in the thirties only to splotch and kill the necessary landings. Together with the damage done by oceanfront development and rising nitrogen concentrations, new crops of spat were all but gone from the harbors for more than a decade—only now returning in numbers the scallopers could reliably fish.

"Come to Bruno's, Bean. Won't you? Let's go have a beer with the fellows." Bev jostled Sabina by the shoulder.

"I can't. I'm sitting for the Fords tonight."

"Just one beer. You've got a few hours still, haven't you?"

Sabina checked the timepiece on her desk. Four o'clock. It *was* nearly Friday night. And her babysitting gig for Captain Ford and his wife didn't start until nine. Without meaning to, she caught herself wondering what Colin Hatch might be getting up to tonight—and whoever might be with him.

"I don't know, Bev." She shook her head. "I've still got to finish my notes for Town Meeting."

"Town Meeting, huh?" Bev frowned down at the pile of research. "You've got the whole weekend to dive into Dullsville. And by the looks of you, Frogwoman, you could do with a pint."

# THIRTY-EIGHT

Isolde and Colin sat side by side, against a glossy, high-backed banquet in the Roma Room of Casaloia's. For tonight's role she wore Pierre Balmain: capped sleeves, sequined bodice, a neckline cleft nearly to the navel, and a cool trail of Moonlight Mist presently atomizing her pulse. The candles had been cut to a prescribed length. The courses epochally paced, according to her emphatic instruction. Pours of Chianti babbled, long and deep, spilling down from a gooseneck decanter that had been gifted to Casaloia's owner by La Divina herself.

Isolde's excitement rather caught her off guard. Already, without eating, she felt full on Hatch's skin, his scent, the little ridge of his chin. What was it about this man? A robustness. An *outdoors*iness—here contained and decorated in silk-trimmed cuffs, besides—like her own private Christmas tree.

"You see this here?" She pointed to the menu. "This is pink champagne flown in weekly from Asti. You have to drink it fresh or else the taste is ruined." All day she'd been planning how she might impress Colin Hatch. Impress him by introducing her knowledge of the city, its secret haunts and charms. Because sometimes when he looked at her—when *all* men looked at her, really—despite her diamond broaches and hand-sewn lingerie, she felt her status on the verge of receding back to that of someone ignorant and pitiable from an ugly town on Lake Erie.

"Yes, I know," he smiled. He pointed himself. "And this is Calabrian eggplant. And that's prawn from Sardinia."

"You speak Italian?"

"I can order Italian."

"Good for you."

"You know, it's the damnedest thing." Hatch shook his head. "I can't figure you out." He flicked a bit of cigarette paper from his lip.

"What's to figure?" She reached into his water glass to extract a shard of ice. All of hers had already been chewed.

"One minute you're as peachy as pie. The next, moody as all hell. Hard to tell exactly who you are."

"A pumpkin, seems to be the verdict," she mumbled.

"How's that now?"

"Look, I started acting before I happened to *be* anybody. Borrowing on other people's words. Their hopes, their dreams. Naturally I'm a muddle of ideas and personalities. A shop girl. A perfume girl. An executrix."

"Oh, that's right. *The Executrix.* That was a good picture," Hatch nodded into the ashtray, remembering. "You changed the old crow's will so that all her money went right to the circus."

"My analyst says that my ego and in fact everything I *do* is actually a by-product of twentieth-century film." She watched him processing. "What? You think that sounds like baloney?"

"I think it sounds like a permission slip to do whatever the hell you want."

"Oh, Christ. Don't start moralizing now. God and sin and all that heavy grubbing."

"Don't you believe in God?"

"With an income like mine, analysis is far less expensive than tithing. Anyhow, religion is derivative. It's all the same act played over and over in different ways. Anyone who says otherwise is fooling himself."

Hatch shrugged. They looked away from one other to readjust their eyes. Maybe their expectations too. Isolde had quite expected to induce another side of her pilot tonight. She'd expected him to transform into someone suave and aggressively freehanded once she coaxed him from the backdrop of his little white-church town. She'd halfway expected to be necking by now. Skipping the entrées. Absconding into the long black car now waiting for them at the corner of Baxter and Grand, where he'd pin her against the door, tearing off her Balmain, forgetting all about the benefit and the poor orphan children.

But the reality of Colin Hatch in New York City was underwhelming. He was exactly the same man: impassive, polite. And another unchanged quality too. As much as ever, he was preoccupied.

"You're not eating." He gestured to the plate that had been delivered in front of her.

"Do you ever wonder," Isolde narrowed her eyes at him, "what all those pretty girls do when you're not around? On a night like tonight? I mean, speaking as a man, does it ever occur to you that one of them might be locked in a tender embrace at this very moment?"

"First off," Hatch sawed into his pappardelle, "where do you get this notion of 'all those pretty girls'?"

"So, you admit that there's *one*?"

"Secondly"—he shook his head, chewing—"why do I get the feeling I'm being indicted on someone else's account?"

"Do you want to know what I'd like? What I'd *really* appreciate?" She ignored his question, stealing the swizzle stick from his cocktail, biting down hard.

"Help yourself to whatever." He leaned backward in the booth.

"I just want to live out one sunny day. Just one day of my life without the threat of clouds. I'm talking about the kinds of clouds that creep in and blot out a person's happiness—do you know what I mean? You can feel them coming. At least I can anyhow. And everything gets so awfully dark. When the clouds come in, the only things you can see clearly are the things you fear worst."

Colin gave her a long look. "What is it that you're so afraid of?" he asked.

She ought to have been ready. On another night she would have jumped at her cue, could have answered so easily—the list never very far from reach. She could have counted off: *spiders, sad songs, lightning, sirens, dressing room mirrors. Getting ill. Going broke. Going crazy.*

But tonight was different. After all, this *was* a date. If only she could get him to see it that way too.

"Aren't you going to eat anything?" he asked.

"There's no time for food." She pushed the plate aside. "Tell me about *you*. When you were a boy. Tell me everything. I need to know exactly where you come from."

# THIRTY-NINE

Bruno's barroom swelled with jukebox music. Fishermen just in from the catch sat atop the counter stools. The Truro airmen had annexed a corner in the back, borrowing chairs from the warped and hobbled dining tables to form a rowdy circle of conversation. Bruno's barmaid dipped and twisted to manage her hips between their rearranged seats.

"Hey there, Sally!" The boys whooped to see Sabina. "Look, fellas! Sally's come out."

"*And Beverly,*" Bev supplied, acknowledging herself.

The girls took up chairs on the periphery of the circle. Bev signaled for two beers, which arrived almost instantly—ice-cold and damp enough to make a pulp of the labels. Bev drank hers straight from the bottle. Sabina looked around, a little bewildered, wondering when a glass might arrive.

"Say, Sally, how come we never see you out like this?"

"Why do you think? She's probably out with her beau."

"Sally hasn't got a beau." Bev leaned in, provoking them. "She gave him the air last month on account of his suspect history."

"No kidding." The boys whistled and muttered an overlapping din of replies.

"Did you really drop him, Sally?"

"What'd you ditch the guy for?"

Sabina blushed. "It was nothing," she murmured. "Just a misunderstanding."

Bev nudged over the beer Sabina wasn't drinking. "He won't tell her about his past. We think maybe he's a fugitive."

"Look, Sally," one of the fellows cut in, "just so that you know, a man is entitled to withhold his romantic past. A modern man, you see, has many affairs. That's practically the point of college these days. First dates. Seconds dates. A man needs to try on an awful lot of first and second dates these days, until he decides he wants a third."

Like a baseball umpire, Bev held up a signal for time. "You're way off base." She shook her head. She waited for their full attention. "Look, Sabina's beau was in the war. European theater. He kept time with a girl over there. Enough to get himself into quite a lot of trouble. And he's not prepared to tell our Sally the long and the short of it. So for now, that's the end of our program. Are you all quite satisfied?"

"What sort of trouble?" The boys wanted to know.

"Don't indulge them," Bev counseled.

"A blue ticket," Sabina said, ignoring her friend's advice. Something inside her wanted to see the group's reaction.

After that there was an uproar. Pretty girl like her (*Sally!*), mooning over some two-bit louse.

"You're wasting your time *and* your tears," one said.

"You ought to forget his name," said another.

"Man with a blue ticket? I wouldn't let him shine my shoes."

"Say, Sally, you even know what they give out blue papers for?"

"Not exactly," Sabina admitted.

"That's good. Nothing any of us can talk about in mixed company."

A few boys kindly offered introductions to younger brothers.

"All right, all right," Bev hollered. To Sabina she whispered, "Never mind all that nonsense. Don't let it bother you. *Does it bother you?*"

"A little," Sabina nodded, tearing up. It was only the first time she'd admitted this fact out loud. She felt a pang of guilt at her own embarrassment. She felt bad about feeling bad about Colin Hatch.

"Well, now that they know his rap, they won't ask you any more questions."

"Yes, but don't *you* want to know?" Sabina's voice climbed high. "Aren't *you* going to ask me?"

"Ask you what?" Bev tipped the brown beer bottle to her lips.

"What's wrong with him?"

"Is there something wrong with him?"

"He's got a blue ticket! I've just told you."

Bev lit a cigarette. She blew a puff of smoke out the side of her mouth. "Lots of boys do. And they aren't all degenerates, I can tell you. Some rotten eggs, sure. But mostly guilty of minor infractions. Sent off too young, a guy's bound to make some stupid mistake. So maybe he skipped out of camp to go see his grandma on her birthday."

"I thought blue tickets were only issued for the worst of the worst. That's what my aunt told me."

"What does she know?"

"Less than she thinks."

"Well then?"

"What about the fellas just now?" Sabina pointed over her shoulder.

"They're drunk."

Doubt in her heart, Sabina's eyes welled. "Oh, Bev, what if I've judged him too harshly? Or not harshly enough? How can I know if it's worth holding out hope?"

Bev shrugged. "You want me to look him up?"

"To do what?"

"Look him up. Pull his record, I'm saying. Find out exactly what he did that was so *other* than honorable."

Sabina reached for Bev's hand and squeezed. All at once, her Friday night offered a glimmer of excitement. "You can obtain a man's military records? Just by—what? Just by asking?"

Bev stood, yanked her hand back, and parked it toughly on her jutted hip. "What do you think I do here? Besides deliver your fruit baskets, I mean?"

"You told me that no one knows what anyone does here."

Bev laughed in remembering her earlier admonition. "I did say that, didn't I? But only because you came barreling into base like Little Miss Cronkite on special assignment."

"I did not."

"No matter," Bev patted Sabina's hand, retaking her seat. "As it happens, what I do here is I screen the Lincoln recruits before they're given clearance. After they finish school we subject them to a whole battery of tests—intelligence, personality—then we interrogate their mothers and brothers and barbers and dentists. And if it all comes back rosy, we process them through the back room of an old bread bakery. Just don't ask me which one. That's classified information, which I cannot reveal."

"Do you ever turn up anything unsavory?"

"If a man has a bum record"—Bev lowered her voice, eyes swiveling in either direction—"heck, if he so much as blew a spitball in third-period French, I can trace it."

"Could you really get to the bottom of things with Colin?" Sabina asked hopefully.

"Do you know his service number?"

"No."

"How about the man's middle name?"

# FORTY

From the crowded entrance of the Court Hotel, big brass notes escaped with each rotation of the revolving door. Inside the lobby, guests' eyes immediately traveled upward, to the elaborate scagliola murals of glowing gods and muses stretched across the barrel vaults of the ceiling, each vignette bordered by hundreds of kilograms of gilded gold leaf. Up the staircase, the second-story foyer rested on Corinthian pillars. Marble statuary lined the hall. Ten-foot mirrors balanced against dark wood paneling. Farther down, gold candelabras sprouted from claw-foot posts along the velvet-curtained walls. Before the fundraising auction even opened, the hotel bar had run out of scotch.

Isolde Martin and Colin Hatch arrived just as the band was finding its stride. Men in serious formal wear had given themselves over to riotous dance steps. A famous jazz performer hopped off the stage to kiss someone's wife on the mouth. Manhattan's wealthy were cutting loose.

"Do you know that man?" Hatch stooped his head to speak into Isolde's ear. The music throbbed in his chest.

"Who?"

"That man who keeps staring at you. The one at the bar, holding two martinis just now."

"Who, Harris? He's next in line for the Massachusetts governor's office."

"Yes, *I* know who he is. Parks his boat at the club. An old crony of Bill Dooley too. How do *you* know him?"

Isolde donned a rare, genuine smile. "Why don't we both go and chat with him?" Isolde suggested brightly. "You fellas travel in similar circles."

Harris Shields was a tall, thin man with silver hair and downbeat eyes deeply set beneath an invasive species of eyebrow. At his side stood Mrs. Shields—strikingly lithe and bearing the most carefully sculpted expression of joy Hatch had ever seen. She wore a column dress in blue silk. Her white gloves ended above her elbows, where Harris's hand easily encircled her bare bicep. As Hatch and Isolde approached, he could see the couple had nearly finished the martinis of only a few moments earlier.

"Isolde Martin, as I live and breathe." Mrs. Shields opened her arms to embrace the actress, so it was only Hatch who could see her facade turn cold once Isolde was pressed against her thicket of black hair. "The committee is so grateful for your involvement. I can't tell you what it's meant to have your name associated with the cause. Oh! And as to names, does this fine gentleman have one?"

"This is Colin Hatch," Isolde pronounced smugly.

"Very pleased to know you, ma'am."

"Charmed. Bitsy Shields." Mrs. Shields held out four limply dangling fingers to be squeezed. "What do you do, Mr. Hatch?"

"I'm a pilot, but I also do a bit of—"

Isolde let out an operatic sigh. "He's a man of a great many roles," she paraphrased, "including ownership of his own feeder airline. For this evening, he is my date."

"A precarious occupation," Harris interjected, extending his hand reluctantly.

"To which are you referring, darling?" Bitsy Shields smiled her displeasure.

"The piloting, of course."

Tonight, as in past run-ins Hatch recalled, the politician looked more like a variety show host than a working-class representative of the people. His wore a flirting grin for everyone, while his eyes told a truer story—constantly appraising and discarding strands of dialogue, scanning for leverage.

"May I introduce Mrs. Bowditch?" Harris Shields clamped a claw on a nearby woman's shoulder. "She's our newest director of the state art commission."

"Harris recommends women to all his posts," Bitsy bragged thickly, trading her empty cocktail for a full one floating by on a passing tray.

"Certainly not *all* of them," Harris chuffed. "Anyway I have my selfish motives for the advancement of women in government. Never had so many surprise *cherry pies* land on my desk."

"And let's remember, too, his nominees are not just *any* women, if I may promote myself," added Mrs. Bowditch, whose tone belied the fact that she hardly needed anyone's permission to promote herself. "Graduated top of my class at Mount Ida. I know every historical date occurring in modern history. Makes me quite an asset among the lawmakers."

"That's fascinating," Isolde replied. "Truly."

"Speaking of fascinating"—Bitsy traced her gloved finger around the circle of her glass rim—"rumor has it you've landed on the Vineyard, Miss Martin. Bought yourself a little house and everything, is what the papers say."

"Then they've gotten it right for once." Isolde's face came to life at this new topic. "Honestly, I've never been happier. If I'd known how tranquil New England could be I'd have settled down a long time ago."

"That's rich!" Mrs. Bowditch smacked her wrist into Hatch's side. "Settled down a long time ago. What is she now? All of twenty-five?"

"Twenty-*nine*," Bitsy declared, too readily, training one bitter eye on Isolde's youthful figure. "Be careful now, won't you, Isi? In my experience, when prominent people come to town, all that tranquility flies out the window."

"Well"—Isolde cocked her blonde head ever so slightly—"I doubt the droves will venture all the way out to my separate island. Now that the

Katama Bay Bridge proposal seems unlikely to pass, despite some people's best efforts."

"Don't look at me." Harris held up his hands as all three women turned to look. "I know that you ladies, as a constituency, are all averse to change, but I'd say Bill Dooley's onto something quite interesting with that land. Did you know the ancient Romans also built condominiums?"

"Yes, and occasionally they fed people to lions," Bitsy put in.

"True enough, they did." Mrs. Bowditch corralled the discussion rather clumsily. From a different cocktail tray, the art commissioner had procured a Polynesian-inspired tumbler, overflowing with fruit wedge garnishes. As she brought it to her thin lips, a bit of pineapple rind went up her nose, and Hatch couldn't help but smirk. "And on that note, why not invite Miss Martin and Mr. Hatch into our game?"

"Oh, is there a game happening?" Isolde's eyes went round the circle.

"Always." Bitsy sipped.

"It's called Before and After," Mrs. Bowditch explained.

"I love a good party game." Isolde wriggled her shoulders, inciting motion along the top of her dress. "How do you play?"

"Well now, it's very simple." Mrs. Shields recreated her beatific smile. "One person chooses a historical event, which he keeps secret from the players. The group then tries to determine the event he has chosen by suggesting their own historical selections and thus zeroing in on the timeframe. So, for example, I might say something like, 'the Burgundian capture of Joan of Arc,' and then Harris would say 'before' or 'after,' depending on how my event related to the idea in his head. Do you see?"

"Let's just play until they get the hang of it." Mrs. Bowditch shook her wrists impatiently. "I have something in mind already!"

"Excuse me, would you, please?" Hatch cut in. "I think I'll make myself useful at the bar if you don't mind. History was never my strong suit."

# FORTY-ONE

"Once upon a time, in a lovely, placid bay not too far from where we sit tonight, there lived a kind and noble spat. A baby scallop, you might say, no bigger than the nail on your small finger." Sabina held up her own to demonstrate. She sat at the end of the six-year-old's bed. So far tonight, she and Kathy Ford had played nineteen rounds of rummy, listened to three records, and baked oatmeal cookies with an improvised, scattershot recipe doomed to fail from the beginning. They were well past the Fords' prescribed bedtime, and still Kathy wouldn't sleep.

"What was he called?"

"The scallop? I'm not sure he had a name."

"Good," Kathy Ford sniffed. "Because wild creatures aren't meant to have names."

And Sabina nodded. The Ford girl demonstrated short patience for tales starring fairies and ogres, which made the two of them fast friends. "Yes, you're quite right. This little fellow lived his life rather anonymously. Contented, mind you, sitting on the softest sand of the sea floor, watching the sailboats gliding overhead. Except that occasionally he'd run into trouble with predators—"

"What are predators?"

"Oh, nasty creatures. Crab, wolffish, whelk. You know the type. They'd have liked nothing better than to make a quick meal of our unnamed hero. Fortunately, he had a cunning spirit. He found he could escape these vile villains if he settled himself atop a tall blade of eelgrass—just long enough till he could grow into a bigger, stronger scallop, capable of defending himself."

"Like Jack Dempsey?"

"Well, maybe." Sabina laughed.

Since leaving Bev and the boys at the bar, she'd tried to keep her mind on the plight of the bay scallops—really, she *had*—all that studying to prepare for Town Meeting. All that energy to embrace a research aim that might matter. To prove to her family she was destined for a science that wasn't just domestic. But wasn't she, herself, now proving the very opposite? Stuck puzzling over the good or the bad of her mysterious pilot all over again. Wondering if she'd ever know—if she even deserved to know—the pieces he couldn't tell her. Maybe, as Malcolm had warned her, she *was* out of her depth. Out of her depth with Colin Hatch. With Town Meeting. This silly ambition of becoming a frogwoman. She certainly felt silly right now.

"What happened next?" Kathy Ford tugged at Sabina's blouse.

"What happened next?" Sabina blinked, checking her emotions. "Well, let's see. What happened next was that things went poorly for our heroic spat."

"A fisherman?"

"Oh, worse. Much worse. Fishermen know better than to snare a scallop before its time. No, the real trouble came from higher up. A giant steel shovel biting into the ocean, ripping up the seabed and, with it, all the tender eelgrass."

"Whadid it do that for?"

"Some men wanted to build large houses on the beach. And the houses needed their sailboats. And the boats needed docks. And the docks needed a certain amount of depth for footings. So, you see, the eelgrass simply got in the way."

"Where did the spat go?"

"To escape, he drifted around. North, south—couldn't find himself a suitable new bed for ages."

"But the grass grew back, right? And he came back to live in the bay? With his family?"

"That's the part I'm still figuring out," Sabina confessed.

"Is that little spat dead now?" Kathy Ford asked, seeking a perfunctory conclusion. Sabina could see the young girl fighting off sleep. She rubbed her eyes. Her index finger traced the seam of her pillowcase. A nightlight above the room's baseboard cast a warm, amber glow onto their faces.

"Well." Sabina hesitated. "Let's save our questions for another night."

"Is he in heaven?"

"I would say so."

"Abraham Lincoln is in heaven too. And three of my uncles. From the war. Do you know people in heaven?"

"My mother is there."

"Was she awfully sick with something?"

"No." Sabina let out a slow breath. "Nothing to do with bad health, I'm sure."

"A car accident?"

"My, you have an awful lot of questions for a little girl."

"Did she die in the war?"

"Never you mind." Sabina shook her head. "Go on. Get your rest now."

"But don't you even *know* how she died? Didn't anybody ever tell you?"

"It's not so important, is it?" Sabina replied, rising to pull the cotton bedsheet over Kathy Ford's skinny shoulders. "Besides, young ladies like ourselves aren't meant to go begging after life's every little how and why."

# FORTY-TWO

Hatch snuffed out his cigarette and made his way down to the lobby, where he'd spied a telephone booth on arriving.

"Long distance. May I help you?"

"Yes, operator. This is Colin Hatch at the Court Hotel in Manhattan. I'd like to place a call to Truro Air Force Base in North Truro, Massachusetts. I know the office code. It's four-two-two. But they've got three dozen buildings over there. And I'm looking for one young woman in particular."

"The Truro Air Force Base in North Truro, Mass, office code four-two-two. Is that right?"

"Yes."

"And what's the name?"

"Sabina McTigue. You can charge it to the hotel's business office. I'll settle up at the front desk."

"All right, Sabina McTigue. Would you like me to call you back when I have someone on the line, Mr. Hatch?"

"No, I'd rather wait, thank you."

"Very well. Please hold."

Hatch held the line while a light hammering sounded off the switched relays. In muffled tones, he heard the Boston switchboard come on, followed by the local exchange operator, followed by several low drones.

"They're ringing the number now, Mr. Hatch."

"Thank you."

"Hello?" A woman's voice came through clearly now. "Truro AFB."

"Miss Sabina McTigue, please," the operator requested. "I have Manhattan calling."

"She's not in the office at the moment," the receptionist at the air base apologized. "I can take a message if you like, but I know she's not on shift tonight. She has a commitment with Captain Ford."

"Mr. Hatch, would you like to leave a message? Go ahead, please."

"Are you sure she's out? McTigue? *Sabina* McTigue?"

"Quite sure. It's every Friday night that Captain Ford picks her up, sir."

Colin Hatch bit the inside of his cheek. "No, no message. Thanks anyhow."

Back in the ballroom, the history game of Before and After had well riled its small circle of players.

"The fall of the Roman Empire!" Bitsy guessed.

"After," Mrs. Bowditch swatted the air wildly to indicate a great lapse of time.

"The sinking of the *Titanic*?" Isolde put in, accepting the champagne Hatch had newly delivered.

"*Before*."

"The assassination of Archduke Ferdinand."

"Before again," Mrs. Bowditch pronounced gaily.

"Oh, but these are all such depressing markers," Harris frowned, sipping at his fresh martini. "What about some of history's brighter days?"

"Yes, come on then, Mr. Hatch. You're a happy fellow. Take us someplace sunny," Bitsy entreated.

Hatch felt less than up to the task. "The discovery of the planet Neptune," he replied, mostly without thinking. It was, after all, one of Sabina's favorite details. She'd told him once, on a bright day at Starbuck, the story of how astronomers located the distant blue star using some kind of reverse mathematics. Gravitational effects on other bodies—something like that—gave old Neptune away. And so brighter minds knew it existed, long before sight gave them proof.

Mrs. Bowditch stopped beaming, looking suddenly confounded. "I haven't the foggiest idea when *that* happened."

"What do I win?" Hatch forced his focus back to the group. "For stumping our resident historian?"

"But that's not how the game works," Mrs. Bowditch complained, slurping from her cocktail straw.

Colin shrugged and reached for Isolde's gloved hand, trying to forget Neptune, forget the island, forget whoever the hell was this Captain Ford. "May I have this dance?"

"But I want to know what the date was," Isolde protested.

"I was thinking of the invention of the printing press," Mrs. Bowditch announced. "In 1440."

"No, not *your* date. I meant Colin's. I want to know when Neptune was discovered."

"I'll tell you later," he winked, wishing he hadn't channeled Sabina at all.

Before they could square off in closed position, the band leader turned to quiet the musicians behind him. "We're going to break for a moment," he said into the microphone, as the dancers audibly lamented, the women slouching into their men. If they stopped now, their weary postures suggested, they might never start back up again. "I'm told we have a special guest who is going to say a few words about tonight's benefit. She is a woman who requires no introduction, but I won't let that stop me. Ladies and gentlemen, your favorite silver screen legend, dazzling in beauty and in heart, Miss Isolde Martin."

Applause and wolf whistles erupted. The overserved guests scarcely remembered the cause at hand.

Isolde made a great humble show of finding her way to the stage. "Thank you, thank you," she said, accepting the microphone.

Hatch watched her become the removed celebrity figure she'd been before she sat in the front of his airplane. Her voice softened and lifted.

Her eyes widened. Her top lip subsumed the lower momentarily, lending to a meek, timorous look she must have practiced before a mirror; it was nothing that came from her naturally.

"I can't tell you how honored I am to be here. I'd like to thank the Homestead Organization for throwing such a bash, and all of you of course, for dancing like hellcats." The applause lit up again. Isolde waited for quiet, for a silence interrupted only by the crunching of flash bulbs. "Much as this issue speaks to my heart, I'm afraid I cannot voice what it means to be a child without a home. Like many of you, I was blessed with a warm, safe haven provided by two loving parents. And so I think a more suitable ambassador, certainly a handsomer one"—she batted her eyelids for effect—"would be my good friend, a man I am proud to know, Mr. Colin Hatch."

She held her hand out toward the audience. Heads swiveled to identify this so-called friend of Isolde Martin. Hatch swallowed. He half-raised his hand, in acknowledgment of the mention, though his face must have revealed his shock and displeasure. For Isolde continued, "He won't be happy with me for saying so, but he's one of the most remarkable people in this room tonight. And as it happens, he was also, once, an orphan. He was a young boy who endured the pain of state homes, lacking so many basic provisions. It was plain to see he was headed down a bleak path, toward delinquency and crime. And then the saving grace of adoption intervened. He gained a home that provided stability, safety. But almost as importantly, maybe more so, he gained a role model in his new father. A pilot. A man who gave him a skill that blossomed into a great talent. And that talent brought forth a national hero, as Colin protected our bomber boys over Europe. To be precise, I can tell you Colin is a flight commander who flew nearly one hundred combat missions, effectively completing two full tours in Italy. More than most of us will accomplish in a lifetime. I'd like to thank him for that. We all should. Yes, let's. Right now, in fact. Let's thank him."

Her coy pause invited the audience to clap, and they enthusiastically obeyed.

"There is more I could say about this very worthwhile cause, but I would much rather toast to the heroes among us. To those who adopt and to those who thrive because of its great good. To Homestead and to heroes," she declared.

"To Homestead and to heroes," the audience echoed. Isolde delicately surrendered the microphone to the band leader before picking up the folds of her gown to descend the stage's staircase, into the arms of the scrum of needy rich—society folks who wouldn't stoop to autograph requests, opting instead for more intrusive, drawn-out favors involving their charity boards and her publicist.

"That was a stirring tribute," chimed a sarcastic voice.

"Beg your pardon?" Hatch wheeled around.

James Whelan, of all people, had suddenly materialized at his side. Whelan was lifting his chin toward the stage. "Beautiful story. I wasn't expecting to see you in New York, much less hear your eulogy."

"Hello, Whelan."

"You coached her well."

"She volunteered a lot of information."

"Made up a few details, did she? I'm struck most by the ones she *omitted*. But then, she is an actress, let's remember. And you're her national hero."

"I don't consider myself a hero."

"You're being too modest."

"I did my bit. That's all."

"Well, it's like I said back at the island. Not everyone can be Ted Williams." Whelan balled his fist as if to chuck Hatch on the elbow, but his gesture was too slow; Hatch took a step backward.

"I'm a Cubs fan, Jim."

"Oh, I wasn't talking about baseball. I meant not everyone can bounce back into service quite like the Thumper did. Thirty-nine missions in Pohang." Whelan whistled. "Remind me, Captain, where were you when all the other boys shipped off for Korea?"

"You're a real creep, you know that?"

Whelan grinned. "Ah. Still a sore subject, I see."

"Where were *you* for Korea?"

"I have an impingement in my shoulder. Damnedest thing. And the asthma too. Go ahead and scoff. But at least I was invited."

"If you know what's good for you, you'll take that drink and go find the rest of the math club. Fast."

"You know what the funny thing is?" Whelan was so smitten with himself he actually began a kind of circular capering routine. "I would have sworn you earned that blue ticket for bunking up with soldiers. Turns out it was some lady dago who got you into trouble. That's what Sabina tells me anyhow."

"Let's take this conversation outside," Hatch offered smoothly.

Just then Isolde returned from her cheek-kissing tour around the room. She saw Hatch's fiery expression and grabbed hold of his arm. "Absolutely not." Isolde planted herself between the two rivals. "We're not here to sort out whatever ancient history you boys are squabbling over."

"Oh, but it's hardly ancient," Whelan smiled at her. "Good evening, by the way, Miss Martin. I'm a fervent admirer."

"How nice. Go admire from afar, why don't you?"

"I guess it's true what they say. Gentlemen, apparently, *do* prefer blondes."

"You don't know anything about Colin," Isolde fired.

"I know that a leopard never changes his spots."

"That's rich. Just look at you, you Freckles McGoosey. You've got more spots than a Yucatan banana."

"Hey, Hatch, your date spars like a street hood." Whelan laughed. "Must be contagious. No wonder Sabina's dean didn't want your kind rub bing off on the nice college girls."

"I'll tell you one last time, Jim—and what's that anyway about Sabina's college?"

"Now I've got his attention, haven't I?" Whelan side-barred to no one in particular. "It's true. The dean at Weston College told Sabina to drop you cold or else she could take up her studies at typewriting school. Thankfully, she came to her senses. Decided she ought to chuck you for good."

Colin lost track of the argument just then. He was remembering the fireworks in the Shreves' backyard. He was thinking of Sabina's face, how differently she had looked at him that night. It all made sense to him now. Florence had faulted him for waiting so long to explain, and yet—he smiled into his drink. Shook his head. Despite Sabina's pleas to hear the truth, her course was already decided. Even then.

Isolde stood close against Hatch's side, shooing Whelan with her gloved hand. "Go find yourself a different audience."

Whelan stared straight into her cleavage, smirking. "I think I'm beginning to understand this guy's playbook."

"What playbook is that?" Isolde's nostrils flared.

"The Bachelor's Guide to Life and Piloting." Whelan snapped his fingers. "Very similar strategies it would seem. Rule Number One: Always keep a backup and a redundancy for everything. Even the girls you're screwing."

Despite having a full drink in one hand, Hatch's swing was surprisingly deft. He felt his knuckles meet Whelan's cheek. The doctor's eyeglasses spun into the air and produced a violent clack against the ballroom's marble floor. His brandy snifter smashed. As he struggled to his knees amid the scattered shards of glass, Isolde picked up her hem and took flight for the door. Hatch smoothed his jacket and shot his cuffs. He pressed his pocket square to a few drops of bourbon now dotting his sleeve. He sipped his drink and took a conscious step to where the glasses had landed, crushing them underneath his polished shoe. Alarmed onlookers gathered at Whelan's side.

"What happened?" cried a woman.

"Why'd he punch him?" cried another.

"S'cuse me, sir. Can I get your name for the paper?" asked a Tabloid photographer. Beside him was another parasite from *Look*. And another from *Life*. Their bulbs flashed in his eyes.

"It's all right." Hatch held up his swelling hand, a little blinded. "I'm a national hero."

Hatch pursued Isolde to the hotel's elevator banks. A few tactless fans had already given similar chase and, all together—Hatch and this group—caught a glimpse of her bright, gelid eyes just before the doors divided them. Hatch commandeered the next car over. He rode it forty stories north, unsurprised to find her hiding out on the rooftop, her small shoulders poking out from the fur of her sable.

Above the city, a stretch of clouds grazed the silver moon. Rectangular grids of light wrapped around the vast blackness of the park.

"Why did you leave?" he asked, shaking the sting from his raw knuckles. "I was just beginning to feel sociable."

"I brought you here to make Harris jealous of you. Or you of him. I'm not sure anymore."

"Why on earth should anyone be jealous of Harris Shields?"

"Oh, who cares? In the end, it's me that's green."

"You oughtn't let him get you so riled."

"Don't you see? I'll never get top billing."

"Go ahead and take a deep breath."

"I try," she breathed. "I really do. But even here, *in my own life*! I wind up second on the marquis. He's got his Bitsy. You've got this college girl. What's the use? I might as well jump."

"Come on now, kid. Get hold of yourself." He took her by the arms. "You can't tell me you haven't got anything to live for."

She fixed her eyes on his with well-practiced intensity. "Right now I do."

"Before you get cute with me, I've got a bone to pick with you. Why did you call me out like that tonight? In front of all those people? Don't you know I've got a rotten rep?"

"So what?" She laughed, genuinely blind to his question.

"So *what*? So, it's a pickle for you just to keep my company, let alone run around calling me a hero. You ought to be careful what you say."

"We're not in Pilgrim country anymore, dear. This is New York City."

"Thanks for the tip."

"Are you angry with me?"

"I was, yeah. For a start, I really was. And then—"

"And then you weren't?"

"Can I tell you something?"

"Everything."

"Tonight, back there—that's the first time in ten years. I'm not saying I deserve it, but I guess, no one's ever offered me a single word of thanks. For the war, I mean."

She cut him off with a kiss. Standing high in her highest of heels, all it took was a tiptoed lean. His good hand caught her waist for balance, while his left took up her cheek, drawing her in. Any remnants of her outspoken star power fell away. He felt her ribs through her dress, as delicate as bird bones—her skin so soft it might've bruised beneath his thumb, at her temple, where he felt her heart—indirectly—pulsing softly, a worn-down machine. As he moved both hands to collect her sylph-slender waist, he realized he was lifting her, without at all trying, several inches off the ground. Her teeth chattered in between kisses.

"Are you cold?" he asked. She shook her head no but huddled against him nonetheless. The wind off the city's rivers bonded them tighter, two allies against a starless summer night.

"I'd like to go home now," she said. "With you. If you don't mind the exposure."

"It's all right." He brushed her cheek. He felt good suddenly—easy, loose—even in his dinner jacket. "I can handle the photographers."

"They won't see us anyhow." Isolde's turquoise eyes flashed through her dark, wet lashes. "There's a tunnel."

# FORTY-THREE

Outside the benefit, press people swarmed. But tonight's driver was very good. "Lose the jokers," Isolde instructed, and he did. He lost the jokers somewhere along the West Side Highway, after the car screeched into orbit around Columbus Circle, past DeWitt Clinton, cutting east across the avenues. Five blocks south of Central Park, Isolde jumped from the back seat, ducking beneath the scaffolding of a dark, anonymous building. She led Hatch down twenty-two precipitous stairs like an advance guard.

"Where are we going?"

"Does it matter?"

Upscale Manhattan hotels had quietly offered subterranean walkways for years—protection for the truly celebrated people—and the Warwick was no exception. Isolde and Hatch laughed all the way through its dark tunnel walls, snaking their way beneath the city, oblivious to the rumbling of the trains as they took turns imitating Mrs. Bowditch with her pineapple cocktails, trying to decide if the major event the other one was imagining had already happened or was only just about to take place.

They'd had too much to drink. But once inside the apartment Isolde poured them more. She wore a roundel ring of pavé diamonds as big as a silver dollar. It glittered on her middle finger as she tilted the scotch from an impressive-looking decanter, sending tiny white lights of reflection fluttering across the sixteen-foot ceiling. The apartment was cool and dark.

Isolde lit two candles on the bar, carried the drinks to the coffee table, and collapsed beside Hatch on the sofa, covering them both with an ermine-trimmed blanket that might once have belonged to a king.

"How are you feeling?" he asked.

"I'm not sure, to be honest." She grinned and clanked her glass against his. She began pulling hairpins from her curls. "But I won't cry again, if that's what you're worried about. Melancholy is such an ugly look for a woman. Men don't like it."

"I forgot that you're the authority on what men like."

"Doesn't take a scientist. A weepy face is just about the least attractive thing to a man. Second only to too much makeup." She pressed her body against his side, grabbing hold of his shawl collar. She traced the lapel's thin curve from behind his neck to the point where his jacket opened at a dégagé cummerbund. "They don't want it rubbing off on them."

"The weeping or the makeup?"

"Luckily," she went on, "*men* actually look all the more alluring when vulnerable. So why don't you tell me what's haunting you instead."

"Why should anything be haunting me?"

"Because you tell too many jokes. Men with clear heads don't halfway bother. Who was she, Colin? The girl from the island you were ready to scrap over tonight? I have it on good authority you've been heartbroken."

"What good authority? Dooley?"

"He's a rotten bastard, but he never misses a scoop."

"No, the story he's telling happened a long time ago."

"Your checkered past?"

Hatch nodded.

"Who was *she* then?"

"I can't talk about it." He sipped his drink. Though, looking at Isolde, with her unmade face, her undone curls—her rather obvious mess of an affair. Maybe he could tell her—of all people—after all.

"Oh no?"

He sighed. "Adele was a student of politics."

"Mmm." Isolde narrowed her eyes. "You do go in for the bookish type, don't you?"

"Bookish?" He ran his bruised hand lightly over his hair. "She spoke five languages fluently. Wanted to change the government."

"Except what?"

"Except everything. By the time she turned eighteen Naples was decimated. Her mother and father were gone. Her husband—well, I guess he fell into her life at a time when so much else was crumbling around her. He had ties to bad people."

"The Camorra?"

"You know of them?" Hatch looked at Isolde with surprise.

"Hollywood does two things very well: diets and corruption."

"What about the art?"

"What *about* the art?" Isolde nodded dismally. She sucked on an ice cube she'd plucked from her scotch.

"Yes, well." Hatch looked into his drink, forgetting his place. "What was I saying?"

"The husband was a brute."

"Not just physical violence, but always threats. Terrible threats to put her out on the streets. She was too clever and too resourceful to accept cruelty of any kind, let alone as a condition of marriage. She fled to Ischia—it's a small island just a ways from Sorrento."

"I've been there." Isolde swallowed hard, acknowledging the particular Italian setting and maybe something else, too, Hatch realized.

"Well, soon enough Naples came calling. As soon as the Allies advanced, she was heading north too."

"And that's where *you* found her. Swooped in to save her! And it was love at first sight."

"It wasn't love." Hatch turned to face Isolde squarely, working through the fog of the booze to arrive at a truer explanation. "Even as young as I was, I knew better. But it was *something.*"

"Formative."

"Right. Yes. All right, so that sounds sappy, maybe, but Adele—that time spent with her—it stuck on me. From the moment I met her I had the sense that if *she* was okay, if I was able to eke out that much of a victory, then we'd all be well enough in the end."

Isolde returned his solemn stare for a second or two. The massive chamber of her apartment stood dead quiet except for the tick of a brass clock on the mantle. Then suddenly the actress broke out into an ugly, howling laugh. "Oh brother. Colin Hatch, you're some kind of card."

"What is it?" Hatch felt his face cracking into a smile. He was drunk. "What did I say that was funny?"

"Say, I've got a tripod and a movie camera in the closet, you know. How 'bout if I film you for my agent? With a delivery like that you belong on a big picture screen, my dear."

Colin Hatch was a man who prided himself on being able to hold his liquor. On the other hand, maintaining adequate perspective so as to avoid the merry stunts and scrapes of an after-party—well, that was a different kind of claim—one he never boasted. Somewhere around three o'clock in the morning, Isolde and Hatch sat working out the mechanics of a thirty-five millimeter camera, left in her bedroom armoire by a screenwriter and his wife who had borrowed the apartment when Isolde was in Europe.

"What do you want me to do?" Hatch glowered at the camera. He stretched one arm along the back of the sofa, propped his feet on the coffee table. His drink balanced on his thigh while his right hand rubbed the haze from his eyes.

"Start from the beginning," Isolde directed from behind the lens. "Where did you meet her exactly?"

"Spoleto."

"What were you doing there?" She spun her hand like a wheel, prodding for more. "Bombing, yes?"

"No, a couple of the fighters and I'd just gotten transfer orders. Reassigned to air-transport duty. Ferrying the damaged craft between depots, MUs, scrapyards, and so forth. My CO owed me one, so I pressed him to send us three ahead by jeep. Goodkind was from Cleveland. He fancied himself a cultured fellow, when it came to food, booze, women. But Clay, he was country. He came from cattle ranchers in Texas. So anyway, I said to the guys, 'Let's make an excursion of it.' Goody wanted to tour Florence, on account of his brother's name was David. And I—"

"Get to the girl, please, Captain."

"All right, okay. *Jesus.* So we were at this little outdoor *catina* in Spoleto. That's like a bar, I guess you'd call it. And Spoleto is just this tiny market village where someone said we might find a memorable meal. It was very beautiful, even with the holes in the buildings and the debris choking out the gardens. The roads all blown to rocks. There were women washing clothes in a fountain, I remember. God only knows how they still had running water . . ."

"Your political scientist was one of these women?"

"No, Adele was on a *bicycle.* See, while we were sitting at the bar we made quite a lot of friends. The Italians were so grateful—most of them, in those parts. They crowded to cheer us, throw us fruit, toast the liberation. The party grew. We were all fairly sauced. And the barkeep handed me this very old, dusty bottle of something, and he was saying—aw, hell, I don't know what he was saying. He wanted me to open it up, I guess. Now, I barely *breathed* on that cork, mind you. It was a very old bottle, as I said. So all of a sudden the top explodes across the courtyard, and, *phisst*"—he shaped his hand like a missile pointing forward—"hits the poor girl on the bicycle, clear across the road."

"You hit her with the cork."

"Yes." Hatch nodded slowly.

"You hit the girl with the cork?" Isolde fell down on the floor laughing. Tears flowed from her eyes. They both forgot the camera. "What did you say to her?"

"I said I was sorry, of course. I asked her if she was—no, I'll tell you what it was. I offered to bring her some ice."

"And what did she say?"

"She said she doubted I could find any ice outside of Rome, which was true of course, at that time. So anyway, I invited her to join us. I asked her to have a drink. She spoke English. I thought the boys would like the company. But I could see my friends back at the bar. Goody and Clay. They were shaking their heads at me, like I ought to walk away. They could well enough guess she was a *gappista*."

"Come again?"

"A member of the Patriotic Resistance. The GAP Brigade was a group of Italians who helped us win back northern Italy. But you have to understand, many of these women, these, uh, *staffette*, they were called. They delivered messages from post to post, like wartime couriers for the partisans. But, I was saying, many of these women were soldiers in their own right. Sometimes they carried weapons or bombs. And we were unarmed, the three of us."

"Three men afraid of one woman. That's rich."

"I didn't want any trouble, was all."

"But you didn't walk away from her."

"No. I didn't. We got to talking right there in the road. She was very pretty."

"*How* was she pretty?"

"Jesus, I don't know. She had dark hair. A nice smile. Smooth skin. *Perfect* skin, just like her face was painted that way. In fact, she *reminded* me of a painting. A painting of the Virgin Mary that used to hang in my church's rectory, back home in Bristol. I never thought about the Virgin Mary as being a woman before. I mean, an attractive woman. But with her skin and her voice—the way she said things like a song—this girl was attractive all right."

"So, what? You invited the Virgin Mary back to your hotel room?"

"No, she asked me if I could fly her to London. Which was *crazy*!" Hatch's voice cracked as he collapsed backward against the sofa cushions. "I had my Class A on. Lots of fruit punch across my chest. She could see I was a pilot. Maybe she assumed I had more authority—or more daring—than I actually had. I don't know."

"And what did you tell her?"

"I said, 'Aw hell, sure, why not? Let's take a trip.'" Hatch laughed, because that was exactly what he'd said to Adele. And he'd been laughing at the time, too, grinning back at his table of friends. But immediately he had seen his mistake. *She* hadn't been joking. Some part of her believed a secret passage might actually be possible. And the way her face fell in realizing, a bit delayed, that he was mocking her hope, it hammered him with remorse. It was the first time in his life he felt responsible for the sadness of a beautiful woman. Her expression, the long pause: it almost broke him. And in that moment—twenty years old, numb to counting all the good men lost and "probable" in the smoke beneath the clouds—he promised he would spend the remainder of his ten-day pass making it up to her. And he had.

Isolde cleared her throat. "Tell me, Captain. How might a good soldier and his beguiling lady friend amuse themselves for ten days in the midst of a war?"

"We kept busy."

Isolde's blue eyes went dark, like steel pennies. "Sounds like a swell time."

"Listen, Isolde, can we cut the camera?" Hatch realized all at once he was tired.

"But you haven't told me how it ended." She was sitting on the floor now. Her eye makeup mottled her cheeks. She looked like a child, playing dress-up in her mother's evening clothes.

"We spent ten days fooling around. What can I say? She woke up that last morning and she left. When I got back to base"—he sighed—"there was a blue ticket waiting for me. A general discharge, they call it. The official heave-ho for the guys who snubbed orders, went crazy. The paranoids, some homosexuals—"

"But why?" Isolde crawled across the carpet, reaching for one of his ankles. "Surely you weren't the only soldier seeking female company."

Hatch stared into his rocks glass. Isolde recognized the look of a man fighting for his next line. "Was just my luck, I suppose."

"I don't think you're telling me everything."

"Look. Do you suppose we could change the subject?"

Isolde clicked off the camera. She stood to open a massive Palladian window. Air from another season breathed into the room. Isolde cuddled close against Hatch's side, hitching her dress up over her knees, so her feet and calves could stretch along the velvet sofa cushions. She ran her lacquered fingers through her hair. "All right. How was it when you first met me, then? Did our first meeting also border on enlightening for you?"

"It was uncomfortable," Hatch admitted.

"You were nervous?" she asked hopefully.

"No, I was tenderized. Probably exactly how I'll feel tomorrow."

"But what were you *thinking*?"

"I was thinking that I needed the latrine."

Isolde clubbed him with a pillow. "Is it really so impossible for you to behave nicely?"

"Okay, okay. I have something nice—an idea you might like." Hatch smiled distantly, picking up her hand with his all-encompassing grip. He pulled the diamond ring off, making room to lace his fingers in between hers. She brought their entwined grip to her cheek, drawing him into a long, sleepy kiss.

"What's your big idea?" She tugged him to his feet. They had to lean on one another to avoid splashing against the walls, down the long corridor that led to the bedroom.

"Have you ever been to a sailboat race?"

"No." Her head lolled onto his shoulder. "But I'm a champ at keeping busy."

# FORTY-FOUR

Regatta day at the island was a tradition almost as entrenched as the fossilized whale bones and prehistoric shark teeth buried in the cliffs at Aquinnah. The list of entrants changed from one contest to the next—a new Kennedy, a fledgling crew from Corinthian—but the lively atmosphere around the town wharf and the brilliant line of kites on the water never diverged from the picture in Sabina's mind's eye.

Neither did the frazzled scene at the cottage, where the business of entertaining out-of-town visitors was its own kind of gut-gripping competition. That morning, Poppy was on her mark, harassing poor Connie over the noncommittal responses of Denny's weekend guests.

"It's lucky I didn't cook a full dinner last night," huffed Poppy, who had not cooked a dinner of any sort—full or otherwise—since the children were crawling. "Do they suppose I'm running a boarding house? Meal after meal, for crowds of come-what-may? How am I to know if a nice-sized leg of lamb is in order? I can't very well pack the icebox *just in case* the weather turns out favorably."

"We can get our hands on fresh scup fillets at a moment's notice," Connie reminded her employer. "How about coquilles Saint Jacques?"

"Perhaps a brace of partridge," Poppy mused.

"Or some of those nice cherrystones with the vermouth?"

"Oh, Connie, please try to think like a proper hostess. How would it be to have guests arriving to the smell of *fish*? No, I think a chicken would be the thing."

"Yes, a chicken would be the thing," the housekeeper placated.

"Nola Dooley's cook has a wonderful way of cleaning birds with salt and lemon. An old method from the West Indies, I suppose. How did they prepare chickens in your native village, Connie?"

"Do you mean East Boston?" Connie asked, turning to give Sabina a weary grin.

"Oh, but even a chicken dinner requires a definitive head count," Poppy groaned, throwing up her hands and slamming the cap back atop her tin.

"A. P.," Sabina began in a tentative tone, "I've some news I ought to tell you. Probably before Denny's company arrives."

"Don't tell me you've also invited friends," Poppy glared.

"No, it's not that. But I did come home this weekend for a reason. I was invited, actually. By the shellfish constable. I'm going to speak at Town Meeting tomorrow."

"I thought the shellfish constable was meant to keep the restaurants from serving undersized lobster."

"Partly, maybe he is, but he's also—"

"I hope he's not going to get in the way of Mr. Dooley's bridge. And you neither. Chappaquiddick needs a road to civilization. Have you seen the vacationists' children over there? They all go barefoot."

"A. P., it's more complicated than simply building a road. Shellfish habitats could be threatened. The bay scallops, in particular, which are a vital part of Edgartown's economy. And its ecology. Bivalves, you see, have a very unique ability to purify contaminated water. Indeed—"

She pulled a notecard from the recipe tin and began sketching digestive glands and pedal ganglia on the back of Poppy's entry for blueberry cake. Instinctively, Connie went to the cabinet to fetch her aunt a brandy.

"Our clams and oysters and scallops," Sabina was saying, "exercise tiny systems of tissue that act as sieves. It's quite remarkable. They can take in any number of marine pollutants and dispense cleaner water in return. I'm going to explain this to the voters so they can see why our bay scallops are so essential—not just as Edgartown's primary cash crop, but as a sort of ecological medicine. And I've got evidence to prove it. Fishing charts and aquaculture data from the fishery at the Milford Laboratory."

Aunt Poppy pulled at the pleats of her apron. She looked as if her lips had been erased from her face.

"Let me ease it up a bit." Sabina tried again, sketching a simpler scallop.

"Would to heaven you'd ease it up *all the way*!" Poppy snatched back her recipe card. "Or at the very least go and bring your scientific lecture over to the shellfish constable's house!"

"But Auntie, don't you see?"

"I told your father. Didn't I tell her father?" Poppy demanded of Connie. "It's the age of child-bossing! And now we're meant to let them pursue every pie-eyed whim, every idle curiosity—"

"Oceanography is hardly an idle curiosity." Sabina stood, defiant. "Just because it isn't the main column in your Saint Andrew's church bulletin, well, where do you suppose tomorrow's weather will come from? Not to mention tomorrow's food supply?"

Poppy was pouring herself a generous glass of brandy when Sabina heard Denny's familiar gab outside in the drive. Two fresh faces appeared then at the screen door.

"Oh look, the young people have arrived!" Aunt Poppy exclaimed, inflating her happy tone. "What a genuine *surprise*! Tell me, Dennis, who have we here?"

The pair of them entered the cottage, hands clasped. Gretchen wore khaki walking shorts with a light linen blouse. Her long, thin legs set her almost as tall as Denny, who'd arrived in faded green swim trunks—shorts that Poppy had more than once reviled as his "Boy Scout fugitive wear."

"This is Gretchen Sanders," Denny smiled as he presented the glowing girl on his arm. "Gretchen, this is my Aunt Prudence. My sister, Sabina. Our housekeeper, Connie."

"How do you do?" Sabina replied. "I like your headscarf."

Gretchen swept the traveling scarf backward, off her forehead. "Thank you. It's dotted Swiss."

"The Swiss." Poppy's nails tapped her glass. "Some fine schools among the Swiss."

"It's very nice to meet you, my dear," Connie put in.

"Likewise," agreed Gretchen, nodding effusively around the room.

Poppy stood before the couple, tracing the furrow of her brow—smiling, but in the way she did when she wanted someone else to verbalize her frustration.

"I'm sorry we didn't phone you, Auntie." Denny pulled his aunt into a one-armed embrace, pecking her cheek before depositing a shabby suitcase onto the kitchen rug. "Gretchen wanted to see Plymouth Rock yesterday. And the other couple I mentioned, Dick and Angela, at the last minute they decided to meet some other college chums over in Hyannisport. So it's just the two of us after all."

"Well, that's no trouble, is it?" Poppy trilled. "And your timing is brilliant. We were just discussing dinner. How does roast chicken sound?"

"Really? Chicken?" Denny slumped against the counter, demonstrating he'd yet to shed certain adolescent postures. "The whole way here I've been bragging to Gretchen about island seafood. The scallops, the oysters. And did I tell ya, Gretch, the McTigues are world-famous for our sweet vermouth clams?"

"No, sir!" Gretchen fawned, taking no notice of Poppy's ferocious scowl. Gretchen had honey-brown eyes, girlish dimples, and an expression that gamely mirrored Denny's as he worked his way to the end of every sentence.

Poppy nodded her resignation at the floor. "All right then. *Fish.* Connie, why don't you head down to the market. I think we've plenty of vermouth in the cabinet."

Connie needed no urging. She was already hurling her apron into the pantry, waving her fingers at the kids as she went.

"This is for you, Miss McTigue." Gretchen held out a small store-wrapped package. "It's a hostess gift. No need to open it now. They're little guest soaps."

"Golly. How lovely."

"They're shaped like bumblebees."

"Imagine that." Poppy winced. "Wherever did you find them?"

"Hey, listen, have you got anything ready to make a picnic?" Denny cut in. "I think we'll probably go freshen up, then head straight for the harbor. If that's all right with you, Gretchen?"

"Certainly," Gretchen replied. "It's so nice of you to have me, Miss McTigue. What a beautiful house you've got."

"Well, thank you, Gretchen. We're very blessed to have it. And doubly so to fill it with such charming company—whether it be *six* guests, or *four* guests, or only just the two of you! Come to find out."

"Auntie, let's let Gretchen freshen up," Denny suggested. "We'd better shake it up if we're going to make the race."

Sabina helped Gretchen escape the kitchen, guiding her to the guest suite above the carriage house. She noticed again what a pretty girl Denny's date was, with glamorously long legs but rather scuffed-up-looking sandals. Sabina wondered momentarily if she was after McTigue money, then decided that was the sort of thing her aunt would wonder enough for the whole family.

"Can I help you unpack?" Sabina offered. "It was so thoughtful of you to deliver me that dress for the Shreves' clambake."

"Oh, I didn't mind a bit," Gretchen said. "I hope it helped. New dress gives a girl a certain advantage, wouldn't you say?"

"I suppose that can be true."

"Denny seemed to think you were aiming to turn some heads. Maybe one head in particular?"

Sabina felt a flush creeping up her neck. With Gretchen it seemed safe to admit she hadn't just come home for Town Meeting.

"I was," Sabina nodded. "I still am, I suppose. I'm afraid it's a complicated situation."

"They all are," Gretchen winked.

# FORTY-FIVE

*Dear "Pining in the Dark,"*

*Some people say you need to know a thing before you can forget it. I'm of the opposite mind—especially where romantic relationships are concerned. You see, the past is a tricky thing; it haunts us all differently. You couldn't know his ghosts even if he introduced you over tea. So why bother chasing them? In my experience, the only thing you need to know is what's ahead of you. Let the dead past bury its dead. Forget whatever may've happened before he ever decides to tell you (for he may never be ready or willing). If you're truly as levelheaded and as unhappy without him as you claim, the only thing to do is look forward, make amends, put your mind to all the good that you can build on together.*

*You say you're "pining in the dark," but I wonder if your compromised perspective is actually a self-made problem. Stand on your own two feet. Love with your own spellbound heart. Friends and family have rights to their opinions, but you'll find—as you get older—your home will become quite crowded if you invite them all to live inside.*

*Sincerely,*
*Emma Dix*

All along the way to the pier, Sabina's head traced over this response from the *Globe*'s advice columnist—and the speech for Colin it had inspired. She'd telephoned Bev at the base, and with nothing to report from that camp, she felt all the more confident following the lead of her "spellbound heart." With each familiar leg of the walk, she grew a little more breathless. She was so busy building up this tender reunion, she nearly collided with Mr. Leahy, who stood outside his market wiping fingerprints from the storefront with scraps of old newspaper and squirts of vinegar.

"And where've *you* been, young miss? I expected to have my currants by now," Mr. Leahy mostly joked, but Sabina felt obliged to explain herself.

"I've been working in Truro. For the Ground Observer Corps. I'm sorry if we left you in a lurch. Has Colin been by?"

"Bah, Colin." Leahy waved her question away. "Can't get an audience with him these days. He travels with the swells."

Leahy pointed his nose at the sky, where a flock of spinning jennies—the fruits of the sidewalk maples—flew and fluttered to the ground like disembodied wings. Samaras were always the first sign summer was moving on. It gave Sabina a little anxious tremor to think something might have changed in Colin since June.

"Matter of fact, if you see Colin," Mr. Leahy wagged his finger, "tell him I'm waiting on those currants he promised me."

Sabina nodded to be polite. When she found Colin today she had no intention of discussing currants or blueberries or the end of the Indochina War. She loved him. That was the simple whole of it. She couldn't care less who heard her say so either, she decided, as she exhaled fiercely through her nose. Her eyes grew suddenly damp with this rise of emotion. She found a handkerchief in her dress pocket just as the race's five-minute signal sounded its short blast. Denny hurried the girls toward the dock.

A crowd of tourists and day-trippers, eyes pressed into binoculars, stood gathered on the small beach by the ferry landing. Casual observers hung about the base of the tower at Lighthouse Beach. Denny, Gretchen, and Sabina chugged out toward the starting-line pin, opposite the EYC racing-committee boat. Dozens of wizened old skippers had already dropped anchor in rows, smoking their pipes, critiquing the form of the Wiannos grouped together on a starboard tack. Small cat's-paws stirred up the surface.

The gun sounded and the thrash began. Gretchen leaned into the action, with Denny's arms around her shoulders and his mouth close to her ear, explaining the strategy of the approach. Several tacking duels were already forming on the windward leg.

"Who are we rooting for?" Gretchen asked.

"Let's see." Denny pointed. "Sabina's friend, James Whelan, is in the Wianno over there. The one with the blue wind vane on the mast. That one to the left, with its head sagging off, that's the Longford crew. J. J. Shreve is farthest out just now. It's his wedding we're going to this month. My money's on his *Carolina*. And over there's Harris, who you know from the office."

"Harris Shields? I didn't realize he was a serious boater."

"He certainly drinks like a sailor. Though I suppose it's his crew who does all the serious boating."

As it turned out, the Weather Bureau's optimistic forecasting proved inaccurate. The wind was all over the lot, sometimes barely there at all. Shreve and Harris got off to a quick lead as the others floundered in the jam on the favored side. The competent yachtsmen—Shreve, Harris, a fellow from Corinthian—pursued their tack with a slow, steady persistence. The middling racers, Whelan among them, chased every header, trying to gain any advantage they could. Windsor Crawford's boat plugged along gamely, a good ways after the fleet—the leaders running one way, Whelan gambling on a split. He ran his Wianno forty degrees off course, tacking down wind.

"Where's he going?" Gretchen pointed.

"He's trying to freshen his wind," Sabina explained. "He thinks he can win this year."

Denny laughed. "He's in for a dumping if you ask me."

Sabina nodded. "His sheets are too high."

"Look at the rap. He's pinching."

"Why doesn't he bear off?"

"Because he's a knothead, for one."

After a while the sails grew too distant to distinguish. The McTigues stayed anchored for another class to start. It was a drifting match among the smaller one-designs—the prams and the beetles—who looked like they might be stuck battling wind shifts until dark.

"Do you think the water's terribly cold at this depth?" Gretchen yawned, sounding a little bored. Just as she was venturing a bare foot over the runabout's mahogany port, the current delivered, alongside their vessel, a shuddering ball of jetsam—black, sleek fur—struggling wildly against the action of the waves. The animal squealed in between hoarse, muted barks.

"Oh, my stars and garters! It's a puppy!" Gretchen exclaimed. "Just a wee thing! I don't think he's quite mastered the dog paddle."

"Well, don't just *stand* there critiquing his form," Sabina yelled from her perch on the gunwale.

"I'll go." Denny began kicking off his shoes.

"No, let me. I'm faster." Sabina jumped up, hoisting her beach dress over her head, glad again for having chosen a swimsuit in place of standard shapewear. She borrowed Gretchen's dotted Swiss scarf from around the girl's neck and tied off a quick ponytail. By the time she hit the water, the poor, gasping creature was a few yards past them, surrendering precious breaths to the larger swells, resurfacing with renewed panic, eyes wide and searching. It might have been a Chow, Sabina guessed, judging by the dog's spotted tongue. An otherwise friendly dog, but bordering on mad in its current predicament. Its claws scratched Sabina's arms and her back, furiously pawing for purchase. She managed to coax the animal under her left arm—a modified cross-chest carry—so she could guide them both back in the direction of the runabout.

She was just thinking what a good name for the pup might be when she spied the *Riva* coasting into view. The nicest yacht in the Sound that day, *Riva*'s well-waxed hull lines shone like crème brûlée. The outboard engine barely whirred, whisper quiet. She knew its occupants, despite her low sightline in the water, from the Norwegian flag that whipped behind the transom. And all at once the pit in her stomach threatened to sink her like a stone.

The way the group looked down at her, no matter who they'd been, it would have been humiliating. The ladies pinching the stems of their champagne flutes, their brightly lipsticked mouths forming ponderous O's. The men dressed in their light linens and immaculate white bucks. But they weren't just anybody, this tony set. They represented genuine royalty: Princess Ragnhild of Norway, her smirking newlywed husband, Isolde Martin, and, yes, it was him. It was *her* him—or so she'd dared to hope, scarcely an hour ago. Colin Hatch.

"*Arvid!*" the princess barked at her animal, pressing her champagne glass into her husband's hand so she could lean over, gripping the cleats for a better view. "You're a naughty boy! Come back here at once!"

At the sound of his mistress's voice, the dog seemed to remember his royal station and poise. He ventured first a front paw, then the pads of his hind feet, onto the flat of Sabina's skull—a bit like a circus seal balancing atop a ball. And from this elevated pose, Colin was able to hoist the dog back into its fine, humming boat.

Sabina arched her neck backward into the water, washing the masses of tangled curls from her eyes. She'd lost the scarf. Her hair must have looked a fright.

"Sabina." Hatch leaned into the handrail. "I didn't expect to see you here." He pushed his sunglasses from his eyes, up onto his forehead.

"I've been busy." She treaded. "You, too, I guess." She tried for a casual, dispassionate tone, but casualness was awfully hard to pull off whilst keeping her chin above the open chop. A cutting wind brought tears to her eyes. Intermittent splashes of waves forced her to blink back the stinging salt. A thousand thoughts crowded her mind. As quickly as the right words came to her they were lost again, driven away by the sounds of gawking gulls and the contoured pitches of a Norwegian dialogue above board.

"What is it you do out there, anyway? In Truro, I mean. Denny says you're volunteering at the base."

"I watch airplanes."

"Is that right? Well, *I'll be.*" He scratched his chin, thinking. "You ever see mine?"

"Sure. Beech 2-2-0-2-2. I've seen you passing by."

"How do I look?" He grinned. Despite the chill water, despite his choice of company, Hatch's smile warmed her as ever. She couldn't bring herself to smile back—not with such regal companions hovering so near. Instead she stared through clenched, slightly chattering teeth.

"Honestly? Very much like all the others."

He laughed this off. "Yeah, well, you keep up these water-rescue routines and you're going to get a reputation."

"I suppose you'd know about reputations better than anyone."

Hatch turned his face from the glancing blow. "Would you care to join us?"

"I can't right now."

"Come to the dance tonight then. The Regatta Ball. Maybe we could talk."

"I can't."

"I mean, I'd like to catch up with you."

"It's a formal. And I don't have a date." She dared him to admit that he already did.

"Find one."

"What's all this now?" At that moment Isolde Martin latched onto Hatch's shoulder, her face beset with theatrical worry. "Darling, is the poor child all right? What's she saying?" Isolde brushed a curl from her eye, all but shouting to be heard above the wind.

"This is a friend of mine," Hatch replied, still looking down at Sabina. "We were just speaking of the dance tonight."

"Oh, do join us, won't you?" Isolde leaned forward a little, clutching Hatch's hand as an anchor.

"I haven't got a date," Sabina said again, just at the same time Hatch was relaying, "She hasn't got a date."

"Well, Colin, you needn't go on advertising it. Let's not embarrass the poor girl." Isolde grazed his bare arm with her polished nails. "Don't worry, dear," she shouted down to Sabina. "Colin will save you a dance. For one night I can be generous enough to share him."

"Will you come?" Colin Hatch did not share his companion's carefree tone. Truth be told, he looked rather sunk. "Find a date and come. Will you?"

He wanted to see her then. That much was clear. Still, the comedown was too much. After all she'd felt and imagined for today. Everything about this scene undid her. She forced a burst of air through her nose and lips, immersing herself beneath the blanket of the waves. She scissors-kicked with all her acquired strength, covering the greatest distance possible in the direction of her brother's boat. When she resurfaced, some twenty feet removed, she heard laughter mounting behind her. Laughter cutting through the gathering fog bank—the kind of laughter certain women use best, not for amusement or joy, but for territory.

# FORTY-SIX

## WESTERN UNION

W. P. MARSHALL, PRESIDENT

The filing time shown in the dateline on telegrams and day letters is STANDARD TIME at point of origin. Time of receipt is STANDARD TIME at point of destination.

1954 AUG 12 3:36PM 1954 AUG 14 1:12PM

EDGARTOWN, MA=P.O. BOX 7786

DEAR ISOLDE: BESIDE MYSELF TO WIRE YOU THIS. WOULD'VE MUCH PREFERRED A PHONE CALL, BUT THAT ISLAND YOU'VE ADOPTED MIGHT AS WELL BE ON THE MOON. LET'S START BY AGREEING CAPRA IS OVERRATED & LARGELY IRRELEVANT TO OUR GOALS FOR YOUR CAREER. THEY FOUND SOME NEW YOUNG THING FOR MILKMAID ROLE. FORGET ABOUT IT. HAVING DINNER WITH HITCHCOCK'S HYPNOTIST TOMORROW. WILL PLANT A SEED. MEANTIME GET SELF ON FIRST FLIGHT BACK TO ANGELTOWN. WILDER'S COOKING UP DELICIOUS NOIR PIC. AGING HOUSEWIFE GONE MAD. JUMPS OFF ROOF. HOW SOON CAN YOU GAIN TEN POUNDS?

TOM

# FORTY-SEVEN

Back on land, Sabina crashed into the ladies lounge, assaulting the door with her bare shoulder, numb to the impact, caring only for shelter at the moment. Nervous energy colored her cheeks and heated her palms. Having hastily thrown it back on, just to cover her wet swimsuit, her dress now hung sopping. Her plan had been to borrow something decent from her tennis locker, then hurry home before the sailors came in. But the *Riva* was already anchored in its slip by the time she, Denny, and Gretchen glided into the dock.

"Hello there," called a low, throaty voice from behind. It was more of a growl than a greeting. Sabina turned to see a woman seated at the wicker vanity, her makeup kit spilled across the glass top, her eyes trained on Sabina's from the rearview of the mirror before her. *Of course.*

*Of course. Of course. Of course.* Sabina grit her teeth against her own shortsighted mistake. This was Isolde Martin.

"Hello," Sabina replied.

"Sabrina, isn't it?"

"*Sabina.*"

"How lovely. And unusual too! Is it Russian?"

"Irish. Well, Latin, actually."

"Perhaps you'd better get your story straight." Isolde picked up her lipstick and laughed, as if her own name were not a complete fiction. "That was quite a stunt you pulled out there. I think the princess might be of the mind to offer you a reward."

"She should be of the mind to pay closer attention to her pets," Sabina replied.

Isolde dotted her temples with a glass perfume dabber, smiling. "Tell me, did you enjoy the race, *Sabina*?"

"Not really." Sabina looked down at her sopping dress. "I was imagining something different for today."

"As was I!" Isolde exclaimed. "That's funny, isn't it? I wonder what sort of person does enjoy bobbing 'round in the wind, watching grown men play sailboats."

"Oh, I do normally enjoy it," Sabina clarified. "*I'm* that sort of person, I guess. It's just that this year—"

"Say no more. I know the problem entirely."

"You do?"

Isolde began to nod gravely as she tossed her complicated tubes and brushes, one by one, back into her enormous leather train case. *A magician's bag. A tackle box*, Sabina mused. "I guess we have a mutual acquaintance, don't we? Colin told me how you tagged after him this summer. What a sweet little helper you were. I'm sure it must have been an awful blow when the flirtation ended."

Sabina grappled for the right response. Of course she didn't care an ounce what Isolde Martin thought of her, but if she allowed this fiction to go uncorrected, didn't it make the actress's version at least partway true?

"You'd have to ask Colin," Sabina surprised herself in saying. She wasn't any kind of actress, but she was keen at human observation. And she realized, without meaning to, she'd assumed the very same haughty tone being leveled at her. She plopped onto the ladies room's settee, wearing her coolest expression. "I didn't have time to wonder how he felt. The government needed my analytical skills. Quite urgently too. And where I work now—taking note of national security—I don't really have the luxury of worrying over just one person. Not when there's a whole country to defend."

Isolde turned from the mirror to regard her adversary head-on. Sabina would have liked to look away, but the actress was so uniquely lovely, it was as though she *had* to keep staring in order to authenticate that face. Its truth held up. Genuine, blown-in-the-bottle beauty. And Isolde, in sensing this recognition, seemed to call her bluff.

"Sabrina, do you know how I can tell when an actress is finally all washed-up?"

"No, I think you'll have to tell me."

"It's when even *I* start to feel sorry for her. Cigarette?"

"I don't smoke," Sabina answered. She turned her gaze to the windows, where in between thickly gathered drapes the afternoon sky was opening up with new color. A band of pink clouds had gathered into tight, cottony curls—like the coat of an Airedale.

"Of course you don't smoke. Listen, my dear. I don't often waste time on the circumstances of others. But right now I feel sorry for *you*. And I think that's telling." When Sabina said nothing, Isolde continued in a falsely sororal way. "You've misplaced your affections. You think he's game to save your seat while you're off, how did you put it? 'Analyzing'? 'Taking notes'? And I'm telling you, he is not. Colin will never want that kind of a girl."

"Oh? Enlighten me then, what kind *will* he want?"

"Someone he can rescue." Isolde rose from the vanity, grabbing her train case by its sculpted ivory handle. "Just like that poor lost girl in Italy."

Sabina's muscles froze. A sting of betrayal fired her blood. Her hands shook inside her dress's wet pockets. "What do *you* know about a girl in Italy?"

She'd flubbed it. Her face, her tone, the way she'd stammered a bit in asking, revealed that Sabina knew less. Knew nothing actually.

Isolde pounced at the advantage. "People tell me I'm very easy to talk to. Good at getting intimate, you might say."

Yet again, Sabina's mind lost track of all the words she knew. All excepting one. She wanted to object, but nothing coherent would form behind her expression of devastated confusion. She didn't know she had the capacity to dislike someone so palpably.

"Will we see you at the dance tonight?"

"I don't think so," Sabina frowned. "I haven't got a date."

"Oh, that's right." Isolde drew her baby pearls into her mouth, biting the necklace like hard candy. "Probably for the best, isn't it? Look, you're a nice girl. Don't get caught up in a romance, Sabrina."

"Sabina."

"Men make paste out of girls like you. You haven't got the right armor for it."

"Haven't I?"

Isolde looked her up and down and sniffed a little laugh. "Not nearly. Holding on to a desirable man, *these days*? It's unbelievably hard work."

"Yes, I think I understand exactly the kind of work you put in," Sabina replied.

"Ah, but if that were true, you'd have a date to the dance tonight."

A light knock at the door breached their standoff. One of the club waitresses poked her head into the lounge. "Pardon me. Is Miss Martin in here?"

"Yes," Sabina very nearly shouted, wishing desperately she'd be called away.

"Who's asking?" Isolde fired back. "Another lousy telegram? Well, I don't want it. I won't read it."

"No, there's a gentleman on the telephone. Your, um . . . he says he's your *surgeon*?"

Isolde's face broke into a bemused sneer. She sat back down at the vanity, unbuckled her case's clasp, and began reapplying Hot Red Revlon, rather like an understudy suddenly called to take the stage. "What's he suggesting?"

"He says he'd like to move your, uh, *consultation* to this evening. Eight o'clock. At the Harbor View Hotel, he says."

"What else did he say?"

"He's on the line still, if you'd like to come ask him yourself."

"No, no." Isolde shook her head with a full-lipped, savoring expression.

Her gold tassel earrings swung and clacked about her neck. "Call me a car right away. Make sure it's a Cadillac with an air-cooling unit or else I'll send it back on your dime. Do you understand? But first go ahead and tell my surgeon I'll be there tonight, won't you? Tell him eight o'clock exactly. And, miss?"

"Yes?"

"Tell him the pain's been quite relentless since I last saw him. So maybe he ought to bring something, let's say, *restorative* with him."

The young waitress searched the tiles of the ladies' lounge floor for a fitting response. When nothing came to her, she ducked behind the door and disappeared.

Sabina moved to follow this same path. "I hope you'll make a full recovery, Miss Martin," she said, scarcely hiding the contempt in her voice. "Sounds like you've a busy evening ahead of you."

Isolde blotted her red lips on a tissue. "Keep taking notes, Sabrina. Maybe you'll learn something."

# FORTY-EIGHT

Colin Hatch drove the inland road to his farmhouse in a fraught silence. He was not conscious of turning or braking or pressing his foot against the gas, though he must have, for the car somehow made its way from Edgartown harbor to the fields approaching his farm—in damned near record time. He turned the truck's radio on then off again. He looked at his passenger seat: empty. He wondered how he'd gotten here—not just to West Tisbury, but *here*. This old place he knew so well.

It wasn't just the drama of the race, the awkward run-in with Sabina, which made him ashamed in a way he kept forcing himself to set aside. These days, he was moving quicker than usual *all the time*. Rushing through daylight without apparent reason. Since his night in Manhattan with Isolde, Colin halfway acknowledged this state, in him, as a kind of fatalistic relapse. He recognized its familiar moods and rhythms. He slept naked. He woke hungry. He allowed the farm to suffer while his vanity bloomed. He wore the sharp clothes she bought for him in the city, at first, for a laugh. And now because, hell, they fit. Florence kept after him with great patience, trying at intervals to restore some sense of normality. But his focus proved obvious, singular. Isolde drew him in like a bright, central vanishing point—a narrowing path toward a distant, burning star.

A star that had, at the moment, drifted clear out of view.

Where was she, after all? This woman who had demanded his notice and compliments all afternoon, only to suddenly make her excuses, duck into a car, and scuttle home to Chappy all alone. *No need*—she'd waved him off with brusque assurance—to pick her up for their date. She'd *catch up later*, at the ball.

*Where's the fire?* he'd called after her, his nose more than a little out of joint. An *earlier appointment in town* was the excuse she supplied, over her shoulder, adding it was *nothing much*, with all the smoke and mendacity of a street con—or, put another way, a damned lousy actress.

He was just pulling up the farm's shell-paved drive when he noticed a young woman beneath the shade of his old horse chestnut. Narrowly in time, his foot slammed the brake.

"Lenore? What are you doing here?" He cut the ignition and climbed out, glancing back down the hill, looking for where the Dooleys' driver might be idling in his Lincoln. But there was no car. Only Lenore standing beside a bicycle. "Are you—is it only you?"

"'Fraid so," Lenore shrugged, more humble than he'd known her to be. "Sorry to drop in unannounced."

"That's no trouble, except I'm only stopping home to get changed for the dance." He stretched his arms wide within his crisp polo. He had the odd sense she already knew something of the day's drama. He wondered if she'd crossed paths with Sabina at the club. Something in him hoped she had. "Aren't you getting dressed too?"

"I'm not going to the dance. Feeling a little under the weather," she replied, though her complexion looked perfectly rosy. "I'm going to do some reading instead."

"Well, here. Why don't you come inside then. Can I offer you coffee? Bicarbonate of soda?"

"No, thank you." She shook her head and blushed further. "I'll only stay a moment."

Colin led Lenore into his bright galley kitchen. He'd left the larder open, so its half-empty shelves now suffered the indignity of display—revealing how incomplete a home he inhabited. But the kitchen counters were more than well supplied with a bountiful harvest of plums and pears and nectarines. Bins of fruit—freshly picked and undelivered—assembled at the dining table and benches. He wove his way around this mess, delivering an unused chair from another room and offering her a seat.

"Is it an upset stomach? I think I've got some ginger root somewhere," he suggested, pulling down canning jars from a high shelf. "If you think that'd help any."

"I'm all right, really. Don't make a fuss over me. I only wanted to give you some news."

Colin leaned back against a well-worn butcher block. On its surface he'd abandoned the project of preserving his haricot beans. He crossed his arms over his chest. "Let me guess," he smirked. "It's to do with your wedding? As entertainment, you've hired a band of sideshow performers who eat stakes of fire and belch five-foot flames?"

"Not quite." She tugged at her traveling gloves.

Colin thought perhaps the girl looked a little dispirited. "Ah, then maybe you've paid a man to release twelve hundred doves at dusk, at the conclusion of the recessional, and now you need all your guests to come dressed in oilskins for the dove droppings."

"I mean actual *news*," Lenore stewed.

"I didn't think you bothered with much actual news. Apart from *Vogue*'s fall preview. Is that what you're reading?"

Without warning, Lenore Dooley jumped to her feet, grabbed an unsuspecting nectarine, and hurled it at him. Colin crouched just in time to let the munition sail past into the hallway. Next thing, they heard a picture frame crashing to the floor.

"Ball one," Colin whistled. "High and outside."

"Are you finished cracking wise?"

"Seems I'd better be."

"Have I got your full attention?"

"You might just have asked for it. No need to weaponize the fruit."

"I'm so tired of everyone assuming I'm weak in the head," Lenore burst out. She wiped a glove below her eyes. "You and Sabina. John. My parents.

I see it in your faces. All of you! But I'm not some little cluck for you to ridicule."

"Of course you aren't." Colin softened his tone. "I don't see you that way."

"Oh, that's flam and you know it. Just now you couldn't wait to poke fun at my wedding plans—the way I dwell on them, more like."

"Well, you have to admit," he rubbed his forehead, "it's not every bride who goes scouting about for confectioners to sculpt her likeness out of—"

"Marzipan." Lenore sat back down, taking off her hat. "All right, so maybe I can't figure cube roots, but I'm not . . . I'm not . . . *dim*. Do you know *why* I spend most days in paraffin wraps in the manicure chair? Do you know *why* I resort to superficial banter, Colin?"

"I don't, honestly."

"It so happens I live in a house where deflection is our family's foremost occupation. Practically an Olympic sport. You either become very skilled at waging war or at avoiding it. I suppose I have found that marzipan and floral arrangements are benign topics, even with my father in the room. A person can manage to chew and swallow her meal while discussing dimity patterns. Less so, I can tell you, when real estate and union strikes and creditors enter the conversation."

"I'm sorry." Colin offered her his handkerchief. He moved a carton of fruit from a chair and pulled it up alongside hers. "I didn't realize. That must be difficult."

The bride shook her head ruefully, sniffling. "It's habit, by now. Burying all the things I know. My father's shell corporations. His sleazy grafts and kickbacks. What else for me, but to invent a life of trifling interests? All right, I'll admit, I *can* be vain. Materialistic, some might even say. I do rather like to visit the shops on Newbury. I enjoy getting noticed in a blond mink. But can you imagine what would happen if I came to the dinner table, thrown together in any old thing, postulating on current affairs like—well, like Sabina might? Giving voice to every moment's headline?"

"No," Hatch admitted. "I can't."

"Someone ought to tell her how lucky she is."

"I think she'd argue she's as penned in as anyone. Maybe we all are, to our different degrees."

"Is that why you go around letting my father treat you as his indentured servant?"

Colin stiffened.

Lenore hung her head, twisting the diamond around her ring finger. "I'm sorry. I didn't mean to insult you. But it is why I'm here in the first place." She reached into her purse and placed a stack of cash on the table. "I wanted to give you this."

"Give me this?" Colin puzzled. "Whatever for?"

"It's a pittance compared to everything our family—my father—owes you. But at the moment it's all I've got."

"Lenore, I don't understand. I'm certainly not going to accept . . ." He drew closer, examining the pile. "Why, there's five hundred dollars here. Where did you get this?"

"I pawned my wedding presents. All the silver pieces anyway. Denny helped me." The young woman nudged the cash toward him. "Five hundred American. That's three hundred thousand lira. I want you to send it to your investigator in Rome. I've got his name and address right here. He's finally found your girl. She's written a letter for you, in fact. Only he won't release this last chapter without payment. Here's his latest correspondence, reminding what's owed. We both know Daddy will never respond."

Colin held his temples to bring her explanation into focus. He reached for the paper she extended—a letter, it appeared, matching the one he'd seen from Dooley outside the seed shed. He read its contents and began to understand exactly where they'd all arrived.

Adele, alive. *Alive.*

And still, the news didn't hit him right. He waited for his reaction. He waited for the tide of warm sense memories: youth, happiness—memories of his life *before*—to rush in and restore him, like a man long held hostage in midwinter, struggling to remember the natural feeling of his unclenched muscles and toes.

But nothing came.

This confirmation on paper—*Adele, alive!*—couldn't even excite the pace of his heart. No great wave of relief undid his captive spirit. No sudden knot undone. Quite the opposite, a toying note of sorrow stirred and mounted. Sorrow tinged with guilt.

"Why do you have this?" he asked finally.

"I've been reading my father's mail," Lenore confessed. "Last month it was just something bratty to do. But life's funny, I guess. The way you find one thing while you're looking for something else."

"I won't take your money." He shook his head. "Not even to hear from her."

"But, Colin," Lenore slid her chair closer to his, "you've got to. It would change everything for you. After all you've been through. Don't you want for people to know the truth?"

"The truth." Colin laughed. He heard an uncharacteristic note of bitterness when he spoke.

"But think of Sabina."

He *had* thought of Sabina. That was the problem. Without fail, for weeks, up until that night in Manhattan. He'd thought almost exclusively of the girl up until his run-in with Whelan. Up until his telephone call to the airbase that seemed to suggest Sabina wasn't thinking very much of him. And if she was indifferent enough to move on with other affairs, then so could he be.

"Look, Lenore, it's no more my job to convince people of my honor than it is yours to convince them of your depth."

"Why did you make that deal with my father then? If you weren't even going to try for a military appeal?"

"I just needed to know she was okay." He picked up Adele's recent photograph from the envelope. The girl was older. The fullness of her cheeks had gone. A shorter style of hair. But there was no mistaking her eyes. "May I keep it?"

Lenore nodded. "I suppose I'm not one to offer romantic advice," she reached for his hand, "but I don't think you ought to give up on our friend, the bookworm. There's a week or two yet before the summer's over and she's gone off to college."

Colin laughed. "I punched James Whelan in the face last week, in front of five hundred people. I'm not sure that Weston College dean of hers will like me any better these days."

"Sabina doesn't care about that old dean. She told James it'd be a snowstorm in July before she'd break if off with you over some dean's silly rules."

"Is that true?" Colin felt his face warming. "She said that?"

"Gotten herself into a ferocious standoff with her aunt, as well."

"Then why hasn't she written or telephoned all summer long? Why hasn't she even tried to see me?"

"She's here now. Maybe she *is* trying. In her way."

"She is here now, isn't she?" He remembered now how she'd looked when he said he wanted to speak with her. Sure, she was angry to find him as he was, on that boat with Isolde and the Norwegians, but maybe . . .

"So what next?" Lenore pressed him. "You've got your answers. But you'll keep working for my father?"

"I haven't decided, to be honest."

"Coward."

"I guess I got distracted."

Colin Hatch looked down at the letter. He read it twice. Adele was alive. She'd actually made it out. She had a son. Safety. A home. If that didn't bring him relief exactly, it brought him something close to peace. And vindication. Not the sort he could ever hold up to the world, but just enough to keep for himself. And for Sabina, too, who maybe hadn't been so indifferent after all.

"Well?" Lenore pressed.

"Your father won't let me off easy. I'd have to pay his farm loan in full. I could maybe sell my plane to swing it."

"Sell the whole company, why not?"

"I can't sell the company. Bill's got rights to that—legally speaking—whatever worth he hasn't gambled away. But one of those airplanes—the one we started with—is mine. I could sell it back to him." Hatch nodded with a shifting momentum. "That would almost square us for the farm."

"My father is flat broke," Lenore leveled. "Don't give him any more bargaining pieces. He'd only take your plane without paying. But maybe . . ."

"Maybe what?"

"Maybe I know of another buyer."

# FORTY-NINE

James Whelan soaped and dried his hands with all the gusto of a man who'd aced Advanced Bacteriology. He combed his hair, smooth and slick, behind his ears. Examined his teeth for any remnants of the club's crab cake hors d'oeuvres. Was his breath all right? He gave himself a gentleman's C, contented in the knowledge that love was on his side tonight. A miraculous night! Resurrected at the eleventh hour, clear out of nowhere, when he'd finally landed his dream date to this very ball.

How had he done it? No matter. She was here, and that was enough, despite whatever caveats she'd claimed about a platonic evening, no monkey business, et cetera, et cetera. His vision was materializing. Sabina McTigue was coming around.

He'd waited *so* long. *How many years now?* It was true what they said about good things and waiting, he chuckled to himself. But Sabina was so much more than a good thing. She was the perfect thing. The perfect woman. And one day, at his side, she would positively thrive as the perfect New York City housewife, as well. He was sure of it now. Could picture her stepping out of their beaux arts building, undaunted by the pace of the streets or the dirt in the air, the way that mousier town-and-country–born girls could be.

She'd appreciate the architecture—the history built into the Dakota, the Apthorp, the Beresford. In fact, she was more perfect still for being someone he could *introduce* to his neighborhood, whereas the native, acculturated girls were all so jaded and snide. Always convinced they knew the fastest way to get from one block to the next. Jesus, James hated that.

He checked himself in the men's room mirror one last time, for good measure. Yes, sir, Sabina McTigue was the only possible fate for him. Brains. Beauty. Not too tall. Dainty feet. Her build was not the type to go all soft and dowdy after children. She already knew well enough what to expect from Mother. And think of it: Whenever he wanted quiet time to go his own way—on weeknights, or weekends, or whenever he didn't particularly feel like being husbandly—she was the kind of girl who could find her own amusements. That was just gravy.

He swaggered back into the function room, stopping by the bar on his way.

"Two whiskey sours," he ordered. "And don't spare the whiskey."

He touched his eye beneath his new glasses. The injury looked better than last week, but it still smarted something awful. *What an animal*, James thought again, *that Colin Hatch*. A real wild animal. And the sad thing, he shook his head in disgust, was how you could find some version of that animal trawling just about every bar and nightclub in America. In the city, smooth guys on the make at least had some purpose. They filtered out a certain type of girl.

But here, on the island, Hatch simply didn't belong.

James had tried, ever so gently, explaining to Sabina the obvious problem with the pilot. And yet she still couldn't see it. Couldn't see how any man who made his money hauling other men's luggage or else tilling about some overgrown victory garden was a man afraid to engage in more intelligent pursuits. A man headed nowhere, fast.

Whelan, on the other hand, was about as forward-thinking as they came. He'd reminded Sabina of that certain difference in the car, lest she overlook the considerable step upward she was taking here tonight. Whelan was a celebrated student of philosophy and medicine and, just as notably, a sensitive collector of arts. His Black Forest cuckoo clocks, for example. Did she remember that surprising fact? Of course she did. Try finding another available doctor with the same level of dynamism. Try finding another man of science who understood what a sin it would be to tack a cheap corsage onto a Dior satin peplum.

James had so hoped Sabina would wear the black Dior again tonight. And she had. But her choice of dress meant that buying her the usual floral accessory was out of the question. Wristlet bouquets were sloppy, in James's opinion—along the lines of public school girls in blue eyeshadow. Moreover, a wristlet would've been beneath this evening's momentous mood. *Our first date!* An engagement sure to be remembered on a Parisian balcony in ten years' time. So James had gone and ordered something altogether different. In truth, he'd gone and ordered it weeks ago, in hopes that Sabina would finally agree, after so many summer seasons, to quit ignoring their shared history and accept the clear eventuality of a life together. He could hardly contain his excitement.

It was a crown.

The thing he'd ordered for Sabina was a flamingo-pink orchid-and-gillyflower *crown.* A massive wreath of silk blooms and hand-sewn leaves designed to be worn just below the hairline, across the forehead, sitting atop the curves of the ears. It was stunning. Sabina nearly fell out of the car when he presented it to her.

And now here she was, a vision come to life, waiting by the dance floor in the clubroom's dusky light. Sabina McTigue was his date. She looked regal, angelic, although the floral crown—he set down the drinks to help her—had just dipped down over her eyes again.

"Are you enjoying yourself?" he breathed on her ear.

"Yes, this is quite an evening," she nodded, steadying the wreath by gripping on both sides. "Overwhelming, one might say. But look, please don't steer me, James."

"Compared to the city, this place is beat," he grunted, releasing his hold on her elbow. "If you're keen on dancing, I could show you some legitimate hotspots in Manhattan. Right off the top, let's see, you've got the Onyx Club, Jimmy Ryan's—I know this one haunt where there's a two-hour floor show, and the stage girls bend like pipe cleaners. They get their ankles up over their ears, and—"

"Gosh. I'd be lost in a place like that."

"You'd manage all right. You only think you wouldn't like it because you grew up in Dullsville. But you could learn to appreciate the Onyx Club. Jimmy Ryan's, for sure. I could show you this one—"

"James?" she cut in. "Would you be terribly hurt if I set aside my crown for a bit? It's so delicate. I just worry I might be crushing the petals."

James was taking the liberty of showing her how better to position the headpiece when the club's most irksome member, Windsor Crawford, sauntered up beside them. Crawford was dressed in the island's requisite yachting ensemble: blue blazer, Oxford shirt, classic Edgartown reds—a brick-colored trouser all the club men owned. "Say, what happened out there today, Whelan? Missed the mark at Horse Shoe Shoal?"

"I didn't *miss* the mark," Whelan protested, inching up his glasses. "It had drifted clear to Bermuda before the RC got out with the reverse-code flag."

"That's not what Connelly said."

"Connelly's a moron."

"He didn't miss the mark, though."

"You can't tell me Connelly studied his course sheet any better than I did."

"Well, some people may study." Windsor stuck out his lip. "Other people just sail. Say, who hung that shiner on you, Jimbo? Must've been quite a punch."

"I think it was a tough outing for everyone," Sabina offered, as a kind of neutral consolation. "The wind was so fluky and then the fog bank that blew in out of nowhere. At one point I couldn't see my own hand in front of me." As she reached out to demonstrate, her gaze caught on something, *someone*, newly materialized across the dance floor. She shooed a silk leaf from her eye, staring straight into the diamond-flecked party crowd.

Whelan followed her stare. Through the bodies of the twirling partners and the sparkling lights of a thousand little mirrors, all glued to the globe on the ceiling, Colin Hatch stood head and shoulders above the other men. A gray-suited island amid a sea of navy blazers.

"Sabina, please. Don't pay him any mind," James instructed. "He's lucky I didn't bring him up on assault charges. God knows I've gone to court over much less."

"Did Colin do this to your face?" she gasped.

"Not entirely," Windsor Crawford put in. "I'd say Mr. and Mrs. Whelan deserve some of the blame for that face."

"That's terrible." Sabina clapped a hand over her mouth, startled to think she was the cause of any injury. "I had no idea. I mean, I knew you were angry with one another, but—"

"Don't feel sorry on my account. He landed one good lick. I could've countered if I wanted, but the press was everywhere."

"Let's be glad for that." Sabina patted his arm.

"I don't know. More I think about it, I've a good mind to go over there and even the score right now." Whelan tugged his lanyard from his pocket, swinging its great many keys around five freckled knuckles.

"I can't let you do that," she said. "You'd regret it, James, I'm sure. You're too classy a person. And a doctor, besides, which means you've sworn an oath to heal people. Haven't you?"

"Not yet, I haven't."

"All the same. Please try to ignore him."

"Do you want to know what he *said* to me? That night?"

"No, really. I don't."

"What an animal. Said something pretty crass about you, and—okay, I won't repeat it. You're right. But, hell, it got me boiled."

"Thank you for taking the high road. Although"—Sabina rubbed her forehead, as if piecing together the clues of a puzzle, and bit her lip—"did you by any chance mention my letter from Weston College? The one that you and your cousin's wife handily provoked?"

"Never mind, Sabina. I'm man enough to put that vexatious ordeal behind me." Whelan swallowed.

"Yes, but tell me first." She dropped her flower crown onto the doorknob of the broom closet. She folded her arms across her black Dior. "Did you mention Dean Budge? The letter?"

"All's I said to the man," Whelan huffed with impatience, "is that his character was sorely lacking. I doubt anyone could argue with that."

"That's all you said?"

"And so"—Whelan poked at the bridge of his glasses—"so no wonder Weston's dean disapproved of him."

"I see. *That's* all you said?"

"And so . . ." He winced. His hands felt clammy. He dragged them against his pant legs. Damned if that idiot Crawford didn't just stand there grinning. ". . . so no wonder you'd decided to give him the brush-off."

"You told him *I'd* given *him* the brush-off? On account of Weston College?"

James knew Sabina was not going to like the fact of that last comment. She often complained that he spoke for her without permission. He watched his date press her lips together, draining them of their pretty pink color. She didn't seem *too* angry. Her expression kept up anyway, pleasant enough. She was only mildly stewing, he judged, waiting, watching the dancers, acknowledging their mutual acquaintances standing here and there around the room.

"Windsor, could you allow us moment?"

"Yeah, Crawford. Clear out, why don't you?"

"James," Sabina pronounced finally, squinting in the curious way she did sometimes. "You were very gracious to escort me here tonight, but I'm afraid I ought to be going. I have a speaking engagement at Town Meeting tomorrow. A good sleep would improve it."

Whelan grabbed hold of her arm. Brutish behavior, maybe, but he couldn't help himself from trying to contain her, this perfect jewel in the vision of his future. She wasn't being fair to him. "*Going*? What, *now*? Sabina, they haven't even played a slow number yet."

"Here you are," she replied, handing him the flower wreath off the doorknob. "Try this on. In my experience, just about everything moves excruciatingly slow while wearing it."

# FIFTY

Isolde Martin swept into the Harbor View Hotel donning the dress she'd worn to the 25th Academy Awards—sequined, sleeveless, bearing five dozen dime-sized buttons from its low-cut back right on down to the floor. Her smile glowed. Her baby blue irises floated higher than usual, riding a span of reddened sclera, framed by black, kohl-lined lids. It was only eight o'clock and already she was trolleyed. High-flying. Hopped up on her special "vitamins" and a bottle of contraband Pernod.

Isolde entered the penthouse without knocking. She smiled in imagining this could have been her first night at the island. *Should* have been her first night at the island—with a proper welcome and her favorite suitor waiting. Harris had already ordered a bucket of ice and a bottle for himself. For her, he'd ordered an exquisitely tiered silver-plated banana split. He was always cruel like this at first, so he could be nicer to her later.

"I didn't enjoy seeing you there with another man," he greeted her. "At the benefit, I mean. That dress?" He whistled, pressing himself against her. "You wore it for me, didn't you?"

"I wore it for your wife," Isolde replied, pushing him away.

"I thought this summer retreat was meant to mellow you. But look, you're as vindictive as ever."

"And you're still greedy and wrinkled." She pinched his cheek. "As long as we're making observations."

"Isolde, I know you're fed up." Harris collapsed onto the edge of the bed, taking her hand in his. She stood stiffly in front of him. She checked the bottle: two generous pours already dispensed. "But I promise you, Bitsy doesn't want the damage to drag out any longer than it has to. She wants one more Thanksgiving in Connecticut. One more honest-to-goodness holiday with Granny and Pop Pop. For the children."

"Granny and Pop Pop?" Isolde deadpanned.

"How much harm in another few months? You travel so often, it'll be October before you're free anyway—"

"That's what *she* wants?"

"Say, Love," Harris swayed moonily, "have you got anything with you? Even a half of something. To wake me up."

Isolde reached into her clutch, fishing for the pillbox. She plucked out her agent's telegram, still folded inside, and wadded it over the wastepaper basket. Outside the closed door, she heard the hoots of the Longford crew—stupid boys still playing in their sailboating clothes, running up and down the stairwells with pliers and mallets, swapping out the hotel room numbers at all the wrong doors.

Harris rose and held her from behind. His shirt hung open. She felt his soft, feathery chest hair brushing against the skin of her bare back. She felt the strength of his hands cupping her chest, felt them even through her rigid baleen corset. The one she'd gone to have made on Chabanel in Montreal, where the French-trained corset makers still knew a proper basque from a straightjacket.

"There's less of you these days," he commented.

"That's the very idea."

She was still hunting in her bag when he said, "I appreciate the little bump. I've got to get back to Boston tonight, and I can't risk nodding off—"

"Back to Boston?" Isolde interrupted, looking up from the task.

"Yes. Back to Boston. And I don't want to fall asleep on the ferry. Aw, hell, why are you angry *now*?"

"Why did you ask me here if you're not staying the night?"

"Because I wanted a bit of time with you." He nuzzled her neck with his hot, sun-flushed cheeks. He was drunk. "Where's the harm in that?"

She turned around and kissed him. His urgency was contagious—warm and unsteadying. She pulled away to pour herself a drink—a big one—to buy herself a moment of clarity. Still, the outrageous dessert on the table was mocking her. *Good luck*, it seemed to say. *Good luck to you*. Harris caught hold of her chin and started up kissing her again.

"It's just," she broke away, pressing two fingers to her temple, "I don't understand. You called *me* at the yacht club. You *invited* me here. If you're not even *staying*—why, the last boat to Boston is just an hour from now."

"Christ. Isolde. Don't be so childish."

"*Childish?*" Her whole body rose up against the accusation.

"Look at yourself. Are you going to tell me you've gotten dressed to the nines all for a quiet night in with me? Just look at yourself."

"Look at *yourself*!" she roared, throwing a pill at him.

Once upon a time, before they'd cast the leading man in her very first picture, a studio head allowed Isolde to sit in on his auditions. He said he wanted to find an actor who "sounded sincere." That was his only criterion, and yet it proved more elusive than the casting call descriptions demanding swordplay skills, foxtrot mastery, a willingness to perform acrobatic stunts on horseback. For hours—maybe days, who could remember? The whole thing was a blur—she'd sat and listened to the same clichéd lines of dialogue, reprised and recreated with comically exaggerated attempts at the sincere. Swings and misses. *Embarrassing* swings and misses. That's what listening to Harris was like. She loathed him. She reviled his words, taken from some other man—from *every* other man before him.

"I'll have you know," he muttered, his head disappeared beneath the hotel bed skirt. He was on his hands and knees, hunting to find where the stimulant had landed. "I woke up at four o'clock this morning. I went to work. I sailed in a goddamned—*fifty-six miles* I sailed in a goddamned *sailing competition*. I shook ten thousand people's hands and pretended to remember all their lousy kids. And now here *you* come in, guns blazing, stirring up some nonsense over where I'm meant to *sleep*, when, well, look at you! Why can't you admit it? You had other plans yourself. Probably still have!"

Isolde watched him crawling on the floor. She wished she didn't love him. She wished she loved Colin Hatch instead. Like the girl at the yacht club, maybe. Isolde remembered how she'd tried to start a fight over the pilot, and how maddening it had been when the girl couldn't be riled. Well, that was being good, she supposed. Doing nothing. Listening. Agreeing. Waiting, forever and ever. No, Isolde knew she could not be that nice girl at the club. Because there wasn't any substance to good, and she already felt empty enough.

After a time, Harris resurfaced holding up the pill to advertise his victory. He knocked it back with a swallow of whiskey.

"I'm sorry," she murmured. She was sitting on the bed now, the ice cream sundae nestled in her lap.

"Are you really?"

"Yes."

"Good. That's good because your favorite surgeon needs to ask you something."

"All right," she agreed. Everything felt easier now. The sudden intake of fats and sugars rendered her instantly, temporarily serene. She ate her dessert while Harris drank. For a moment, the room was light and calm.

"I would like to ask that you make an appearance at Town Meeting tomorrow."

"Do what?"

"The Edgartown Town Meeting. It's tomorrow. Just before the polls open on the new warrant. I'm saying maybe you could drop by. Tell some folks why the bridge is so important to you."

Isolde's eyebrows went high. "I didn't know that it was. So important to me, I mean."

"It's not worth debating. Just say you'll go and wear something decent."

"Aren't you afraid I might reveal myself childish?"

"Look, you're making a fuss again. And all's I'm asking is that you say a few words about the bridge and perhaps your upcoming role, which is perfect for you, by the way. And just, all the things we've discussed."

Isolde collected a big breath in her chest. She looked to the window. She watched the red beacon at Lighthouse Beach blink on and off against the darkness outside. "I didn't get the role."

"What's that?"

"The Capra film. I didn't get it. My agent sent a telegram today. He paid three dollars per word and he wrote in full sentences. That's how badly he needed to let me know."

Harris lit a cigarette, watching her devour the dessert. "I'm awfully sorry, darling. But let's face it. Capra doesn't deserve you."

"Why do you want me at that Town Meeting, Harris?"

"Because I'm *asking* you. To go."

"Because you expect the people here are dim enough to actually care what I think, is that it?"

"Because it's a simple favor. I do them for you all the time."

"And because *Bill Dooley* can't afford to see that bridge get blocked. Isn't that right?"

"It's a simple favor to me *and to Bill*." His voice rose to eclipse hers. "And I do favors *for you* all the time."

"And because," she spoke louder still, the sleepiness in her eyes replaced with a belligerent conceit, "because this whole ruse—the house, the island, your meeting me here—it's all been for this!"

He laughed at her. Took the glass sundae dish from her hands and let his laughing eyes tread all over her. "You give yourself too much credit, you know that?"

"Three dollars per word, Harry. That's the going rate to reject me. Where's your wallet?"

"You're dotty, Myrna."

He used her real name to provoke her. It worked a charm. "It's *all* been for *this*!"

"Why don't you cut out the ham act already? Do you realize, if I had to explain every political preference of mine, we'd be here until Christmas?"

"I don't need you to *explain* anything," she hissed at him. She hid her face in the crook of her arm; all at once the room became oppressive. A cold, prickly flash shot down the back of her skull. She felt faint, nauseated. The room shrank all around her, the air too odious to fully inhale. Isolde collapsed her head against a mirrored wall—the blanched curves of her face coming at her peripherally, with terrifying effect. She felt weak. She felt as though she might never feel well again.

"We would be here *until Christmas*," Harris repeated.

"Right. Except that you're *not staying*."

"*And neither are you!*" he roared.

The herd of stomping Longford sailors barreled past the closed door again. Something hard or else thrown with a good bit of force hit the other side of the wall. Laughter erupted—hooting cries that gradually dimmed and settled into a frightening silence. Through the open window, Isolde heard tires screech. Four floors down, the cars were peeling out onto North Water Street. Having quite a time, they were. Quite a wonderful time.

Isolde looked at herself. A long, chocolate stain bled down the front of her dress. Across her face, a visible heaviness was descending. It weighed on her shoulders, her eyelids. She fought to sit up straighter but landed further slumped. She thought she might like to rest a spell. To close her eyes and drift. She heard Harris gathering his things. Heard the door slam shut. The lights were out and the room stood still. But something in Isolde flickered to life just then: a memory, an impulse, a dream she'd once had and couldn't quite remember.

*There's nothing you can do wrong that I can't fix.*

# FIFTY-ONE

*Where is Isolde? No Miss Martin tonight? But isn't she coming?*

Since Colin had arrived at the Regatta Ball, this was all anyone could think to say to him, and now the question—or lack of an answer—was beginning to get on his nerves.

"Evening, Colin. You come stag?" Denny McTigue and his girl from the office came swanning over.

"Not on purpose," Hatch laughed.

"Sabina seemed to think you were spoken for tonight," Denny added. "But maybe Isolde's not coming then?"

Hatch had to admit, yet again, he hardly knew. She had said she'd be sure to meet him here, at the dance, sometime before the trophies were presented. But that part of the evening had come and gone. The Venona Cup now sat abandoned on a shelf in the coatroom, along with fifty-seven pairs of high heels, belonging to the girls with sore arches from trying to keep pace with Bill Haley.

"I don't know." Hatch yawned, checking his watch. "I don't know where she is."

"Say, what about Lenore?" Denny leaned across his date to ask this second bit somewhat discreetly. "Have you seen Lenore tonight?"

"Lenore isn't coming," Hatch replied. For this much he did know.

"Is that a fact?" Denny's shoulders caved a little.

"I saw her at the farm today. Said she wasn't feeling quite well."

"Is she sick or what?"

"For someone who didn't offer up two words at dinner you're awfully interested in whoever's *not* here," Denny's date complained.

"I'm sorry, I—listen, Gretch," Denny checked his watch. "Maybe we ought to be heading home. I've got a flight lesson in the morning. And maybe, it turns out, I'm not feeling quite well either."

"Heading home? At ten o'clock? I paid eighty-seven dollars for this dress, and you've hardly given four and a quarter's worth of notice."

"I know. I'm sorry, Gretch. It's just that I remembered something about tomorrow. An early start I've got to make."

"Dennis McTigue, are you giving me the slip? Because if I didn't know you better, I'd think this was an awfully crafty play. That old Sigma Phi tactic of hot, cold, and repeat. I suppose you'll say you lost my telephone number next."

"No tactics, I promise. I just—"

"I'm not going to *beg* you, if that's the idea. Some girls may go in for the artful, complicated type, but not me. Not me, buster."

Hatch slapped McTigue, the poor bastard, on his back—a gentleman's goodbye—and excused himself to the lady, who was too wounded to notice. He circled the floor, patting his chest for his cigarette case. Only three Luckys left. He supposed he'd have to make them last. His palm held steady to protect the lighter's flame, so his still form stood all the more pronounced against the fast, jumping music and the full-skirted dancers whirling like rainbowed eddies.

Across the room, he saw Sabina catch him staring. She'd just handed James her fairy garlands in a quick little pushing match, like reverse tug-of-war. Her gold bracelet came undone. He watched her snatch it up from the dance floor, only to hurry away in the direction of the coats.

It was the sight of Sabina that did it finally: woke up his heart to Adele and that Italian letter, confirming her safety. Earlier, back at the farm, maybe he hadn't been ready. Maybe two months of doubting Dooley hadn't equipped him to hear the news just yet, never mind hold up its full weight—as though someone had handed him a bag of gold, while he floundered, treading water, in the middle of the ocean. But here, now, with his two feet on steady ground and his best girl before him, he let himself try.

He felt himself reawakening to those early mornings in June. The beach. The farm. Everywhere he and Sabina had moved and laughed together. All their long summer days and nights melded into one bright, strident moment. And for the first time since that yacht club bruncheon—heck, since he was a kid—he felt like flying—*really* flying. Taking off just to go. No one in his ear, on his back. He felt that heady, dumbstruck bliss most guys only get to feel once, if they're lucky—like his wildest dreams weren't even halfway drawn to scale with the actual possibilities of the world. Like the best things that could come from a moonlit night might be *so* good, *so* beautiful, he couldn't even begin to predict.

"Excuse me." Colin burst forth, pushing his way past Windsor Crawford, past Mrs. Shreve and the commodore, past the Ewings and the Nashes and the rest of his Sunday-night card partners. The band started in on a familiar Sinatra tune.

# FIFTY-TWO

"You look like a girl in need of some repair," Colin Hatch announced himself. His glinting eyes dared her to feel any which way except swooning. By some romantic's deft hand, the lights faded three degrees dimmer just as a familiar ballad—their very first dance song—came to life from the bandstand. "A dance partner too."

"Is that a proposition, or are you just making small talk?" Sabina replied. She toed at a strand of tissue streamer that had fallen from the rafters. She scanned the other couples in their orbit. Loose-limbed embraces began forming on all sides, a sea of bodies lapsing into smooth, steady rhythms. A part of her considered rejecting the offer of his arm, wondering how quickly she could flee the room, how successfully she might keep her tears (of sadness? anger?) at bay. But instead she looked up at Hatch with steely eyes, determined not to repeat any displays of immaturity. She'd gone and endured James Whelan all night for a reason.

"I could fix that clasp for you." He gestured to the bracelet in her purse.

"Where've I heard that old promise before?"

"Sometimes a first try doesn't take."

Sabina let out a laugh, which she hoped came off sounding wry and breezy and ultimately above it all. "How many tries do you expect you deserve?"

"That's a trick question." He pulled her into a close box step before she could object. "Feels like I might get socked no matter how I answer."

"From what I hear, you're the one doing all the headhunting."

"Aw, hell. That's just Whelan and his glass jaw. Whatever his complaints, at least I fight barefisted."

"Meaning what?"

"Meaning, he's as underhanded as a fifty-four-card deck. You can't count on him for the full story."

"You've got some gall, you know that? Standing here grinning like a big-time smoothie."

"I'm only following your cues."

"Yes, but I'm smiling for appearance's sake. *You?* You're genuinely delighted."

"I can't actually pretend otherwise when I'm with you." His hand at her back drifted upward, for a moment, to stroke the smooth curve of her French twist. She made a little head jerk to discourage him.

"Honestly, Colin," she whispered. "Did you expect I'd just melt into a puddle after seven weeks without so much as a word?"

"Didn't you get the tomatoes?"

"I'd have preferred an honest explanation." Sabina glanced up at him. His nose and cheeks proved newly flushed from the ocean sun.

"I didn't think you college gals were *allowed* to keep time with a hound like me. Tomatoes seemed safer than love letters."

"I don't care what I'm *allowed*. And anyway, I'm an altogether different person these days. What with everything I've learned and seen. So you'll have to try a bit harder than that."

"Look, I'm not claiming any medals. *I'm* to blame for this summer. I know that. And I haven't exactly made things better. I haven't been perfect . . ." His speech trailed off into the room's many shadows. In the space he left dangling, Sabina supposed she could imagine what "less than perfect" looked like. Less than perfect with Isolde Martin. "But in my heart . . ." he was saying.

"Please don't wax poetic." She pressed her cheek to his lapel. While her words fought, her body surrendered to the powers of the soft melody. Even as she found herself plotting harsh gambits, she recognized the cooperative motion of their coupled arms and legs, the reflexive nearness she assumed—her chest pressed to his, her head tucked beneath his chin. "I've heard plenty about your heart today. In particular, how it's bound to cherish some timid creature in need of rescue."

"Is that right? Says who?"

"Isolde Martin." She looked up at him for a reaction.

"Oh." Hatch's smile vanished. "I didn't realize you'd swapped notes."

"I wish we hadn't. Then I mightn't have known how well you're willing to confide in her. Whatever dark past you couldn't share with me. The war? Your girl?"

"I admit, I told Isolde too much. In truth, I *started* to tell her everything. But I didn't, I swear. Not what really happened. And the bits I told her, that was only because—she's not like you, Sabina."

"I'm aware of that." Sabina's fingertips roved the seam of Hatch's suitcoat—a surprisingly mesmerizing path over the mountain of his shoulder. She recalled Emma Dix's advice, asked for and answered, and quoting Longfellow besides: *Let the dead past bury its dead.* Past was one thing, Sabina supposed. Isolde Martin seemed rather immediate.

"No, wait now. I'm only saying that to mean, just that she's made her share of mistakes, same as me. Gotten tangled up in some ugly jams."

"Tangled up, I'll say. She was draped around you like a clinging vine today. Out on that boat. Calling you *dear* and *darling*."

Hatch's eyes leveled her. "I don't remember any clinging vines, but while we're examining the record, I might put in that I *did* try to reach you, actually. The other night. It was Friday night and, as I recall, you were otherwise engaged with a *Captain Ford*." His head tilted in the direction of said other night—an enemy he'd apparently been ruing.

"A man who's keen on a girl doesn't wait until a Friday night to telephone."

"Noted. Now who the hell is Captain Ford?"

"Captain Ford is a colleague for whom I *babysit*," Sabina countered. "He and his wife have a standing bridge game."

"Is that right?"

She watched a sheepish smile materialize across his face.

"Bridge game, huh? I suppose I owe you an apology, then. And answers. I owe you answers, Sabina."

"Let's finish the dance." She frowned. *Forget whatever may've happened before he ever decides to tell you . . .*

"I've gotten news from Italy. It's what I hoped for."

"They found her?" Sabina swallowed.

Hatch nodded. "What if we went someplace quiet to talk? Look, I'll even carry your fairy crown."

"I wish you wouldn't crack wise." Sabina shut her eyes against his shoulder. She let him stroke her hair. Maybe she was tired, after all.

"You're right. I really ought to pipe down and leave you to your puddle melting."

"Now, look." Her head flew up. "Don't go thinking you've won me over just because you've gotten your arms around me."

"Like a clinging vine?"

"A Virginia creeper, no less."

"So I've lost you then?" He made a somber expression, but she could see a smirk trailing just behind. "I'm all out of luck? Out of chances? Is that what you're telling me?"

"I didn't say that exactly." She closed her eyes. She felt his hand at her cheek. She didn't dare to imagine more than two steps beyond this moment. *The only thing you need to know is what's ahead of you.*

"I'm awfully glad to hear it. Let's get your coat, then. Come on. We're going for a ride."

# FIFTY-THREE

Sabina and Colin strolled the Oak Bluffs' streets backlit by the glow of a thousand Chinese lanterns. The Grand Illumination had begun as an advertising scheme—the nineteenth-century version of a neon sign, beckoning mainlanders to make "Cottage City" their summer retreat. Now, of course, the island hardly needed gimmicks to draw in summer traffic, but the tradition remained, growing more elaborate each year, at the end of each summer, perhaps reminding those who knew the place so well that there were still greater depths of enchantment to be carried back home, dreamed on and recounted until it all came back to life again the following May.

The Oak Bluffs homeowners and shopkeepers took great care to arrange their luminaries in uniquely colorful displays. The lanterns took on a variety of shapes—some cylindrical, some spherical, some like inverted Bavarian domes—strung gaily from the fretwork of the town's gothic cottages and gingerbread-style shops.

"It's breathtaking." Sabina marveled at the lanterns, performing a slow spin from the gazebo on the flat of the hill. They walked the loop around Trinity Park, past the Tabernacle and the campgrounds, through the crooked side streets that smelled like grape jam for all the wild vines left baking in the day's heat. Her small toes screamed inside her heels, and she had to keep her eyes trained on each footstep, watching for places in the sidewalk where the oaks' roots tunneled underneath, buckling the path. Hatch offered his hand to steady her.

"You should see it from the sky," he said into her ear.

His warm breath sent her blood rushing. Her heart thumped unevenly. "I can only imagine."

She shivered, and he gave her his suitcoat. She ducked her head and stepped away from him for distance. The suntanned flesh of Colin's throat smelled too deliciously of sandalwood, oak moss, and mint. His voice on her neck had been compelling. It would have been so easy to turn and melt against him. All night, in fact, she'd caught herself sinking back into the dream of their early summer connection. His fingers in her hair felt so familiar. His jokey lines—delivered in voices he invented for all the comical-looking tourists—brought them back into an easier rhythm. And she had laughed without being able to help herself.

But in other ways, Colin Hatch showed the imprint of a slick, careful molding. His shirt, for example, she noticed as a European label not sold on the island. Something like what his new friend Erling, the princess's husband, might wear to a Brazilian polo match. His cologne was—well, it was *cologne*, in place of his usual citronella soap smell. And although the effect was heavenly, she couldn't help but distrust its influence. Seeing Colin again tonight, she realized, was like pulling back up at the cottage, that first weekend every May—taking in the familiar lines and pitches. Still, she could always tell a little bit of life had happened to it without her—little scraps of paint or shrub or fencing, worn away by rain or frost or gale. There was always that momentary appraisal and silent reintroduction before the place was all the way hers again.

"So, tomorrow's the big day, is it?" Colin cleared his throat. "The day you save the scallops?"

They'd paused to stand at the water's edge, where a young willow wept into the bay—its lances nearly brushing the waves. The tide swam in, showing its backbone on each approach—up, up, up and then dissolving against the seawall.

"I'm not sure what good I'll do. If any." Sabina shook her head. "People have such strong opinions."

"That's true."

"Colin, why did you bring me all the way out here?"

Hatch looked relieved that she'd finally come to the point for him. He took out a cigarette, struck a match against his shoe. "I suppose I have some things to confess. None of it easy. But I agree it's time that you knew."

She watched the fire of his lit Lucky deepen as he inhaled. His face looked so fresh and so young, yet so fretful at the same time. She felt her eyes fixating on that face—discerning its mood. Trying to brace her heart for the worst kind of story, whatever that might be.

"I sold my Beechcraft," Hatch deflected. "Going into Boston tomorrow to finalize the papers."

"What will that mean for your work?"

"Means I'm quitting, I guess." He blew a breath of smoke. "Haven't mentioned it to Bill Dooley just yet. But starting tomorrow, the farm alone will have to support me. And my family." He gave her a meaningful look.

"Colin, before you say too much more, let me say *my* piece, starting with the fact that I'm leaving next week."

"Weston College? So soon?"

She shook her head. "I'm going out with a team from the Woods Hole Oceanographic Institution. Haven't mentioned it my '*boss*' yet, either. Aunt Poppy, you know? But I'm going. On a diving excursion."

"You're not going to Weston?" He threw down the cigarette, looking a little alarmed.

"Not anymore. But not because of you, either, despite whatever James may have fabricated. I'm going to find the things that interest me. See how life works in other places." Her words came out quickly, in a high voice she didn't much like, let alone recognize. She lowered her head to breathe. A person watching from afar, peering through the dusk, might have thought she'd lost something on the ground. "There's a research trip starting in September. All men, naturally, but I, well, I've learned how to dive with the Aqua-Lung. We'll have the freedom to explore hundreds of feet down, practically, with tanks on our backs. Leaves your arms unencumbered for swimming." She did a weak little breaststroke to demonstrate.

"I'm glad for you then." He touched her shoulder. "Sounds like quite an adventure," he said, though his face looked glum.

"Yes," she agreed. "I think it will be."

"Always nice to be *unencumbered*."

"What's that remark supposed to mean?"

"I didn't intend it any way."

"Like fun you didn't."

"Well, all right then." Hatch stuffed his hands in his pockets. "Frankly, I think it's dangerous."

"You don't know anything about it."

"I know *hundreds of feet* under the water is a risky proposition for anyone. Divers can still get drunk on nitrogen—can't they? Get disoriented, lose their way?"

"Well, I can promise you that I won't lose mine."

"Well." He smiled at her again. But this time she didn't feel reassured. "You're just young enough to believe you can keep a promise like that."

"Colin Hatch," she quivered, "I won't go with a boy who doesn't believe I ought to do new things, to *learn* new things. Or old things, for that matter. Who thinks me so delicate that I ought to be spared life's unpleasant details. I've spent nineteen years sheltered from dark and difficult truths—outside the circles of privileged communication. Why, I don't even know the story behind my own—well, what I'm trying to say is that I won't go on that way."

Moonlight filtered the blue night air. Here and there, through the branches, amber lights from cottage windows formed warm pockets in the dark. Two quick bats swooped overhead, chasing mosquitos back into the trees. Somewhere far off, Sabina could hear the familiar *whisk-slap* of a screen door slapping shut.

"You haven't got any faith in me, have you?" she said.

"That's a rotten accusation."

"What am I supposed to say?"

"I don't know. Try saying you'll at least hear me out. I thought you'd be *happy* to, actually. I thought that's what you've been waiting for."

"Happy? Why? Because *you've* made up *your* mind? As if I haven't got one of my own? And please don't imagine I've spent my summer waiting on you to reclaim me, because I can tell you—"

"Sabina, I—"

"You're standing here, announcing how you've chosen your farm, chosen you're ready to explain, chosen *me*, after all's been said and done, deciding for the both of us it's full steam ahead and—" She kicked a stone into the water. "Oh, what's the use?"

"Sabina, I'm trying to tell you that I love you."

"Is that right? Quick, someone run and get the smelling salts. My knees are weak."

He tapped his ear with a finger. "I notice your sarcasm's holding up just fine."

"I suppose you think I ought to go to pieces just because *you* say it's time. I suppose you think every love story ought to end with the man getting down on one knee, and there being no question as to the girl's answering yes. I suppose you think I'm just dying for a ring."

"A boxing ring, at this rate."

"Go on. Keep making cracks. Must be nice to have a smart line ready for everything."

"I don't have any lines ready for this." He pressed his fists into his pockets, taking a slow step backward. "I can tell you that much."

"I'm sorry to quarrel," she mumbled. She watched the negative space between them grow. A young couple, holding hands, hurried past. Their date was going well, and they exchanged embarrassed giggles to happen upon this other that was not. Sabina collected herself, smoothing her dress against her thighs. She took off his suitcoat and checked her wristwatch. "If we keep on this way I'm worried I may miss curfew."

After that they drove back to Edgartown in silence. A few times she watched Hatch try to find a song on the radio. But all the jump numbers sounded too loud for the quiet mood in the cab; all the ballads made them clumsy and shifting in their seats. Sabina knew that this moment—this result—was at least halfway her own fault. Probably more so. She *had* been waiting all summer for him to explain. So why couldn't she admit it? Why had she dreamed so long of having him back, only to block his path—*their* path—to whatever came next? Did she want him to fight harder or go ahead and leave her alone?

The only thing she knew for certain was her fear. She felt it plainly, on that ride, in the dark. She'd been so busy resenting her place on the outside of Hatch's story that she hadn't spent very much time imagining how well she'd do to own it right along with him. And now, as the time to hear him came and went, as the night's end drew nearer, she realized she wasn't any bit more freethinking than Lenore, James Whelan, her aunt. She was afraid to share his black mark, his blue ticket, afraid of being disliked, cast aside, sneered at. She didn't know how to apologize for this new and certain smallness. Not even when Hatch's Ford arrived back at the yacht club. Not even when he walked round to open her door, to kiss her cheek goodbye.

"You'll go home with one of the girls?" he asked.

"Yes, I'll find someone inside the dance, thank you."

"Sure I can't drive you to your door?"

"Aunt Poppy will be asking whatever happened to James. It's easier this way."

"Well. All right then. Have yourself a fine evening." He smiled weakly, leaning back against the side of his truck.

The streetlamps shimmered in the centers of his eyes. He looked as cool and collected as always, but Sabina saw the uneasiness about him. He was waiting for her to walk back into the ball. He was waiting, she supposed, for her to decide.

When she didn't, he asked, "What gives, McTigue? Why are you looking at me that way?"

"I don't know." She stood in the middle of the road. She'd given him his coat back, so she had to hug her own shoulders for warmth. A vast circle of clouds crawled overhead—a slow-moving caldera—blown open at the center, where the sky was studded with starlight, like syenite rock flecked with a million bits of gold. "I guess I'm suddenly picturing you as an old man."

"That's a new one." He laughed. "How bad do I look?"

"Well, your ears will be larger, I'd say. Some wrinkles around your eyes and maybe some folds along here." She stepped toward him, reaching out a gloved hand to touch his cheek where a laugh line sprang from his dimple. "From all the smoking you do."

"You paint a grim picture."

"You'd still be quite handsome."

"That's your cup of tea then, is it? Wrinkles and oversize ears?"

"More importantly, you'd still *sound* the same. Your voice. That's what got me thinking just now, I suppose. Because sometimes when you say quaint things like that—'Have yourself a fine evening'—you sound like a proper old English gent. Very sweet and grandfatherly."

"Grandfatherly?"

"Yes, that's what I said. *Grandfatherly.* In this light, I can practically see you silver-haired, walking the farm in some tweedy old coat, maybe trailing a loyal dog at your heels. And when the sun goes down, I can picture you retiring into your armchair with your Dunhill and your pipe. Calling after the girls who come to bring you your supper, 'G'night, girls! Have yourself a fine evening!'"

"Tell me more about these generous girls bringing my supper." He winked. "What do they look like?"

Sabina shook her head at him. "They'd be the nuns from Saint Andrew's. The ones who visit the old folks who don't have anyone else." She walked another ten steps toward the club, lowering her glance into her handbag. She hadn't meant the comment to sound so cruel, but of course it did. Of course it did. Muffled music drifted out from the club, along with the rings of a hundred halyards, clanging against a hundred aluminum masts. She made herself busy routing for her lipstick and her handkerchief inside her bag. Something was stinging in her eye.

"That's swell, Sabina. Real swell. And where are *you*, by the way, in this grim premonition?" Hatch called out to her. Without looking, she could tell he wasn't smiling anymore. "While I'm growing ancient and confined to my armchair? Why aren't I bidding *you* a fine evening?"

"I don't intend to live here forever. Maybe the occasional summer. Maybe you and I will still be island neighbors," Sabina replied in the direction of the water, her best imitation of an offhanded person.

Hatch rubbed his eyebrow with the back of his wrist. "That's a mighty sad ending," he said. "I mean, if it turns out that's all we'll ever be."

She took in a breath and held it. The ocean sounded heavier than she ever remembered. It was a fair night, still summer by rights, but the wind—when it gusted—threatened the island with the roaring violence of fall.

"Sabina, believe me. I've got faith in you plenty," Hatch said suddenly. "I tried to fix things for us, more than you know. I thought to call you every day. But I couldn't. I couldn't bring myself to say the words I needed with some old operator listening in on the line. I drove by the cottage, too, in case you'd come home by chance. Made up all sorts of excuses just to ring the bell. I went and found that beehive your aunt was all afire about. I read the Carson book you lent me too. About the sea and where it all started. I can see why you like that kind of reading now. At least, I think I do. Been wanting to talk with you about it."

Sabina clenched her jaw to keep it from quivering. She looked out at the sky. The clouds and the air floated together, as illusory shapes, gray on white, white on gray, assuming the background in turns. It made her think of how the ocean played a similar game with the land—not just in its coloring on the horizon but in the space it claimed, as the surface on which the continents floated or the currents that swam above and between deeper mantles of stone. How they took turns holding fast, alternately, bodies fleeing and also joined forever.

She'd been so scared that it could never work. That she and Hatch would never work. She'd hoped and lost and hoped again. Her thoughts were blurring now, making it impossible to pin down any truth.

"I'll let you go then," Hatch was saying, turning his back when she still hadn't replied. "But wait, for one second, will you? I made you something. You'll probably think it's corny. It's just"—he was reaching into his stake-bed now—"I remember you saying you wanted it. And I hope you haven't changed so much after all. Because I don't know any other girls going off on worldly adventures who might need a thing like this."

He handed her a large picture frame, the hanging wire slack against the brown paper backing. Balancing the frame on her knee, Sabina turned it frontward in her outstretched arms. It was a map. It was *her* map of the world. Clusters of pin tacks denoted the cities, the islands, the rocks of Saint Paul: all places she'd visited in her books and journals.

"How did you—?"

"Mrs. Lyons lent me your borrowing history."

"Yes, but how did you know to pin here at Sumburgh Head and Pentland Firth and—"

"I read them too. Well, most. The blue pins are for the places I've been along with you. In a manner of speaking. I hope you don't mind the intrusion."

From that same primal circuitry that commands the chest to breath, Sabina's sudden need to hold him began deep within. A gateway—in her head, her heart, her stubborn pride—opened on its own. The gathering knot in her throat gave way to a fraught, tiny wail of his name. She set the map down carefully against his tire.

Every muscle the body requires to hold a thing flexed until it ached. She clutched him tight by his coat, at last letting him draw her face up from the bedrock of his chest and kiss her, genuinely, while she undid the damage of two months of silence. She told him all she'd feared, admitting absent apologies, nodding into his lips, the transitive power of so many soft, brushing movements overcoming their lapses in words. She gave him confessions and affirmations strung together in long, complex sequences.

And he gave them back to her—his hands moving up and down her cold, bare arms—holding safe her wind-chilled fingers, until his forehead came to rest on top of hers. For a minute, at least, they stood that way, connected.

"I promise you, I don't care about whatever happened." She pressed her face to his cheek. "I know everything I need to know."

"Are you sure?"

"Yes," she nodded. She meant it. She couldn't deny how happy he made her, what it did to her heart to hear him hinting at a life together. Or, just as much, to hear herself testing that awful vision of a future lived apart. However the world might react, she knew she didn't want their story to end. "And I don't need you to fix it. And I won't care whatever anybody says. 'Let the dead Past bury its dead!'"

"What's that now?"

"That's Longfellow."

"What's he got to do with it?"

"I'll tell you some other time. Did you really find Poppy's bees?"

"Caught the queen." He grinned. "Moved the whole colony to my farm last week."

Sabina smiled. "Selling your airplane—does that mean you've got enough to buy the farm outright?"

Hatch held up a small pinch of air. "Nearly. Good news is Jack Crowder took a look at the contract terms. He says there's no way Dooley can pull out the rug, no matter how peeved he is."

"And Miss Martin?"

"Miss Martin will be a Mayflower Airlines passenger from here on out. She won't like it, but I'm sure she'll live."

"You *have* been busy, I guess."

"Still one more errand to make it all official." He touched her cheek with his hand. "I'm due in Boston tomorrow."

"Can I help at all?"

"No, but I *am* sorry I'll miss your talk at Town Meeting."

"I can give it again if you like." Sabina looked up at him. She studied his face, and she wondered if this was what life became for people in love—in the endless pages after the ending—bouts of hopeful wagering built around the chutes and ladders of an inconstant world. An endless succession of antes and bets staked on who one chose to love. Staked on who one chose to *be*, all in the same bargain.

She'd woken this morning in a state just shy of bliss, prepared to declare herself and her fully realized, overriding devotion. And then a bad day, and a worse night, and now—and now that her bet was coming 'round again, she felt herself swimming in the warmth of his voice; chasing that rare glimmer of his eye; surrendering as she always would to this man who sent her up and up and up . . .

"Hatch!" Mr. Shreve bore down on them with a grave and sudden presence. "Colin! Where've you been?"

"Oak Bluffs. Why?"

"You're needed urgently up the block. Never mind your hat. There's no time."

After years of duck-and-cover drills, and now six weeks spent strategizing against the Russians, Sabina's mind instantly conjured some kind of attack. Maybe Hatch's did too. "What is it?" Hatch held Sabina closer. "What's happened?"

"It's Miss Martin. Up at the Harbor View. She's damned near leaping off the roof. Police are trying, but they say she won't back down for anyone except you."

Hatch turned to Sabina in torment. She could see his conflict, his unwillingness to shatter this delicate mend. "Go," she told him.

"It's not because I have feelings for her, you understand? Not like that."

"Colin, go!"

"But I do . . . I do care."

"You'd be a stone not to."

Hatch gathered her up by the shoulders. "I will make this up to you. Not just tonight but everything. *Everything*, Sabina. I swear."

"Don't worry about me." She hurried alongside Hatch and Mr. Shreve.

Cop cars blaring two-toned sirens sped past. Some of the yacht club members were just now drifting outside the dance, craning their necks toward the uptown hotel.

"Bean? Let's be clear. You're not so very different than you were," Colin called over his shoulder. "You've always been this person. Someone I happen to love. And, for the record, because I know you are always keeping one, I don't think every love story should end with a man getting down on one knee. I only think it should start there."

# FIFTY-FOUR

"Say," Hatch lit his last cigarette. "What's a girl like you doing in a place like this?" He climbed over the balcony railing and took a seat along the overhang, where Isolde Martin stood like a maidenhead, carved at the bow of a tall ship, facing off against the harbor.

"Sightseeing."

Hatch nodded. "Never get tired of this view, can you?" His long legs dangled in the wind. He sat a yard's distance from the actress in her stocking feet. From the corner of his eye, down and away, he could spy the lamp lights of the cars and the cruisers gathered at the hotel lot. Someone must have telephoned the press, for now and again a flash bulb exploded against the blackness below.

"I'm afraid I've grown tired of them all," Isolde replied. "Ocean views. Look at it down there. Like a dark, dead pool."

"You won't sell many postcards with that slogan."

"Ha!" Isolde wheeled around to glare at him, and he flinched for how nearly she lost her backward grip on the rail. "Tell them this is the spot where I offed myself. Tell the magazines that. Then you'd sell postcards plenty. Condominiums too."

"So you're really going down, are you?" Hatch clicked his tongue, took a drag. "Care for a cigarette first?"

She nodded sullenly. "Don't make pretend like you care."

"*Pretend?*" He stood slowly. With one hand he held the rail behind them, while the other extended his lit Lucky to her lips. "Sister, I care plenty. Right now I'm pitching a perfect game when it comes to talking lovely women off of ledges. But if you go over, my average is sunk."

"You've done this before?" Isolde's expression betrayed her disappointment. "Saved some beautiful woman whose heart you'd broken?"

"That depends on your perspective." He inched himself back down. "She wasn't all that beautiful."

"I think I'd feel better if you didn't tell me any more of your war histories."

"Well, look. I'd feel better if you sat yourself over here for a while."

"It's a fitting end for me," the actress declared, marvelously producing one perfect tear to trail from each eye.

"Eh." Hatch looked down to the hotel lawn. "With a couple more stories it might be. But at this height, you'll probably just break both your pins. Sit down, would you?"

She crouched against the cedar planks. He managed his arm around her waist. They sat like that together for a time, with the breeze blowing at their faces. Wind pressed into the branches like invisible fingers playing at piano keys. Isolde picked at the sequins of her thousand-dollar gown.

"Colin, they've used me."

"Who's that?"

"Harris. Bill Dooley. They've brought me here for a scheme. And I'm no better for letting them."

"Come on now, kid." He shimmied his hips a mite bit closer to hers. She let her head flop down on his shoulder. "You're being too hard on yourself."

"I'm not. It's true. *This* . . . this is all I'll ever be. A girl who waits around on men's lousy ideas. Only they never give me the ending."

"Who cares about them anyway? You've got your own affairs. Your career—"

"I didn't get the part," Isolde sniffled into his jacket. "The milkmaid. The Capra film. I didn't get it."

"Okay, so that's a rough break. But look, you'll bounce back."

"Hitchcock will never think of me now. Why should he? Who am I, after all?"

"*Who are you?* I'll say who. You're a gal who makes up her own ending." He squeezed her hand. "You might as well be Lillian Hellman up here. Writing your very own stage play. *You* decide."

He watched her thinking. He watched the wind toss the curls about her cheeks, a little mirror image of the moon shining inside her damp eyes. "How do you know Lillian Hellman?"

"I talked her off a ledge once." He winked.

Isolde laughed in spite of herself. "And what will I tell them all?" she asked eventually, gesturing to the crowd below.

"Tell them the truth."

"Harris says I wouldn't know the truth if it arrived gift wrapped in gold."

"Well, there's your answer. Right there. Tell them you're tired of no-good, scheming men."

"That's rich." She stole another puff from his cigarette. "Could I really say that?"

"Sure. Why not? Cast him as the louse that he is. And you? You're the hero."

A rush of wind billowed her dress skirts from below. Isolde tamed them between her knees. "The hero of what? Aging film queens? They ought to have named that road to my cottage Sunset Boulevard."

"You could be the hero of your little island. The woman who demanded a halt to Dooley's build and the bridge right along with it."

"It's true." Her eyes opened wider. "I could say I'm awfully bothered by the idea of all that crowding. So much blare and hurrah in a place that ought to be restful."

"That's the ticket. This isn't an attempt." He mussed her hair. "It's a protest."

"Like a publicity stunt?"

"You've got it exactly."

She hiccupped. "But, Colin, I must look like the wrath of God right now. I'm a perfect mess. And beyond drunk, besides."

"Do you think Gandhi made his Salt March sober?"

She leaned over and kissed his cheek. Her hand pressed down on his thigh. "We're swell chums, aren't we? You and me?"

"Sure we are."

"So take me home then. To California. Take us both."

"Is that a request?"

"It can be whatever you want it to be." Her eyes held on to his. "So can I."

He looked her over, taking a long drag from his cigarette, tossing it down four floors so they could both watch it fall. He didn't reply right away. And he realized, with a tremor of guilt in his gut, his hesitation was not entirely feigned to buoy her ego. In a second—maybe less—he pictured a life with Isolde Martin. Days and nights spent breathing the air off a different ocean. Extravagant highs and lows set against the Pacific's constant, comfortable calm.

"We *are* swell chums." He kissed her hand. "But I can't take you home. Not this time."

"Why not?"

"I don't fly that far anymore. I'm meant to stay grounded."

# FIFTY-FIVE

"Ladies. Gentlemen. Good morning. I call to order a special session of Town Meeting, on this the twenty-second day of August, 1954." The moderator lowered his gavel, and the residents of Edgartown promptly withdrew the last bits of their independent chattering. It was a cool day outside the Old Whaling Church. Litter from the regatta festivities dotted the downtown lawns. A gang of summer youth could be heard outside, playing on the grass, attacking one another with sassafras slingshots, taking turns collapsing against the white fence posts, uttering their final words for posterity.

"Almighty God," the priest began, "we pray thy presence and thy guidance be with us as we . . ."

While the priest and the voters prayed, Sabina studied the crowd through a series of furtive glances, tugging at her white gloves, afraid to make eye contact with the wrong person—a friend of Dooley's, a proponent of the bridge; the Nashes, the Crosbys, the Crawfords. She knew these investors stood to gain considerably from the passage of Article One. But the fishermen weren't on that list, nor the bay scallop openers who made their winter livelihood prying shells at one dollar a gallon. Neither were the scallops themselves on any list of beneficiaries, though they were as vital a part of the island as Bill Dooley or Harris Shields times ten.

"At this time I would ask our appointed tellers, Wendell Carlson and Andrew Buckley, to submit an official count."

Mr. Buckley stood. "Three thirty-seven."

"So we have a quorum?"

"We do."

"Very well. Shall we read the warrant?"

"As the warrant has been printed, I move we can dispense with a reading today."

"Seconded? Yes? All right, so voted."

"On petition of the shellfish constable, Merton Greene, I would like to recognize our special speaker, Sabina McTigue, of twenty-two Acorn Street, Boston, Massachusetts. Here to educate our voters on the matter of bay scallop habitats and coastal development of the sort outlined in Article One. Miss McTigue?"

Sabina stood. She took slow steps for fear of stumbling. Her gloved hands pressed deep in her pockets to hide their shaking. By the time she reached the podium, she worried the microphone might capture the sound of her heart.

"Everything dies," Sabina leveled at the room. "Plants. Animals. People." Some of the women gasped at this austere opening. The men cleared their throats in gentrified criticism. Aunt Poppy, seated in her aisle seat, pressed her forehead to the curve of her cane.

"We all know this much, don't we? But here's a fact you may not know." Sabina paused to remove a photograph and a stack of notecards from her handbag. Her wrist caught the clutch and the bag upended, sending combs and cosmetics flying across the dais. "Here's a fact you may not know," she repeated, waving the photograph to distract from the ridiculous rattle of her lipstick tube rolling off and away. The aerial image captured a toxic algae bloom in the Western basin of Lake Erie, where the fires had been burning all summer. "Can you see this in the back? It's meant to illustrate that water dies too."

"Sabina, if I may." The town moderator stepped up beside her, covering the microphone like a small child's ear. Murmurs ensued.

Mr. Crawford shot up in the front row. "Pardon me for interrupting, but has this girl any education at all pertaining to the business of this meeting?"

"Miss McTigue is a member of our community," the constable countered from his place behind the podium. "She has volunteered—"

"Hank's right," Mr. Nash now backed his neighbor. "The McTigue girl went to high school with my own daughters, and I can tell you they've barely mastered scalloped potatoes, let alone scallop habitats."

"Where's Bill Dooley?" Another man stood up from his pew. "Shouldn't Dooley have an opportunity to refute this pseudoscience?"

The crowd noise flared. Riled voters began to shout pro-bridge slogans and anti-bridge jeers, while the town moderator, Mr. Gibbs, tapped his gavel ineffectually. Sabina stood back to watch the proceedings dissolve, noting—from the corner of her eye—a familiar form emerging from the audience, approaching the stage at an equally familiar slow and crooked pace. Her efforts up the staircase eventually subdued the crowd noise. Voters ceased their shouting and hushed one another in deference to the old woman (for she looked suddenly so old to Sabina, from this new vantage point). Finally it was only the solemn knocking of the oak cane on the floor to be heard throughout the church.

"I'd like to speak with my niece a moment," Aunt Poppy nodded to Mr. Gibbs. "We'll just be a minute in the wings here, as they say."

"Now?" asked Mr. Gibbs.

"*Now?*" asked Sabina.

"Well, I'm certainly not up on this stage to twirl my baton. Come here please, miss."

The crowd resumed its buzzing and soon thereafter its roaring, and Sabina felt powerless but to obey her aunt's command with all the town watching and all her confidence withering besides.

"What are you doing up here?" Sabina hissed behind the shield of a column that held the church's arched portal. She wondered how long Edgartown would wait for her to speech to resume.

"Sabina, don't look so overwrought. You and I are past due for a little colloquy."

"A colloquy? Mightn't you have suggested one this morning? Or yesterday? Or any other time excepting right now?"

"I didn't quite understand the situation before, but—strike that." Poppy shook her head, tapped her lips as if scolding their false words. "That's not true. I didn't *want* to understand it."

"Didn't want to understand what?" Sabina felt her anger fading. Her aunt's tone was so quiet, her face so transformed, so defenseless. No prim smile, no presumptive eyebrows. And honesty. A look of genuine contrition.

"Sabina, it's an odd affliction. Getting old. You probably think I was born old, don't you?"

"Certainly not, but I—" Sabina was puzzled.

"It's all right. I haven't given you much opportunity to see me any other way. Any other way besides old, I mean. Old and afraid. Why, since you first set off for elementary school, I've dwelt on every harm that might befall you. The croup. The measles. That sly-looking boy who cajoled you into his soap cart and sent the both of you tumbling headlong down Acorn Street. Remember how I scolded him?"

"He never talked to me again," Sabina smiled. "Practically ran past our house every day."

Poppy glanced back into the church's antechamber, where a row of whale oil lamps lit the walls, bringing to life the fading antique murals of tall ships on the water. She scanned the unruly crowd. She turned back to her niece and whispered, "But then *you* stopped building your soap carts too. It was me, I—I made you distrust them. Distrust yourself."

"Auntie, I'm sorry. I think I'm confused. I don't want to build any soap carts."

"Don't be obtuse. *Hear* what I'm saying. Will you, please?"

"What are you saying, Auntie?"

"I never imagined you'd last the summer in Truro. I'm not sure what

I supposed would repulse you first—the paperwork, the constant indoors, the suits and the blouses. But you've grown up, you have. I'm a fool not to have noticed sooner."

"You're not a fool, A. P."

"Do you really want to study this sort of thing? This fiddler crabs and jellysquid business?"

"Yes?" Sabina inquired of the floor.

"Don't say so like you're asking me. Do you or don't you?"

"I'd like to *try*."

"Good. Very good. Then you shall! You shall do exactly that."

"What about finishing school? Switzerland?"

"Oh, Sabina, don't be daft. I hate the idea of you all alone in Cape Cod. Did you really think I'd send you unaccompanied to the Alps?"

"But then—"

"Sabina, listen to me. I've been angry at your mother for a long time. Too long. If she were standing here in front of me, if I had the words, I don't mind confessing that I'd scold her too. She had no business—no business, let's say, building up soap carts in her way. No business leaving you and Dennis to such a tumble when she left. She was careless, and it frightened me. How quick and how cruel this world can be. It frightened me. But I can see now I oughtn't let my worries hold you back. Not anymore."

"Auntie?"

"Come along, now. No tears. None of that. Let's straighten out these insurgents before they start hurling stones." Poppy took Sabina by her dress sleeve back out to the stage.

"So as we may proceed with this meeting in *civilized* fashion," Aunt Poppy said into the microphone, gazing disapprovingly at her neighbors, "I can tell you Miss Sabina McTigue has just accepted a post as a research assistant at the Woods Hole Oceanographic Institution, studying under an esteemed group of scientists, who have read Sabina's preliminary reports on this, our bay scallop issue, and firmly back the testimony you are about to hear. Starting—*again*—exactly now."

Sabina tried to hide her astonishment. How did A. P. know of the research post? *How did you know?* Sabina mouthed.

"Your certification arrived in the mail," Poppy whispered in her niece's ear. "For the diving classes. And a note from that Dr. Hughes, who evidently thinks the world of you."

"Does she?"

"So do I."

The crowd's quiet held—for the moment—and Sabina recognized the need to go on. But not before shooting her aunt a broad smile, fully returned. She walked back to the podium without any notes or papers or photographs to hide behind. All the words and details seemed to take up easy residence in her brain. She didn't doubt them now.

"Some of you," she continued, "are old enough to remember a time when Long Island Sound flowed full of shellfish. When the oysters in New York Harbor were still edible. When you wouldn't catch typhoid just by visiting Chelsea Piers. More locally, you may remember the days before the Neponset and the Assabet ran brown and lifeless, like aquatic deserts. When a person could canoe along the Charles River, reliably encountering more than just tin cans. Or when the clean, broad flats around the Edgartown lighthouse still colored the bay with dark bands of grass. During our town's last building boom that grass went away. Our scallopers were lucky to catch a few thousand bushels in those years. Bushels full of cluckers. Empty shells, no meat. Sure, the grass came back in some places. The scalloping came back too—in *some places.* But can you remember how much less?

"I'll admit, I haven't seen as much of the world as I'd like," Sabina proceeded, clearing her throat. A baby called for its mother in the room's echoic quiet. A bench creaked. A motorbike passed outside in the street. For good or ill, her audience was listening again. "But I've read about people who have. I've read their reports—warnings, I suppose you'd call them. I've read about the building crews in Narragansett, where they've backfilled the coast for the new casino, the beach club houses with the private docks. I've read how they're dumping dredge spoil on top of delicate plots, burying the skate eggs and worm tubes and everything else that once lived there. I've followed news of the sludge from the pipes of Atlantic City hotels feeding putrid slurry into Egg Harbor. It's not an accident the fish are abandoning these places too. Maybe you've heard about that. Or maybe you haven't been listening.

"Water dies when you yank up all the trees at its edges, making way for new houses with splendid carports—or worse, golf courses and croquet fields for the sort of folk, no offense to anyone in this room, who like to host their garden parties on perfectly lush beds of green. Water dies when you dump your trash and toilet water into its tributaries for decades—or even just a few years, assuming there are enough of you squatting around the privies." She now summoned the courage to deliver a pointed stare at the owner of a popular waterfront hotel, whose habit of dumping garbage off the Edgartown dock had only recently inspired the hiring of a night watchman to patrol the shoreline.

"Water dies when you churn it with a factory's heavy metal, with the dripping guts of modern machinery, cars and oils—or even just the mounting midden heaps of a crowded marina and its traffic." She nodded at the president of the Automobile Owner's Association, pausing to catch her breath. "Water dies when you choke out the few precious creatures capable of cleaning it. When you kill the quahogs. The bay scallops." She locked eyes with George Mattos in the front row.

"Article One will kill the water. Maybe not this year, or even in this same generation, but eventually, I'd wager. And before the water dies, the bridge in question will crush its most important creatures with a cutter head. Dredging will pulverize, *emulsify* our native colonies of clams and scallops—animals who have within them the capacity to restore dying water. When the shellfish we once lost come back, *if* they come back, their beds will be gone. Their larvae will drift away with nothing to cling to."

She looked up again. She saw her aunt smiling in the same new, naked way. She felt a flush of sadness—or was it fear?—whisking through her, like a breeze. She paused a beat to let it pass. For now, she was prepared only to speak of the island's water. Of its rhapsodic mood at daybreak, rising as vapor off the ponds—a peaceful, next-to-nothingness that of course was just the opposite. The water's ability to rise, to transform, to rain and rise again: that was not nothing. That was everything, *everything* about this island where they lived.

# FIFTY-SIX

"Bless me, Father, for I have sinned. It's been six weeks since my last confession. Although, to be fair, I *did* mail you."

"Yes, William, I received your many postcards."

"So, we're square then?"

"I keep telling you, son. I can't accept penance via US post."

"Not even for a regular?"

"It's still high season," the priest pressed on. "What are you doing back in Boston?"

"Getting a haircut."

As evidence, Dooley whisked his derby off his head. Ran a finger along the dark grosgrain ribbon. He was only forty-something or other, but in the last eight months his hair had all gone silver, while his complexion bloomed two shades redder than a Falstaff rose. It was true he'd blown into town for a trim. But also true that his barber ran a popular horse room, complete with eight ready telephones on the dark side of the shop's back wall. Dooley opted for a more forthright answer.

"All right, then. You got me, Father. I'm here taking chances. What else?"

"The bangtails again? I thought you were broke."

"Beyond broke. Sailed past broke in April. You might say *shattered* by now. But the kids had some Series E bonds they've surely forgotten about. So that's what I did yesterday."

"What's in the box?" Father Keneavy inquired. Through the clover screen, the priest eyed a neatly wrapped package balanced on the builder's knee.

"Profiteroles."

"From Danko's or Zanetti's?"

"Christ, you wouldn't catch me dead in Zanetti's." Bill forced a laugh that sent him coughing.

The priest nodded gravely. "Presumably"—Father Keneavy paused, waiting for the penitent's fit to subside—"if you are borrowing from the children, I gather your island bridge problem has not been resolved?"

Dooley subconsciously tugged at the end of his little Errol Flynn moustache. He kept it pencil thin and broken across his philtrum, in a style his daughters often described as criminally old-fashioned. This morning, at his Hanover Street barber, Dooley had regarded himself in the mirror with equal measures contempt and despair. It seemed to him quite plain: he couldn't even build a bridge beneath his own nose.

"Resolved?" Dooley shook his red face at the floor of the confessional. "It's regressed, more like."

"*Romam uno die non fuisse conditam.*"

"What the hell is that supposed to mean?"

"Rome wasn't built in a day."

"I'm not asking for cathedrals, Father."

"What are you asking for then?"

Dooley pressed his palms to his cheeks and pulled the skin down taut, in a way that set his eyeballs bulging. The morose little mouth now nestled between the heels of hands murmured, "One lousy break."

After an uncomfortable silence, the priest finally asked, "Where do things stand at the moment?"

Bill set aside his profiteroles and knelt at the kneeler for full effect.

"Vote's today. Polls are open *right now*, in fact. I'm not hopeful, Father. Yesterday was a disaster. Walt Ewing spilled the beans about my West Chop plan, so naturally all the buzzards on the Steamship Authority payroll went berserk. Murphy cited the mounting crime rates in Coney Island, as a view of what's to come for Edgartown, I suppose. Isolde Martin went out on a ledge, blaming me—*me!*—when they asked her what for. Came down from that rooftop like Moses descending Mount Sinai, declaring Chappy sacred land. Calling me a heretic—"

"Maybe she's got a point." The priest yawned.

"A point? She's got a bed in the psych ward just now, where she belongs. Still, the damage is done. Today, five Beta Thetas chained themselves to the fence at the statehouse in solidarity, which Harris did not appreciate. The McTigue girl rendered everyone comatose with her blasted bay scallop soliloquy. And if you think any of that earned me an ounce of sympathy at home, think again. My wife has all but run away with the florist. They're off in their own dimension, counting out waxed orange blossoms."

"Remind me again. What is your West Chop plan, as you call it?"

"The other bridge, Father. The *real* one. From the Cape Cod mainland. So as Martha's Vineyard wouldn't be an island anymore. Jesus. Sometimes I wonder how well you listen in there."

"Being that you're back to see me every two weeks bemoaning all the same troubles, I might wonder the same of you."

Bill sniffed. "Next time I'll bring my Dictaphone." He tugged at the red-and-white twine securing his bakery package. The unyielding little knot got him flushed and sweating. He settled back onto the bench. Ripped a hole in the cardboard. With a mouthful of profiterole, he went on complaining, "I've got people demanding money. *Now.* Twelve buyers pulled out on Wasque."

"But you've still got their down payments."

"The bet-taker behind Suffolk's pari-mutuel window has their down payments, more like."

"So, what is it that you're telling me? You've squandered the funds? You can't build your apartments after all?"

"I don't think so, Father. Maybe not even if I win the damned vote."

"William, I do wonder. Have you talked to your wife?"

"I've thought of it, Father. But she's not a very sensible woman."

"I see."

"Any other bright ideas?"

"You might stay away from the track. For a start."

"I intend to." Dooley checked his watch, wondering where Colin Hatch might be carousing at this hour. And how hard he'd have to press for an upstate flight. "Right after the Saratoga Stakes."

# FIFTY-SEVEN

Colin Hatch dealt a hand of cards into seven tidy piles. Half a dozen peanut bowls overflowed with cash. A breeze carried in the wafting scent of fry batter from Murphy's Seafood on the wharf. The goat room air felt especially heavy.

Denny sat squared off against John Shreve, engaged in some private, silent dueling match. The other club boys looked edgy too, waiting out the verdict from the town's bridge vote, chewing at their fingernails. But Colin felt fine. More than fine: he felt free. After his day in Boston, finalizing the airplane papers, pocketing that giant cashier's check, preparing to cut his dock lines from Dooley once and for all, Colin hardly stopped to wonder at tonight's titled chip count. For the first time ever, he was winning every hand.

"Pair of threes."

"*Again?* Jesus. This guy took my cards away from me *again*."

"My very deepest sympathies."

"Where's the pin?"

"It's two to raise, Ellie. Pay attention."

"There's a raise."

"All right, I'll go high."

"Ace."

"Ace."

"Next one better be low or I'm gone."

"Hey, you still splashing around with Mae West, Captain? I heard she went berserk or something. Off her nut, is she?"

Hatch looked up from his hand. He'd been expecting inquiries.

"I'm not sure what got into her last night," he murmured, more in defense of his own judgement than Isolde's. With the boys it was always best to move things along. Like crows, they had a nose for weakness, and when they sensed it, they were apt to swarm. "She's got a complicated perspective."

"That's just women. They all do."

"Women turn faster than cut flowers. It's why I don't bother with 'em."

"They don't bother with *you*, more like."

"Say, Shreve, any hot prospects coming to the wedding on Sunday? Single gals?"

"Yeah, Shreve, give us the lineup. I've been stuck stag all summer."

"I don't know anything about who's coming." Shreve scanned his cards intently. "Not my department."

"He's not even sure if *he'll* show up. Are you, John?" Denny instigated.

"Count yourself lucky," said Shreve, ignoring the comment. "You want the fastest way to kill a good time? Get yourself a steady girlfriend."

"You'd know too. Wouldn't you?" Denny kept at him, nodding. "Seeing as how you've always got two or three on the line."

"I'd lend you one, McTigue," Shreve tossed a chip, "if you weren't such a dammed prude."

"Stand-up guys don't 'lend' and 'borrow' women."

"No kidding. They go home alone."

Denny folded his hand and pushed his chair away from the table. Grabbed his flat cap from its hook. "Deal me out, boys."

"Ouch."

"*Ouch indeed.*"

"No friends among enemies."

"Speaking of twos or threes—"

"Would you give it a rest, Ellie?"

"Who made this cake, by the way? This is a damn decent cake."

"Dinah Shore."

"Any update on that bridge business?"

"Radio says vote's too close to call just yet."

"You think it'll pass?"

"Of course it'll pass."

"Like hell it'll pass."

"You know they tried this once already? Back in '24. Some old fool with a waterfront mansion on the Chappy side."

"And did it pass?"

"Do you see a bridge outside?"

"Of all the *shit luck*. I'm out. Ellie? In or out?"

"I'm *thinking*."

"Better get him a helmet before he hurts himself."

"I'll say one thing." Ellie leaned his husky chest into the table's felt.

"Do we have to listen?"

"This vote's a preamble. Just a lot of shadowboxing, if you ask me."

"He's right. Town's only greasing the wheels for a *real* bridge. Three miles long. West Chop to Falmouth."

"Are you talking or playing?"

"Statehouse wants to sink the Steamship Authority. Take over the ferry business, I'm saying."

"Raise."

"Buck."

"Buck."

"Why'd they want to do that?"

"Why do you think? Special interests. Harris Shields and his gang."

"Special interests like what?"

"Say, I have a special interest. It's called *make your bet before I die of old age*."

"Think about it." Windsor knocked on his head. "Bridge goes in. Cape Cod traffic skips the boat altogether. Town gets all that bridge-toll money. Maybe a five-dollar fare—each way! Somebody's favorite contractor gets a Golden Gate–sized job—"

"Hold up. Did you hear that?"

The players were still pondering the implications of a passed measure when a violent noise erupted. Uproarious noise. Hoots and brays tumbling down the hill from Edgartown center. The boys crowded together at the window to catch a glimpse of the cavalcade.

George Mattos bounded first into the frame. He blew the sort of tin noisemaker young children collect at New Year's Eve parties. Doc Kemp followed behind, limping, wagging pep-squad pom-poms in tassels of red, white, and blue. More little islanders' cheers of victory could be heard clear across the boatyard. One particularly tall form, passing under the glow of a streetlamp, proved to be Hayden Roon on horseback. He gulped foam from an overly agitated champagne bottle, singing "The Battle Hymn of the Republic."

"Oof. There goes your special interests."

"We lost?"

"Just like that?"

"No bridge."

"No bridge?"

"Say, Hatch, you think Isolde swayed the vote? Playing the flying elephant out on that roof? Mugging for all those magazines, way she did?

"She wasn't playing." Hatch tilted a Ballantine to his lips. "Or mugging."

"Nope. Wasn't her." Roger cracked a peanut, threw his shards out the open window. "Sabina read everyone the riot act. Today at Town Meeting. Took the whole town to school on bay scallops."

"How'd you know?" Ellie balked.

"Maybe your sister told me. At the boathouse."

"Keep it up, Roger. I'll break your beak."

"All right, all right." Hatch diverted the boys, sorry again that he'd missed Sabina's speech, wishing he'd had a chance to see her before she shipped off for Truro. He didn't fully understand this new aim she'd proposed—this open-sea diving. But he meant what he'd said last night. She had his faith. She had all his faith. And if she wasn't afraid to hold her breath and jump, who was he to demand she ought to be? "Back to your hands, gentlemen. I've got an appointment with my pillow, but I haven't stolen enough of your money yet."

"There's a flush."

"Hot dog and a bucket of slaw!"

"Say, who invited this sharpie, anyway?"

A clink-clanking avalanche suddenly sounded in the club hallway. Empty beer cans. Someone tripping over the pile of rolling tin.

"Evening, fellas," Bill Dooley said as he tumbled into the goat room. He pinched his porkpie in one hand, scissors-held his omnipresent cigar in the other. An ivory suitcoat swung from the crook of his elbow, a polished flask sprouting in its pocket. "Grab your purse, Mabel," Dooley commanded in Colin's general direction. He swallowed a belch. "We're headed for Saratoga."

"Evening, Bill." Colin looked up from his cards, nettled. "Care to join us for a hand?"

"Eh. What'd be the point?" Dooley chomped the wet end of his extinguished H. Upmann. "At this table? Half of you are gambling with your mothers' costume jewelry."

Ellie took the jab as an invitation to banter. "Sounds like the bridge ain't happening, Mr. Dooley, huh?"

"Too close to call. There's going to be a recount," Bill frowned. "No kidding, Hatch. Wrap it up. I need to be in Saratoga by breakfast."

"Look, Bill." Hatch set down his cards, keenly aware they had a circle of curious auditors. "I know we've come to terms in the past. Heck, I've bent over backward when you've asked. But I'm not interested in going on that way. And I think you should know—"

"Tell me more." Dooley squinted his eyes, drew his lips together in the sarcastically ponderous way that Hatch had long hated. "Tell me more about what I should know."

"—that maybe I'm through taking orders."

"I see," Dooley nodded, setting down his hat. His red cheeks deepened in color. His neck twisted in discomfort above the crease of his starched collar. "Well, ain't that a sticky wicket? Because you know what? I'm not quite through giving them."

Hatch scratched at the edge of his eyebrow. He could feel his shoulders tensing. "Don't get me wrong, Bill. I appreciate our work together—"

"This is what *appreciation* looks like to you? Sitting on your duff? Playing pinochle with the Andrews Sisters when an old friend's stranded? We had an agreement."

Hatch stood. "We did. We agreed you'd find Adele for me. Except that you never followed through, did you?"

"You'll have to ask Mr. Wunholm about Italy. He's handling all that business."

"Mr. Wunholm is some seedy stiff you pay to ignore people like me."

"Bullshit!" Dooley spat. "I *encourage* him to ignore people like you. I *pay* him not to bother me with the nonsense either way!"

"Give me one good reason I shouldn't grab you by the scruff and throw you out of here."

"Because I own you, Hatch."

"I don't think so," Hatch asserted. "Not anymore."

"Oh, I see what's happening," Bill chuckled as he pulled up Denny's empty chair, straddled it backward. "This is the part of the story where you run away to Hollywood. Like some sweater-girl gigolo. Isolde Martin's money must be greener than mine."

"I sold the plane," Hatch leveled. "And I'm handing in my notice."

"You sold our plane?" Dooley sucked his cigar so that his cheeks sank in. He blinked his pink eyes.

"*My* plane. Don't worry, though. Saratoga will still be there by morning. It's a nice night for a drive."

"You must be nuttier than a fruitcake if you think I'll let you weasel out of our deal. The bank will side with me, of course."

"I'm betting the bank has bigger issues with you right now."

"That's a goddamned fool's bet."

"No worse than building a geriatric resort on an island without a bridge."

"There's *going to be—*" Bill spat brown bits of cigar at the floor, choking on his words. "There's going to be a recount."

"I wouldn't hold my breath."

Dooley unbuttoned his shirt collar. His face shone damp with sweat. He checked the flask in his pocket, frowning when its emptiness betrayed him. Though they held their tongues, Hatch could tell the audience of club boys made everything worse for the drunk little man. Dooley's feverish eyes scanned right and left, hunting for a direction. "If you were any kind of man, you'd back it."

"You're talking ragtime, Bill. Go home and sleep it off."

"You made a bet, didn't you? About my bridge? So back it."

"Right now I'm going home." Hatch stood from his chair. He didn't understand this new charge the old man was leveling.

Dooley walked 'round the table to block him. "I'll bet you everything in my pocket against everything in your pocket I can turn that bridge vote around. You want to bet?"

"No, thanks." Colin shook his head. He pushed Dooley aside. He wasn't certain, but it seemed the island's most notorious gambler was on a bit of a tear. "My wallet's pretty thick tonight. And I'm too impatient to wait and see."

"Play a hand then." Dooley bucked his chin.

"What's that?" Hatch wheeled around.

"Play me a hand. One hand. All in." The developer's watery eyes at once looked ravenous and pitiable and sad. "Everything I've got," he said, yanking out cash, breath mints, a pocket comb, a toothpick—turning his jacket lining inside out over the green felt table. "Plus," he licked his finger, counting off bills, "the deed to your farm."

"What did you say?" Hatch stood stunned in the doorway.

"The deed to your farm. I'm saying you'd own it, outright. Or I would. One hand decides. Dealer's choice. Crawford!" Dooley barked, "Shuffle that deck."

Windsor Crawford obeyed the command with a quick, expert riffle.

"You couldn't give me that deed in a cardroom bet," Hatch blurted. "You'd need a lawyer. Closing papers."

"We're in Edgartown. You think I can't roust a lawyer on a Sunday night?"

"I don't know." Hatch rubbed his brow with the back of his wrist. "Let's settle down. You've—look, we've all been drinking."

Dooley's eyes twitched. He settled his gaze on the miniature refrigerator in the corner of the room. "I can have Jack Crowder in this room, with closing papers and wallpapers besides, in all of about twelve minutes. *Get me a beer, Ellington!*" He held out his hand for Colin to shake. "Now prove it. Are you in?"

Hatch looked around the table. He thought of Sabina. His farm. Tonight he actually was winning every hand. "All right." Hatch shook. "I'm in."

"Good. So put it on the table." Dooley waved his arm like a traffic cop. "Everything you've got. All of it."

Colin Hatch dug into his pants pocket, a slow smile dawning across his face. He threw down the crumpled wad of singles and fives he'd already won from the boys tonight. His own money clip held a few folded twenties. His father's gold cigarette case. His lighter. The keys to his truck, his old boat. That giant cashier's check, practically still wet with ink. He checked Dooley's face. The old drunk was salivating. Nothing he'd offered just now could be taken to heart. High or low hand, it didn't matter. There was no way he'd win anything—not ever—from making another deal with Bill Dooley. He'd played this game before. Been playing it for years. And yet somehow, he also knew, starting tonight, he couldn't possibly lose.

# FIFTY-EIGHT

Denny shuffled home from the card game nursing an indefinable complaint. Something he'd eaten. A knot in his neck. The allover malaise of a coming flu. But really, none of those was the case. At his back, Edgartown blared with the news of the vote. Celebrants who'd fought against a bridge and a great many more—the sailing crews and vacationists, who hardly knew anything about the road that might have been, but the moon looked so lovely, and it was an unusually fine evening—they all filled the decks of the downtown, together hooping like coyotes for their different kinds of joy.

Up the hill, where the streets grew darker, quieter, Denny could picture where the girls would be sitting just now. A. P. and Connie, sipping their tea. Maybe an angel food cake on the table with the checkered oilskin cloth. They'd have heard the bridge news on the radio. Sabina would be proud—ought to be proud—for speaking up the way she had. And he knew he ought to be there with them, telephoning his sister at the airbase to celebrate.

Denny felt sorry all over again that he'd skipped Town Meeting. He should have manned a seat at the Old Whaling Church, front and center, given his kid sister someplace safe to focus. Instead, like a coward, he'd paid extra and doubled his flight lesson, in an effort to avoid anyone who might chance to ask how he was doing today. He feared, given the question, he couldn't be prevented from answering straight. *How he was?* Baffled. Dismal. Fierce. The only reason he'd shown for cards was this crackpot idea—an impossible dream—that maybe Shreve would've been ready to fess up by now. Maybe some stitch of courage or grace had materialized, and the town could know this unhappy couple was parting ways. And then maybe he'd say, *Gee, I oughtta go tell her how I really feel.* And then maybe Lenore could actually hear him for once. But it would never happen that way. She never let him get that far.

So when he reached the edge of the McTigue's cottage drive, he found that his legs kept on. A little breeze spurred him. The wind, where it brushed at his arms in short sleeves, felt exactly the temperature of the air, and for a moment the effortlessness of the walk felt like swimming—like floating, rather—along with the night's natural current.

Like a kid, he avoided the bell at the door. Instead he scooped a handful of pea stone from the garden and pitched a few up toward Lenore's warmly lit window. He saw a hand at the curtain. Her face coming into the light.

"Denny?"

"Hi."

"Hi yourself. Why are you lurking in the dark? What are you doing here?"

Her question, reasonable though it was, caught him off guard. He hadn't planned on starting with an explanation. "Guess the wind just got a hold of me." He looked around for something more material. "Your grass is dead." He checked his shoes. Underfoot the Dooley's grass, always perfectly lush, in fact now crunched like toast.

"The gardener quit last week."

"Huh," Denny replied, noticing too the herd of hydrangea that normally pushed at the gates like little lambs' heads. Instead their cones drooped with doubt they might ever again see rain.

"You won't want to be out there when Daddy gets home. He just telephoned. I overheard Mother trying to get a word in. Sounds especially rabid tonight."

"I know. I saw him. In town."

"Oh." She looked embarrassed.

"Why weren't you at the dance?"

"The Regatta Ball?"

"Yeah. I was looking . . . I mean, I expected to see you there."

"No one asked me."

"You have a fiancé."

"He didn't ask either," she smiled, pulling at a tangle of bittersweet from the trellis that bordered her window. "I suppose he realizes he already got one yes from me. The important one. How many more does he need, really?"

"So you're going to go through with it? This weekend? Even if there's a good chance he doesn't show?"

A little absently, she plucked the fragrant leaves apart and let the torn bits drift down to the hay-colored lawn. "I have a plan."

"You mind cluing me in? So I know what I'm walking into on Sunday?"

"After everything that's happened this summer, I've found it's best not to worry too far ahead." She brushed her hands together. "It's an awfully nice night, Denny. Go home and kiss your girl."

Again he wasn't ready. She was telling him goodnight and he hadn't said what he needed to say. "Lenore, you don't deserve this."

"Me, personally? *I* don't? Come on, Denny. You're acting as if you've never heard such a thing. I'm not the first—"

"Don't go giving him a pass now."

She sighed. "Men will act foolishly. That's a given. They chase us girls. They catch a few. They put their favorite one in a cage to keep her at home. Then they go out and chase some more."

"Is that what they're teaching at Vassar these days? How to get kicked around and not complain?"

"Buzz off, Denny." Lenore lowered sixteen squares of double-hung glass between them.

He held up his hand. "Wait!" His voice climbed so loud the dog next door began to bark.

"Shh! What is it?" She allowed a small opening.

"Just answer me one thing. Do you love him?"

"What difference does it make?"

"*What difference*? You're going to marry the man. You ought to know—"

"I *do know*, Denny. I know exactly what I'm doing. I already told you, I have a plan."

"Oh yeah, what's that?"

"None of your business."

"Great. *None of my business.* I'll remember that the next time you call me from . . . from . . . wherever it is you next find yourself ignored, or stewing, or utterly stranded."

"You're a fine friend." Lenore moved to lower the sash again completely, palms flush against the meeting rail. But after a moment she stopped, then whispered through the screen, "And how often *really* do I call you?"

"I don't know. How often do you need to know the next line of the song that's stuck in your head? How often do you need to hear there's not a ghost in your attic? That you still look pretty? How often are your parents scrapping so loud you can't sleep? And parties! How many parties that you needed to sneak out the backdoor? How often have you needed collecting from Vassar? From John's fraternity house? Or how about the train station?"

"Honestly then. If my friendship irks you so much—"

"It doesn't *irk* me, *Jesus*. But it might . . ."

He wanted to say that "it" might be something to think about before hitching her life to the man responsible for ignoring her or abandoning her—or never showing up in the first place. It might be a clue perhaps Cupid's arrow was not the real McCoy but in fact one of those novelty, sight-gag arrows people wore on their heads at Halloween—something that fooled the eye while defying common sense. He wanted to say—or, more honestly—he just wanted her to *know*, that it might be the very thing slowly breaking his heart. But of course he couldn't. And she couldn't press him to hear it. For a million complex reasons he couldn't say a thing like that. Instead he said:

"She's not my girl anymore. Gretchen, I mean. Left the island this morning. Took the first ferry home. Said I was giving her the Sigma Phi treatment or something like that."

"She must not know you very well."

"Oh, and *you* do?"

"Dennis McTigue, I know you perfectly. That's why I'm not telling you what's going to happen on Sunday."

## MONDAY, AUGUST 30, 1954

# Lost Pilot Identified as Hopes Dim in Search for Lost Aircraft

EDGARTOWN, MA (AP)—Darkness persists across the island and beyond, as electric power companies remain unable to restore power with so many torn, live wires strewn across flooded streets. Along with Martha's Vineyard, residents of Nantucket, coastal New Hampshire, and vast swaths of Maine are entirely without electricity or communication. Police dispatchers and ambulance crews are employing two-way radios to locate the injured and imperiled.

Damage estimates now hover around $3,000,000, according to William Baird, chairman of the Board of Assessors. Officially, more than five dozen people—including the crews of two ground-fishing trawlers—are reported dead. Dozens more are still missing.

### *No Flight Plan for Missing Pilot*

Dennis McTigue, twenty-three, of Boston, Massachusetts, was behind the controls of a Beechcraft Bonanza, piloting over Cape Cod Bay at the time of a blinding rain thought to have jeopardized his trip. McTigue filed no flight plan and was flying on Visual Flight Rules (VFR), according to CAA's airway traffic control center in Boston. A resolution to ban all but good-weather flights to the Vineyard was today proposed by island community leaders.

McTigue, who left Boston College during his freshman year to serve in Korea, saved fifteen men from the Fifty-Third Field Artillery Battalion, Eighth Infantry Division, during a six-day retreat at Chosin, battling enemy forces and temperatures of thirty degrees below zero.

The Coast Guard has dispatched seven rescue boats to the vicinity of the supposed crash site, based on eyewitness testimony of a small, burning aircraft entering Boston Harbor early Friday morning. Five patrol boats were sent from port security detail and two cutters, the *Chumash* and the *Kennebec*, from the USCG base.

*SEARCH cont. page 13.*

# August 26, 1954

Ten hours before the storm

# FIFTY-NINE

The commodore pushed his chair away from the dinner table and patted his paunch. "At this rate they'll have to roll me down the aisle! What about you, Bill? Gotten your cutaway back from the tailor?"

Bill Dooley, more than a little hungover, suddenly realized he was the only one around the table still tunneling into his sorbet. The Shreves' maid, Solange, stood at his arm, waiting to clear the crystal goblet. The Welsh corgi camped at his feet, poised to catch any falling morsels.

"Most people lose their appetite in the heat, but Bill's always expands." Nola made a little laugh to go along with the excuse—another excuse on his behalf. She stroked his hand and he smiled around the room, obeying his cue. The kids sat next to one another assuming equally strained postures. J. J. looked down into his water glass like a man at the edge of a cliff. Lenore bit into her lower lip. The grandfather clock in the hallway chimed nine o'clock. Bill wondered how much more time would have to pass before it would be acceptable to call it a night.

As always, dining with his future in-laws sent his blood pressure soaring. Even before the unpleasant news that had yoked them all together and the mad scramble to set a wedding date, Bill had long struggled to endure the stage-play atmosphere at the Shreve mansion. Fruit bowls filled with fruit that wasn't intended to be eaten. Hand towels hung with an absurd orderliness. Even the chessboard on the coffee table, with the center pawns squared off at midcourt, gave Bill the distinct impression old Shreve had started a game with himself sometime back in '51 and thought his maneuvering to be so masterful that the household should preserve it—a kind of still life exhibit for any guest who might wonder what a gas it was to live in the midst of a real-life Shreve. Bill often found himself wanting to stand on his chair, pointing and laughing, or else to grab the wife and plant a wet one on her creased, wine-stained lips. Just to see what the unscripted Shreves might do then.

Meanwhile, the husband yakked like a woman and the wife drank like a man. Like a pelican, better yet. Tonight, Bill had taken great pains to focus on the food in front of him because he'd found that if his eyes lingered too long on a particular vase or portrait on the wall, he'd be confined to hearing the object's hundred-year history along with all the unfathomable twists and turns old Shreve had endured to acquire it.

The only reason Bill hadn't outright canceled on this affair was that he needed Nola in good spirits. The best of spirits, actually. He needed to continue playing up the joy—as though they'd come upon a coronation day rather than a shotgun wedding—so that later this evening, the smiling rosiness still fresh in her cheeks, he could deliver his confession.

Yes, it was time to tell Nola the truth, he had decided—with some gentle prodding from his friend, the priest. Bill Dooley's money was all gone and then some. His neighbors wanted answers. An unpaid Baker wanted blood. He'd defaulted on three loans, bounced seventeen checks, emptied his daughters' savings accounts, and—just this morning—casually considered various means of suicide. The tide was coming in all around him. Nola's Dublin account was the only way out, and just at this very thought his wife quaintly patted his hand again; he realized someone must've asked him something.

"What's that?"

"I was just saying," old Shreve repeated himself, "you've certainly started a stampede. Crawford tells me everyone is fighting to sell back his stake in your Wasque build. I hope it won't come to blows at the wedding."

"Bill never discusses business at the dinner table," Nola volunteered.

"How about you kids, then?" Shreve turned his unnerving attention to the young people. "What sorts of last-minute errands are topping your lists? I know John Joseph hasn't done a lick of packing for Europe. I keep telling him, you can't get away with blue jeans in Paris."

"Sure, I'll get to it, Dad."

"Take the boy out shopping, Lenore, will you, please?" Shreve continued, while his wife caught hold of Solange's arm, gesturing to the travesty of her empty wine glass. "If he spent as much time on the factory floor as he spends on that boat of his, we'd be the preeminent *papetier* on two continents. You see, Bill, a *papetier* is the word you'd use in place of 'stationer' to describe what I do overseas."

"It's not the word I'd use," Bill grumbled.

"Maybe the ladies would like to move into the living room?" Nola suggested. "I have a sample of the bridesmaids' gifts to share."

"Wait, before you get up." J. J. looked first to Nola, then to Bill, then to Lenore at his side. His suntanned face somehow drained of its color. "I have a confession to make."

"Let's save the confessions for the church next week," Shreve barreled over his son, rising to move the party all in a big hurry. But Dooley was lethargic, weighted down by two helpings of seafood casserole, and now, for the first time ever, he was interested in his son-in-law besides. He didn't move an inch off his dinner chair.

"The reason I haven't packed for Europe, you see." J. J. ran a hand through his perfectly sun-streaked hair. "Well, I was planning to leave."

"Leave?" giggled Mother Shreve, a ring of purple tannin giving her mouth a clownish effect. "Leave to where?"

"Men, let's reconvene in the study," Shreve commanded sharply. "I think some sensible conversation is in order."

Bill laughed. He couldn't help himself. His whole life was in financial ruin, and soon he'd have to go groveling to his wife for the keys to her family's treasure chest, and even still—this was so very much like a stage play.

Shreve moved to physically evacuate his son from the room. But J. J.

stood firm and shrugged off his father's arm. "What I'm about to say concerns everyone here. I'd just as soon get it out in the open."

"What is it, J. J.?" Mrs. Shreve elicited, certainly the most well-fortified of anyone to accept a difficult announcement.

"I was given the opportunity to act as partner in a sailboating company, with an old friend, Randall Simms. He lives in the Leewards now. A little port town called Marigot. Sailing practically all the time. He's doing very well for himself. And you see, I thought it'd be a lot like Colin Hatch's charter business, only on the water."

"And in a different country," added Mrs. Shreve, less than helpfully.

"Down in the tropics, there are all kinds of little islands and atolls where a person could get lost," the bridegroom continued. "Folks on vacation need help finding them. That's the whole idea behind Simms & Shreve Adventure Company."

"Marigot is not an *opportunity*." Shreve thrice slapped his knuckles into an open palm, giving the clear impression he'd already made this argument before. In dredging it up again, his tone deteriorated into a snarl. "Marigot is a fairytale. A lot of 'don't fence me in' nonsense—yes, I know that old tune, sonny. But it will never happen. Not in my lifetime."

"Aw, hell. Would you let me finish, Dad?"

"Do you think me so old I can't remember my own days of wine and roses? Do you think *I* wouldn't have liked to cruise through calypso country on a catamaran all day long? To watch the little rich girls sunbathe across the webbing? To trade in my father's business for a goddamned *adventure* company? Do you know why I didn't?"

By his face, it appeared to Dooley that Junior did not know.

"It's because I'm a *man*!" The father pounded the table. "*We* are men. We are *virtuous* men. We go to work. To respectable jobs that will secure the futures of our families, who, by the way, have deeper roots in Boston than all the coconut trees you can count."

"But wouldn't you all much rather I be honest with you *now*?" J. J. cut in. "Shouldn't I stand up and tell you that I don't want to run a paper factory? Spend my life folding lousy greeting cards? Look, I could have gone ahead without all this fuss. Run away like a thief in the night. Taken a powder. Disappeared. Never to be heard from again."

"Frankly," Nola interrupted the boy's impassioned monologue, her eyes twitching between apoplectic blinks, grabbing hold of her daughter as if to shield her from a gathering storm. "Given the choice between such an utter disgrace of a man and a curious disappearance, I'd have much preferred the latter. At least that way we could all have hung on to some possibility of your having had a noble character. Not anymore, I'm afraid."

J. J.'s jaw fell open. Bill's did too. He'd never heard Nola attack anyone with such venom. He loved his wife in that moment. He loved her deeply. The way she stood clutching Lenore with such resolve, such firm detachment from the holy institution known as "Shreve."

"J. J., is all of this true?" Mrs. Shreve whimpered into her napkin.

Lenore's blue eyes grew wide in the chaos. Bill could only imagine his youngest daughter's pure horror. Probably picturing herself confined to knee-high waders and a pith helmet, trekking through some tropical jungle teeming with overgrown bugs and snakes. Instead, the girl looked around the room and held up a firm hand, as though she had the answer they'd all been waiting for.

"No, it's not true," Lenore said.

Mrs. Shreve dabbed her eyes. Nola exhaled. Junior looked puzzled.

"It's not true because . . . because, you see, the opportunity that John's referring to is gone now. *I* took it. After some talking, Randy Simms and I have decided to go in together on the adventure company, since of course John is needed here. At home. At the factory."

Dooley nearly fell off his chair. Junior looked as if he might sock someone, only he wasn't sure who.

"Lenore, you can't be serious." Nola threw down her napkin.

"I'm quite serious. I've known about the boys' adventure company for more than a month, to be honest. But, just as Mr. Shreve has explained, I realized that John is indispensable here, keeping the family business humming along, whereas I'm not needed for very much of anything. And besides, I enjoy piña coladas."

"But why didn't you tell us what was going on?" Nola looked tortured.

Lenore smiled at her ironically. "Would you have liked the idea any better in July?"

"Darling, you don't know a single soul in . . . where is this place? Saint Martin's?"

"Never mind that." Junior had regained his ability to form words. "You don't know how to sail! You don't know the first thing about boating. You don't know a rhumb line from a conga line. How do you expect to serve as anything but a nuisance down there?"

"I know how to speak French," Lenore countered in an instant. "As I recall you barely managed to cheat your way through two semesters. I know I weigh 115 pounds soaking wet and you're at least eighty pounds more. That's eighty pounds of champagne our tour can carry without your excess baggage. I know the difference between a real Colombian emerald and a bit of polished glass. Randy says he'll be awfully glad to keep his clients from getting scammed the way they sometimes do. I know how to samba and cha-cha—remember you didn't want to learn? I could lead a party to the Purple Parrot and keep them entertained because as it happens I can conga too. Men tend to like me, women tend to want to be my friend, and Randy's pretty certain he and I will double the profit of his first year. Especially now, since we're bringing a charter airplane to join the fleet."

"Whatever do you mean, dear?"

"We bought an airplane." Lenore shrugged, ever the confident shopper.

"*We*? What we?" John turned to her in question.

"All right, *I* did, that is. *I* bought Colin Hatch's airplane. A Beechcraft Bonanza. One hundred eighty-five horsepower. Surprisingly light and manageable."

"But how could you afford such a thing?"

"I had a bit of extra cash lying about. *And*," she inhaled, "I hawked my engagement ring. Gosh, I hope you won't be angry."

All at once, five sets of eyes around the table focused on the impeccably white stripe of skin circling Lenore's fourth—newly naked—finger. Bill thought first of Colin Hatch. Second, of rage. Third, of the seafood casserole he'd just consumed and how it would keep him tormented half the night with a hellfire case of indigestion. Somewhere too, in this muddled soup, he thought of how he couldn't possibly burden Nola with another grim revelation. Not tonight.

"That was my grandmother's diamond," the old pelican moaned, pouring more Bordeaux down her beak.

"Well, *this* is—this is perfect madness." Shreve set about pacing the carpet. "Whoever heard of such a thing? Bride and groom get married. Bride goes off to sail the seas . . . with *another man*? They'll crucify you."

"And so what if they do?" Lenore blurted. "So what if we all agree that it—the marriage, I'm saying—can't work? After the vows and a respectable amount of time"—she took in a deep breath—"we can divorce. Go our separate ways."

And then the yelling. From all sides. Crying, screaming, unscripted Shreves.

"Maybe we ought to take a moment in the study," Bill finally cut in, uncharacteristically calm. "I don't think the children need all of us bearing down on them at once." No one heard him.

"I don't understand. Is there going to be a wedding this weekend or not?" Mrs. Shreve, apparently, felt they'd arrived at the point where it was appropriate to remove her high heels. They dangled from the prongs of her fingers like dead game birds.

"Of course there's going to be a wedding. Don't be deranged, Mavis."

"I was thinking we'd elope at city hall. Boston," Lenore corrected.

"City hall?" both Shreve men balked in unison.

"It's the easiest way. And we'll all be less embarrassed when the whole thing gets dissolved in Reno sometime next year."

"Pardon my intrusion, but am I the *only one* who is going to ask?" Nola Dooley broke in. "While we're all busy licking our personal wounds," she addressed the senior Shreve, "has anyone stopped to think about the child? I mean the actual child?"

Five sets of eyes looked to Lenore's pregnant middle. Lenore turned to her mother, then back to her fiancé. "Plenty of women raise children alone these days. Husbands leave all the time. And the mothers simply find a way. I won't say *it's not difficult*"—she stared pointedly at John—"but the alternative, in this case, would be ever so much harder."

The shouting reached new peaks and pitches. The Corgi fled, as did the poor, tortured maid. Dooley heard Shreve's wailing as if he were listening to the din from underwater. He couldn't take it anymore. The threats and barbs. The tears and sufferings. He simply hadn't the space. And, hell, he knew these kids never had a chance anyhow. Would've bet on it. But for all the revelations delivered inside this one, crowded hour, he was still stuck on that bit Nola had spoken. How grimly she'd said it. How clearly she meant it.

*Given the choice between such an utter disgrace of a man and a curious disappearance, I'd have much preferred the latter. At least that way we could all have hung on to some possibility of your having had a noble character.*

He would never shake that image of Nola from his memory. Nor could he ever pretend, when it came right down to those true, naked moments of crisis, that he didn't know of her preferences.

# SIXTY

Small things kept Lenore awake long past midnight. The toilet ran, like a steady exhale, into the farthest corners of the night. The peepers' cries, urgent and viscous, evaporated into hot, heavy air. The waxed orange blossoms meant to decorate her bridal veil—she spied the silk purse of them waiting on her dresser. She supposed they'd look awfully out of place at a city hall elopement.

Inside the house, the Dooleys had all fled to their separate corners, to process the events of the evening. Her mother might still be up sewing—tugging at her embroidery hoop to avoid nervous gnawing on her cuticles. Her father would be in his den, puffing his pipe, his dinner shirt pleated open between buttons, revealing the paunch of his white belly as he lounged backward into some illusory distraction. Her sisters would stay out, stay *away*, bleeding Edgartown of its last summer reveries, until the lights of the cottage were all extinguished and the threat of an uncomfortable conversation proved safely past.

For all the hours it took to assemble a wedding, Lenore marveled, it hadn't taken any time at all to pull the thing apart. A few muffled phone calls in the den. Some skittering on Clara's part, whisking away the most glaring remnants of an aborted party. Some poor lackey at Shreve's printing outfit, rousted from his Dedham bed, instructed to immediately engrave 427 notices of apology.

*Mr. and Mrs. William Dooley*
*announce that the wedding of their daughter*
*Lenore Margaret*
*to*
*Mr. John Joseph Shreve IV*
*will not take place.*

Her mother then got lost to an exceedingly lengthy shower, followed by a dose of sleeping pills served with Connemara tea.

Now Lenore climbed from her bed with the same careful quiet she'd once employed to meet J. J. at the end of her dock. She unzipped the garment bag that cloaked her massive bridal gown. Yards of pleated satin and old family lace spilled out like Mallomar filling. Even in the palest of ivory's tones, the dress was still too perfect for the occasion at hand. Or *at heel*, rather. She riffled through the wardrobe trunk containing her trousseau—silky slips and stockings and French-made underthings. Stacks of monogrammed bed linens, eiderdown quilts, tray cloths, fingertip towels, bath towels, guest towels, kitchen towels—towels enough to sop up an entire ocean.

She laughed. She had the idea she might like to bicycle down North Water Street and tour her wedding tent on the hotel lawn. It was already built and garlanded, after all. Beds of bluebells had been specially installed. Lighthouse Beach had been swept and cleared and swept again, so the hem of the sea lay as smooth and spotless as her unworn gown. There was primrose planted along the footpath to Saint Andrew's. The lampposts, up and down the waterfront, had been festooned with five-foot-high pull bows for her arriving guests—and indeed all the island's late-stayers—to admire. She wondered if anyone would notice the tent, the bluebells, the pull bows coming down, and no royal wedding having happened in between.

In stocking feet, she crept down the stairs to duck past her father's office. A green banker's lamp cast a weak glow over the confusion of his desk, but she could see him well enough. His index finger perched across his thin mustache, below his nostrils, as if he were stifling a sneeze. He sat poring over a nautical chart—one of those massive sailing leaflets a person can continue unfurling—square after square, longitude after latitude—until whole kingdoms of open sea beckon. His chair squeaked with a listless rocking. To her great surprise, the shelves and nooks perpetually buried by paper had all been cleared. A fire roared in the hearth. Beside the desk, on the floor, Lenore noticed that her father's ditty bag lay open, revealing its various pins and resins, cotton cord and boltrope. A second bag, waiting to be packed, sat guarding a neatly bound stack of cash.

"Nola?" Her father startled behind the desk. He sprang to his feet with great alacrity, like a member of the help caught loafing. "Oh, hello there, darling. You're not your mother."

"I'm wearing her beach robe," Lenore pointed out. "Just going out for a ride by the water."

Her father stood silent, visibly setting aside whatever thoughts he'd been chewing just to take in his youngest daughter. His attention—his full attention—came along almost as rarely as an eclipse. And childishly, Lenore realized, it was a prize that still delighted her. "People often mistake you for your mother, don't they?" He smiled. "That's lucky. More Hoobin than Dooley blood in you, I suppose."

Lenore contemplated her father with equal measure. His forehead nearly level with hers. He'd never amounted to much in physical stature, but *to her*, of course, he'd always been about as imposing as Paul Bunyan and the Holy Ghost. She'd never once doubted his ability to clean another guy's clock, if need be. Never doubted his natural immunity to the fevers and flus his little women suffered around him.

"No," Lenore concluded, without saying more. She didn't quite have the nerve. It was very late. She felt awfully sad. She wanted to tell him "lucky" wasn't the word. And anyway, she liked to think she had more Dooley than Hoobin in the balance. *Hidden strength*, a person might say. A latent kind of inherited quality to be fed and fully revealed, maybe, every *other* generation.

"I have something for you." Her father raised a finger, suddenly remembering, whisking himself back to his desk despite his bad knee.

"What's this?"

"You'd know better than I." His eyes flickered, handing her a thick envelope. "Seems you've got the jump on quite a few stories this summer. Wanda says you asked her to wire some cash internationally. And here is the result."

Lenore's cheeks went red. "It was my own money to send."

"I know it was."

"It's just—Colin deserves to find out the truth."

"My girl." Her father pulled her into a firm hug. She let herself be heavy in his arms. "The truth is not something we find. Not us Dooleys, anyhow. It's something we *create*. Remember that, will you?"

She nodded.

"And Lenore?" her father stepped out to check the hall. "Lenore, I want you to promise me something."

"All right."

"Suppose I were to . . . I mean, supposing *you* were to come into some property, as a result of my . . ."

"Passing?"

"Moving on, yes. I'm talking about Wasque."

"Yes, I know."

"Promise me you'll never sell it."

"Daddy, don't talk morbid. You're perfectly healthy."

Her father shook his head emphatically. "You can always build on it. Build it up as high as the sky. But never sell it, no matter the price. Promise me? It's worth more than anything anyone'll give you. I'd bet my last dollar on it."

"All right." Lenore blinked away the tears filling her eyes. "But—"

"Hush, hush. Never mind that business now. Where did you say you were going?" He squinted. They both looked out toward the front door, where the sidelights revealed a low moon, nestled in clouds, a misty ring around its edge.

"For a bicycle ride. By the water. I have some letters I want to drop. Where are *you* going?" She tilted her head toward the ditty bag, the chart, the rather obvious pile of cash.

"Shh." Bill Dooley smiled at his youngest daughter. His eyes grew bright and busy, like a boy with a scheme for sneaking out of catechism class. "I haven't decided."

# SIXTY-ONE

Sabina listened to the low drone of the mercury vapor ionizing inside fluorescent tubes. Around her, the Operations Room hummed. She heard the stereoed ticks of eight dozen data processing machines, the pip of a plane on the pulsing radar. The calls that night had been quick and routine. A *mult-eye* motor, as the Worcester County observers liked to say, headed west. A single jet going north. All of them flying "high" or "very high." A housewife from Rehoboth testified that spotting gave her a welcome respite from managing bedtime for her six children. A retired watchmaker buzzed in only to complain about raccoons invading his observation tower. She was just hanging up when she realized, in fact, she had company.

"Good evening, ma'am. Do you mind if we join you for a bit?" Two men appeared at the door. They wore civilian sport clothes. No coats or hats. In another setting they could easily have passed for golfers just strolling in off the back nine.

"Not at all." Sabina sat straighter, looking around to see if anyone might object. Lucille was dozing at the status board. "Pleased to meet you, Mister . . . ?"

"My name's Wigeon. This is Mr. Wicklow." They held out their hands across the plotting table. "We come from Bedford, the Cambridge Research Lab. Do you know it?"

Sabina nodded.

"We're here to borrow your FPS-6," said the shorter of the two. "The height finder radar," he clarified.

"Have you intercepted something serious?"

"Possibly, but it's not coming from the East, if that's what you're thinking."

"Another aggressor, besides Russia?" Sabina stood up from her stool.

"It's bad weather," Mr. Wicklow cut in, relieving her alarm. "For enemy aircraft, they don't usually send in the PhD students," he added, smiling.

"What sort of bad weather?"

"That storm that's been loafing off the Carolinas for three days?" Mr. Wigeon stepped toward the plotting board map, swirling his finger just east of Charleston. "Looks like she's headed our way. Are there any airmen who can relieve you ladies? You should get back to your families as soon as possible."

"But the Weather Bureau said the worst of it was moving out to sea." Sabina ignored his attempt to dismiss her.

"The Weather Bureau is about as sophisticated as Beetle Bailey," Wigeon said flatly.

"Not for want of talent, of course," Wicklow objected.

"They lack equipment." Sabina filled in. "Isn't that right, Mr. Wicklow?"

"Call me Peter. And yes, that's exactly it. They haven't got half the budget they need. Right now, for example, their mid-Atlantic weather ship isn't even stationed at its post. How could they possibly warn New England about what's coming?"

"What *is* coming?" Sabina looked from one man to the other.

"Look here," Wigeon instructed. "The reporting stations last night measured from her weak side, to the west. Sixty-five mile-per-hour winds, they thought. But our reconnaissance fliers say she's twice that. And gaining."

"She, *who*?" Sabina puzzled.

"Carol," they said.

Seated at the FPS console, Mr. Wigeon spent the next hours on and off the telephone with MIT's Lincoln Lab in Lexington. He called in the position of Carol's eye while Peter made rapid calculations on a sheet of graphing paper. The vertical plotting board usually used for airplane positions became a roadmap for the storm—a string of dots and dashes indicating her progress up the Atlantic coast.

"How far out can you see?" Sabina swiveled her attention between the radarscope and the paperwork.

"Regular surveillance radar can pick up maybe two hundred statute miles," Peter replied, pencil between his teeth. "But this one you've got here is working triple that distance. Radar transmitter sends out these little pulses, you see? Electrical energy radiated from its antenna. When that pulse comes up against something in the sky—an airplane, a large flock, or a storm in this case—some of the reflected energy shows up as an echo. That's this curl of whiteness showing here against the black."

"But how do you know for certain Carol is a hurricane?"

"Precipitation is already showing us a characteristic pattern. You can tell she's a hurricane by this line of echoes here—that's what we call a squall line. Here's her rain shield. Can you see those spiral bands? If we go back and speed them up, you can see her moving counterclockwise. That's a hurricane all right."

"And what about that ring there?" Sabina leaned in. "That little doughnut?"

"That's the wall cloud."

"I've got a definite eye fix," Wigeon interrupted their lesson. "See if you can get hold of someone at Flight Advisory. Cancel all flights for today."

Sabina sat back on her stool, eying Peter's reflectivity charts, trying to digest what the different intervals and echoes represented. She realized she needed to telephone the island. Somehow get hold of Colin if she could. The Weather Service could issue a hundred warnings, and, even still, most islanders—the many without television sets in their summer homes—would be oblivious. Someone needed to patrol the beaches. Check in at the cottages that sometimes took on water. Warn the kids off their boats.

"Miss? *Miss?* If you're only going to sit there, could you get me the governor's office on the line?" Wigeon broke into her thoughts. "Tell them it's Truro AFB and Carol's moving twice as fast as we thought she would. And coming in strong. Massachusetts ought to get the whistles ready—especially Cape Cod and the islands. First gales will hit before breakfast."

After that, it seemed, everything began to happen rather quickly.

# SIXTY-TWO

*Dear Denny,*

*If anyone's looking for me, please tell them we've gone and eloped. I know what you'll say, which is why I'm sneaking this letter under your door at God knows what hour. I'm sorry I couldn't explain my little plan the other night. I wanted to, truly. But I know what you'd have said. I know what you'd have done. (I can read your eyes so easily, you know.) And you getting mixed up in this thing wouldn't be right either. John and I getting married—quietly, briefly—is the simplest way.*

*We'll be on the 5:00 a.m. ferry into town. Service at noon. Boston City Hall. After that I'm off to Marigot. John is trying to convince me we ought to go down together. Maybe I'll cave, who knows? Either way, I promise not to call you for a ride home.*

*Mostly I wanted to thank you for all your help this summer. For every summer, I guess. For every summer and every season in between. If I had it to do all over again, I would go with you—only you—to that junior prom of mine. Guess I'm a slow learner. Don't hold it against me?*

*Love always,*

*Lenore*

*P.S. I'm enclosing a letter that's meant for Colin. It's from an old friend of his. He isn't expecting any word, but I think he ought to read it as soon as possible. Will you see that he gets it?*

# SIXTY-THREE

James Whelan woke to the sound of his cottage telephone ringing. He felt for his eyeglasses on the bedside table, hauled himself upright and down the corridor, past his odd asylum of Black Forest cuckoo clocks, treading lightly down the hall in slippered feet. If any sort of racket woke up Mother, there'd be hell to pay.

"Yes?"

The operator announced long distance from Florida. David Hammer—his lawyer.

Whelan cleared his throat to reply in an unnaturally lower register. "Very well. Put him through."

The operator invited the caller to go ahead.

"Hiya, Hammer."

"Did I wake you?"

"Oh, no, Dave. I don't mind the hour at all. I'm up at five o'clock normally. Hitting the heavy bag and so forth."

"My wife said you called last night. Pretty late, she said. Some kind of emergency?"

"Yes. Well, no. Not exactly. I did give you a bell yesterday. Something has come up on that case we discussed. The assault charge."

"The soldier who punched you?"

"He *assaulted* me. And he's no soldier. Not anymore, Hammer. Listen, I'd like to get those charges filed after all. And I think I can dig up some dirt to go along—"

"James, we've talked about this."

"It's not just rumors, Dave. I don't deal in rumors either. Medicine—that's my vocation—it's a concrete science. But supposing we knew for a fact just how unprincipled this assailant was."

"You're after that girl again, aren't you?"

"What girl?"

"The girl. The McTigue girl. The one we've written in and out of your will sixteen times now."

"It's got nothing to do with her."

"Mind you, Jim, I'm just your lawyer. But I don't think dragging an adversary into court is going to win over any young woman's affections."

"Well, no, I don't imagine it'll get me too far either. But let's be clear, Hammer. I'm not the only one who stands to lose. Public safety, sir. It's a simple question of public safety. And if *you* won't work to make our streets safer . . ."

Whelan could hear his lawyer sighing all the way in Palm Beach. "I'll file the charges this afternoon. After my golf game."

"Good. And I'll be out looking for character witnesses. Maybe this way we can all know the truth—the *full truth*—about Colin Hatch."

# SIXTY-FOUR

"Son? It's like I say, son. Airport's closed today. Storm's coming."

Denny McTigue went on untying his plane, ignoring this mild, raincoated man: Katama's overnight manager. He struggled against the tie-down knots, stopping every few seconds to wipe his dark hair from his eyes. Normally Denny would have felt obliged to explain. He liked the guy. Respected the guy. But he didn't have the composure or the time. Lenore was getting married. Today. In Boston. And for all the wrong reasons. He couldn't let her go through with it.

"You're liable to get knocked around," the manager persisted.

"This time I intend to fight back," Denny nodded.

"The weather, I'm saying. Ain't you the same fella who lost his lunch over a little downdraft last Saturday?"

"Haven't had any lunch today."

"Wind like this could bust your wing. Never mind the hail."

"What hail?" Denny paused to consider the clouds.

"Don't doubt that lightning'll bring hail. And I've seen what hail can do to an engine like yours."

"I'll jag around it," Denny replied. He was a full fifty hours shy of earning his pilot's license, but today that hardly mattered.

"Jag *around*?" The manager panted out a series of bewildered laughs. "*Around* this front is somewhere near Albany. And with the crosswind at . . . where is it you think you're going?"

"Boston."

"I'd wager they won't even land you in Logan."

"Squantum, then."

"Squantum's closed, son."

"You're full of good news today, pops. Say, take this letter, will you? It's meant for Colin Hatch. I expect you'll see him before I do."

"If you take off in that plane right now, I don't expect you'll see too much of anyone anytime soon."

"You'll have to pardon me if I don't stick around and debate the point."

"What's the harm in waiting an hour or two? Come back inside the office. I've got an extra sardine sandwich and a year's worth of *The Hollywood Reporter*—"

"No, thanks."

"You don't belong up there today, son."

"Says who?"

"Says me and the Flight Advisory and whichever god you worship."

"I haven't been to church in ages," Denny smiled, climbing up into the bird. "But I do know the way to city hall."

# SIXTY-FIVE

"Looks like you're loaded for bear." Colin surveyed the scene at his secretary's house. She sat camped on the sofa with her black tea, her crumb cake, and an economy-size pack of Welch's Junior Mints. An old Emerson battery set droned at her ear, delivering dire premonitions from Providence.

*All flights from Logan International Airport . . . grounded . . . Visiting hours at Plymouth Hospital . . . canceled . . . Massachusetts's letter carriers . . . summoned back to their stations . . . Livestock and yard dogs should be confined to storm cellars or else garaged . . .*

Colin didn't bother too much over the frenzied pitch of the radio men, but he knew bad weather made Florence uneasy. So he'd come by to tape up her windows, deliver water pails for flushing, check the kerosene in her hurricane lamps.

The telephone rang. Hatch looked up at his secretary. "I'll get it."

Outside the sky dimmed. Sallow clumps of foam whipped across the cottage yard, pelting its leaded windows. Along with the keening wind, Colin could hear a sound like river rock churning in a canyon rapid. Twin braids of seawater bled across the lawn, carrying pebbles and swirling mats of spume.

"Hatch here," he answered, and quickly distanced his ear from the voluble torrent coming through. "Who's do you mean? Slow down there, Stan. I can't . . . Denny? Denny McTigue? Put him on the line."

Florence sat up straighter for a better listen. She whisked her hands together, dribbling bits of crumb cake onto her plate.

"Tell him he can't go up. That's all. No one's flying today and . . . Stan. *Stan!*" Hatch set the tape roll down on a windowsill. He shook his head. He crossed the room to quell the volume of the Emerson. "All right, yeah. I understand. I'm on my way." He looked at Florence before setting the receiver back down. "Get your boots on, Flo. I'm taking you up the hill to my place. It's safer, and I'm not sure how long I'll be gone."

"And where are *you* going?"

"Katama. Stan needs my help talking a damned fool out of an airplane."

A high wind rattled the old walls. The cottage's lamplight flickered.

"Should you be driving in this?"

"Don't worry about me." He handed her a wax-coated jacket he'd brought down from the farm. "Don't I always find my way home?"

# SIXTY-SIX

Sabina ran to shed her office clothes in exchange for heavy weather garments. According to the Bedford boys, she hadn't a prayer of making it back to Edgartown before the ferry shut down. But she had to try. Working the telephone was no use. No answer at Colin's farm. The line to Florence's house proved busy. Her own Starbuck cottage couldn't be reached. She knew there was only one phone cable between the Cape and the mainland. When storms loomed, its party line system almost always overloaded. Hurriedly now, she stashed belongings into her gripsack: woolen knee socks, her rain bonnet, the letter from Dr. Hughes—officially welcoming her to join the research fellowship. She was just squeezing into her overshoes when she heard a knock at the door.

"Rumor has it you're heading home early." Bev peeked in. She looked an odd interrogator, her watchman's flashlight aimed at Sabina's face, her peasant-style nightcap with its hanging ribbons.

"There's a terrible storm on the way," Sabina confirmed. "You ought to stay in your room for the next twelve hours or so. Save your bulb too." She pointed at the light. "You may need it."

"I know you're in a hurry, but there's something you need to hear. It's about Colin Hatch."

"Oh, but, Bev." Sabina's face grew contrite. "I ought to have told you. I've decided not to go rooting 'round Colin's affairs after all. I've been unkind to him. And it's like you said, lots of boys got blue tickets back in those days." She was whispering so as not to wake their sleeping floor mates.

"Sabina, how much time have you got to spare?" Bev's half frown lingered.

She took in a quick breath. Checked her watch. "Five minutes maybe."

"That won't do it. I'd better get dressed and tell you along the way."

"But, Bev, it's barely dawn. And about to be bedlam out there, besides."

"Sabina," Bev said sharply. "Colin Hatch didn't earn his blue ticket for setting off cherry bombs. Nor for skipping camp to go see his grandma on her birthday."

"Well of course he didn't."

"No, dear," Bev persisted, taking hold of her friend's wrist. "What I'm saying is that it was worse. Much worse."

Sabina shifted the sack on her shoulder. She lowered her gaze to the floor. "It's like I said. I'm not sure I want to know anything more about it."

Bev swatted at the wall plate, showering the room with a bright, startling light. "Well *I* want you to know. I insist on it, in fact. Colin Hatch earned his blue ticket for desertion."

"*Desertion?*" Sabina felt the breath leave her lungs. Her green eyes went wide. "How can you say so?"

"Miss Arthur doesn't graduate ninnies, my dear."

Another knock at the door. This time it was Lucille popping her head into Sabina's dorm room. The young woman snapped her gum.

"Shh!" Both Bev and Sabina turned to address the new visitor, still sporting her plotter's grease pencil behind her ear.

"Sabina? I think you ought to get back down to the OR. Those men are asking for you. Something's just popped up on the screens."

"There's a storm coming, Lu. A big one. I know it already."

"No, it's not the storm. There's an unidentified. Two of them, actually. Single engines both. Small planes. Could be flying IFR, though it's hard to imagine why anyone'd be out for a joy ride this morning. And we can't find them on any of the documented flight plans."

"Headed for Boston?"

"One, is, yes. Circling the city for the past ten minutes."

"And the other?"

"Headed straight for us, actually."

Sabina looked to Bev and back to Lucille.

"Do me a favor, Lu, and keep trying these numbers." Sabina scratched out the cottage telephones on a pad. "Ask the operator to cut in if this one is still busy. Meet us down in the OR once you've reached someone. I'd be very glad to know none of them is out of doors just now."

# SIXTY-SEVEN

George Mattos didn't like the temper of the morning's sky.

"Don't dawdle getting home now, will you?" he asked. He took another measuring scan of the clouds, blinking hot with lightning. "Looks awful mean up there."

"I should only be an hour or so." The young man spoke his pretension from behind a pair of thick lenses. He crossed his bare, freckled arms. The wind had picked up, and George—himself clad in flannels and an oilskin—could see his passenger was cold.

"I'll wait for you then." George leaned into his wheel, taking extra pains with it. He didn't relish the idea of waiting for anyone this morning. "Thirty minutes. But not longer."

The young man nodded, settling back against the seat of his miniscule convertible. George sniffed. He'd owned hunting dogs that were bigger. He could almost laugh to watch the young man fuss around with the latch for his protracted roof, and the wind, all the while, stirring up his hair.

"Might want to call someone to ride you back home," George put it, after a few moments of silence. After it seemed the roof wouldn't go up after all. He looked dubiously at the convertible. "Hate to wager how far you'll get if the roads wash out."

"Do you really think it'll be so bad?"

George shrugged. "You see that ceiling of clouds? Coming down quicker now, aren't they?"

"I'm not frightened by rain."

George shrugged again. He knew enough to know that fishermen told stories for a reason, and that this particular sky was no fiction. His father had been a great collector of heavy-weather stories. Hurricanes, precisely. Oh, how he'd loved to rank and compare them. To trot out the ugliest of the island's storms like long-forgotten sweethearts in an unfortunate kind of pageant.

And the captives too. The deflected birds. George's father remembered every storm for the displaced creatures that had landed woozily on his masthead or paused to catch their breath on the rocks of a deserted causeway. Terns, jaegers, xemes, petrels—after seventy years of unsettled Augusts, he still remembered each one. Each rare thing he'd seen tumbled by the wind. Big storms pulled birds by the hundreds, miles removed from their natural flyways—for an hour, a day, an entire lifetime, maybe, of misspent wingbeats—arriving someplace fearsomely distant, someplace completely unknown.

"It can't be all that bad." The young man judged the sky impatiently. "They'd have shut down the steamship."

George shrugged yet again. He didn't feel he needed to defend his opinions. Least of all to this city slicker in his matchbox car. "I'll wait for you one half hour," he repeated the bargain. "After that we're sinking her." He gestured to his wheel, estimating he and the boys would have time—but not much more—to secure long ropes at each corner and weigh her down, so as the little scow wouldn't later smash into the harbor's unattended boats or drift off out to sea. And because he was irritated now, he didn't even bother to ask where on earth—on Chappaquiddick, as it were—the young man was presently headed.

# SIXTY-EIGHT

"You've got a phone call," Captain Ford greeted Sabina back in the Operations Room. Out of working habit, she moved to smooth her hair back and remembered her silly rain bonnet. She tugged it off. Outside, leaves darkened the sky like swarming bats. The girls had run clear across the base, skating and slipping across mats of wet pine needles, raining from the trees, erasing the pavement.

"*I* do?" Sabina wondered aloud. She looked over to Wigeon and Wicklow, still charting the storm. More of the base men had joined the researchers by now, standing at the screens, watching the pips blink across the displays.

"Boys at the gate picked up a friend of yours, apparently. A pilot."

"*Colin?*"

"I don't know his name. I just know he's damned lucky we didn't deploy any interceptors."

"He's *here*? What for?"

"Why don't you ask him?" The captain held the telephone out for her to take.

"Put him through, please," Sabina addressed the operator. "Colin, is that you?"

"Yes, it's me. Awfully sorry to drop in unannounced."

"Colin, they were getting ready to send fighters up after you. You're not on any of the planned flights. And there's a terrible storm coming."

"I know all that," Colin said through static on the line. "Listen, Bean. Something's happened."

"Is it A. P.?" Sabina held her breath.

"No. It's Denny."

# SIXTY-NINE

"Ding-dong," Isolde Martin answered the door by mimicking her own tinny bell. Her blonde curls looked as though she'd slept on them. Her eyes flushed an unhealthful pink. Not even Technicolor could have saved her complexion. "Bit early for Halloween, aren't you, junior? Who are you supposed to be anyhow?"

"Good morning, Miss Martin." James Whelan whisked off his hat. The wind was too quick; he had to chase it a ways along the dooryard. Chappaquiddick's tall, parched grasses rustled under the gray-smoke sky. Bits of macadam from the newly completed roadway launched and sailed across the lawn, clacking hard against the stone wall of Isolde's water well. "I'm here for you, actually."

"The reaper then, ay? Aren't there meant to be four black horses as well?" Isolde looked past the doctor, searching out a distant object on the sea.

"Beg your pardon?"

"I think you'd better come inside." She led him to her cottage living room. A scene of total disarray. He looked down at a pile of sheets and pillows occupying the sofa. "You can throw those anyplace."

"We've met before, of course," Whelan smiled, setting the makeshift bedding aside, somewhat pleased she couldn't place him from the scene at the Homestead benefit. "I'm a doctor, you see."

"Oh, dear. Did I skip out on the bill?" Isolde murmured through her teeth, biting into a long, lit cigarette. Her bare feet swung erratically beneath her chair. “Hospital ought to start a tab for me.”

“Would you mind if I sat with you for a moment?”

Isolde shrugged. “I haven’t any plans.”

“To be frank, I’ve come to ask you a few questions about Colin Hatch.”

Isolde laughed her sharp, mocking laugh. Upstairs, the wind blew a heavy door shut. “The bellhop.”

Whelan felt sorry for the girl. Suffering some sort of psychotic break, he judged. Another fine mess, no thanks to . . . “*Colin Hatch*.” He repeated for clarification.

“He’s not here.” Isolde looked around defensively. “Probably out with his girl. Diving for pennies off the pier.”

“I don’t care where he is. I’m only interested in his behavior. He’s about to be handed some criminal charges. And the prosecutor is keen to know what else he’s been up to.”

The sound of hard rain filled an awkward pause. Isolde’s attention wandered.

“Look, Miss Martin,” the doctor attempted again. “I need to know the nature of your relationship with Colin Hatch this summer. It’s a serious matter.”

Outside the little island cottage, treetops nodded in the wind like great green nags’ heads. The bamboo shades began to levitate and slap back against the sills as salted rainwater spit cold drops onto the floor. Whelan stood to lower the glass. All along the shore, dune grass furrowed. Inside, on an old sideboard, he saw Isolde’s breakfast buffet of pill bottles and cigarette ashes.

“It’s all a little too much, isn’t it?” the actress said, following the doctor’s eyes. Whelan thought he heard a note of lucidity coming through. “The way that people swim in and out of your life?”

# SEVENTY

Muscular clouds patterned the sky over the water. Heavier anvils loomed and flashed in the distance. The gaps were slim, but he wouldn't need much time. Maybe fifteen minutes, Denny thought, wheels up to wheels down. And anyway, he knew how to fly by his instruments if things got rough.

He turned ninety degrees toward a gap in the buildup. He'd always been told to steer at least twenty miles clear of lightning. Then again, he'd also been told the girl he loved was about to marry a total creep of a guy when she sure as heck didn't have to. When she had another option—a much better option—ready to stand up there with her, if only he could find his way through to smooth air.

*Low and slow*, he told himself, looking up into the cloud towers overhead. *Low and slow.*

But this sky was charged, all right. Convection atmosphere. Static danced from the bird's nose. He tried to stay focused on his instruments. Out ahead, the propeller swept through a haze. Clusters of buildup closed in around his windscreen until everything was white. Like flying in a milk bottle. He couldn't see a thing.

Wasn't any cause for alarm, though. Plenty of fuel on board. Plenty of time to pick his spot. Small planes like his rarely ever caught a strike mid-flight. Plane like this, hell. More likely to take a hit of lightning tied down on the ground. Every good pilot knew that much, and besides—

*Crack.*

A blinding flash. A sudden shock. His head hit the canopy. He thought he saw Saint Elmo's fire glowing blue in front of him. One last blip, and then blackness across the dash. Denny turned to check for his instructor, but of course the seat was empty. What the hell to do now?

*Start climbing. Give yourself every opportunity to gain altitude—to gain time.*

# SEVENTY-ONE

"Denny? In *this*? Where is he going?" Sabina practically shouted into the mouthpiece.

"Can't say for certain. Katama manager thinks he mentioned city hall. Boston, I guess."

"Not likely," Wigeon interrupted, pointing with his pencil to the radar screen. "He may have started out for Boston, but he's not headed that way now."

"You've lost him?"

"*I* didn't lose anyone," Wigeon argued. "I'm just telling you he's flying the wrong way."

Sabina dropped the phone and ran for a closer look at the screen. Without question the tiny pip was heading east, away from the storm but also away from the land. When she picked up the receiver again, Colin was saying, "Bean, I'm sorry. I went up after him just as soon as I could."

"So he's diverting around the wind, right?" Sabina asked hopefully. "That happens. Pilots do that."

"Or he's lost," Wigeon put in. "Unless he's intending on the Canaries."

Sabina shot him a look. "Can't ATC radio in to guide him?"

"He wasn't responding last we checked. I'm sure Stan's still trying, but—"

"We can try him." Sabina looked to the men. "He'll answer if it's me. Can't we try him?"

"Not if his radio's shot."

# SEVENTY-TWO

"Why do you suppose they name storms for women, anyhow?" Isolde settled herself next to the doctor on her powder-pink davenport. It was the only modern piece of furniture in the cottage. By now, much as the rest, it smelled of pine paneling and the faint wisp of decaying sea life. "Care for a sweet?" She gestured to a bowl of caramels on the coffee table.

"No, thanks all the same." Whelan removed his eyeglasses and rubbed his nose.

"How about a Dexamyl?"

"I'm just wondering if you have any letters or photographs. Something tangible from Mr. Hatch this summer. Speaking to his *character.*"

Isolde threw her head back in mock death, like a child fantastically bored. "You say you don't know why, so I'll *tell you* then. It's because women are merciless."

"Holding a grudge against someone, are you?"

"Let me explain something." Isolde stood, her voice suddenly plummy and Hollywood again. "Are you listening? It goes like this: A man has an affair. He may be terribly in love or not at all so. Either way, he burns the silly letters. Burns them straightaway. To save his wife the embarrassment. To save his mistress the shame. That's what a man does."

Whelan leaned in, accepting the offered caramel after all.

"Women are different creatures." Isolde lit herself another cigarette. "A woman has an affair, and what does she do? She saves *everything.* Every faintly scented handkerchief. Every hotel matchbook. Every stupid, careless note. Every coat check ticket. And instead of destroying these treasures, she burns herself. *Inside*, I'm saying. She burns every day with her souvenirs stashed in the closet, afraid of being found out and questioned. Interrogated and abandoned and *hated*, ultimately. She is terrified, you see."

The actress delivered her monologue while making *en pointe* jumps from one wooden floorboard to the next. Whelan reached out his hand to steady her. The actress kissed it and curtseyed.

"Do you want to know the very worst part?"

"Tell me."

"A woman loves every moment of that burning. That torturous, incessant, hell-on-earth burning. It becomes her favorite kind of sensation. The constant panic. The walking about while mortally wounded. It's like a slow death played out in dozens and dozens and dozens of meetings and all the days in between. And soon she comes to crave her torture, not just for herself; she wishes it on everyone actually. Like some kind of *emotional plague*. Do you see? Do you see what I'm saying? That's why women are merciless."

Satisfied, Isolde fluffed her negligee ruffle around her knees. Whelan straightened up to get a better look. She dragged an old step stool from the coat closet.

"Now, look, you oughtn't be climbing anything." He stood behind her, hovering, ineffectually. He picked up her pill bottles to read their labels: Dexamyl. Desbutal. Ambar. "Not after the breakfast you've had."

"You want dish on Colin Hatch?" The actress took a clumsy swipe at the doctor, aiming to poke his chest and succeeding, instead, at grazing his beefy chin. He noticed her wrist still bore its Mass General hospital bracelet. Since he was curious now, he didn't endeavor too much to stop her; she persisted in climbing barefoot, stretching her calves to retrieve a Roger Vivier shoebox from the closet's top shelf. Her fingers shook and fumbled with the lid.

"Are those your mementos?" Whelan craned his neck, unable to hide his excitement. "Letters you've kept? From Colin?"

"These? These are clippings. Critical reviews," Isolde explained with a facial expression of great malaise, tossing paper from the box onto the old yarn rug.

"Yours?"

"No, Eva Gabor's. Yes, naturally *mine*. Except for *somewhere* in here, I do have *one* thing Colin wrote. One thing . . ."

James Whelan sprang to her hip, rabid, nearly choking on caramel. "Did Colin Hatch profess his love? Promise devotion? That evening in Manhattan. What was the buildup exactly? What'd he do?"

"Doctor, please." She stood atop the little ladder and got lost in the view out the window.

Whelan followed her gaze to where a huddle of ancient lobster traps—only props by now—had begun freewheeling toward the mainland. Far out, rusted smudge pots dotted the way to Dooley's looming build. She looked as if she were trying to determine the way of the wind.

"He didn't *do* anything, I'm quite sure. Not with me, anyhow." She descended in a sulk. "That's why, if I were in my right mind, I wouldn't give this to you. That's not the sort of girl I am. Is it?"

Whelan grabbed at the paper, nothing short of a viper. He studied the letter, front and back, while a fresh gust rushed through the trees. A For Sale sign skated over the sand plain. Utility poles swayed at precarious angles. Scraps of shingle and clapboard crawled, then scudded down the road. Off in the distance, the smudge pots tipped and rolled. Everywhere, in small pieces, the manmade world was breaking apart.

"This . . . this is . . ." Whelan stammered his glee. "Why, this is a confession—a signed confession—of theft. And desertion. Maybe worse."

"Is it?" Isolde shrugged. "Merciless."

"He ought to have been thrown in jail! *Still* ought to be." Whelan wondered how much Hammer knew of military law. Perhaps, if he hurried, he could catch someone more familiar at the yacht club. "Listen, Isolde, I've got to run."

"Run? Run where?"

"Back to Edgartown."

"Take me with you."

"With *me*? You're not dressed. And you're bevvied besides."

"I'm coming anyhow. I've got a motorbike outside."

James Whelan looked out the window, looked back at the actress. He laughed. "A motorbike? You'd have better luck hitching a cab."

# SEVENTY-THREE

"Can you see him yet?"

"Nothing since we first lost sight."

"Why don't you come out here to the gate," Colin suggested. "I could sit with you at least. They won't let me come inside where you are."

"No, I want to stay where I can keep an eye on the screen."

"I hate that I can't be any help to you."

"Stay on the line with me. That's help enough."

"I hardly know what to say."

"That's never stopped you talking before." Sabina made a little laugh, though it took all her strength not to open up crying. "Why don't you tell me a story?"

"What kind of story?"

"One with a happy ending."

# SEVENTY-FOUR

"Dammit to hell." The young doctor checked his watch. He'd promised the ferryman he'd be back in thirty minutes, but it'd been an hour at least. Getting back to Edgartown by boat would be impossible now. He scanned the shoreline. Just west of Wasque, Norton Point was narrowing—disappearing—melting fast into the waves.

"You won't make it," the actress called from her open window. Rain wet her face, and yet she smiled through it.

"Watch me," the doctor sneered, ducking into his Austin-Healey.

"Let some pressure out of your tires first."

"How's that?"

"Air down your tires, you silly old reaper! Or you'll sink into the sand."

Whelan paused to consider this advice. And its source, presently bent over the open sill, delighting in the rushes of air that filled and lifted her curls.

"I'll do it for you if you don't know how," she said, giggling. "But you have to take me with you."

"I'll do it myself," the doctor muttered, getting out of the car, wiping his glasses on his sleeve. He got down on a knee before the first tire. A sudden gust knocked him over. He planted his front foot again. Isolde kept up laughing. *Let her laugh her way back to the loony bin*, Whelan thought. He had what he'd come for. Soon enough everyone in Edgartown would know about it too.

# SEVENTY-FIVE

"It was spring 1944. I'd just been assigned Air Transport Command duty. That means flying the damaged aircraft away for factory repair. Bringing mended birds back to the fighting fronts."

"You were in Italy still?" Sabina sat half listening, watching the radar for her brother's airplane to appear. The base men stood by taking notes, pacing the floor. Lucille snapped her gum. Colin's voice kept her calm.

"Yeah, outside Florence. The Allies had gotten a manufacturing plant back into working order. Producing parts for busted Hawks, Mosquitos, Bolos, and all the rest. Plum gig. I didn't want it at first."

"But you took it anyhow?"

"I'd flown so many missions," Colin reflected. "More than my share. The big brass said I ought to sit out a few. They worried about our morale and so forth. You sure you want to hear this right now?"

"Yes. Please. Really, I do."

"About that time I got word my father was ill, back in Bristol. Guess I'd started to think maybe it could happen to me. The possibility of not coming home to them. To the old man, especially. I always promised him I'd come home."

"So you took the assignment?"

"Right. I agreed to ferry the junkers for a few months. Long enough to send some honest letters about my being out of harm's way. That's when I met Adele. She was working as a courier for the Italian Resistance. The end of the war was coming into view. After the role she'd played, and with an angry husband on her tail, she needed to get out. She wanted *me* to fly her out. Of course I couldn't do that."

"So what did you do?"

# SEVENTY-SIX

While the doctor knelt at his tires, Isolde made for her raincoat and rubber boots. She tied a scarf around her curls and fixed her lipstick before the mirror. Soon enough the effort of standing made her dizzy. She stopped to rest. She may have dozed off. And then the lipsticking, it turned out, took a bit longer than usual. She spent a box of tissues fixing the edges, making it work. She needed Colin to see she was all right, even if she wasn't exactly. She needed him to know she was trying, and failing, without him. She needed him to say, "Good morning, kid," in that way that he did. Or who else would? Who else ever, ever would?

She checked the window. The doctor's polished convertible now leaned like a junkyard wreck on two perfectly flat tires. "Idiot," she laughed. The doctor himself was gone. Her Lambretta bike too.

The trees along her road swayed their leafy fringe. Their naked fronts—where they'd been sheared to make way for last month's power lines—shivered and dipped. Flat and exposed on one side—like a dollhouse. Like a life sliced open for casual study. Isolde swore her favorite swear word and nearly fell down laughing despite herself. Her scalp tingled. Tiny white crystals danced before her eyes. She didn't quite know what she felt like. Perhaps a bit of fresh air.

# SEVENTY-SEVEN

"We had ten days. It wasn't much time, but she was—she was like you, in a way. Her mind worked like a machine. Goody, Clay, and I, we'd been given a guidebook for all the different aircraft we might need to ferry. Different procedures for cold starts. Different power settings. We went through that book twice and Adele knew it by heart."

"But to what end, Colin?"

Colin gave out a little sigh. He'd told the story in his head a thousand times. Or maybe it was his own defense he was so used to repeating. "She wasn't ever meant to *fly* anything at all. Just play the part of *knowing how.* She was only meant to play a part, you understand?"

"Not remotely."

"The plan was to pose her as an ATA flight engineer. See, the Allies had these women helping us in the auxiliary. Attagirls, the Brits called them. And they came from all over—Australia, Canada, South Africa. Civilian pilots, the whole lot. When they had to move the heavies—bombers, I mean—they flew in pairs: pilot and flight engineer. We figured Adele could pass for an FE. All she'd have to do was get her name on a manifest and pretend to monitor the control systems while some other gal pilot flew her home."

"Without any badge? No license?"

"Sounds flimsy, I know. But the ATA was about as regimented as a traveling circus. Hell, they let one-armed volunteers into that ferry pool. I figured if I briefed her well enough, if she could read the instruments and speak the lingo . . ." Hatch shook his head. "For all the supplies we lacked in the war, there was always a surplus of blind trust. Had to be. I'm telling you, Sabina, I could've delivered Judy Garland as an ATA pilot and they'd have taken my word." Colin paused. He flicked his lighter. "The only real obstacle was her getup. She needed a uniform."

# SEVENTY-EIGHT

Lenore pressed her face against the tall, arched window, looking down at the city streets toward Granary, the old patriots' burying ground. Outside, the wind whipped up the leaves and the litter—parking tickets, sheets of newsprint—landing them on the building's grand pavilion or sending them aloft, up and about, helicoptering away on paths impossible to follow. Lightning flashed. Rain battered the glass. She supposed all of this was just deserts.

What had she been thinking—leaving that note under Denny's door?

Was she trying on an idea? Testing a theory? Or just—in a lingering bit of habit—sporting about carelessly? No. She shook her head for the benefit of no one in particular. It was more than that.

"And you say the island ferry has already shut down?" she called back to J. J. He sat behind her, fuming on an oak-paneled settle bench in the second-floor lobby, watching the department secretaries—one by one—lock up their offices and venture back outside in frightened pairs. Clearly he was ready to give up on the idea that anyone of any authority was coming into work today.

"The *ferry*?" J. J. burst out, as if he'd been waiting to unleash something all these hours stuck together, thwarted by an absent city clerk. "Lenore, *everything* is shut down. The banks. The restaurants. Are you half-blind? You are looking at a hurricane in front of you."

"A hurricane, you think?" She bit her lip.

"I'll be lucky to manage us a hotel room across the street. In fact, you stay here while I go try."

"John." She turned to face him.

"What now?"

"Get two rooms, will you?"

He shot her a look. Thunder cracked. She didn't quite believe in God. And yet, this morning, she suspected he was trying to tell her something.

"On second thought, get three. Three rooms."

She wasn't surprised to hear his derisive laugh at this request. "What an excellent idea. Are you expecting friends?"

"No," she turned back to the window. "Something more than that, I think. Something more, I hope."

# SEVENTY-NINE

Dennis McTigue first saw the film *Frankenstein* at Back Bay Cinema, with his father, at a tenth-anniversary screening on Halloween night. He was ten years old. His father prefaced the movie—maybe five or six times—by saying they did not have to stay to see it through. They could go home at any time. It was only a movie, and boys his age would likely be frightened by some of the high-drama scenes. Denny still remembered going to bed with a faint tremor in his hands; he'd gripped the armrests so tightly—refusing to exercise the quitter's option.

*Keep your eyes peeled for land—any land. Shit, am I still headed west? Or is the wind taking me out to sea?*

From there, the easy outs never disappeared. Denny rarely accepted them. His mother had died young. His father sought to flush the grief from his system by talking to computer machines in speculative mathematical formulas. What Denny had lacked in parental figures he'd been compensated in games and toys and Canadian fishing trips with uncles who offered to let him sit at the bar and order his own beer when he was fourteen. There were certain things he *had* to do: school, church, teeth brushing. But even these prerequisites were open to interpretation—executed according to his own ideas—while his primary guardian, Aunt Poppy, was busy harassing his sister into some approximation of Doris Day.

*Okay, so you've lost visibility. You've still got daylight on your side.*

*Eventually you'll come upon a landmark. Unless—unless this is open ocean below.*

Denny had never felt any worse off for his upbringing. Being spoiled was not the fabled curse his bedtime stories might have led him to believe. In fact, lots of people told him he was a "good kid." He'd turned out all right. Did he own things he didn't quite deserve? Probably. Had they ever done him any harm? Up until his twenty-third birthday, the answer was a resounding no.

And then he'd petitioned for this plane.

And then lightning had struck.

And for the first time in his life, Denny McTigue had only one option.

*Sit back and cruise. Perfectly safe to cruise. There are no mountains on Cape Cod.*

But whereas lightning had brought life to the monster Frankenstein, this eruptive jolt had erased the heartbeat from his plane. Altimeter: dead. Radio: dead. Artificial horizon: gone. The only working components that remained were his engine (still receiving power thanks to a pair of permanent magnets) and his whiskey compass.

*Let me find a place to set this bird down. Just one flat stretch of earth.*

Infinite seconds passed. He willed his eyes to find something, anything besides the unrelenting whiteness of the sky. In his mind he reviewed crash-landing protocol, straining to visualize an emergency touchdown, even if touchdown was, right now, just a far-off prospect.

*If the wing flaps don't respond, be ready for a wheels-up landing. Cut the ignition before impact. Try and slow her to eighty.*

Visualization wasn't working. He couldn't focus. Couldn't help but think of Frankenstein. That old Halloween showing with his dad.

*We can get outta here whenever we want, Denny. Anytime at all. Just say the word. And we're home.*

# EIGHTY

"The ATA girls were civilians. Many of them couldn't shell out for official service dress. Some made their own. We found a seamstress in Spoleto who agreed to take on the work in exchange for half our pocket money, six cartons of cigarettes, and peppermints besides. We gave her exact instructions: dark wool, slacks and blazer, embroider the sleeves with a trumped-up nationality title and gold rank lace. Sew a purple backing behind the gold. That was what the flight engineers wore."

"And she got it done? Your seamstress?"

"Well enough, yeah. The day we were due to report, we brought Adele along with us. A gray day. Looked like weather to come. We told the brass we'd picked her up at the embassy, on account of she was delivering medicine and supplies."

"Did she pass muster?"

Colin laughed and Sabina could picture him nodding. "Remarkably, she did. ATA officer took her in with nary a second glance. Gave us some proper British glad-handing and sent us off to find our own transport assignments. I heard him saying she was bound for Oxfordshire. Striding off, she kept up with the ruse so well, talking up the Faringdon Tower and its lovely views of White Horse. How she knew that place is anyone's guess. Goody and I clapped backs, thinking we'd done it, that we'd saved her. She'd have been in Britain in two hours, except—"

"Except that something betrayed her?"

"The jacket. The old seamstress forgot our purple fabric behind the rank stripes. Adele was only meant to play backup. But that uniform, as it was, told everyone she was a proper pilot, not any tagalong flight engineer."

"So what did she do?"

"She climbed in and took off."

# EIGHTY-ONE

Isolde saw the doctor now. Up ahead. Standing in the water against the crutch of her bike. He was kicking it, actually. The bike went over, lost beneath the waves—as neatly erased as a mistake in a child's drawing.

She called to him, realizing she didn't know his name. She called, "Reaper!" and discovered her voice went nowhere in the wind. Still, the doctor turned and saw her. She felt relieved, though lightning scissored the sky and the rain bit at her cheeks like bees.

Big waves knocked against her. Up ahead she could see the banks of South Beach, the promise of safety on higher ground. Behind her the sand spit was gone, swallowed. But why was he turning? Why was he going on ahead without her?

She waded out the only way she could. Waves rolled in higher, and she stopped minding the shock of wet cold. She let the water soak into her clothes, swirl around her with its thick, drenching weight. She kicked off a boot to feel the sandy floor of the earth. The other wouldn't come. She crossed her leg over her bent knee to pry it loose just as another wave came and went, sucking her heel into the riptide, knocking her sideways. She struggled to her feet spitting mouthfuls of sand.

The cresting waves had a cruel way of catching her off guard, one right after the next. The rain and the waves became indistinguishable. The saltwater stung her eyes and bled her spit-block mascara down her cheeks like black tears. She used her hands to shield her face until she needed her hands completely for balance, to help herself back up again, to tread water, to swim.

# EIGHTY-TWO

"I thought I'd killed her. Her and the actual flight engineer because there were two of them in there we could see. Adele at the controls."

"What did you do?"

"Only thing I could do. I went up after them. Ran across the airfield, grabbed my own assignment bird, tried to follow. Everything was happening all at once, you understand? I chased a smoke tail I thought was theirs. Half an hour went by. Turned out to be a buzz bomb. By the time I realized my mistake I was coming up on Bern. That's when I spied the RAF on my tail."

"He recognized you as friendly?"

"Thankfully. I couldn't reach him on B channel, so I only waved, fell into formation. Crossing the border, two Swiss fighters met up to convoy."

"And you landed?"

"In Switzerland."

"And you were taken in?"

"I told myself right then I'd killed her," he repeated. "Good as killed her."

"But what could you have done at that point? Admit to smuggling an anonymous girl into some subset of the Royal Air Force? Our closest allies? It'd have been grounds for treason, Colin."

He took in a deep breath. "That's what they court-martialed me for. Theft. Desertion. Treason. The Corps put the screws to Goody first, so as he had to talk. Poor bastard. I don't blame him. He already had a wife, three kids. He spilled everything about Adele and what we'd done. I was given a life sentence."

"A life sentence!"

"Once I got stateside again, I was able to secure American counsel. Lawyer chalked it up to combat neurosis, said my mind was *unduly affected* by all those extra missions. I refused to stand behind his lie, but it never even came to that. He'd demanded a rehearing or else a dismissal of charges. War Department vacated the sentence."

"And just that like, you were vindicated?"

"Well, no one could prove Goody's story. They never found a trace of Adele. It was easier for everyone to believe I'd gone crazy. They handed me the blue ticket. Fifty cents for bus fare."

"What about the airplane? The two women inside? You never got any word?"

She could hear him, over the line, taking a slow drag. "Not until this summer. I mean, not until Lenore did her part."

"Lenore? What's Lenore got to do with all this?"

Hatch paused. "Sabina, I got a letter this morning."

"How is that possible?"

"Lenore delivered it to Denny, and Denny dropped it at the airpark, just before he took off."

At the mention of her brother, Sabina's eyes went to the radar screen, but there was nothing to see. "I'm not sure I understand."

"You wanted a story with a happy ending. If you're still up for it, I think maybe I should read this letter to you."

# EIGHTY-THREE

The pinwale trench coat confined her. Isolde tugged it off. The doctor, up ahead, had lost his body. He'd transformed to just a dot atop the waves, like a little fishing bobber getting pulled in on its line. Distantly, she heard hurricane whistles bleating into the brume.

Stray bits of fencing tossed past. Driftwood. A CLOSED BEACH sign. A hand pump. She caught sight of these objects only as flashes. Cedar shingles. Lengths of rope. There, then gone. She decided she didn't want to follow their paths, making a panicked bid for shore, for the grass on the hillside she'd skirted just minutes prior. But the grass was gone. The hill was gone. The land between the bay and the ocean had disappeared. The option of retreating back to her cottage appeared to have vanished. Another wave caught the side of her head, driving her whole body backward and fully below the foam. She gagged and gasped upon surfacing, misjudging the amount of time she had to recover. Another wave came. She screamed underwater. She could see the sky, just not long enough to breathe it.

Isolde thought suddenly, stupidly of stars. How she'd always loved them. There were so few to admire in the city, but here on the island they were plentiful, far-reaching, bright. And wouldn't it be a shame if she'd seen her last one but never known it. She coughed. She searched the sky for stars. It was morning, she knew, but unlikely things had always had a way of finding her. She only had to look out long enough. To look up. To keep her head *up*. Oh, but how her eyes stung, blurred, and swam. Water crashing everywhere. The sky elusive, faraway. Retreating.

A beat passed. A beat without inundation. She tested her eyes again. Above she saw sky. She looked up and saw, at the edge of the false night, a patch of blue infiltrating the gray. She swallowed another mouthful of saltwater. Her sinuses stung. Her arms proved too heavy to thrash. But it was coming. She could see it brighter now: the clean, blue light edging its way into view—calm and perfect and completely without flaw.

# EIGHTY-FOUR

*Dear Colin,*

*I was as happy as Easter to hear I might have this opportunity to reach you. I knew you once, for not so many days. And still I have been certain, always after that, you would be guessing at my fate. Guessing probably in an unhappy way. You will want to know, naturally, if I made it to London—how I made it to London, because, yes, I did. You may have thought, these many years, perhaps I was injured or dead or just a bad dream from the war. I think it too, sometimes, about that day.*

"I don't think Sabina ought to hear any more of this just now." Bev commandeered the telephone, breaking into Colin's reading. "By her face, I don't suppose your story hour is helping our friend very much."

"It's all right." Sabina patted Bev's arm. She glanced back at the men manning the radar. "There's nothing for us to do just now except sit tight. And pray."

"We can take a break from this," Colin offered.

"No, please. Go on," Sabina urged him. "I'm listening."

*If I'm to thank you properly for saving me—for surely you did, save me—I must acknowledge your accomplice in the affair. I'm sure you have never been introduced. How exactly did we meet? As with a dream, the order of things is difficult to recall. You delivered me to the airplane. I felt in my chest il batticuore, you understand? I was practically sick with fright. But then the door, like a great clamshell, opened and the staircase tumbled out. She was waiting. Waiting and smiling at the top. American. Such pretty green eyes. I shook her hand. Her nails were black with grease.*

*She could see I was tentative, I suppose. She started talking right away about the weather, the clouds, anything to steady my hands, which were shaking. I remember she wore a wedding ring. You can imagine my surprise that any husband would let his pretty bride fly away across the ocean to witness a war she needn't ever have seen. But it wasn't such an odd bit of duty for her, she told me. She was checking her list: the fuel, the radio, the lights—still talking to me all the while. Her husband came from Boston. Her two children were with him there. She asked if I had a huband, children. She asked, of course, why I'd come to help.*

"You're trembling, Sabina." Bev offered an arm around her shoulders. "Can I bring you some tea?"

Sabina sat silent. Only held up her hand for Beverly to stay quiet.

*I said, "You first." She wasn't shy about her reasons. The Allied army hadn't enough manpower for delivering supplies, correspondence. The men were needed in combat. So, who else? Who else would deliver the letters? Years before, she had fallen in love with her husband, you see, through letters. Hundreds of lovely letters trusted to unknown carriers and the miles between them. But for all that, maybe there would be no happy marriage, no beautiful children, she told me. When she read about a volunteer pool—women helping soldiers secure their sweethearts' letters from home—she had to come. She was instantly decided. She'd arrived in England at the early start of things. They were glad to have her, too. She was skilled with engines and small machines. She learned the bigger ones—the bombs, I mean—as the war went on.*

*I am ashamed to say I told her everything before we even found our seats. How I'd never once piloted anything. How we were not as alike as she assumed. How I was nothing more than a rebel, homeless, fleeing. She didn't ask me any questions. I remember how well she understood from just a few scant words. Soon enough we were moving. We were leaving. Coming off the ground. She drove. She talked. Did she know how to fly? Maybe a little, she said with a wink. We were both so stupid, I think we laughed. I asked her why she was helping me. I think I almost couldn't believe it real.*

*She said she liked to tell her children stories. Not about little rabbits or bears in short pants, but real stories. Like ours. She would tell her children—her daughter especially—a real tale about two women, taking to the sky, pulling a little thread in the web of the world, with what effect, who knew? Two women flying up and up and up . . .*

"He's back up!" Wigeon shouted.

Sabina gasped.

Colin stopped reading the letter.

A small green blip pulsed into view, and the men crowded together—heads and necks—blocking out Sabina's view. Lucille grabbed her grease pencil, climbed her plotting board ladder. Sabina set down the telephone, extracting herself from one drama just in time to take up this current one.

"It's him! It's Denny!" she cried, pushing her way between the men. "Heading westbound now. He's turned around!"

Bev drew in for a better look, only to see the faint green marker disappear.

"Gone now," Wicklow observed. "Just birds, you think?"

"That's not birds." Sabina shook her head, tears welling up in her eyes. "Not in this wind. That's my brother."

"What was his last position?" Bev demanded of the room.

"I'd say right about here. Forty-two, nineteen, nineteen north; seventy, fifty-one, fifty-two west. Give or take," Lucille answered. "I know because that's right around the Kiowa site. The old shipwreck. He's coming in south of Shag Rocks."

"You don't know that's him," Widgeon frowned. "You oughtn't give false hope."

Just then the second phone in the Operations Room rang out. Lucille jumped for it.

"Air Defense, go ahead."

Sabina held her breath.

"Altitude? Speed? Uh-huh . . ." Lucille drew up the data across the Plexiglas. The room listened in silence, not quite believing they had an observer phoning in just now with visibility so limited and common sense dictating anyone in range ought to be indoors. "That makes sense," Lucille nodded. "He's too low for the radars to pick him up."

"He's too low," Sabina picked up the phone to tell Colin. "Do you suppose he's lost control?"

"He's just looking for a place to bring her down, I'll bet."

A third line rang. And a fourth. The men pitched in grabbing telephones. Four conversations overlapped like a kind of perpetual canon calling out the same questions for the different observers on the lines. An airplane was tearing through the clouds. Lovells. Fort Warren. A ranger at Bass Point. They all agreed. Small craft. Slow. Low. Seemingly bound for a crash landing. Sabina could sit still no longer.

"I need to get to the harbor islands right now." She jumped from her seat. "It's him. I know it's him. Colin, will you take me?"

"I'll take you," Hatch said. "Except, Sabina, are you sure? It's bad. And you don't fly."

"You've got a good window coming up," Wicklow offered. "The eye. Maybe ten minutes at the outside."

The mood inside the room had shifted—the most dramatic of wind shears—from gravely expectant to briskly apace. Everyone talking over one another, barking orders and prescriptions of what next. A rescue flight was ordered and announced. Sabina was given permission to join. Without her asking as much—she was already gone from the room—it was determined Colin Hatch ought to go along with her. Standby fliers at Otis received their commands and were already en route for a touch and go landing in Truro. And while the indoors was this way bustling, the space inside the storm's eyewall brought a temporary calm—even a spray of sunshine—to the air outdoors. A small flock of whimbrels, entrenched in this oddly quiet pocket, flew overhead—eye-riding, as it were—tired, hungry, as eager as anyone to see where this latest storm might land them.

## TUESDAY, AUGUST 31, 1954
## Crash Landing Survivor Found! Other Losses Loom Large

BOSTON, MA (AP)—A Boston pilot, earlier feared lost at sea, was today located—alive and well—among the trash heaps at Spectacle Island. Dennis McTigue, twenty-three, dropped from the skies last week, when Hurricane Carol came to call on New England.

McTigue's quick thinking landed his powerless bird in Boston Harbor's spectacular trash pile—which reaches heights of eighty feet in some spots—without any instruments or landing gear to aid him. The pilot suffered minor burns and dehydration. Rescuers say they might never have happened on the crash site but for the timely assistance of advanced radar devices lately in use at the North Truro AFB on Cape Cod.

Sadly, not all of Carol's missing made it home to tell their tales. Chappaquiddick's most prominent resident, Isolde Martin, was found drowned on the sands of South Beach last night. An investigation is underway, following the discovery of an abandoned automobile on the actress's property and eyewitness accounts of an unknown man calling on the Chappy celebrity in the hour preceding the storm.

Arrangements have yet to be finalized, but Cristobal Balenciaga, speaking from his home in Paris, told the French Press he had been especially commissioned by Miss Martin's estate and was already at work on her final frock.

Meanwhile, the governor's office has vowed to clean up Spectacle Island, newly thrust into the spotlight, highlighting long-time complaints about its unsightliness and overpowering stench. Contract bidding opens next week.

*SPECTACLE BIDDING cont. page 8.*

# EIGHTY-FIVE

The beach lay empty at daybreak. Behind heavy drapes, the tourists slept off their revelry while clear waves rolled softly at the foot of their grand hotels. Silver thatch palms twisted in the breeze. The blue-water yachts of Carlisle Bay appeared to shudder and nod. Down toward the pier, an old local woman baked bread inside a tin drum. The comforting smell of the rising dough, intermingled with the ocean air, gave off a fleeting impression of home. It almost could have been Boston. But it wasn't, of course. Far, far from.

Standing with his short legs planted apart, bare feet dug into the powder-soft sand, a bald man touched the dome of his head. It proved badly sunburned, and he wished he still had the hair of his youth. He must have looked like every other overzealous retiree, so starved for escape he hadn't bothered to think about exposure. But there was some consolation in that. Foolish people were everywhere. They went unnoticed.

The horses were just coming in now. And that's what he'd come here to see. Thoroughbreds, taken out to swim—their long faces, eyes agog, seeming to express the massive effort required to pedal ashore.

The manager of the hotel appeared silently at the man's side, his hands pressed together in prayer, his linen suit as clean and pure as the white sand shining through the shallows.

"A coffee for you, sir?"

"No, thank you." The man shook his head. He would have liked a cup, but he wasn't staying long.

"Tea then? We have good Irish labels."

The man looked up and sneered at the hotel manager. He wondered if his accent had betrayed him. Were Barbadians that perceptive? He quickly checked his temper, forcing his face into a smile. He was trying to pass for Canadian. "No, thank you again."

"Sailing out today?"

"Yes," the man nodded.

"Mind you watch the big rollers out there. Mean water to the north."

"Oh, I've been through storms," the little man laughed. He laughed maybe too loud for that particular hour of the morning, when the sky still held on to its violet cape. For a moment, a familiar confidence swelled inside the man's lungs, and he felt rather like himself again. "Call me when they think up something worse than weather to send my way."

The manager smiled politely. "Some tomato juice, perhaps, for you?"

The man shook off this offer with a condescending little grimace. It was one of the stock faces he made—a distinct face, an expression he'd been forming all his life—though he didn't know it until the children had come along, and he'd seen it mirrored back to him in the countenance of three young girls, girls forever condescending and grimacing at him.

He gave the manager a dollar to make him go away. Then he thought better of it, calling after him, "You *can* do me one favor, friend."

"Sir?"

"Tell me what time's the early race at Garrison Savannah?"

"Nine o'clock, sir. Local time."

The horses came rising from the waves now. The trainers held on by their halters and throat lashes, urging the sleek brown bodies out from the depths that had concealed so much of their forms. They looked an act of magic, if not a full-blown miracle, like an unknown species just now, this instant, materializing—evolving from secret aquatic existence into some new giant of the land. They were marvelous animals, but also, in the morning's violet light, a little unreal.

"Can I confess something to you?" The man looked hard at his new acquaintance.

"I am a witness to Jehovah," the manager nodded, as if he'd expected to be called on in such a capacity this morning. "I can see that you are lost."

"I'm not even a guest at your hotel," the sunburned traveler smiled.

"I know, sir. But you are a creature of god. And you've come here in good faith."

"Have I?"

"There is an assembly at the Kingdom Hall on Bay Street this afternoon. I would be delighted to bring you along, Mister . . . eh, Mister . . ."

"Wunholm," the man nodded slowly, as if they'd both just now agreed this would be the case. He pressed both palms to his red, shining forehead. He laughed again. The baking bread smelled too perfectly wonderful for any honest man to pass up. "I appreciate your invitation, but I think I'll probably go now. I've some business to explore on another island."

The manager closed his eyes. "God bless you, sir."

"Yes. It's true. He certainly does. Some days more than others."

# EPILOGUE

*September 1954*

*Dear Bean,*

*As I write, your beau is on his way back home to you. You'll have heard my answer by now, of course. I imagine we'll all have toasted and hugged and begun to think about a guest list. Still, I wanted to write this down, my blessing, which I give you both with the very best of wishes. Thought you might like a memento for your hope chest. Or else some sappy reading material for your children's bedtimes one day. (Read quickly, when they come. Children don't just grow up fast; they catapult.)*

*Colin is a fine man, and he'll do well by you. As I told him today, I admire his service. His ambitions tend toward the natural world, as do yours; that's good fertile ground for a marriage. He spoke lovingly of his parents in such a way as I'll never doubt his ability to cherish and care for a family. We spoke of finances, at his insistence. I told him that wasn't any kind of prerequisite for me and that you didn't care a lick about money either. It's only one of the hundred reasons I'm so proud of you.*

*Oh, and speaking of fatherly pride, I have a small confession to make. Blame it on the latest Hitchcock release (Rear Window, you'll hate it), but I've done some spying of my own, by way of our friend Dr. Bassett. Marshall tells me his biology department would be thrilled to have you, after your tour of duty with the Woods Hole team. He recommended an advisor, currently studying marine bivalve filter feeding and bioenergetic flux. You'll have to school me some evening over dinner. Chicken, I suppose. Have I mentioned that I'm proud?*

*I'm ashamed it's taken me so long to accept it: your being an adult and all. But here you are. Here you've been, rather. And in turn, here's a little something I owe you. It's a letter from your mother (enclosed). She wrote it before she left to go help with the war. To explain herself, I imagine. When is the right time to share such a missive with a daughter? I always thought "not yet." Your Aunt Poppy always thought "never." I wonder now if you wouldn't have appreciated its contents much, much sooner. I hope you can forgive another man's imperfect timing.*

*For now, here's a little sketch for you and your engagement. It's a drawing of a man I saw today—preposterously—riding down Storrow Drive atop one of those antique penny-farthings. So absurd, I had to capture it right then in the cab. Didn't look awfully safe, but then, nothing interesting ever is.*

*May your and Colin's life together always be interesting. May you keep your beautiful moments "flying," as Goethe wrote, as all curious minds ought to proceed. Be contented at the side of one another. But be restless, always, with your place in the world.*

*Yours now and forever,*

*Bud (Dad)*

## THURSDAY, SEPTEMBER 23, 1954

# Boston's Own Warm-Blooded Mermaid Reaches Astounding Depths, Resurfaces to Tell the Tale

*The Gazette begins today publication of a series of articles informed by a local woman who has mastered Cousteau's Aqua-Lung apparatus and seal-skin diving suit.*

FALMOUTH, MA (AP)—September on Cape Cod is time for the wives and children to migrate back to their winter homes—back to the inland Wellesleys and Winchesters of New England—where Dad's been living like a bachelor all summer long, excepting those two short weeks of R and R a working man's entitled to spend by the water, attendant to his brood. Only this September, one of the kids is staying on. Miss Sabina McTigue, a twenty-year-old Beacon Hill native, says the diving bug caught her quite by accident. We'll chronicle her unusual journey in this new weekly column on scuba diving and the exploration of our region's fascinating marine resources.

"We're heading out on a bottom-sampling survey," McTigue explained of her upcoming expedition with the Woods Hole Oceanographic Institution, commissioned by the Cape's commercial fishing association. "Our study is twofold in scope. Ocean quahogs aren't as vigorous, in terms of their reproduction, as some other species. They can only survive low levels of fishing before their stock is depleted. So we'll be listening, along the continental shelf, for any new beds, as well as assessing the stock in known beds." Research scientist Malcolm Lambert adds that the ocean is a plentiful source of food and resources but perhaps not inexhaustible. "We've only but scraped the surface of what's to be found and leveraged for the benefit of future generations."

As to maneuvering with the experimental Aqua-Lung, McTigue has proven herself a resilient student. "That first time I came up and took off my helmet, everyone screamed, 'Sabina, your head is bleeding!' I'd only ruptured an eardrum. Anyway, it didn't feel like much." The young lady science enthusiast, as pretty as she is brave, says her new role did require some convincing at home.

Miss McTigue, newly engaged to be married, says her fiancé worries some but not overly. Asked about a potential strain on the courtship, the plucky adventuress replied, "None hardly. We've been divided often enough before. It's the natural rhythm of things between us." McTigue hastened to add the WHOI's expedition vessel comes equipped with its own telegram equipment (for printing and sending handwritten facsimiles) aboard.

*FROGWOMAN cont. page 12.*

## *Wasque Land Given Over as Nature Preserve*

Lenore McTigue (née Dooley) of Marigot, St. Martin, granted eighty acres of oceanfront land to the Chappaquiddick Island Association, on terms that her parcel remain forever unaltered and undeveloped. "I made a promise I would never sell this land. I think a gift of this kind preserves the virtue of that promise, and acts as a kind of insurance policy against those who might love a big idea today but fail to see its folly in the long run. A lot of people disagree with me, I know, but whenever I think of the island, of its many chapters over time, I think of family and of children. Children and families of all sorts. Even the complicated type. This last chapter is for them."

*THE ISLAND cont. page 7.*

# Acknowledgments

*Ways of Virtue* began in the spring of 2017 as little more than the eponymous Sumner Barton line from a 1954 *Boston Globe* article connecting hurricanes and radar systems. My first note of thanks necessarily goes to the team at Boston Public Library responsible for digitizing one hundred–plus years of news into an archive, where I was lucky enough to happen upon inspiration. The manuscript would not have grown much beyond its first pages without the encouragement and optimism of a few steadfast cheerleaders. I am grateful to the early readers who recognized where I was going (or at least kindly claimed to) when there was still a decent question as to whether or not I was going anywhere: Robyn Bradley, Francesca Uberoi, Kerrie O'Mara, Cathy Bracey, Stephanie Borgia, Kate O'Neill, Brantley Aufill, Katherine Smith. To Miriam Parker and Megan McDonald, for the free advice, I still owe you flowers. Much thanks to Sally Petersen and her generous book club.

For the sake of story, I have borrowed a place and conflated its eras. The manners and mood in WOV are decidedly 1950s; the environmental slant is of 1970s vintage; with the exception of a few noteworthies, most of the fancy people didn't arrive until the nineties and beyond. For those who truly know Edgartown, I hope you can forgive this creative license.

I am indebted to the many local historians and scientific experts who took time out from their important work to answer oddly specific questions or connect me with resources that might: Bowdoin Van Riper and the Martha's Vineyard Museum; Helen McNeil-Ashton, the Truro

Historical Society, and the Cobb Archive; Emma Green-Beach, Rick Karney, Paul Bagnall, and the Martha's Vineyard Shellfish Group; also Clyde Mackenzie, whose contributions proved so much larger than bay scallops. For their many insights into piloting and aviation, I thank Jon McNair, Buddy Wyatt, and most especially Tom Corcoran, who not only talked me off the ground but enriched this book with his priceless humor and character. Special thanks to Dr. Kenton Clymer, who helped paint a picture of the GOC post he manned in Naperville as a boy; Dr. Carl Ipsen, professor of history at Indiana University; John Sheehan and Ron Raitt, for your service and shared memories of North Truro AFB and Lincoln Laboratory training; and Michael Smith of the National Model Aviation Museum.

A debt of gratitude to the owners and staff at the Harbor View Hotel, where much of this book was written—in two- or three-day sprints—during my annual winter escapes from a day job, laundry, and dishes.

I wouldn't be equipped to write anything worth reading without the guidance of my favorite teachers, starting with Caroline Demeo, who instilled in me a love of good books and abided many a messy "project time." Nothing could better describe my writing process, so I think this artistic preparation must have been crucial. Also thanks to Joanne Crescenzi, John Bisicia, Lynn Parker, Kerry Johnson, Jessica Treadway, and the entire Creative Writing Department at UNC Wilmington. To Ben, a secret story genius and celebrant of classic films, thank you for letting me stay up past my bedtime, and more recently for access to your card games. For helping me find a way out of the maze I'd created, thank you Emma Dries, brilliant fixer and loving godmother to my characters. And finally, Katie Grimm, my non-agent, who offered more than she knows at one or two critical junctures.

For the July and August weeks we never wanted to end—with the ocean at our windows, everyone camped together on Wellington and Crowell Roads—all my love to Ed and Mary; to Mary and Bernard.

To my Westborough family, who have made this lucky life of mine magical, art-filled, and also possible: Charley, Carolyn, Katie—I'm not much for music; let this be my party piece in exchange for all of yours. To John O'Neill, who has done so much and yet hardly wishes to have it mentioned. Your kindness is forever in my mind. To Declan, the hero of my world, you are a wonder and an inspiration—too much goodness for me to take (even half) credit for—and there are pieces of you that I find, in small moments, tucked into these pages. I know you would've preferred that I footnote them.

And to Matt, my best reader and best friend, for not only remembering the details but for inventing all the ones worth keeping. You gifted me my favorite stories ever—my favorite *summers* ever—complete with perfectly curated soundtracks and grilled English muffins. I will always be smitten with your backward cap, your elite hand/eye, your stripes, your hidden arsenal of superpowers—the sort that can fix leaky sinks and engineer elaborate Halloween costumes but also, occasionally, conjure a family of deer across a snowy wood on a dark night, the two of us driving—forever driving—the farm road back to the earth.

# About the Author

photo credit: Carl Pickett

**Liz O'Neill** earned her MFA in Creative Writing from the University of North Carolina, Wilmington. She currently works at the Boston College Center for Corporate Citizenship, where she supports major brands looking to make better environmental, social, and governance choices. She lives outside Boston with her husband, son, and black Lab, Jiggs.

**Looking for your next great read?**

We can help!

Visit www.shewritespress.com/next-read
or scan the QR code below for a list
of our recommended titles.

She Writes Press is an award-winning
independent publishing company founded to
serve women writers everywhere.